PRINCESS OF
PARK AVENUE

PRINCESS OF PARK AVENUE

DANIELLA BRODSKY

BERKLEY BOOKS, NEW YORK

THE BERKLEY PUBLISHING GROUP
Published by the Penguin Group
Penguin Group (USA) Inc.
375 Hudson Street, New York, New York 10014, USA
Penguin Group (Canada), 90 Eglinton Avenue East, Suite 700, Toronto, Ontario M4P 2Y3, Canada
(a division of Pearson Penguin Canada Inc.)
Penguin Books Ltd., 80 Strand, London WC2R 0RL, England
Penguin Group Ireland, 25 St. Stephen's Green, Dublin 2, Ireland (a division of Penguin Books Ltd.)
Penguin Group (Australia), 250 Camberwell Road, Camberwell, Victoria 3124, Australia
(a division of Pearson Australia Group Pty. Ltd.)
Penguin Books India Pvt. Ltd., 11 Community Centre, Panchsheel Park, New Delhi—110 017, India
Penguin Group (NZ), cnr. Airborne and Rosedale Roads, Albany, Auckland 1310, New Zealand
(a division of Pearson New Zealand Ltd.)
Penguin Books (South Africa) (Pty.) Ltd., 24 Sturdee Avenue, Rosebank, Johannesburg 2196, South Africa

Penguin Books Ltd., Registered Offices: 80 Strand, London WC2R 0RL, England

This is a work of fiction. Names, characters, places, and incidents either are the product of the author's imagination or are used fictitiously, and any resemblance to actual persons, living or dead, business establishments, events, or locales is entirely coincidental.

PRINTING HISTORY
Berkley trade paperback edition / December 2005

ISBN: 0-425-20537-1

Berkley is a registered trademark of Penguin Group (USA) Inc.
The "B" design is a trademark belonging to Penguin Group (USA) Inc.

This book has been cataloged by the Library of Congress

PRINTED IN THE UNITED STATES OF AMERICA

10 9 8 7 6 5 4 3 2 1

For David

ACKNOWLEDGMENTS

It's true what they say! The second time around *is* a lot more difficult. But it's the heart-wrenching talent of the authors who've done it before that keeps you moving. And for other kinds of help that keeps me trudging along, I'd like to thank the following people. My sister, Niki—for being, honestly, the best sister ever, never mind her public relations efforts at the elementary school level, my little brother Ryan—who is a genius Bionicle engineer (and *Oy!* So cute!), my mother who claims everyone is somehow from Brooklyn, and my Grandma Sylvia, whose Brooklyn apartment always feels like home . . . no matter how long you've been away. A shout out to Steven, who is an irreplaceable part of our family, as are Kevin and Rey—who represent another borough with more than a fair share of home-decorating flair and curb appeal: Staten Island.

My new Connecticut family is wonderful, too: David, thanks for making life magical every day, always making me laugh, and for inspiring fabulous male leads—who may or may not do the dishes. And a special thanks to the whole Colwick clan for much warmth and caring—and to its newest member, Miss Grace, for being so darn cute. And all the folks at "my" Starbucks rock.

A world of thanks to my editors at Berkley Books: Cindy Hwang, Leslie Gelbman, and Susan McCarty. It's been an honor to work on this book with all of you and to continue to learn and grow under your direction. Jodi Reamer, my agent, is a constant source of support and education, and as a fabulous bonus, she always laughs at my jokes . . . really loud. Thank you to the library and book communities in New York and Connecticut for welcoming me with open arms.

Ahhh, friends! Deborah Marrocchino, the Italian expert *(Madre Mia!)*, and world-traveler; Mimosa Montag—Brooklynite extraordinaire—is a second sister to me; Amanda Berke—a living definition of "good people"; Heather Imbey—the most generous, stylish friend on earth; and the girl who is a bona fide expert in the area of friendship: California girl, Courtney McQuade-Lundie.

Research is hard work and would have been impossible without the altruistic aid of hair guru Christopher-John, Edita at Mark Garrison, and publicist Ronna Reich. For the inspiration they lent to this book: Julie Lindh at Exhale, color genius Paul Labrecque, the women of Butterfly Salon, Bendel's department store: where I attended my very first press event and had to ask Monica Lewinsky what she thought was "romantic," the personable celebrities that keep you company via television late at night when you sometimes need them to, and last but certainly not least, New York City—hands down the best city in the world (and that includes all the five boroughs, *of course*).

Princess of Park Avenue

Dear Mrs. Machuchi,

I have enclosed Lorraine's January 3rd poetry assignment, as I think it may shed some light on Lorraine's recent daydreaming and the severe drop in her marks. If I may a caveat, though, she does have an excellent grasp on language arts and the rhyming schemes we covered in class. And she has great hair.

Yours truly,
Mrs Fontana

January 3, 1986
Lorraine Machuchi
Mrs. Fontana's Class
P.S. 126
Brooklyn

There once was a girl named Lorraine.
A boy called Tommy drove her insane.
She'd ask him questions he'd pretend not to hear.
Still she'd want to kiss him on the ear.
Chrissy'd tell him to go away;
She'd say "Lorraine he did the same thing yesterday!"
But Lorraine could see only hearts in her eyes.
And say to Chrissy who wasn't surprised,
"So put down those stones you plan to throw!
Or he may come back for more tomorrow!"

eBay auction block #1
Description: Document pair including 2nd grade homework assignment and letter to Lorraine's mother regarding said homework assignment. With the hindsight of twenty-two years, Mrs. Machuchi said she regrets not taking this more seriously. Her comment on the topic was *"Madre Mia!"*

Opening bid: $250
Winning bid: $875 by LorraineBKLYN@Bgirl.com

Comments: MOM! Stop trying to make money from this stuff!!!!!!!! If you want something, just ask! We are RICH NOW!!!!!!!!!

ONE

♥

"SWEET CHERRY, MAKE IT AWFUL"
—HOLE

It was a Tuesday, a fact that, Lorraine mused—as she did about most days—didn't lend it any particular distinction from any of the other days of the week.

"Tuesday, Tuesday, Tuesday, Tuesday." She sang it until the two syllables were robbed of any significance, and then sighed at herself in the mirror, frustrated that it never would mean anything. Not just those two syllables, but any of it. Of her twenty-eight years on this earth, she'd spent twenty of them in love with Tommy. And with little exception, she'd gotten the same disappointing results every day. That realization hit her every morning that he wasn't next to her; filling her tummy with the same hollow feeling. And after that came the familiar sinking idea—that no one seemed to let her forget—that she didn't have anything to show for herself as a result of her inability to let go of him once and for all.

Regardless of what it was called, on Tuesday evenings Lorraine and the same old people she'd hung out with for God knows how long *did* break their regular routine of hanging out in the corner of the schoolyard at the abandoned elementary on Sixty-fifth Street, and went to the Bay Ridge Bowl instead. But, since she'd done the same thing *every* Tuesday since she was fourteen, it probably would be considered a routine of its own. What was worse, on that particular freakin' Tuesday, it was raining. And Lorraine didn't like to get her hair frizzy.

"Lorraine, just come on already. Tommy is gonna be there! So your hair's gonna get wet! Big woop. All the girls are wearing it all frizzy and wavy like that in the city these days anyway."

"Do I look like a city bi-atch to you?" Lorraine wasn't having it. Chrissy always tried to get her to do what she wanted her to do by dangling Tommy in her face. What was the freakin' point, though?

She thought of that first night—the first time Tommy himself had dangled hope in front of her. She didn't know if it had made things better or worse. God, it was the only time she'd ever wished on a stupid star. And when they'd reached Tommy's house with nothing but a car alarm in the distance, one locust rubbing its legs together, or whatever they did to make that noise, everything had stopped. The whole world, she was sure, had stopped spinning, the guys on the corner had stopped throwing that stupid football, her mother had even probably stopped yelling at her dad for not making enough money to get them back to Italy, as Tommy turned around abruptly to face her. He'd dropped the cool act, let the smug smirk relax, and really looked at her. After a second it had been a lot to take—the weight of him looking so directly at her like that; the fact that everything she'd always wanted was now glaring at her with so much force.

"You want to kiss me, don't you, Lorraine?"

They were fifteen then! And for the love of God, yes! She'd wanted him to kiss her, had never wanted anything else for as long as she could remember. Would she take it back if she'd known how things would be now?

She'd dreamed of that moment for so long, with her mother's voice shrill in the background shouting, "Johnny! Would it kill you to clean up your dishes for once, you good for nothing piece of shit!"

(For the record, her father was not a piece of shit, nor was he good for nothing. But you couldn't tell that to Lorraine's mother, just as you couldn't tell Lorraine's father that her mother meant any of it. He was so smitten with her, the words changed to sweet music before they reached his ear. At least that's how he'd described it to Lorraine. If only Lorraine and her brother had the power to hear the sweet sounds their father did!)

And there it had actually been happening—with the bonus of her mother's voice being, if slightly, out of earshot. Thinking quickly, she'd realized the best move would be to stay quiet. Make him work for it a little. She'd already learned about what men wanted, for crying out loud—she and Chrissy had watched both *Knots Landing* and *General Hospital* religiously. So she'd stared him down. And just like that they'd stood, daring each other in their own way, silently accepting the mutual challenges. Seconds, minutes passed, and still, nothing had happened. Lorraine's limbs had throbbed with the absence of breath. She'd known she'd never survive if her dreams were quashed this close to possible realization. The throbbing had turned into a smoother, easier beat, her temperature rose—still nothing. Finally, when it seemed she'd lost her chance, she turned her head to go, to follow the same disappointed route she had hundreds of times—God, since she was ten years old! *What was one more night?* She had already been trying to console herself.

She'd started walking.

And he'd made her pay for it. He'd made her think he was going to let her go—down two streetlights, or five twisted shrubs, or four driveways, or twelve cracks in the sidewalk, whichever way she felt like counting how far she slept from Tommy each night.

But not two light posts later he, grabbed for her hand with a roughness she'd not attributed to him before, staring her down like that again, making her throat go dry.

She was looking out her window to that very spot right now! If only she didn't think of it every time! But she did! For the love of God, she did! And she could see it, like a movie playing out right in front of her from her balcony seat. Sick! She was sick! She could remember every moment: She'd stood there—her hair so big it could engulf Tommy's head entirely—and she'd thought, *Oh my god. It's happening.* Take any experience she'd ever had, times it by ten, add it to a million, and still . . . it had nothing on that moment. How could she have desired someone so much? What had she known of it back then? But she had known! She'd been the *Firestarter*, anything she touched a finger to would've gone up in flames.

He'd looked down at her mouth until it felt like he'd kissed it already, so hot did her lips feel by then. She'd say, when she told the story, to the one person she told it to no less than 10,000 times—she'd say, "Chrissy, I swear on my great-grandma's grave, it was like he kissed me without kissing me."

Fourteen years later, and Chrissy thought she could *still* get Lorraine out by putting the idea of Tommy in her head. Lorraine scowled. It was true, she could! But she felt more comfortable attributing her change of heart to her desire to try the wavy hairstyle. Chrissy was right, she had just seen one of those chic city bi-atches on the subway wearing her hair like that, the kind of girl who only came to Bay Ridge because she'd heard they stock Michael Kors in the Century 21 on Eighty-sixth. "But that's the only reason," she told Chrissy. "The *only* reason." She repeated it, as her voice trailed off. She didn't even believe herself.

As she retraced that route now on the way to the Bay Ridge Bowl, in the heavy grayness of the early evening—five twisted shrubs, some of which really weren't all that twisty anymore, Lorraine felt the sensation that time was racing ahead and she wasn't catching up. After all, shouldn't she have more than this by now? Some of her friends had married. One just had a baby, for heaven's sake! She'd held it in her own hands, ran her finger down the soft baby arm, choking back the tears that blurred her vision with the distinct feeling she'd never have this for herself. But this was out of her hands. This was the part she just couldn't explain. If there were a way to flick a switch and just turn it off for good, maybe that would be a different story. But even that remote, unrealistic scenario couldn't play out too far in Lorraine's mind, because she wasn't so sure she *would* turn her feelings for Tommy off, even if she could.

You see, he *had* kissed her that night, thirteen years ago. He'd (*finally!*) kissed her and kissed her, each time pulling her in deeper and deeper like he couldn't get enough of her. Oh, the way his hair actually felt—thick like a lawn, but soft at the sides where there wasn't gel and hairspray holding up perfectly imperfect spikes. He was skinnier back then—all the guys were—but his arms had been strong as she felt them around her, and what a feeling! The veins, their green—it was wild what she had noticed! She'd locked every detail away in her mind, storing them in a place where she could always return.

They'd sat under a tree in his backyard. Lorraine could see the crippled tops of its branches now, and her breath caught in her throat the same way it had on that night. It had been an old tree—even back then—and half the boughs were completely bent over. Under there they had been secluded, in their own little Tommy-and-Lorraine pod. To this day, she could remember exactly the sound of the raindrops hitting the leaves, the sound of a leaf giving into gravity and pouring a bunch of raindrops down onto the ground at once. In fact, with the rain now picking up its ferocity, she thought she heard that same sound. It had been humid that night in their tree world, and they had been soaked through, their clothing stuck to them like it was never coming off.

She'd thought she'd known what it was like to be hungry for Tommy before, but actually having him . . . once she'd gotten a taste of that, she'd been STARVING, pulling at him and grabbing at his hair and the back of his neck and his soaking shoulder and the very bottom of his back, right at his jeans waistband. After that very first kiss, after the smoothing over of each other's tongues and the tasting of each other's lips, and the grabbing so tight that you don't even realize, he'd looked at her and she could see what it was about Tommy that made her love him—the very same thing that kept her so paralyzed now. In him, there was knowledge of a Lorraine that no one else shared. In those tiny glimpses he'd tossed at her over the years like bits of confetti on New Year's Eve, she saw it was possible that she could be so much more. And then, finding herself face to face with him looking at her full on, she'd seen it more deeply. The way she'd read his look, the things she saw in his chocolaty eyes with their watery glaze, so big and framed with thick black lashes, and his boxer cheekbones jutting out right underneath, those were things she couldn't get enough of seeing. "I've never met anyone like you, Lorraine."

She resolved now, for the millionth time, not to look up at his window as she passed by his house on her way to meet Chrissy at the bowling alley. Their lives, their words echoed there. Despite that, certain weeks she could will herself not to look. She would say to herself, Lorraine, under no goddamned circumstances are you to look at that boy's house! Don't look for the pearly rock of his snake tank in the window. Don't look for the American Flag spread across the top third of the window. Don't check to see whether his 2000 Mustang GT convertible in K7

Bright Atlantic Blue, with 17 inch 5 Star rims is there or not. *Just don't do it. Don't do it. Don't do it.* Painful as it was, she could walk by. She could let the echoes of their words just roll over her, and not pierce through the way they sometimes could. Somehow she now turned the corner without looking at Tommy's house.

"Home free," she said to the garbage pails whose lids were sloppily tossed in the street. She was proud of herself, knowing all the while it wouldn't last, couldn't last. She was kidding herself was all. But what other games had she to occupy her time?

That very first night, he'd hooked her. Every day and night after that, Lorraine had done everything with Tommy's drippy look in mind—with the image of herself she saw reflected in it, in mind. She would wear this lacey underwear and that bra and spray this eau de parfum and chew on this breath mint, and arrange her hair up away from her neck on that side. Anything and everything to be that Lorraine! To be looked at as that Lorraine! To have him say something like he'd said before, "I'd never noticed, Lorraine, how your neck curves like that, so soft up beneath your hair." And he'd put two fingers there, pulling the tiny hairs at her nape between them, over and over and over. Deep down, she didn't want to be Lorraine. She wanted to be Tommy's Lorraine.

They'd kissed like that every night for two weeks, and it had rained then, just as it was now, unrelenting and continuous, like a sheet of water . . . running, running. She'd been afraid for it to end—all of it— Tommy, the rain. She would stay late. Too late, until Lorraine's mother would yell, "Madre Mia! Where is my daughter? Where is my *daughter*?"

Her mother would scold her: "Do you want the whole neighborhood to hear me screaming for my own daughter that way?"

She hadn't wanted to hurt her mother, but how could she help it?

She walked now two blocks past their own with a heavy heart, but managed to keep herself in that far off place from all those years ago. On one of those late nights, those beautiful, stormy nights, under those dreamy tree boughs, the rain had cleared and revealed the moon high above and stars intermittently visible in the slight breeze that swung the branches just the slightest bit to the left or the right. They'd lain facing each other, with their sides on the moist grass.

It had been silent some time and Lorraine had been taken by the dramatic change in the landscape. "It's true, I guess, what they say—you can't appreciate the good weather without the bad."

Tommy had looked into Lorraine's eyes in that way again, like there was a deep truth in there. "I never met anyone like you Lorraine Machuchi. You are so different." He'd said it in a casual way she never heard him use with other people. But to them, he was the Tommy people wanted to know, the hot guy with the tight shirt and the dreamy brown eyes. *That* Tommy didn't let people know him like Lorraine had.

Where was he, so deep in those eyes? People had wanted to know, but Lorraine already did. She'd known just exactly where he'd been taken. And when he had took her there, she could see that he didn't understand science too well, and wasn't sure if the way his father hit him sometimes wasn't more than he should. Tommy was real, more real than anything else she could see around her. He *mattered*. Math class didn't. Her mother's yelling didn't. But Tommy . . . well he did, unmistakably, he did.

For Lorraine, it had been as if her whole life was happening to her right then and there and she knew she could never want a thing more. When she thought of it now even, when she would see him at the Bay Ridge Bowl, it was unmistakable to her that they were joined somehow. It was the wanting that first hooked her in—the highs after the lows of it, the satisfaction of finally getting there, having him look at her like that again. Everything else would melt away on a drift of slower breaths and higher consciousness. And he'd say, "Ahhh, Lorraine," like she was the antidote to it all.

Those two weeks had ended just as abruptly as they'd begun. One night, after the group split up, he'd given her a painfully friendly kiss on the cheek, and with his hands in his back pockets, walked the cracked concrete path up to his front door. At first Lorraine had thought he'd come back, that he'd pop out from the front door and hoot, "Just kidding!" And she'd waited and waited. But after an hour it had become obvious that he wasn't coming out. "Moron!" she'd screamed at herself, at the hateful moon peeking through the trees outside Tommy's house, where she sat with her feet in the flooded gutter, water rushing down into the sewer so loud it sounded like the ocean. But she couldn't help herself. She'd gone up to ring the bell. Tommy's mother had answered.

"Oh, hello Lorraine. I'll go get Tommy." Lorraine had tried to gauge something in Tommy's mother's tone—anything at all!—but she was warm and welcoming as she'd always been. Lorraine had waited there, looking into the deep weave on the carpeted staircase that led up to Tommy's room. Brown, brown; it seemed the whole house was his gaze, that the slippery chocolate of him had spilled out all over it and would overtake her. She'd never survive.

And then he'd appeared at the front door, and Lorraine had started to let her breath out, the breath she'd been holding in all the long hours by the oceanic sewer. But when he'd looked at her, her breath had stuck right there in her throat, because his look was now completely empty. It didn't say anything!

"What's up Lorraine?" he'd asked like an acquaintance she'd only just met. The chocolate of his eyes had turned to sturdy, waterproof leather. Nothing was getting in or coming out. Suddenly the whole house re-pelled her.

She didn't know what to do or say. And so she'd just excused herself. "I'm sorry. I thought I left something with you."

"Nope. Nothing," he'd said.

And so she'd run, hard, harder, home and retreated to the memory of him that was more real than this unbelievable thing that had just happened. Inside Lorraine, the thing Tommy had found there, she felt it cramp up and then shatter up into a trillion tiny pieces.

That had been the first of many endings for Lorraine and Tommy, and each time, the in-between grew more deeply aggravated. When you pick at a scar, you leave no chance for it to heal. If you could somehow make yourself forget it was there, allow it to close up; it would slowly blend into your skin, never to be seen again. That's what she'd been told, anyway. But no matter how hard the fall, how deep the wound, she always took the leap when his eyes opened up to her again, let her in, saw her. *This time!* She'd always think that this time it might just last.

She wasn't surprised to find herself walking aimlessly by the bowling alley, hating herself all the while she indulged her thoughts. In her mind's eye their arms were interlocked as they glided in and out of the world—restaurants and weddings and their friends' basements and backyards and pools. The angles of their elbows seemed solid, unbreakable, when she remembered them that way.

"Lorraine, pain, strain, drain . . . boy, that's a depressing name you've got there Lorraine." He'd said this to her when they'd been barbecuing in Petey's backyard. That had been two years ago, and their fingers were laced together—why did this always look so fantastic? The weave, the pattern of them.

"Crane—that's a good thing, isn't it? Used in building new, beautiful things. How could that be bad?" It had been a stretch.

"What about Tommy?" she'd tried to change the direction of the conversation. "Tommy Salami," she said. "That's bad for your cholesterol."

And he'd smiled, from teeth to eyes to hairline, the way all those girls tried to get him to do. "I bet you want some Tommy Salami. . . ."

She'd smacked him—playfully of course. But then he'd turned serious, his swimming eyes at the peak of their power, the tide of him high. Everyone else was scenery.

Fears of the end aside, she'd been dizzy with happiness then, not really experiencing life so much as feeling around for everything through the haze of it. She could stay up in her tiny bed for hours just thinking of the way he'd had trouble saying good night, the way he'd said, "I just can't let go of your hand Lorraine," and then how he'd looked down at it as if it must be true. *Please be true,* she'd thought.

He'd never used ordinary words such as "I love you." For them, there were other words. "You are everything, Lorraine." And she was bolder and brighter still. A Broadway marquee, she'd been, dressing at the foot of his bed. How could she have known it would all come crashing down again?

So different than she felt now! She knew at that moment, as she walked heavy-footed, the only way she could muster with her jean cuffs so weighed down with rain, back toward the bowling alley, soaked all the way through to her matching lace bra and panty set by the now hard-falling rain, that she'd wasted her life. Her whole fucking life—for Tommy. And she'd given him up—ten, fifteen, twenty-five hundred times. *Because he obviously doesn't love you. Moron!* But she always went sneaking back, hurling rocks up at his window at midnight if he asked her to, meeting him wherever he'd begged, until the frowns said the whole neighborhood knew anyway.

Standing outside the bowling alley now, her hair was wavy and messy. It wouldn't dry, not with the water coming up so hard from the sidewalk it felt like knives stabbing at her ankles. She forced herself to go inside, into the bathroom, where she looked at herself in the cloudy, cheap bathroom mirror. Despite how terrible she felt inside, she did look good like this. Sexy. *You are everything, Lorraine.* No, she couldn't believe it now. But she forced herself to walk outside. Walk toward the lanes where she knew she would see him.

All the cute guidos wore tight shirts, but Tommy's were the tightest. And not only Lorraine, but *all* the girls appreciated it. All he had to do was flash that freaking smile (which she personally knew he owed to Crest White Strips—a fact he'd revealed when he was particularly down on himself. Teeth whitening was one of the tiny ways in which he tried to make himself feel better about life in general) and Tommy could get a girl to come right over and make a fool of herself, proudly running her fingertips over her hair, each thinking herself the bravest, most novel, the *first* to ever do that, to walk right over that way.

At nine on the dot he smiled at a girl who looked as if she charged by the hour (and not a lot at that), who wore glittery gold chains and hoop earrings and leopard in at least three different representations. On cue the girl came over. It wasn't five minutes until he bought her a frozen strawberry daiquiri in a plastic cup with a Chinese umbrella, and had his hand laid out far enough up her thigh that you knew she was in for it.

Tommy never bowled. Despite the shockingly colored posters advertising special discounts, taped up half-heartedly over the shoe rental desk, barely anyone did—except for the really old guys that lived in the senior home down on Seventy-second and the really geeky high school guys with the pocket protectors who didn't even bother trying to skirk their stereotype. There were at least twenty people in Lorraine's group, who hung out at the Bay Ridge Bowl on Tuesdays. It was two-for-one drink night was why. Even before that, they were drawn by the night manager named Decker who always served the underagers as long as they paid him and turned an eye when he pocketed the cash instead of throwing it in the register. Decker was long gone now, but they were old enough anyway. Too old, really.

The group had somehow split in two—guys huddled around one square wood-look table, girls at another. They often tended to revert to those old formations. Lorraine wasn't interested tonight, couldn't bring herself to care—it was clear she was hitting some lower than low point with this addiction of hers. She had no idea what the girls were talking about, just heard snippets.

"I just saw him look at you," Susan had said to her best friend Mary. Lorraine didn't have to guess who they meant. Mary had a thing for Petey for the last couple of years. Even if Lorraine hadn't known, she wouldn't have cared to ask. Their gossip never interested her. She had enough problems with gossip, she didn't need to add to the worldwide epidemic. Like recycling, she thought, if *she* could just do her part . . .

"I'm not sure," Chrissy had her eyes narrowed to little slits, Lorraine knew without looking. That was how she always delivered her commentary, like every word should be handled with the utmost gravity. The seriousness she conveyed bore no reflection on the effort Chrissy exuded to actually change things—none—and to work on what she looked so disturbed by.

"Haven't you had enough of this?" Chrissy asked Lorraine, despite the fact it was her idea to come. It was obvious it hadn't been a good idea. But Lorraine knew she would have gone no matter what. Besides, Chrissy had the same problem she did. You had to want to change something to put the effort into it. And neither of them were there yet—although Lorraine could feel herself getting close.

Lorraine knew that it was frustration of the sexual sort that made Chrissy want to get the hell out of Dodge. (That had been their saying the whole summer. Lorraine couldn't remember where they'd heard it. But it was permanent, now that the nights were getting a slight chill. It was staying, just like everything else in her life did, without changing, losing significance along the way.) Chrissy was so worked up, she was peeling labels off of every bottle on the table. Her boyfriend hadn't slept with her in two months, and she was pissed. That's why she wanted to come to the Bay Ridge Bowl in the first place—she wanted some attention. She thought she'd dressed for it, but Chrissy was a good Christian girl and her idea of dressing tartish was to wear a boatneck and matching earrings. It didn't matter, though. Nobody was gonna screw with her because her boyfriend was connected, and no girl was worth that.

Now she was regular frustrated on top of the sexual frustration. Which, if you think about it, is a lot of frustration.

"The Diner."

They both needed it. Lorraine knew Tommy was gonna take that girl back to wherever it was she lived, to show himself he could have that life if he wanted it. She knew just how he'd kiss that girl and where he'd put his hands and for how long. She'd seen enough.

Bay Ridge Diner was another place so familiar to Lorraine that she could tell you with her eyes closed how many booths were torn and which ones stunk like puke—from her own friends who drank too much late at night. She knew where the beveled mirrors were cracked, where the tacky chandelier light fixtures never worked anymore, and that the waitresses dumped the coleslaw you didn't eat back inside the plastic bucket and reserved it.

"Large fries and two Cokes." Lorraine didn't need to ask Chrissy what she wanted. They'd been eating this for nearly fifteen years. It was a wonder they stayed so thin.

They weren't gonna talk about Chrissy's problems with Big Bobby. There was nothing to talk about. He was cheating on her, but she wouldn't do anything about it except project her frustration onto Lorraine's own hopeless situation.

Lorraine could count the seconds from the time the waitress brought their Cokes in those old pebbled brown plastic glasses to the moment she knew Chrissy would start in.

10, 9, 8, 7, 6, 5, 4, 3, 2, 1.

"Seriously Lorraine, what the fuck is wrong with you?" She readjusted her boatneck, which Lorraine knew was a half-hearted commentary on her own low-cut top.

It was as pointless to explain to Chrissy that the deep-cut blouson-style chiffon top wasn't slutty, but stylish, as it was to explain that Tommy would call later. He would call to make Lorraine see there was hope despite what she might have seen earlier, and still saw now; he would call to tell her that she was someone too special for him to screw around with like he did that other girl, and that he had to be *ready* for her. She'd gone through all of this before, and Chrissy never bought it.

So she took a long sip of her soda instead, watching it zip up through the straw, and then she let it fall from her mouth and watched it slip back down into the cup.

Back in her bed, in a warm sweatshirt washed down to a soft finish, with a big neckline cut so it hung off her shoulder, and tight pants, sliced open to flare at the ankle the way the girls were doing when Lorraine was in high school, she thought how cozy and reliable her bedroom was. She just loved it in there. The door was heavy enough so she could barely hear her mother screaming at her father, and her father ignoring it and making smooching noises all the while "(Look at this plate we have to use—chipped!" "Oh, give Pappa a big hug!"); it was far enough upstairs so her brother and his stupid high school friends (she really liked them, but had taken to calling them "stupid" so long ago she had to stick with it now) could be in a different country for all she knew, rather than just down in the basement.

Her hair did look cute like that, she thought, after she'd pulled the sweatshirt over her head and saw her waves pop out in her bureau mirror. There wasn't too much room in that mirror for looking at yourself, what with old pictures of her and Chrissy and Tommy and other people from the group—some of which she'd been closer with at some point or another, some of which she could care less about, but still hung around with out of habit.

It was silly to be getting herself fixed up—some more deodorant, a little Bath & Body Works Watermelon Spray, turning her head over, shaking out those waves. But she knew he would be calling soon. She lay in her bed and thought about the day a bit, while she waited.

She worked at the Do Wop Shop for Hair, where she was a senior colorist. She loved coloring hair. When she looked at a head of hair, Lorraine could see exactly which shades should be painted where—it seemed obvious to her. So, understandably, it pissed her off when Carlo, the no-talent owner of the Do Wop Shop for Hair, wouldn't let her apply color in the way she wanted.

"One head! One color!" he screamed it so many times, sounding like an old Benetton ad. Only it was the opposite of the open-mindededness Benetton had in mind. One color means flat color. It's cheap and extremely archaic, just like the salon itself. Why didn't they just use coffee grinds like friggin' Cleopatra did? *Mrs. Jacobson, would you move over to the Columbian Dark Roast vat so we can do your roots?* It shouldn't have angered her after so many years, but it did.

"You're the most freakin' stubborn man in all of Brooklyn!" She screamed along with mumbled profanities under her breath, and plenty of exaggerated kicks at the papers and things that are always swept all over the floor in salons. But he barely listened, barely heard her anymore. He was her uncle and so he was never going to fire her, or Lorraine's mother would kill him.

An hour and a half later Lorraine's telephone rang. She had her own "teen line" (*What a joke, you're almost thirty!* her brother said when he saw that on the bill. He was a real comedian, her brother). Her parents had installed it when she was in junior high. When Lorraine's phone rang, as it very often did, in the middle of the night, it never woke anyone.

"Hello?" she acted surprised, like she had no idea who it was. Like all sorts of men called her in the middle of the night.

"Hey." He sucked in a deep breath after he said it.

Lorraine took this as a signal of comfort. Finally he could be himself. When he could be himself, she could see a glimpse of that Lorraine she was always looking to recover. Thoughts like that could soothe you while you watched a leopard-printed ho bag stick her skanky tongue down Tommy's throat. But she wouldn't mention that now. The way their conversations had evolved over the years, there was no other girl in the world aside from Lorraine, despite the reality.

"Went to the diner?" Tommy asked her.

"Yeah." He always wanted to know where she disappeared off to. She knew that had to mean something.

"Cool. I was there just now. You know that waitress, Sandy, is quitting? She saved up enough to move to Florida."

"Nah, I didn't know that," Lorraine said, trying not to wonder how Tommy came to know this, trying not to picture Sandy—Lorraine thought she might have been the coarse redhead with the real curvy body—telling him about that, sharing a cigarette, undressing somewhere.

"What was up with that hair tonight, Lorraine? You looked like you wanted something. Something hot."

Lorraine couldn't help it; a smile hijacked her face. She knew she was grabbing for crumbs, but when crumbs were all you got, you found ways to make them into a satisfying meal.

"I have no idea what you're talking about, Tommy. None whatsoever." She pulled her stuffed lion from the Bronx Zoo a little tighter. Tommy had bought it for her. She'd come out of the bathroom by the polar bears and there it was, in his hands. And he'd kissed her, smoothed her hair back, like all of her dreams were coming true. Whenever Tommy was in her room and looked at that lion, there was satisfaction on his face—he knew a piece of him would always be there. "You're the real thing Lorraine, the real thing," he'd whispered while they were still both holding on to it.

"I think you do," he said, and what hung between them doubled and tripled in meaning in the minute of silence that followed.

They were silent for a little while, as Tommy switched CDs to some old house music that functioned as a time machine for Lorraine, bringing her to age sixteen, dancing in a street like she had the whole world in her hand. She imagined she could hear the clicking and clacking not only through the phone, but through the window. It increased their connection when she could picture that, concentrate on it. One, two, three songs they listened to that way, not saying a thing, until Tommy spoke.

"Remember that?" he asked.

And she did. They'd driven upstate one Memorial Day weekend, all twenty of them, to someone's sister's house—a real dump, with peeling paint, scratchy upholstery, and basement mold. That music played the whole time, while they punched a volleyball around the pool, drank way,

way too much during games of flip cup, roasted marshmallows and bar-becued hot dogs and hamburgers, and ate coleslaw and giant sour pickles she'd fished from a barrel. It was one of the times they were on again. She could remember his arm over her back, rubbing up and down, the feel of her T-shirt tickling her under his palm—that was what she remembered.

"What happened to all that hope, Lorraine? Where is it in this world? What am I *doing* here? What's my . . . purpose?" He seemed to consider the question, as if it were just then uniquely conjured in his mind, like people didn't think that very same thing with every other breath. Lately, he'd been doing this more. He'd get far-off and moody, drifting where Lorraine couldn't reach him. She was doing a crazy dance trying to.

She could see him staring up at his ceiling, those old glow-in-the-dark stars and planets still stuck up there. There wasn't a person in the world he spoke to like this. That Lorraine knew for a fact. *You're the real thing, Lorraine. The real thing.*

And then he actually said it. "You're the real thing, Lorraine. The real thing."

She felt the tears burn, but tried to swallow the sound. She knew it was true. So why could they not just share their lives? Soon, soon, she hoped she could stop asking herself that, and just accept things the way they were.

After more silence and more songs, during which Lorraine's tears had multiplied and finally stopped, Tommy started to tell her more, the way he had very recently started to do. And when he had revealed too much, he covered his tracks by shoving the conversation over to more meaning-less topics, like the new cheese he thought they should introduce at Bay Pizza, how Tommy wanted to start Pepperoni Fridays with two pies and pepperoni stromboli and a two liter of Dr *Pepper* ("Get it?" he said. "*Pep-per?*") for twenty bucks, tell that son of a bitch he worked for that you need to change and stock things like chocolate ice cream pizzas for dessert, or else you die.

She didn't ask him why, then—if change was so damned important—did he still live in the same town, do the same things, play the same games with her, bring her so close to everything she wanted and just pull it away until she was spinning around like the dough hook they used on the electric mixer at the pizzeria? More and more she was feeling anger poke through her desperation. It surprised her, and she just held her breath until she had to let it go for a refill.

"I just wanna go someplace, do something real. Don't *you* wanna go somewhere, Lorraine? Or do you wanna die at the goddamned Do Wop?"

God! She thought with sadness how he was patronizing her when she'd given up all her chances to do something better for a chance to be with him. She squeezed the belly of that lion, until she'd pierced his fur and her fingernails were scraping against each other. He was so hostile tonight!

"Where the fuck are you *going*, Lorraine? Where?"

He pushed it so far, she couldn't stop the tears rolling now, and the embarrassing moan that accompanied them. Her hair quickly sopped them up, her pillow, too. Would this be her whole life? Or was this it—the point where things would come to a horrifying halt, finally, once and for all, sealing the fate that she would never get back to that place with him? Which would be worse?

She knew Tommy was projecting his own self-disappointment onto her. But when you're in love, you can't *see* things even when you can guess at them in some remote part of yourself. You only see yourself through that person's eyes, and you want to be everything they want you to be so they can love you, and so you can breathe. When you can't see anything in their eyes, you are nothing. And so she didn't answer, only dug the hole in the lion deeper and deeper, staring so hard at one spot on her wall that her eyes ached.

Finally she whispered in as steady a tone as she could manage, which wasn't all that steady, "I'm not sure what you mean."

"I knew you wouldn't understand. Jeez, Lorraine. I hate to be the one to tell you this. But Lorraine, you're a round-the-way girl—plain and simple. And that's what you'll always be. And *that* is why you and I will never work, Lorraine. Because *I'm* going somewhere. I'm sorry, Lorraine, but I gotta go."

Lorraine and Tommy. Their names were knotted up for better or worse like old necklaces at the bottom of a jewelry box. You could knead them between your fingers, try whatever means you could to yank them free of each other, but still, there they were—through all his phases— joined up and not letting go. Whenever anyone ran into Lorraine, they'd think right away of Tommy, "Meet someone else already!" they'd say. Everyone had an opinion, or a single relative. They wanted to be the one to save her. "Have you ever met my nephew Bartholemew (or Christopher or Bryan with a *Y*)?"

Or they'd be hopeful. She loved the hopeful ones. They'd ask, "So when is he going to pop the question already?" as they spread mayonnaise on her turkey sandwich or rang up her Snapple iced tea. Everyone had an opinion about them—whether they approved or disapproved—but always that opinion encircled them both, drew them together, created an inevitable union that no one could deny. Never in all the days she waited, anticipated, thought she might just starve to death for even the scent of his deodorant, a glimpse of his ankle under the white cotton of a sock, did she ever think that in the end, they would wind up apart.

But that night, a giant meteor came hurling through her twisty telephone cord and crushed her right where she sat. *It might not happen between us. It might not happen between us.* Before she knew what had happened, she'd torn into the hole in her lion, pulling a tiny string of stuffing out. It was the cheap kind that mixed itchy crimped grays and browns in with the more choice white fluff. And soon she was clawing it out—clumps at a time—digging her inch-and-a-half acrylic nails deep inside until there was absolutely nothing left inside him. The stuffing littered her bed and the floor surrounding it, but the lion was completely deflated, with a telling hole in his underbelly. She knew just how he felt.

Lorraine took the lion over to the window with her, together, they looked beyond the five (un)twisty shrubs and caught a sliver of that tree where everything had started with Tommy, where they had really become knotted up, twisted, and pulled tight and mottled, one tattooed with traces of the other, for the very first time. Her chest was heaving as if all of her insides were being ripped out as well. She had the sudden shock that everything that filled *her* had also been of the cheap variety, the kind that couldn't, wouldn't last. She tried not to make a noise, and when she thought she might, she mashed the deflated lion over her mouth to muffle the sound. Admitting it to herself was one thing. Sharing it would be something else entirely.

Lorraine and the lion shell could see that the tree was not what it once was. Those boughs which had been lush with greenery—*Ah! The sound of those raindrops!*—were mostly dried out and cracked under their own weight. Looking out the window, it became obvious to Lorraine that something had changed . . . forever.

May 4, 1994

Dear NYU Admissions Officers,

While I am grateful for the generous scholarship offered to me, I regret to inform that I will have to decline your offer of admission to NYU.

Sincerely yours,
Lorraine Machuchi

eBay auction block #2
Description: In this letter, Lorraine Machuchi emphatically decided to skip college at NYU so she could stay in Brooklyn with Tommy, whose feelings she wanted to spare from the despair of realizing he'd not gotten in when Lorraine had.

Opening bid: $325
Winning bid: $785 by <u>tommyl@aol.com</u>

Comments: See! I knew it! She loves me! So take THAT Mr. Mercedes!!!!!!!!!! Sucka!

TWO

♥

OPPORTUNITY KNOCKS
AT THE DO WOP

Rotten is how Lorraine would describe her mood the next day at work. The day after that wasn't much better. Everything annoyed you more when you felt like a round-the-way loser who wasn't going anywhere—and had been told as much by the boy you'd spent most of your life torturing yourself over. Lorraine barely knew what to do with herself, other than create long flowing lists of what exactly she was lacking, that when found, would bring him into her arms once and for all.

So she continued to do just that in her mind—*she could smile more; wear red—everyone always said it was her best color.* She colored head after head of hair finding every client more annoying than the next. *Lorraine, why don't you settle down? Isn't it time?* That's what she wanted to know, but Lorraine knew Mrs. Stephano had more on her mind than an innocent hope for Lorraine's happiness. She wanted Lorraine to forget about Tommy. And so she made Mrs. Stephano's hair just a slight tint cooler than really would look best on her olive skin.

But creating an imperceptible stroke against Mrs. Stephano's looks was not going to make her feel better. *Why?* Because everyone wanted to know about Lorraine and Tommy. And today their meddling was just irritating. No, it was always irritating. Today it was *intolerable*. Every nerve ending on her body itched to punch something, eat something, turn someone's hair purple with lime green stripes. Even the things she herself did seemed intolerable. Why did she eat tuna for lunch EVERY SINGLE DAY? Why did she always put two sugars in her coffee, and not fill it all the way to the top, but just an inch below the lip of the mug? It bothered the crap out of her.

So when Carlo had volunteered Lorraine to attend a color class in Manhattan, it just felt like another in a long string of pains in the asses she'd been suffering for far too long. She'd have to get up early. She'd have to dress cooler. She'd have to talk to a lot of people who were full of hot air. She'd have to see the world outside of her neighborhood that she'd shunned for so long.

"What the hell do you want me to go to a color class for? You never let me do anything new, so why should I learn anything new?" She knew she sounded like a bratty teenager, but she didn't care.

"Because, you bratty teenager, daughter of my sister, or else you wouldn't be working here, because L'Oreal is demanding it if we want to continue to use their color here."

This, all in front of two blue-haired women in shiny silver robes, following along in the mirror as Carlo and Lorraine painted what looked like purple mud on their ever-thinning roots. They glanced at each other, looking glad to have some gossip to share tonight out on the stoop. They were Harriet Sussman and Constance Mazzarolla, and they came to the salon just as much for gossip as they did for hair color and oversized blow-dries that were guaranteed to last three days. In some more sophisticated neighborhoods, salons offered things like fancy tea cakes and shoulder massages. At the Do Wop you got a Lorraine-Carlo scream-off story you could dispense at your will all through the week—the gift that keeps on giving, you might say.

Even as she responded, "Why does it have to be me?" Lorraine took in a big breath of mildew mixed with questionably carcinogenic chemicals. It dawned on her that she was glad for the break in routine. The last couple of days had felt suffocating. *Loser! Loser! Loser!* The word played in her head all day long. While the hum and familiarity of Lorraine's neighborhood and schedule had always given her a great sense of comfort, they now felt stupid, empty, dull, and embarrassing, the way she imagined Tommy saw it all.

And so the next night Lorraine overly prepared herself for a day in Manhattan. The attention she paid to her outfit and packing her purse slightly lessened the gaping hole in time during which she normally spoke with Tommy, and got her excited about possibly learning some new techniques, even if she'd never happen upon the opportunity to implement them. Lorraine filled in the cracks in her acrylic nails. She still preferred the long nails she'd always worn. Exactly one inch from the top of her nail bed. She filed the tops into dainty half moons, not razor sharp rectangles, the way most girls in her neighborhood had done. They would be red or hot pink exclusively (these were her trademarks), and she'd airbrush (freehand, mind you) a bold, seasonal, floral motif along the top of the right pointer finger. For Christmas, the bud might be green; in the springtime, yellow or pink; at Halloween, orange or black or some years, both. No matter what the season, on the left pinkie, she always applied a tiny gold B—B for Brooklyn. It was difficult to work the tiny gold charm and have it lay flat on the upper corner of the nail at a 45-degree angle like that, but she'd always thought it looked really cool. As the years flew by, the cursive design of the letter retained a retro charm of the variety that you didn't find in a lot of places these days. And a little edge like that would do her good on a day in Manhattan, a place which, despite her cynicism, could easily intimidate her.

At 5:45 A.M., Lorraine woke, showered, and decided to let her hair dry in that wavy way again. It was starting to grow on her, and besides, it was a huge time-saver. She got dressed, ate some Frosted Flakes for breakfast, drank a jumbo coffee and refilled her insulated jumbo mug to take with her. She locked the door on her sleeping family behind her, thinking how peaceful it was with them all quiet for once.

Lorraine's mother hated Brooklyn. Her mother, Lorraine's late Grandmother Lorraine, whom she was named after, was off-the-boat Italian and had only come along with her husband to make money to buy a *casa bel-*

lissima back home, in the village their whole family lived in. Every day she woke to work in the toy factory in Mill Basin, making parts for those frightening jack-in-the-boxes that rang out an eerie tune and then scared the crap out of you. And then she'd come home and make a big pasta dinner for the family, but all the while she hoped to get back home to what she referred to, with the shaky, sandpaper manner in which she spoke, as *paradiso*. But God help the woman, she was made for birthing . . . and before she knew it, Lorraine's mom was born, and her uncle Carlo. Then Lorraine's grandfather fell ill with leukemia.

When he died, Grandma Lorraine knew she could never afford to get back to the Old Country. She never even saved enough to visit. Lorraine's mother grew up learning to despise the cramped neighborhood, the gossipy women she loosely called friends, the attached house she'd grown up in, always called home. But mostly, she hated Lorraine for throwing away her chance to leave it all behind. *Lorraine, hai un talento dio-benedetto!* (Lorraine, you have a God-blessed talent!) And she didn't shy away from sharing that fact with her daughter—or anyone else who'd listen—whenever she got the chance. It got so bad that Lorraine couldn't walk down a single street in the neighborhood without somebody shaking their head in pity at her. What would her grandmother say now? Perhaps it was better she wasn't around to see this—it would have killed her for sure.

It was strange to be out this early, while it was still dark outside, the sun just starting to shoot tiny rays between the buildings. Lorraine normally got to the salon at around ten-thirty, which meant she woke up around nine. Now, even at this hour, many people were running, just as she was, to the R train, because if you missed it, there wouldn't be another train for fifteen minutes, at least. That's the way it was in Brooklyn—just a little slower.

All the regulars, with their handy, savvy commuter MetroCard keychains, knew exactly where the doors opened along the platform, which was why people were huddled in small clusters every few feet for as far as the eye could see. Lorraine remembered this detail from the bunch of times she'd gone regularly to the city for her scholarship interviews—to prepare her essays with the counselor at NYU in an old-fashioned office in a forest green with chair rails and loads of old-smelling, important-looking books just as she'd expected. She'd gone over finances in a much less beautiful office that was all lines and numbers like at a deli counter and nothing else. Lorraine returned to get her acceptance before they were even mailed out, on a blustery winter day. Because the counselor was from the Bay. And that was they way they did things where Lorraine was from.

Lorraine would never forget the day she'd declined her admission, because her mother had cried for ten hours straight—ran a river right through their living room. She told her she wasn't taking it, wasn't going to college in the city, wasn't going to college at all. She could still see her mother's eyes turn heavenward, asking God, in Italian (because that's the language God understands, according to her mother): *Perchè me? Perchè ho ottenuto una figlia che desidera scavarla una tomba in anticipo dal dolore del cuore?* (Why me? Why have I got a daughter who wants to dig me an early grave from heartache?)

She'd made her decision for the wrong reasons—Lorraine saw that now. She and Tommy were on again at the time and that's where he'd wanted to go. He'd talked about it nonstop for months while the three of them—Lorraine, Chrissy, and Tommy—half-heartedly went through the process of SATs, applications, graduation. And he'd been wait-listed, which wasn't an exact rejection. It meant you just waited a few more months to see who was declining admission and leaving a space open for you. So, when Lorraine had received her letter, it was only a short moment of bliss until she went and found out about Tommy's wait-listing predicament.

She knew how sensitive men were about being beaten by women in any arena. And their status as a couple was already shaky at best—Tommy's head turning here and there like an oscillating fan, and her trying to ignore it and make up excuses. *He has a tick! He is studying for a project on the distinct characteristics of women in the outer boroughs.* They had been off-again for so many years, and now that they were on-again, Lorraine didn't want to give it up—even for an education. It didn't seem possible that a piece of paper could compare to an evening watching a movie in Tommy's bedroom, the anticipation of a kiss and more dancing between them like magic.

At the time, tucking the letter in a secret spot underneath her mattress seemed like the best idea. "Yeah, I was wait-listed, too," she said, hanging on to the hope that maybe the both of them would be able to go to NYU. They'd bond, adjust to city life together, become academic, wear felt berets and ribbed black turtlenecks, discuss Chaucer and saving the whales, or maybe how reading Chaucer could somehow save the whales.

In the meanwhile, Lorraine pursued the scholarship opportunities her acceptance letter had detailed. "We rarely provide anyone with a free ride," they'd told her. And that was okay, because she had a little nest egg—a savings account she'd been making deposits into since she was a little girl. Every birthday, Christmas, milestone Catholic event in her life for which her name got longer and longer (Lorraine Catherine Mary Francine Roberta Machuchi is the complete version, or was it Roberta Francine?), she put that money directly into her bank account for college. It wasn't that Lorraine was dying for college or anything, it was just that you were supposed to do that. "Get good grades, Lorraine, and you'll get into college." It's what her mother screamed any time her father forgot to pick up a fresh Italian bread on the way home, because he'd been so busy picking up the pastries, milk, arugula, and red potatoes: "If you don't go to college, Lorraine, this is what you have to look forward to—stale, defrosted bread with your dinner." Lorraine thought each household probably made their own bread in Italy, but she wouldn't dare say so.

When July came around, and Tommy was rejected, Lorraine sent in her own letter saying, *"Thank you for the opportunity to attend your school, but I have chosen to decline admission."* It hadn't been difficult. She hadn't stood at the mailbox, her hand hovering dramatically over the slot or anything. In fact there hadn't been any other choice, as far as she was concerned.

Now, as she stood in between two of the groups at the R train platform, that word stuck out in her mind: *decline*. In light of the recent call from Tommy, she thought now that's just what her life had done since that day she'd mailed her letter to NYU, only she hadn't realized it. Still, she didn't think she'd made the wrong decision. College hadn't been for her. She was a fabulous hairstylist, this Lorraine knew. Everyone in town knew it. And she still had her bank account. And there had always lingered the chance with Tommy. Until a couple of days ago, anyhow.

The train came through with a screech. The doors opened right in front of the expert commuters, which made Lorraine the last person on the train, the person with no seat. Still, as she watched the faded tile walls flash by beyond the window, and then the darkness of the tunnel, she was surprised to feel glad about the prospects of the day.

The building where the class was held was down in the SoHo area—Broadway between Prince and Spring Streets. Lorraine looked at the engraved signs of the other occupants in the building without much recognition: Bliss, Skincare Labs, some kind of yoga that looked difficult to pronounce. She felt the same mix of emotion she always did in the City—vaguely incompetent and at the same time superior, based on the idea that she wasn't dying to know what everything was and exactly what she should be overcharging on credit cards at 24.5% APR today. She looked down at some impossibly cool girl, dressed in that downtown style that made you look like you fell off a garbage truck but must have cost $2,000, at the least. Her nails were filed short, nearly to the quick, and painted in a pearly purple that made her skin appear green. Lorraine recognized from the *Vogue* ad that the color was new—from Chanel. She shook her head at the blind faith in fashion these city people devoted themselves to, and then looked at her own long nails, done up so pretty, like a real woman's nails, and smiled. She couldn't help it if she had a knack for style.

The space here, she always felt, was closing in on itself, threatening to up and leave for good at any second; smooshing the entire city in like sardines for eternity. But the loft where the class was being held was spacious enough, with high ceilings and old decorative plaster work that was beginning to crack around pillars and at moldings—the sort of shabby space New Yorkers wasted millions on, calling it "charming" God forbid they buy something brand new and clean, properly functioning. With everyone always rushing around being late for everything in the City, she had her pick of any of the twenty sink/stylist's chair stations. Not even the instructor was there when she arrived.

Lorraine pulled out the issue of *Vogue* she'd lugged on the train in the oversize leather tote she'd resurrected from her high school days. Lately, she'd again taken to the worn softness and slouchy shape of the leather.

She was reading and thinking, God that wavy hair *is* everywhere. She was glad—the style reminded her of better days, when her own hair was wild and everything was still full of potential.

Twenty minutes later the seats were full and the tiniest man, straight from central casting, began, with a singsongy voice and dramatic hand gestures, to address the class.

"Well, a glorious morning to all of you!" He was in head-to-toe black, except for purple shoes.

Lorraine wondered what you could learn from someone in purple shoes.

But the class didn't seem to notice. They muttered assorted greetings ranging from "yeah," to "whatever." Lorraine thought with wide eyes, that she heard someone pull that old trick, "fuck you very much." Clearly, no one was glad to be here not making any tips. But Lorraine was. The Do Wop clients worked on the old tipping scales anyhow: two dollars for color, one for cuts. Wash girls were lucky if they got a quarter or two.

None of it fazed Mr. Tiny, who was nothing if not all smiles. "So, we're going to go around the room"—his finger danced around the group—"and we're going to say where we're from, what we hope to learn here today, and a fruit that begins with our name."

Oh, great, Lorraine thought, a cross between Liza Minnelli *and* Mister Rogers.

As if he'd heard her thoughts, Mr. Tiny looked right at her as he sang, "I'm *Geeee*-orgio and I am from the West Village by way of Yonkers, by way of Ohio, and I hope to learn something from each and every one of you, and that's *Geeee*-orgio, with a 'G' like Green *P*epper." He said it all with extra pauses and lots of swirly palm waving, without stopping to consider any of it, as if he'd said the same thing to every class he'd ever taught.

Lorraine knew he'd said the pepper thing to get everyone chatting—purple-shoe guys lived for that sort of thing. Of course someone bit the line.

"Isn't that a vegetable?" A girl with blond highlights took the bait.

Lorraine thought she'd add a few dark whiskers along the girl's crown, and some whiter chunks in front, top it all off with a dark curtain of chocolate at the nape.

Geeee-orgio said something, doubtless having to do with seeds and how that sets boundaries between what is a fruit and what is a vegetable. And Lorraine zoned out, hearing only scattered chuckles and "hmph" here and there. She went around the room imagining what she would do to each head of hair topping the colorists in the chairs. But then she came upon a boy still wearing his leather bike jacket, sporting a pink mohawk, and Lorraine thought something she rarely did: that this boy's outrageous hair was absolutely perfect for him. She was intrigued. He caught her checking his hair out and she smiled, never one to shy away from anything. Well, unless you counted Tommy . . . and a college education, dating other men, trying new things . . .

The boy rolled his eyes and cocked his head toward *Geeee*-orgio to indicate their shared viewpoint on the importance of classifying vegetation.

When a few minutes passed and people started shyly pointing out potential "partners," as *Geeee*-orgio had instructed them to pair up, the boy with the pink mohawk shuffled right up to Lorraine and introduced himself as her partner, Don.

"Lorraine Machuchi."

"Yeah, I know, from Bay Ridge. Lorraine, like linguini."

"I don't much like fruit," Lorraine said. "I'd rather leave it for all those anorexic Park Avenue Princesses."

That struck Don as funny. "I should know—and by the way, nobody eats fruit anymore."

"How should you know? You don't look like a Park Avenue Princess to me."

He also found this funny. "What? You mean you don't like my hair color?"

"On the contrary." Lorraine picked a section up, rolling it between her fingers. "You used Manic Panic and then rinsed with Metal-X shampoo and oil bleach, right? I think it looks wonderful. I would have done exactly the same thing." Then she stepped back, tilted her head to the side, squinted her eyes, and said, "You know, now that I think about it, I might have added a little . . ." and then they finished in unison with a mutually delightful meeting of the minds, "clear gloss."

The pair smiled and got to work on *Geeee*-orgio's first assignment: what he called "the brand-new chocolate highlights trend."

The "new trend" was exactly what Lorraine would do when she

thought someone should stay a little darker, only she'd use a lot more colors than the two Georgio was instructing them to use. She said as much to Don.

He lifted his lids, as if it were a really novel idea.

Next they moved to a lighter blond highlighted look, and then to a reddish two-tone, done with a hand-painting ballayage technique, rather than foils—the way Lorraine always preferred to do highlights anyhow. Each time she commented on how she would perform the look if it were up to her, and performed the assignments barely needing to pay attention. It was simply second nature to her.

They were waiting for the apparently mute model to process under the bonnet dryer. Very often the "models" were quiet for two reasons: a) they weren't models in the magazine and runway sense, they were really just everyday people, used as Barbie head mannequins with the added bonus of being human, and b) they'd never done this before—and with an important event waiting on the weekend, and a dislike of affordable Supercuts prevailing, there they'd landed—and were completely frightened they would come out looking horrid.

But when the "model" was done, her hair looked fantastic. Don leaned back in his chair and said, "Wow, you are awesome." He had a warm, gravelly voice she automatically took to.

"Thanks," she said, "you're not too bad yourself." Secretly she was flattered. She rarely heard those types of comments, mainly because she didn't have the kind of clientele who could tell the difference. That, and the fact that her uncle found creativity a threat to his steady business.

"No, really, though." His eyes grew wide like he'd figured it all out. "Wait, are you, like, one of those secret shoppers, hired to spy on *Geeee*-orgio and make sure that this class is up to snuff?"

"Yeah. Just call me Bond. Lorraine Bond." She raised a brow for emphasis. People always liked that she could do one at a time.

They both laughed. "I could never do that eyebrow thing," said Don. Lorraine knew she liked this guy.

During the break Lorraine and Don went to eat at Dean and Deluca, enjoying the rush of new acquaintance, filling in life details along the way. Normally, Lorraine would shy away from such pleasantries—after all, she already had enough friends—but she really took a liking to Don. He was a good guy. And besides, wasn't this whole day about new experiences?

"Ten bucks for a freakin' turkey sandwich on rye?" Lorraine expressed her outrage as she bit into what would no doubt be considered a lean sandwich in her neck of the woods. "And I don't even get a pickle!"

They were sitting at a window bar, so cramped their elbows were touching when they lifted up their matching sandwiches.

"You think this is bad? Come on . . . this sandwich would cost double up on Park Avenue."

"Again with the Park Avenue? Whaddayou work up there or something?"

"You mean *you* don't work at a Park Avenue salon?" he asked, halting mid-chew as if his heart had stopped from the shock.

She shook her head.

As if he'd been swimming around lost and just regained his perspective Don said, "Oh, you work on *Madison* Avenue?" A sliver of turkey plunked to the paper below.

They both watched it before Lorraine answered.

"Nope."

"Fifth?"

"Na-ah." Before Don's head exploded, Lorraine clued him in as to her whereabouts.

"Woah. So you don't know anything about the earning potential a stylist like you has got, do you, Lorraine?"

She'd heard stories in the trade magazines. Carlo subscribed to them under the guise that his salon was keeping up with the Joneses. *Sure,* she thought often, *if the Joneses were the owners of the dusty Elegant Coiffeurs on Fifth.* Jokes aside, though, everything she'd read had turned her off to the idea. She wasn't about to go through the feudal system of the Manhattan salon world and die an assistant.

"You could make like $300,000 a year."

Now, just wait one minute. Could he have really just said that she could make $300,000 a year? That's more than everyone on her block put together made—well, except for Chrissy's boyfriend, but nobody wanted to know about that.

"Did you just—"

He cut her off before she could finish. "Lorraine, you're a follicular superstar. You're like J. Lo stuck in the Bronx. You're like Johnny Depp in some shit Florida town. You're like . . ."

"I get the picture," she said, rolling her eyes. She always knew she was good, but was she really *that good?* And even if she was, what would she do up on Park Avenue? The idea was ridiculous. Lorraine fit in on Park Avenue like Paris Hilton fit in at the Bay. Not at all. It was a bad coupling. Surely he could see that? Right? She sat back, waiting for him to recognize his mistake. In case he didn't, she fanned out her nails, waving the B around until it caught the light. Surely *that* would stick out on Park.

"Okay. Ha ha. Funny joke," she said when he didn't move or let up on his stare down.

"It's not a joke, Lorraine. Whaddyou have some kinda confidence issue or something? I wouldn't have pegged you for the sort."

It wasn't confidence she was lacking, was it? The whole thing just didn't seem . . . *natural* was the word she was looking for. Besides, maybe Lorraine wasn't at her peak self-esteem at the moment, all things considered. *Where the fuck are you going, Lorraine? Where?* The words crept in whenever she let them. But, after they had swished around a few times, now the question seemed almost a challenge in the face of what she'd just been told. Could this be where Lorraine was meant to go?

She barely liked the city. Lorraine was always looking for some excuse to turn her nose up at it, to claim her borough the superior one once and for all. After all, no song's lyrics claimed "Manhattan's in tha house," did they? Even while she was eating her ten-dollar sandwich, trying to swim to one or the other shores of this idea she'd been tossed into, she couldn't help herself from thinking how much *better* they made these at Jimmy's Delicatessen on Third.

Still, the more she thought about it, the more it seemed to make sense. Wasn't this the sort of opportunity Tommy had said she'd never get? She knew he was attracted to success; it was the common theme in all of Tommy's women—they had something he coveted, be it a home, job, residence outside of the neighborhood, money, the power to do something he couldn't.

None of those things were what Tommy needed. She knew that! Of course she did, but what he needed was someone like Lorraine who understood all of those things about him. And if she had to become one of those women to convince him of that, well, was that such a bad thing? Rather than listen to the voice telling her she'd hit rock bottom only to find a secret trapdoor to a lower chamber, the voice that was screaming—do this FOR YOURSELF!—she chose to acknowledge another thought: probably it would hurt them in the long run if she didn't experience *something*. Besides, it was merely a matter of changing her whole entire life.

"At least say you'll think about it," Don pleaded, dabbing at his mouth with a napkin.

"Oh, fine!" She wasn't sure if she was frustrated with Don for insisting or for the apprehension she was still experiencing in the face of such an obviously exciting venture.

She crossed herself for luck before picking up her sandwich again. Lorraine crunched away, with a concerted effort to accept this New York City sandwich with an open mind for what it was. She did the same for the blinding jewel of woman screaming into her cell phone, carting around her tiny dog in a beach house worth of purse as it yelped up a squeaky storm. "Shmoosy!" she yelled the dog's name every now and then. Lorraine tried to keep positive. *She could be a very nice person. She could deserve everything she has. Maybe she's just coming back from tutoring underprivileged children in Spanish Harlem. Or volunteering at the NICU at Beth Israel as a cuddler for the premies. Or . . .* Okay, it was clear Lorraine was going to have to work on this open-minded thing if she was going to start looking for work in Manhattan. But at least she'd recognized her problem, and everyone knew that traditionally, this was the first step in solving it.

When Lorraine checked back in, she noticed Don looked sort of sad. She guessed it was because with all this talk about Lorraine's talent, or whatever, Don couldn't help but compare. If she'd left it to him on that last assignment, the model's hair would have looked not unlike the shade of orange you might find on the cartoon character Garfield. She didn't know him well enough to say anything, but she couldn't help wondering why he stuck with this job. At best, he appeared indifferent toward hair.

Lorraine's mind was working overtime, thinking of all the ways she could find out which salons were the best, how she might design her résumé, what she'd say in a cover letter. For a little while they ate in silence. Then Don dropped his crusts onto the paper he was eating over. "Lorraine, you've got to come work with me at my brother's salon. He's in Bendel's. He does all the Park Avenue Princesses."

He seemed surprised when, rather than throw herself over him in excitement—a top salon, some of the most powerful clients in the world—Lorraine said, "Oh, yeah, sure. And why don't you come over to my uncle's salon. It's in the Waldorf-Astoria. You should see how much a sandwich costs over there." There was a nastiness to her tone she hated to hear. Change is hard! She wanted to cry it out loud, but even in her head it sounded infantile.

"It's true what they say, you do find talent in the weirdest places," he said, looking down at Lorraine's nails and shaking his head. "Lorraine, I'm serious. And by the way, hotel salons suck. Everyone knows that. Boy, you've got *a lot* to learn. Now, hurry up and finish that sandwich. I know this great place up the block for a mean garlic pickle."

"Well, if it means Don will shut up already, I'd love to give you a chance," Guido, a very tall man in an expertly groomed Fu Manchu and a red velvet cape, said, extending his hand out to Lorraine. He noticed her nails and said nothing, but raised his eyebrows. Eventually, he gave a slow nod of approval as if realizing something profound about them.

Don had apologized beforehand for her having to test with Guido right after coloring all day long, but Lorraine didn't care. She had gotten so caught up in the excitement of the offer once she'd given herself over to it, her instant bond with Don, and the conflicting feelings of love and hate she felt the second she walked into Bendel's, that a little more work was the last thing that could bother her. The hard part should have been the decision—for someone like Lorraine, as someone had put it, so "round the way,"—but after the initial hesitation, it hadn't been. In fact, like many things in her life, it didn't seem to be much of a decision at all, just a point plunked in front toward which she was slowly moving. Besides, she needed a way to prove herself to Tommy, to her mother, and to everyone who shook their heads at her on Eighty-sixth Street when all she wanted was a damn gyro sandwich with extra hot sauce. And here, God, Don, Guido, whoever, had placed it right in her hands.

She painted with ease—her favorite, signature five-shade color, designed to look different in every lighting environment—on the sister of one of the other stylists. Afterward, Guido sent her out with a huge stack of employment papers and a manual about the guidelines of styling with the Guido Method, *Book 1: Color*. Lorraine was spinning.

Don was turning her around toward the elevators that led to the clothing department, telling her a thousand things at once. "I know you're overqualified to be an assistant, but you'll see in the end, it's worth it. I know my brother. He was blown away by your talent, so don't get discouraged about the shampooing and the gloss-only work you'll be doing. You'll see."

Don circled Lorraine around the denim area—the $180 jeans with Swarovsky crystals on the butt pockets, the cute ones with the pink "A" embroidery. Sure they were beautiful; she knew a good thing when she saw it. But she was never paying $180 for jeans. She was brought up better than that. She could just picture Chrissy's face now, if she came home with something like that! *If it isn't the Queen of England!* She'd said that once when Lorraine had sprung for a cashmere tank, although it had been marked down to 70 percent off.

A girl was walking to the dressing room, followed by a salesgirl carrying a mountain of denim, matching T-shirts, and Juicy hoodies in every color of the rainbow. Lorraine couldn't help but shake her head at the wastefulness. That girl was about to try on a kid's first year of college. And why? Because some magazine told her to. She fumed her way by shoes, accessories, formalwear, lingerie, cosmetics. But by the time they reached the ground floor, she'd realized she'd completely abandoned her promise to be more open-minded. What the hell was she so *angry* about? What the hell did she care if a woman could buy a wardrobe double the worth of Lorraine's house in less than twenty minutes?

She breathed and swore to herself she would loosen up.

And the vow came not a moment too soon. An elevator whisked the pair down to the basement, where Don gave Lorraine a long sigh, placing both hands on her shoulders. What he was about to tell her would make it a hell of a lot easier to open herself to the ideas of extravagant consumption. "Now listen," he said seriously. "You're about to receive one of the most coveted items in the world. A Bendel's discount card."

So, she opened up. Way up. In fact, by the time she set off for home, she'd done five shopping bags' worth of opening up, Lorraine noted as she looked around, realizing her shopping bags were taking up three subway seats. With fifty percent off, who wouldn't? She was still Lorraine Machuchi, from Bay Ridge, just trying to go to that ever elusive "someplace" that could settle her once and for all. Maybe, she considered, she'd finally arrived there.

The train screeched to a halt, dropping her safely, once again, at Seventy-seventh Street and Third Avenue, where the schoolkids were skipping familiar cracks on the sidewalk and drawing chalk games on the dead-end streets, and Lorraine realized she was smiling—for the first time in a long time.

"Hey, Lorraine," one little girl said as she passed by. It was Lorraine's cousin Antoinette. Lorraine watched her sometimes when her parents went out to eat at the steakhouse on Ocean Parkway.

"Hey, Tony. Whatchyou girls up to? Jump rope?"

Antoinette smiled in that shy way girls do, and shook her head.

Lorraine looked up at the sky, could see the bridge in the distance. Suddenly she dropped her bags, pulled out a glittery scarf, and artfully twisted it around Antoinette's neck. Then she playfully pushed Antoinette's friend, Lilly, over a little, and grabbed her cousin's hand. Together they jumped and sang the same songs Lorraine sang as a girl, the same her own mother had sung, until the sun was all the way behind the buildings and the moon was taking its place, way up high.

Strawberry Shortcake, cream on top. Tell me the name of your sweetheart. . . .

"Lorraine! Your scarve!" Antoinette screamed the word in an adorably mistaken way as Lorraine walked away.

"Keep it!" Lorraine turned her head back to the girls and smiled.

When she got home, there were no messages from Tommy. She didn't think there would be. He wasn't the type.

There was only one more thing Lorraine had to buy before she started her job in the city in a couple of days. It was nothing fancy, which was a good thing considering all the money she'd just dropped at Bendel's. What she needed had a practical purpose, which was to keep her father from freaking out over his little girl working in the Big, Bad City—the vision of which he'd garnered from the 1973 film *Serpico* and hadn't altered since. Her father hated Manhattan. Fifty-five years in Brooklyn, and never had he gone there. Not even once. He was so relieved when she didn't go to NYU, although he'd never tell that to Lorraine's mother and risk getting hit over the head with a wooden spoon. What she needed was a cell phone. It would be easier to break the news to him if she had the instant communication device all ready to show him when she did.

She picked up Chrissy in the gently bruised family Honda in its conspicuous shade of sea green, beeping as she pulled up to her friend's house—attached brick, just like her own, only a mirror image on the left instead of the right.

"So what's this big secret you have to tell me already?"

Lorraine noticed Chrissy had gone back to the straight hair again, and said so.

"Yeah, well, old habits die hard. You should know." Everything was loaded with them lately.

Lorraine didn't feel like getting reamed all night about Tommy when she knew the real problem was Chrissy's relationship, so she just came out and asked. "Are things any better with you guys?"

"Well, I told him if I ever find his fat ass underneath some skanky blond whore ever again, I'd have Little Joey put a bullet right through it."

"Yeah, but you've said that a million times already." Sometimes she'd alter the body part, but overall, the idea was the same.

Chrissy breathed deeply. "I know. I *know*. You're friggin' right. But what am I gonna do?"

There was no answer. They both knew this. Chrissy loved the fucker. And Lorraine wasn't in any position to judge.

They drove a couple of blocks in silence.

"So, why you getting a cell phone when everyone you know lives in a two-block radius?"

"That's the news, Chrissy. I got a job at a Fifth Avenue salon. I'll be working in the city starting tomorrow." It felt good to say it; the power of it seemed right.

But rather than filling her with awe, the news set Chrissy off in hysterics. She started smacking the dash, as if Lorraine had said the funniest thing she'd ever heard. "Really, you're such a good friend, Lorraine, cheering me up like that," she gasped. "You should think about going into stand-up maybe. You're a lot funnier than those *Blue Collar* idiots." Chrissy wiped some stray tears from the corners of her eyes.

Silence ensued. Lorraine didn't say anything, merely stared her down as much as she could while watching the road. Chrissy's eyes bulged as the reality of the statement dawned on her.

At a red light Lorraine turned her full attention to her friend. She couldn't help but smile. She knew Chrissy would be thrilled—her friend was always pushing her to take her career further. *God, one of us should, for crying out loud.* She'd said that a million times if she'd said it once.

Every time Lorraine would style Chrissy's hair—very subtly, just to cover the few premature grays Chrissy hated to see—Chrissy would look at herself in the mirror and say the same thing. "Unbelievable. It is unbelievable how hot you make me look. Look at me. I'm a friggin' supermodel." And it was true. A few delicate, barely detectable hints of a medium toffee, a couple of loose layers framing her cheek apples, and Chrissy's most beautiful features beamed. Sometimes, Chrissy would look through *Allure*'s makeover pages and exclaim, "You did a better job than that one . . . and that one . . . and that one . . ."

"Are you gonna friggin' say something, or what?" Lorraine was gonna cry right there in the car if her friend didn't stop looking at her like that.

"*Or what* . . . seriously, though, Lorraine. My gosh." She fluttered her eyes dramatically, wiped at imaginary tears—maybe a couple real ones, too—and sniffled for effect. "I am so proud of you."

"Shut the hell up." Lorraine stepped on the gas hard, sending Chrissy back into the seat with a thump.

"You better watch the driving, you City Bi-atch."

Another guy from the group, Stevie, owned the cell phone store with his cousin Petey, the guy Mary had a thing for. "Well, well, if it isn't the Bobbsey Twins," he said. It's what everyone said when Lorraine and Chrissy went anywhere, ever since about 1978, which is why it sounded so old-fashioned and lame. Some nicknames were timeless, classic. This wasn't one of them.

Lorraine was filling out the papers for her new Motorola flip phone, which she was surprisingly excited about despite the fact she'd never really wanted one before, when the door opened. She knew before she looked, because she could smell him, sense him even, after so many years. If only she could hold on tight to the counter, maybe she wouldn't drown.

"Stevie, Petey." Tommy nodded to each before he came over and invaded the space between Chrissy and Lorraine. She knew it wasn't right, him coming over and making her all tingly and hungry, when he'd already crushed her dreams of anything happening between them. Here he was dangling her on a thread all the same, and here she was letting it happen. That fabulous Lorraine of the day's previous hours gasped for breath.

He had made a wall between the Bobbsey Twins with his muscular frame, in his head-to-toe black outfit (three buttons open!). His nose was nearly touching hers. He picked up Lorraine's cell phone and pressed a few buttons.

"Lorraine, Lorraine," he sang her name in a whisper that meant who knew what.

"What'd you do?" she asked when he'd replaced the Motorola on the counter. She hoped she sounded angry—but not too angry. She picked up the phone. She hadn't quite figured the phone functions out yet and couldn't find anything that looked different. But the warmth of his hand was still on it, so she pressed her palm firmly around it. Who knew? This might be the last time she felt his touch.

He didn't answer, just looked at her and said, "Cell phone, huh, kid?"

like he'd noticed something different, knew this to be so unlike Lorraine. He didn't smile. The way he looked at her, the way he evoked their familiarity like that—it was enough to just forget the hurt, or at least look past it. How could you let someone be that close? Mean that much to you? Despite the hurt, his words echoed in her head, vibrated in waves around her chest. It was good she was getting out. The idea was a tiny seed, but it was there—undeniably it was there. Still, she didn't want to say anything just yet about the job. Better if he found out from someone else.

"Yeah, she needs it because she's a real City Bi-atch now," she heard her best friend chime in. Chrissy smiled proudly.

The only thing worse than changing yourself for the guy you're mortifyingly obsessed with is the guy *learning* that you changed yourself all on his account—a fact that seemed embarrassingly obvious just then, like maybe it was written in red marker on her forehead.

But as glaring as it felt to her, she wasn't sure if he'd gotten it. Tommy looked from Chrissy to Lorraine, his face scrunching a bit as if he were pondering some elusive idea. He snuggled his hand on Lorraine's back, just below her shoulder blade. He'd once said it looked as if their pieces were made to fit like that. "Good luck." He kissed her close to, but not on, her mouth. Then he turned to Stevie and Petey and started talking about the Yankee game. The Bobbsey Twins exited the store. Lorraine found herself back in that place between heaven and hell she knew all too well.

Chrissy was playing with the phone on the way home. Lorraine was deciphering Tommy's actions, trying to attach meaning where she could. Just like the card game Memory she'd play with Carlo's daughter. If you could remember what this was under here, you could pair it with this over there, pile it neatly away with everything in order. She tried to make matches—meaning to action—to cover everything she'd seen.

"I found it!" Chrissy was thrilled with herself. "He programmed his phone number in there. What a pompous piece of shit. Hopefully you'll find someone better in the city, you Bi-atch."

If only either of them believed that. If only the spaces in between their laughs didn't hold so much pain.

★   ★   ★

It was with pure excitement that Lorraine woke up the following morning for her last day at the Do Wop. As far as she was concerned, the best part of her new job was that she got to tell Carlo to shove it. How many times had she proposed changes and updates to him? How many times had he told her, literally, to shove it? It was a second name to her, "Shove It, Lorraine." *Miss Shove It, you've got a client coming in at two.*

Lorraine arrived at the Do Wop ten minutes late, on purpose. Tardiness drove Carlo bananas. Of course, she had never been late the entire time she'd worked for him, but she knew, even this once, he'd flip out, and that would make for the kind of grand finale the silver hairs would remember forever.

"Go to Manhattan for one day and already you're walking in late like you're the Queen of England!" There was a silver hair crowned in purple mud already beneath his hands—Mrs. Aranian—and next to her was Chrissy's grandmother, Mrs. Vioto, who was wide-eyed. Lorraine wondered if Chrissy had already told her the news, because Mrs. Vioto looked as if she were ready for a show. It wouldn't have surprised Lorraine in the least if Mrs. Vioto had pulled out Cracker Jacks and Mike and Ike's from her purse.

"I didn't know Mrs. Vioto was scheduled for today," Lorraine ventured.

"Last-minute appointment," Mrs. Vioto quipped, locking eyes with Lorraine in the mirror.

Hmmph.

Lorraine ran her fingers over Mrs. Vioto's hair, flattening it, rubbing a few strands between her fingers to see how the color had held up, if she needed any extra conditioning. It was too quiet; she knew they were all up to something.

"You know," Carlo screamed, his thinning hair swaying slightly with the force of it, "I could fire you for tardiness alone! I could just . . ."

She finished for him, "Toss me out right into the street."

"If only . . ."

"My mother wasn't your sister."

"You know, Lorraine? *I hate it* when you do that! Can't I just finish my own sentences?"

"So be more original next time."

"Original, original, that's all I ever hear from your big mouth!" Carlo waved his comb around for effect.

Both Mrs. Vioto's and Mrs. Aranian's eyes flew back and forth like Ping-Pong balls. They were making mental notes, already smiling with the juicy stuff they'd bring to the stoop.

"Well, guess what, Carlo? I'm . . ."

"Leaving!" He finished for *her*.

"Yes, exactly, I'm leave . . . *Wait a minute*! How did you know?" There was nothing worse than being cheated out of your own news.

"*Mama Mia*, how long you live in this neighborhood, Miss Shut It? We're all horrendous gossips!" And Carlo was the ringleader, she knew.

The Silver Ladies tried to cover their faces, by looking down, fidgeting at what remained of their eyebrows.

"Oh, Mrs. Vioto, you know it's true!" Carlo was not going to take the brunt of this all on his own.

"Oh, fine, it is true!" She got up from where she sat and walked over to the coat closet by the door. "Here, I made you a lasagna." She handed over a big silver tin, covered up, the garlic intoxicating all the same.

"Thank you," Lorraine said. "But how did you know?"

Mrs. Vioto pulled her limbs in like a crab and mumbled, "I overheard you and Chrissy in the car last night when you dropped her off."

Lorraine shook her head, but smiled at all of them simultaneously. Sometimes you couldn't fight tradition. Sometimes you didn't want to.

"Oh, Miss Shove It! What are we gonna do without you?" Carlo was sincere.

Lorraine guessed she'd known deep down he always felt like that. But they'd had their routine down so long, she had stopped thinking about it. She saw now she would miss him, despite the frustrations he caused her. She would miss the familiarity and the gossip and the language of rolling eyes and shrugged shoulders they'd silently perfected over the years. But there was more out there for her, and she wasn't going to find it doing the same thing day in, day out. She'd gotten a potent taste of something bigger and she couldn't underestimate the truth in it now.

Around lunchtime, her mother came in, the way she always did, as if she owned the place. Mrs. Machuchi may not be living in Italy, but she could be the big shot of the Do Wop! Although they repeatedly asked her to, she never made an appointment, just moseyed in and sat right down. But, another reason brought her in. Today there was her daughter, leaving this neighborhood! And *that* was something to hold your head up high, high above everyone else's for!

"My little girl! She's so special! Too special for this tiny place! *Madre Mia!* If only it hadn't taken so long!" She was holding her daughter so tight Lorraine could feel the imprint of her fingers pinching in at her side.

All day, clients had come by to wish her well. She could just see the rumors spreading from brownstone to brownstone, attached house to attached house, like that old game, telephone. Probably, after Mrs. Vioto complained of her bad hip to Chrissy, she pogo'd around to everyone handing out plastic cups strung along lengths of yarn. They didn't need to rely on AT&T in this town! Everyone just added their own editorial regarding Tommy and what might happen as a result of Lorraine's new city life as they passed the story on, and on and on.

Mrs. Stephano had obviously been on the receiving end of a larger than life version of reality. "I made this for you last night!"

It was a blanket. She had crocheted it to say, "Forget about Tommy!!!" in a curly script with three exclamation points over hearts.

Lorraine held it up, tried to inspect the quality of stitching, rather than the content. What was she expected to *do* with a blanket like this? And how did Mrs. Stephano make this blanket in one night? And never mind *why*?

"Turn it over!" Mrs. Stephano was so excited you'd think she'd just met the Pope.

On the other side Mrs. Stephano stitched the words that could win her the title of Yenta of the Year (they really did award this title in the Bay). It read, in big block letters, . . . AND BY THE WAY, DID I EVER TELL YOU ABOUT MY GRANDSON JIMMY?

The day was quietly turning into a food festival. Lorraine had accumulated three afghans, two bunches of begonias, and four dozen rainbow cookies from well-wishers. Everyone was sad to see her go, but everyone was glad for her new job. And *everyone* had something to say about

Tommy. He would either see his mistake, realize he was a moron, or start looking to Lorraine like a round-the-way loser himself.

As people continued to flock into the shop, Lorraine resolved to seriously start searching her room for bugs. "How'd you find out?" Lorraine asked her mother as they tucked into the lasagna.

"Oh, your grandmother told me."

It wasn't strange to Lorraine that her mother had been communing with the dead. In her crowd, it was pretty common to be visited by dead Italian ladies. In fact, some of them still held their voting rights in the Ladies' Club at Our Lady of Perpetual Grace. Her mother claimed Lorraine's grandmother spoke to her all the time, often to give her new pasta sauce recipes from the Food Channel. As for Lorraine, she'd been visited in dreams a few times—mostly to be hollered at—but she'd taken it with a grain of salt.

"Oh, speaking of your grandmother . . ." Her mother dabbed at the corners of her mouth daintily. "Your grandmother's best friend, Mrs. Romanelli—I'm not sure if you'd remember her, dear, she moved to *Park Avenue* over in Manhattan years ago—well, she was over at Jimmy's Delicatessen on Third before. She says she won't get her meats from anywhere else! Well, she heard about your job and she wanted to know if you wanted to have her *Park Avenue* apartment when she ships off to Italy in a couple of weeks—for free."

Lorraine always took whatever her mother said with a grain of salt. Talking dead Italian ladies she could believe, but free apartments on Park Avenue! Lorraine wouldn't put it past her mother to have made the whole thing up so she could say "Park Avenue" a couple of times in front of everyone at the Do Wop.

"I'm not saying you have to move to the city, but just think about it a little bit. It would be really great to be there at night, and then you could go out down in the Meatpacking District. I was watching that Style Channel, you know? And *Mamma Mia*, you should see the rich men that go over there! I wrote down a few places for you."

Lorraine breathed deeply. In a little less than twenty-four hours, she'd be escaping to another borough. Even if only for eight hours a day, just then it felt as if she was set to embark on a Caribbean vacation.

After twelve pounds of lasagna had been consumed and ten silver hairs had been colored at Lorraine's trusty fingertips, she plopped herself onto her stylist's chair, surprised at how exhausted she was. It hadn't occurred to her how much the change would take out of her. This was the last time she'd look at herself in this mirror, this chair, as a stylist at the Do Wop. Now it seemed so formally announced, so final—her last day behind her, the first day ahead, Lorraine felt doubt and fear settle in. What ever happened to "If it ain't broke, don't fix it?" That was something she'd said before, hadn't she? Now she couldn't remember if it had actually come from her lips, or if it was just something she'd heard too many times. Who *was* this Lorraine, filled with all this doubt? She couldn't even recognize herself. She'd never faltered before. Then again, there hadn't been many chances to, hadn't been many risks or changes to face.

She heard the door open. Underneath the *Good Luck, Lorraine!* sign stretched over it, in walked her father. "Don't start doubting yourself now, Quichy."

She knew it meant a lot for him to say that. He hated to have her go off to the city. But her dad could always put his own feelings aside in the best interest of those he loved. They'd always had that kind of respect between them.

"I kind of wanted to be the one to tell you," she said. The tears that had been threatening all day were choking up in her throat. But she wasn't about to let them out. She was going to do this without crying—she was going to show her father he had nothing to worry about.

"That's okay. Not too easy to keep anything a secret around here." He rolled his eyes.

"Oh, you've gotta see this." She showed him the afghan from Mrs. Stephano, and they got a good laugh out of it.

"Oh, the old Stephano matchmaking blanket." He threw his palm down at it. "Show me something new."

She remembered the cell phone and pulled it out of her drawer. "I got a cell phone, Dad, so you can check in with me. Here, let me write down the number," she said and did so.

"Just don't forget, Lorraine," he said, after she'd taken time to shut down the salon for the last time, pull her tiny wad of tips out of her drawer along with some business cards and paper scraps and hair elastics. They were standing in front of the store, her father securing the metal gate for his daughter. "If you don't like it, you can always come back. Not everyone's cut out for everything, and sometimes there's more dignity in knowing that than forcing yourself to be something you're not."

"Thanks, Dad," she said. The greasy garage hug he gave her before opening up the car door for her made Lorraine realize she always had this. No matter what, she always had family. It was something she didn't take lightly. Inside their less-than-perfect Honda, they drove the few blocks, past the hopscotch girls—Antoinette was still wearing the *scarve*—and the old silver hairs on Mrs. Mazzorola's stoop assembled in a rainbow of lawn chairs. They continued on, moving closer to tomorrow.

```
                    M V M   R E C E I P T


    M T A   N Y C   T R A N S I T
    7 7 t h   S T .
    B R O O K L Y N   N Y
    M V M # :   0 2 1 6   ( A 0 3 4     0 7 0 0 )



    THURS 23 JULY 04      6:57

    Trans: Sale OK
    Payment Mode: Cash
    Amount:                    $10.00
    Bonus:                      $2.00
    Card Value:                $12.00

    ATM Card #:  XX2553
    Auth#:  162562
    Ref#:  053414182236
    Serial#: 0919013985
    Type: 012
    PRE-VALUED



                  Q u e s t i o n s ?
            C a l l   ( 2 1 2 )   M E T R O C A R D
```

eBay auction block #3
Description: This was Lorraine's first subway receipt during her time at Guido's Salon.

Opening bid: $300
Winning bid: $1500 by crazymetrocollector@crazymetrocollector.com

Comments: DUDE! If you find any more of these Metrocard receipts, please e-mail me. Will pay good money for them. Also, not sure what a Metrocard is actually for. If any information at all please write to P.O. Box 1234567 Louisville, KY 55555. Peace out . . .

THREE

♥

THE APARTMENT SEARCH

The commute wasn't exactly wonderful. Traveling early in the morning and relatively late in the evening, Lorraine had to learn to carve her own place amongst the huddles along the platform, find a seat for the long ride that wasn't already taken by the lifers. The train was packed with all kinds—a young guy with a heavy *thump-thump!* spilling out from underneath his studio-size headphones, his chunky hoop earring smushed against his neck; a woman she vaguely recognized from somewhere she couldn't place—maybe the bank. The woman did nothing but stare directly across at something far beyond the window for the entire ride. But the commute wasn't the reason she'd really started looking for an apartment in the city.

The reason was her mother, and the fact that she hadn't stopped bugging her about it. It wasn't exactly that Lorraine wanted to please her mother, but she was sick of facing the disappointment in her eyes, in the slight downward turn of her mouth, every time she came home from work. After all these years Lorraine thought she'd grown used to being met without praise or warmth from her mother, and she had. But now she was doing something to change herself for the better, and her mother *still* wasn't happy. It seemed she'd never be satisfied with Lorraine. Each smirk, each *tsk* cut her deeper than the last. And to be honest, she was feeling wonderful in general about the changes in her life—every day a new person to meet, a new store to peek inside, another street to explore. If she wasn't meeting her new life with "open arms," at least she was meeting it—making the effort to have an open mind. She couldn't stand to be hit with her mother's negativity on a daily basis. So she agreed to start looking.

"Why won't you just take this apartment from Mrs. Romanelli! *Mama Mia!* It's waiting for you!" Her mother raised her hands to heaven, looking for an answer.

Why wouldn't she? Well, maybe she didn't want to take this advice from her mother. Maybe she thought, like many of her mother's lofty, romantic dreams, that it might turn out to be nothing like her mother had thought. It was possible the woman hadn't even mentioned Lorraine could have the apartment. It was also possible that in her mother's dreamy mind, she'd transformed the idea into something it wasn't. Then again, it was also possible Lorraine's mom *did* have it right—then Lorraine would be forced to listen to her mother's opinion on everything in the future. Otherwise she'd be met with "You doubted me about Mrs. Romanelli's apartment, and look how great *that* turned out! See, now listen to me about Mrs. Stephano's grandson Jimmy." It wasn't a fantastic scenario. Besides, wasn't it better to do this on her own?

She'd been doing it on her own at Guido's through the week, and that seemed to be going well enough. Like any salon, there was a pattern, like the borders on a kindergarten bulletin board, that stylists fell into. Lorraine was used to patterns, that was for sure, but she wasn't used to watching other stylists do the work while she held out clips, gripped sections of hair to pass over to someone else's fingers.

Lorraine hadn't gone in blindly, though. She'd known about the assistant duties—she'd been given the entire book! But it was tough, this holding back your potential, not being all that you could be. However, she was determined to see this experience through, to see if maybe there was more for her outside of the Bay.

That was the spirit Lorraine held fast to on Saturday, her first day off, when she and Chrissy drove into the City to meet up with Don and check out all the open houses listed in little boxes in the *Village Voice*.

The "Aquatic Honda" (Chrissy's description) made its way up the FDR and over toward Park Avenue. Floating through the Upper East Side in the vehicle, it occurred to Lorraine that the whole place looked different from this perspective, as if you weren't quite in the midst of it, but looking inside a giant fishbowl Manhattan. And she smiled at that idea—that she now knew the City enough to know what it *was* like when you were *really* swimming around.

"That place is great for sticky buns," she pointed out to a blasé Chrissy as they pulled up to Don's apartment. He lived in his brother's humungous place on Park Avenue, and was leaning against the stone building casually, holding a foam coffee cup. Lorraine loved how he looked simultaneously *out of* and yet *exactly in* place. She knew just what that was like.

Their vessel was a two-door coupe, and so Chrissy opened the door and stepped out to pull her seat forward for Don.

"Holy shit! You guys are like the friggin' Bobbsey Twins!" he commented before even introducing himself.

The girls laughed and shook their heads. Sometimes it seemed as if there was no escaping the past.

"Yeah, well, you're already talking like her, stealing Lorraine's *friggin'* like that! I'm Chrissy, Bobbsey Twin Number One." Her tone was bubbly.

"Hey, *I'm* number one!" Lorraine yelled out to them. "Chrissy, Don; Don, Chrissy. Now get in the friggin' car and let's go."

They started uptown over by Columbia and worked south to the Lower-Lower East Side. Everything was either taken or sucked beyond belief—no sink in the bathroom; or even no bathroom at all. Forget about the condition of the walls, ceiling, fuse boxes, and of course, the smaller-than-Lorraine's-bedroom-at-home-sizes.

"Oh, look, a walk-in closet!" Chrissy exclaimed at one apartment on Eleventh Street on the West Side.

"That's the bedroom," Lorraine said.

"Well, at least you won't have to spend a lot on furniture," Don offered with an easy smile.

But even that one was taken by the time they got through looking at it.

Zero for fifteen, Lorraine crossed the last tiny box off her *Village Voice* page. To lighten the mood, Don insisted they take Chrissy to the dining room at Bendel's for lunch, since he had a tab there and could therefore treat the three of them. It sounded good, so they both agreed.

"What the hell is *foy grass?*" Chrissy wanted to know, scanning the dainty menu.

"I think it's like the new thing after that slimy green wheat-grass crap. Those Park Avenue girls will drink *anything* if they think they'll lose an ounce," Lorraine said, thinking of the bright orange, and even worse, muddy-colored drinks she'd seen them sipping in clear plastic take-away cups.

"You guys seriously crack me up," Don said, wiping tears from his eyes and holding his belly.

The Bobbsey Twins were firmly holding furrowed brows. They didn't enjoy being funny when they didn't intend it.

"It's called *foie gras,* and it's goose liver. Like chopped *liva,* Funny Girls. That's a good one, you really sounded just like Babs, exactly. You gotta do that for Guido—honestly, he loves that shit."

They hadn't been joking, but whatever. They both hated chopped liver anyhow. Don ordered the *foy grass,* just to be a little funny, and admittedly it was. Chrissy went for the *gourmet* macaroni and cheese and Lorraine opted for the roast chicken with lobster mashed potatoes. Since the whole thing was free, she ordered a glass of the house red.

"*Mademoiselle,*" the waiter said after Lorraine had given the final order, "zee chef recommends zee vino blanc wit zee rrrrroast *chiiiick*-en."

There was nothing, and she meant nothing, that pissed Lorraine off more than pretension. And the more time she spent in the City, the less patience she had for it. "Well, you can tell zee chef zat *Mademoiselle* is aware that restaurants create balanced meals so that patrons can drink either white OR red with *any* meal zey serve, and so *Mademoiselle* will be sticking with *zee red.*"

The waiter looked to Don, a regular, for some kind of aid, but Don just shrugged his shoulders and said, "You heard zee *Mademoiselle.*"

"How the frig did you know that?" Chrissy wanted to know when the waiter retreated to input their order and probably spit on it.

"From that Sonoma trip for Frankie and Samantha's wedding last year. Remember we went to tour Chateau St. Jean, but you were too mad at Big Bobby to come with us?"

Chrissy quieted at that, grmacing before turning a deep shade of eggplant.

"Who's Big Bobby?" Don wanted to know. He was two years younger, but you might guess more from his sweet, innocent nature. He never thought twice about saying anything, and even if he was being sarcastic, you never took it to be nasty.

Chrissy breathed, and surprised Lorraine with her answer. "He's the f'er I should break up with but can't. Same old stupid story. Just like Lorraine."

"Whaddya mean, just like Lorraine? I didn't think you had a boyfriend, Lorraine." Don looked confused as the waiter came by, white-faced, to place the red wine in front of Lorraine.

"Never mind about that," Lorraine said, and picked up her glass.

The other two held their Cokes in the air.

"To Don, thanks for a sweet lunch," she said, tipping her glass, wanting to change the subject fast. You didn't come all this way just to have the same reputation.

"To Don," they both said, laughing.

"Damn, that's good stuff," Don said of his soda.

Lunch was long, filling, and fun. It looked as if Chrissy felt just the same bond with Don that Lorraine had when she'd met him. In fact, she couldn't stop talking about him on the way home.

"Whaddya love him or something?" Lorraine said after they'd crossed the Brooklyn Bridge and maintained the moment of silence they always did, following the loop around to the Brooklyn Queens Expressway, where the best views of the diminished skyline were to be had.

"Yeah, I'm freakin' in love with him. You found me out. I wanna have his kids, with little pink mohawks. We can make a million doing perms on Eighty-sixth Street. Just think how we'll all fit in at the Bay Ridge Bowl."

Sounded to Lorraine like someone was being a little sensitive, but it had been a long day, so she let the subject go. Besides, Don was younger and there was no way Chrissy had a thing for a guy with a pink Mohawk who styled hair. Did *anyone*? Furthermore, Chrissy was an accountant. She did the books at the Waldbaum's over by Fort Hamilton. She had a 401k and retirement benefits. The second Big Bobby asked Chrissy to marry her, she'd change to part-time status and start popping out kids. That had always been her plan. Unfortunately, Big Bobby kept sleeping with skanky blond hos.

The following week, all Lorraine's mom did was drop hints about the apartment in the city. On the list of Pork Store items she handed to Lorraine one evening, number 10 read, *Call Mrs. Romanelli about the apartment before your mother dies of a heart attack thinking of you in some hovel in Alphabet City.*

Lorraine had always done her best to ignore her mother's schemes and ideas, but after the fruitless weekend search, she was feeling a bit more amenable. So, when her mother burst into a theatrical display of tears, hanging on to the painting of the Virgin Mother and begging of it, "Why me? Why me?, *Perchè me? Perchè me?*" Lorraine figured she might as well take a look on Monday, if only for the peace it would restore to her family's home.

"Fine, Mom! I'll do it! Would you get up already, please?"

"Oh, Santa Maria, thank you! Thank you!" Her mother kissed the Virgin Mother's face.

Lorraine, her brother, and her father rolled their eyes. Lorraine's brother offered the code phrase they used in place of "She's crazy": "Can you pass the bread?" he said with excess blinking.

Lorraine nearly spit out her cavatelli. "Yes, *please* pass the bread," she said.

"BREAD! PLEASE!" her father confirmed before they all broke into hysterics.

"What's wrong with all of you?" her mother asked. When they didn't answer, she said, twisting her own piece of bread into two pieces, "You're all nuts."

That night in bed Lorraine determined that, whichever way it turned out with Mrs. Romanelli, she was done looking for apartments. Even in dreams, she couldn't stop thinking about how badly they sucked. In the dream she couldn't fit her bed in the bedroom and wound up throwing it out the window, only for someone to cart it off with her screaming out, "Hey, that's my bed!" which pissed her off. Not because she lost her bed, but because normally, Lorraine dreamed about Tommy. It was a time that he would always be hers. And now, it seemed clear to Lorraine, she couldn't even have him in her dreams.

On Monday at two P.M. there was a free hour in the schedule of the colorist Jacqueline, whom Lorraine was assisting that day. Jacqueline, the only stylist at the salon who even hinted that she thought the whole Princess thing was ridiculous, had told Lorraine she was going to use the hour to "Run up and down Fifth Avenue shooting every fake blonde with an Uzi."

"Have fun," Lorraine said nonchalantly, without looking up. It was the perfect opportunity to check out her mom's kooky apartment connection. As she turned down Fifty-eighth Street toward Park Avenue, Lorraine couldn't help shaking her head at the pointlessness. Who ever heard of a free apartment? If there was one thing Lorraine knew; it was that you didn't get something for nothing.

Still it was a nice day, and the walk to Seventy-sixth Street was pleasant enough. You could almost breathe up here, what with the wider avenues and the trees and the lower buildings that actually afforded a glimpse of sky. Lorraine kept waiting for the neighborhood to turn bad, look like something someone from the neighborhood might know about, but it didn't. If anything, it got ritzier-looking, with friendly doormen nodding, and one dog tinier than the next trotting happily along in what appeared to be lime green mink vests and matching UGG boots.

At 562, Lorraine asked the doorman if Mrs. Romanelli was in. Even through the telephone, Lorraine could hear the voice on the other end change in pitch from its dainty, "Why, yes, who is it?" to "Oy! You mean Lorraine from the Bay? Send that girl up already!"

Even the doorman seemed surprised to hear a tenant at this building speak that way. He cleared his throat and swallowed a smile before saying slowly and with deliberation, "Ms. Machuchi, Mrs. Romanelli says, please go right up. It's 5P." And as she stepped inside the ornate gilded elevator, with its velvet red bench and its matching sullen attendant, the doorman added, "the *big* one."

There was no way this was working out. Where were the roaches? The burnt-out hall lights? The cracked linoleum? Lorraine pinched herself to ensure this wasn't just a continuation of the mattress-out-the-window dream.

The elevator doors opened to a softly lit hallway that also beheld a soft velvet red bench to wait comfortably on. These people knew how to live. God! How she hated to wait on her feet. That was the worst.

The second she approached 5P, at the very end of the hallway, the door opened as if by magic, without any of that creaking that ordinary doors are known to emit. From behind it, Lorraine was greeted by a rather tall, rather old gentleman in a tuxedo.

"Is that Lorraine?" a tiny, shaky voice asked from somewhere indiscernible, somewhere behind the world's largest tuxedo.

Finally a tiny, nearly balding head to match the voice nearly stripped of all its own heft, popped out from one side and said, "Oh! You must be the granddaughter of poor Mrs. Lorraine Machuchi, my old, dear friend."

Lorraine was shocked to hear the name of her grandmother, and by the tears that sprang to her eyes at the mention of it. Her grandmother's death last year was still a fresh wound.

Ten minutes later Mrs. Romanelli and Lorraine were drinking tea by a huge picture window overlooking Park Avenue and all the tiny regal dogs and their jeweled owners who called the block home. From up here, Lorraine thought, it looked so peaceful—and while admittedly there was an overindulgence to it—all the stopping and chatting and familiarities reminded her of her own little neighborhood on the other side of the bridge. She thought she would definitely like to live here.

Mrs. Romanelli was whispering something in the humungous ear of her humungous butler while Lorraine busied herself watching one rather remarkable little Yorkie Maltese on the street below. Her furry little head stood straight up, and looked remarkably like Queen Elizabeth's head pulled through that ruffled collar she was always painted in. There was one point of distinction: a tiny pink nose pointed north. The dog's tail swung ten beats per second, reangling itself with each jerky movement of her body. Around her miniature neck sat a pink rhinestone collar.

But the most remarkable thing about the Yorkie was her owner—who was a man! And not the kind who worked at the salon with Lorraine either (excepting Don, of course)! This man was waving around to everyone in the neighborhood as if it were nothing at all to be walking this frou-frou dog. In fact, it seemed the women were *waiting* for him, like characters on a stage, each at their respective X's. And when, on cue, he came closer, each flew his way, growing more animated and flirty as they rushed over, pushing hair back, fussing over the tiny dog, sticking chests out, brushing imaginary lint from blouses.

Lorraine smiled at the scene and turned her head back to Mrs. Romanelli, who'd just finished her chat with the butler and sent him off on some errand which called for his closing them both in the rich oak parlor alone.

"So, darling, tell me, does everyone tell you how much you look like your beautiful grandmother? My God, girl, you could *be* her at your age. You've got her stormy gray eyes, her lips, those long arms and legs, the dark coloring." Mrs. Romanelli's mind wandered, with all probability to somewhere decades back, when Grandma Morano hadn't met her grandfather yet.

"They do. They do." Lorraine was trying to fight the glum mood settling over her chest.

"Well, I hear you've got a problem like your mother—God how she drove your grandmother crazy! What a complainer that one! You're in love with a neighborhood boy, a pizza boy."

Unbelievable! Lorraine could not believe how wide the piteous head shaking had spread. It was a friggin' epidemic. Apparently, there was no escape. But Lorraine was smart enough to know this wasn't the time for angry responses. Besides, hearing it so out of place like this, the whole thing did sound a little trite—likely the way Mrs. Romanelli saw it—even if she still knew it to be true. She just shrugged and shook her own head at herself, like she couldn't help her own weaknesses.

"I want to hear, I need to hear your love story, darling. You may not know from looking at my old raisin-y, widowed self, but I am a romantic. A romantic with barely a hair left on her head! But I *know* about romance. I have quite a reputation."

There was something about her—the faint fluff of her white hair, her warmth, her open arms with their swingy flesh, the way she refilled Lorraine's tea with a pinkie held out, even the way she sat back with her legs crossed at the knee, smoothed her skirt, re-folded a scarf about her neck—that was all very inviting and comforting.

And so, Lorraine told her. She told the whole story. Mrs. Romanelli asked questions, and noted answers as if she was committing them to memory for a precise purpose, rather than just casually listening. Before Lorraine knew it, a half hour had passed.

When Mrs. Romanelli saw her glance at her watch, she said, "Oh, you have to get back to work, don't you, dear? I'm afraid I've kept you too long. Come, I'll show you the apartment. It's yours a week from today. I'll be in Italy for the year. All you have to do is watch my dog, Pooh-Pooh. He gets walked twice a day, at seven A.M. and seven P.M., fed an hour prior. Pooh-Pooh is at the groomer's right now getting a trim, so unfortunately, you can't meet him. However, I know you'll grow to love him. Everyone does. And the other condition, darling—you need to forget about that pizza boy. Promise me you'll forget the pizza boy."

Lorraine found herself following the woman around a never-ending apartment—a series of rooms, one more well-appointed than the next, done in the warmest style, making you feel like you could just plop down and make yourself at home here. There was a deep sofa piled high with pillows in contrasting hues of orange and green, and a large coffee table, stacked with cool-looking art and decorating books in hardback; flickering candles added spicy aromas. Books also lined shelves in many of the rooms, as did games and photos—tons of photos of smiling people hugging and kissing and laughing, framed in patterned silver. All the lights were soft and inviting. The bathroom was a full-size spa, with a Jacuzzi and steam room and every product you could imagine, stuck with French-looking labels. And when she was shown the bedroom she'd be staying in, Lorraine had to hold herself back from diving right into the deep pile of box spring, mattress, feathery comforter, and dozens of tasseled pillows. *Yes! Yes!*

When, once again, they were at the door, Mrs. Romanelli dropped the keys into Lorraine's palm and instructed which were for the front door, back door, trash, mail, and added that a detailed instruction sheet would be laid out for her when she arrived the following week. "The dog is my family. I know you will love him."

Before she knew it, Lorraine was headed back to work with her home situation all settled. She'd never really been one for taking care of dogs, but how difficult could something named *Pooh-Pooh* be? She thought of that little Yorkie with her unlikely owner, and figured Pooh-Pooh couldn't be too far off. This was Park Avenue after all.

MACHUCHI'S GARAGE

Directions to Lorraine's new apartment:
Brooklyn Bridge to FDR
north, 71st St. exit
Straight all the way East to Park
 Avenue
Turn left on 76th St.
562, Apartment 5P

eBay auction block #4
Description: Directions to Lorraine's first NYC apartment

Opening bid: $3
Winning bid: $400 by MachuciDad@aol.com

Comments: Aw, I love you, Lorraine. And I'm so proud of you. You're good people.

FOUR

♥

THE PIZZA BOY, POOH-POOH, AND A PRINCESS

"You're not coming out *again?*" Chrissy was rightfully pissed, as Lorraine had uprooted the patterns that had kept their lives intact for the past twenty years or so. "And what the heck am I gonna do when you're not even here anymore? Shit."

Lorraine was starting to feel bad. She didn't want to hurt her best friend. It sucked when changes wound up hurting the people you loved. It was one of the reasons she'd never made any changes before. "You can come and stay with me. Wait till you see this place! The whole Bay could stay there with me."

Chrissy was quiet, so Lorraine assumed that had calmed her friend a bit. "Oh, just come out one last time! Maybe Tommy will be there. He's working, but deliveries are always slow on Sundays."

Normally, this would get Lorraine going, but not tonight. Not when she saw all her belongings in piles all over the floor, which needed to be boxed up and somehow stuffed into the Honda before daylight.

What felt like twenty hours later, plan B went into effect. The twenty boxes she'd packed were empty again, their contents now being transferred into large, but smooshable black garbage bags on the front lawn.

She was in the process of smashing one last pair of jeans into a bag when she saw him. It turned out Chrissy was right—deliveries were slow, so Tommy had cruised around to Lorraine's. It wasn't an odd thing for him to do, if there wasn't some other girl he was wanting to spend time with, or if there was, and he just wanted to make her jealous by spending time with Lorraine. Or the other way around! Lorraine had never quite figured it all out, but whatever his motive may have been, she'd never been able to resist the temptation.

"Becoming a bag lady?" He kissed her half on her mouth. Closer than last time, but that could mean nothing. You just never knew, only caught your breath before it choked you, halting and starting with such ferocity.

"Yeah, thought I'd hide out behind the Bay Pizza Dumpster. I hear there's a lot of trash that hangs out around there. I'd never go hungry." Although she was just being herself, saying the sort of sarcastic things she always would, she could feel the sting of his words reverberate after such a long absence. There had been no late night phone calls for a while, and it put her on the defensive. Lorraine could feel hostility bubbling like a witch's brew. Every word he said felt like a turn of the great cast-iron spoon.

Tommy half-smiled. "I don't know if you'll be able to carry all that."

What are you doing here? Don't you remember? I'm not going anywhere. I'm not good enough for you Tommy, Pizza Boy. Besides, I'm supposed to forget about you. "Well, that's what I've got big, strong guys like you around for," she said, choosing to be a good witch, giving his arm a squeeze.

He pushed her arm away from his, grabbed her hand instead, and without saying anything, kissed Lorraine in the sort of silence that allowed her to attribute whatever she wanted to his thoughts. Then he clutched at either side of her waist, fiddling with the bottom of her T-shirt, pulling it up to explore the skin beneath.

"I like a city girl who can handle heavy lifting," he said.

She couldn't explain it even if she tried to, how she'd wound up in Tommy's bedroom at five in the morning, with the sun beaming into her eyes. *God!* He was so friggin' hot like that, with his jaw so strong and that chin already shadowed with a touch of beard, its tiny cleft magnified somehow, and the way one lock of hair had come un-gelled and grazed his forehead.

Lorraine fell back into her pillow, knowing it was hopeless. Even if she moved to Tennessee, she would still be in love with Tommy. It didn't matter what he said or didn't say, how many ways he could find to hurt her, Lorraine would always want more. It had been five months since the last time she'd had him this way. She couldn't help wanting him just one more time. And so she ran a finger over his arm, its familiar constellation of scars he'd touch sometimes without thinking—some of them he'd got when they'd been together—until he stirred suddenly. He slipped her finger inside his mouth and sucked on it. Smiling, he turned over on top of her, pulled her hands around his back, and she got her wish.

When the hour was as late as she could push it, she got dressed. Lorraine hoped in the way she always would that he would say something, give her a line of hope to tug on when he wasn't around tomorrow. But what he said was confusing: "I'll miss you." He looked far away when he said it, like maybe it was hard for him, or maybe there was something else he'd already put in place of this role of hers. If she started wondering what he might have realized, she couldn't go through with it. There was always a possibility—but it was possibilities that could do the most damage to the best intentions.

"Missing is so yesterday. Just kiss me and we'll call it even," she joked over the horrible possibilities of lost chances and replacements both, rather than let him see it affected her that way. She kissed him quickly, too quickly, and turned to go without looking back. Because if she'd looked back, she wasn't going to be able to do it.

Lorraine knew the dog would have already been walked that morning. The butler was doing it one last time, before he started his year's paid vacation, according to Mrs. Romanelli's telephone message yesterday. Lorraine only had to empty her belongings into the apartment with her dad, before he brought the Aquatic Honda back to Brooklyn.

He was a quiet guy who didn't see much use for chitchat. At the garage he owned, Mr. Machuchi worked, rather than talked. "Time is money," he'd say if the guys got too chatty, pulling his jeans up under his belly. They knew that to mean they'd better shut up and get working. So, when they were just about done crossing into Manhattan—the first time her father had ever been there in his life—and he turned to her, Lorraine knew she'd better listen up.

"Sweetheart, I'm not in love with this whole idea of you moving to Manhattan, but I want you to know I am very proud of you—I've always been very proud of you. I know you're a smart girl, smarter than I ever was, and I know you've always done what you wanted. I was never disappointed in any of your decisions. I trust you did what you knew to be best."

Lorraine felt a pang, because she'd always thought doing things for Tommy was what she considered "the best" to be. She didn't think her dad would see things the same way.

But he surprised her when he said, "Lorraine, people do crazy things for love. Crazy. I've tied myself into pretzels for your mother. God, I love that feisty little pain in the ass."

They both laughed, her dad's voice lively and deep, the way she thought the Buddha might sound if he yucked it up, and Lorraine saw this problem of hers in a whole different light. Maybe she couldn't help it. Maybe it was in her blood. Wouldn't it be easy to give up all responsibility in the face of that fact? *I'm a hopeless romantic.* She knew then, with his hand clutching her own, that it would be hard not living with her dad, and even in a weird way, her mom.

"Hey, no crying, sweetheart," he said to his daughter when he saw her tear up. But the tears had pooled to capacity, and the warm water slipped quickly down, before she could catch it, and spotted her pants leg, tiny and dark. He pulled her under his arm, to his chest that was always warm, as far as Lorraine was concerned, as he used to do when she was a little girl. Back then, when no one paid too much mind to seat belts and car seats, she could ride like that with him for hours at a time, fall asleep on the pillow of his Buddha belly. When she woke they'd be right where they were supposed to be. Like magic, she'd always thought. That memory sent a frisson of fear through her. Moving into Manhattan was quite the opposite of being right here at the Buddha's belly. What had made Lorraine think she could handle this?

She didn't fall asleep this time. Instead, she watched through the open window past her father, as all the things that she'd known seemed like an empty movie set. Suddenly they had a plaything quality, like if she stepped outside, she might find that the street was merely a piece of painted plywood, that she could kick a storefront over with her foot. And then came the highway, so familiar with its old billboards and empty-looking factories alongside, debris here and there. A dusty tire resting against the median seemed to tell Lorraine she'd made a terrible mistake. A broken-down Chevy Cavalier before Exit 21 mocked her. If it couldn't even make it to Manhattan, what made her think she could live there?

She was thankful for the silence. Lorraine didn't think she could keep up a conversation. After a few more minutes, she felt her chest tighten and the tears start to flow. Her father's free hand tightened on her shoulder. Maybe he could feel the tear on his T-shirt; more likely, he could sense what she was feeling. They were one in the same those two—always had been.

And then the last stretch of the BQE, and the bridge and the glorious sun on the water, off the glass facades of the skyscrapers in a city she'd always been part of, if only a little to the south. Wasn't New York New York from the Bronx to Brooklyn to Staten Island? Weren't they all just New Yorkers? Yes! It was overwhelming to her at that moment, this feeling of camaraderie. It was so strong, she was convinced that surely everything would be just fine.

At H&H bagels Lorraine asked her dad to stop so she could show him how great those NYC bagels really were, so she could give him some link to her new home. Who knew? Maybe it would become their thing. She'd call and say, "Dad! I'm coming home tonight!" And he'd respond, "Oh, please bring some of those wonderful bagels from H&H!"

She took a number and waited: 96. They were currently on 93 and so she started daydreaming. These were her neighbors! One guy with a tie tucked inside his third shirt button had an IPOD buzzing out from tiny white earbuds. "Next!" the man with slick black hair yelled from behind the counter. One woman was wheeling a baby in an old-fashioned pram. Another woman of around the same age was dressed in a tasteful taupe suit with a long lariat necklace hanging down to the waistline of her pants.

Lorraine looked out to her dad and he waved, smiling. Looking at him like that, in their little Honda, as taxis and buses zoomed by, Lorraine was filled with respect for her father. She knew how difficult it was for him to let her go, to let her run off and live in Manhattan—a place he thought to be filled with dangerous lunatics. But he was doing it because his daughter thought it was best for her, and he only ever wanted her to be happy. Her father was so generous and selfless. It was all Lorraine could do to stand there and wait her turn, when at the moment, all she felt like doing was running back out to the car and having him envelop her in all of his goodness. She knew she was leaving her family, but now it really hit her: She was *leaving her family*.

Lorraine turned back to the glass case of bagels. Each kind had its own basket: egg, super egg, everything, onion, plain, cinnamon raisin. She felt her father with her, and she realized how silly she'd been to think they'd ever need a "thing" to keep them connected. She already had something. And it was something inside of her, that she took around with her every-where. He'd been right there during her entire life.

And so it wasn't such a disappointment, when it turned out her father wouldn't be eating any of the H&H bagels that day, anyhow.

After they'd helped the bellhop drag all the stuff up to the apartment, with the bellhop trying in vain to explain they didn't need to do anything at all, Lorraine finally opened the door to bring in the mountain of black garbage bags they'd erected outside 5P. She had almost completely for-gotten about Mrs. Romanelli's dog, Pooh-Pooh. But when she opened the door, and a dog the size of the butler who'd opened the door the last time, came barreling out and knocked the three of them into the black garbage bag mountain, her memory was jogged.

"Pooh-Pooh!" she screamed in what would be the first, but certainly not the last embarrassing exclamation she would make at her new canine charge.

After the three of them piled Lorraine's belongings into her new bed-room, which Lorraine thought, looked even more inviting than it had the first time, she picked up the crumbs and nickel-sized scrap of brown paper that was all that remained of the bag formerly holding the bagels and a half pound of scallion cream cheese (never mind the plastic container that it came in!). She looked at Pooh-Pooh, a Greater Swiss Mountain dog, in the face and said, "Pooh-Pooh, we've got to have a talk later. Please do not eat anything expensive-looking while I'm gone."

A dog the size of a horse did present a sort of roadblock to what had been a somewhat smooth move so far. If she'd known his breed name had the word "great" in it, maybe she'd have known how big he was! Still, he was very cute—mainly black with brown here and there and white spots in the middle of his face and belly, and on his paws. But, cute or not, Lorraine had never had a pet before. Excepting the one weekend she was allowed to bring the class turtle, Mr. Boxer, home for the weekend in the first grade, Lorraine had never been entrusted with the care of any animal at all. And even that hadn't gone so well. *He's looking a little—well, dry, Lorraine.* Still, she decided she'd meet Pooh-Pooh with everything she had after work.

The eary part of the day went quickly, jumping from one client to the next and one task to the next. There was a rhythm, if not exactly a satisfaction, to the work she had to do. Fold the towels—flatten, fold both edges in toward the middle, top down, and then fold the left side over, smooth down; next. Fill the shampoos—unscrew caps, clean off with damp towel, insert funnel, pour; next. Sweep hair—well, that one wasn't exactly rhythmical, it was more of a battle against choking. *Don't breathe in!* No, she couldn't convince herself there was any positive to that particular task. What she had to convince herself of was that if she walked out on the basis of being too good to be sweeping hair off the floor, then she'd never get to show the world how good she really was. And there was a rhythm to that. It went: You're too good for this; just leave. No, you have to stay; stick it out. And on and on and on.

At two-thirty Lorraine learned Pooh-Pooh wasn't to be her only big surprise of the day. Scheduled, right there on her time sheet, was Lorraine's first encounter with a Princess. Not the kind you see in *Hello!* beneath a sparkly tiara, straining her back straight under the enormous weight of diamonds, nor the kind at the end of the Super Mario Brothers levels. No, this was a very different type of Princess, as Don explained it.

"These girls *are* New York City. Mallory Meen is the central Princess. The other three wouldn't switch their lipstick brand without asking what she thought first." He started speaking as if he were explaining the inner workings of a terrorist network to the CIA.

Lorraine knew the Princesses, of course; everyone did. But the way he spoke of them! She tried to meet his level of seriousness, but it wasn't easy.

"Lorraine, these girls make and break businesses in a second. If one of them goes to your shop and doesn't like what you have, your windows will be shuttered by the end of the week. Their fathers are all board members at no less than four Fortune 500 companies apiece. They started going to benefits, press events, club openings when they were twelve. If you don't invite them, you might as well cancel the venture. Mallory's fellow Princesses are Stacey Reed, Tracey Levin, and Katharine James. They are the muses to Marc Jacobs, Michael Kors, Oscar de la Renta, and Peter Som respectively."

Then, without looking, he pulled a pink folder from a filing cabinet next to where they were standing. As if readying himself to pass on the word of the Lord, Don closed his eyes, steadying his head atop his neck before he spoke.

Lorraine had never seen him this way, and found it increasingly difficult to keep from laughing. The pink hair, the pink folder—it was difficult not to joke about it all.

"The Princesses get their hair color done here with Guido." Don put his hand over his heart and then crossed himself, apparently to thank God for such a gift. "Lorraine, as you know, this is the holiest of holies. You, being a good Catholic girl, should appreciate that. Those four glorious girls are why Guido has been so successful. They each have a card that guarantees them an appointment whenever they feel like fluttering in. It doesn't matter who Guido is doing at the moment. He will stop and will begin working on the Princesses. Today, Mallory has phoned ahead of time, which means we need to be doubly attentive."

Lorraine stood smiling, waiting for the punch line, so she could sock him in the arm and say, *Oh, you really got me there.* But it never came. "Amen," she said, her hands in prayer, her head bowed, buttoning away a smile with her teeth at her lower lip.

Don remained serious, which really didn't suit him. His eyelashes were too light for serious. Still, he fanned out the lined index cards he'd removed from the file and handed them to Lorraine. "There are four cards here. One for each Princess. Typed on the cards you will find their preferences—how much conditioner they like, how vigorously they like their scalp massages, whether they prefer lemon or lime in their water, sparkling or still, you'll find what topics they like to discuss, if any at all. You'll see how much styling product they allow, if any, how much time they like everything to take and whether they like to have you call a car for their ride home or take their own. You'll find their pets' names, what their pets like to eat and drink while they are here, whether they like their hair blown out super curly, messy wavy, sultry wavy, or angular wavy—don't even suggest straight, it is so last season for dogs."

Lorraine leafed through them and turned her head so she could roll her eyes without him noticing; it was apparent he was taking this seriously, so she didn't want to offend him. She was glad, at least, that he was done talking such nonsense. Okay, kiss ass. She could understand the concept. But this was plain disgusting. Never in her life did she think she would miss cursing Uncle Carlo. *Miss Shut it!* It sounded almost operatic then—a follicular tragedy that spanned two boroughs. When Don started talking again, it became all the more clear that she did feel that pang of loss. *What had she done?*

"In the beginning it was just Mallory Meen, daughter of Alias and Isabelle Meen. It is said that when Mallory was born she was so beautiful that all the other babies in the nursery cried out of jealousy." He held his face serious as a monk reciting a Bible story.

And then, Lorraine thought, *she was turned into a pillar of salt.* She liked that one. "Lemmie guess, Don. And then she was turned into a pillar of salt."

But he hadn't heard her. Or if he did, he didn't let on. Just turned his gaze heavenward and lowered his tone to an even more serious one. "She was always extraordinary. Excelled in her classes. Most popular girl at Spence. It was only natural she'd grow up to be so powerful. This story they just did on her in *People* will really teach you a lot."

Don reached into the drawer again and passed her a color copy of the story.

Lorraine thought maybe he was having a seizure. Or perhaps his body was being confiscated by aliens? She stood, still waiting for the punch line.

He stopped speaking. His face turned back to the regular Don expression—a tight-lipped smile—although it wasn't at all clear he hadn't been joking.

"Jeez, I thought I lost you there for a minute," Lorraine said. "What the hell was that all about? *And on the third day he created Mallory.*" She swept her hands through the air. "Oooooooh," she added for effect.

"Lorraine, you do understand you have to take this all very seriously, don't you?" He was as serious as a guy in a pink Mohawk with blond eyelashes could pull off.

She forced herself to get serious. Don was not Carlo. "Dude, I understand. But you were possessed. I was scared an alien was gonna pop out of your stomach, or something!" She was only half kidding.

"Lorraine, as crazy as it sounds, the Princesses *are* that serious. Please think about what I'm telling you. They could really help you, like they have with Guido, but they could hurt you, too, if you piss them off. And that's why you'll see that Guido will do *anything* they ask of him—no matter how outrageous. As a Guido employee, you are a representative of Guido, and so I'm sure I don't have to explain to you that as crazy as it seems—you're to handle this as seriously as cancer."

"Okay, okay. Hey. I'm sorry I was being kind of callous. You know how a Brooklyn girl can get sometimes. *Shut it, Lorraine!*" She screamed it to herself, singsongy, and smacked the side of her own head, but the effect was lost. She held out her hand in an act of peace. Don was on the level, and if he was taking this so seriously, the least she could do was try to understand. It was a trait of her father's she'd always admired. If he could always give people the benefit of the doubt, well, then, she could try it this once.

"I know, Lorraine," he said. And then he seemed to drift off. His gaze turned floorward when he murmured, "You can't just break all the rules and expect to change the whole order of things." Lorraine got the sense it may have been something he'd often wished for.

Seeing her otherwise lighthearted friend act like that, Lorraine tried even harder to show compassion, understanding. Besides, maybe he was right. He'd been right about everything so far. "All right. Let me take a look at those cards."

She could be understanding of Don, but it didn't mean she could really understand how a couple of girls could become so powerful. People could really make her sick. What the hell was so great about those girls that they deserved so much? Lorraine doubted even her own mother knew how much conditioner she preferred to use in her hair. Give Mallory Meen one day in Brooklyn and see if she survived, Lorraine thought.

"Lorraine, I know you understand how this business works, but really, I need to stress to you one more time how important it is to put your personal feelings aside with this and just kiss ass."

She shook her head. Surely he didn't think she'd embarrass them? That she might be jealous? Or maybe he just understood what she was thinking deep down. Lorraine realized she didn't know Don well enough to be sure what he thought. But if she had to guess, she'd say he knew just what she felt, only he was paranoid where this Mallory was concerned. And if she really thought about it, she guessed she understood. It was his brother's business, and that was the most important thing.

Lorraine took a quick look at the other cards when Don went off to his client. The head Princess would be there in twenty minutes for highlights. Great, Lorraine thought, first the Pizza Boy, then Pooh-Pooh, and now the Princess. It sounded like a fairy tale, albeit a pretty screwed-up one, and she'd never cared much for alliteration.

While she folded up the pristine white towels all fluffed and warm from the dryer, Lorraine tried to think whether she felt any different knowing she officially lived in the City. She tried to think whether she felt any stronger knowing Tommy would not be sleeping down the block. But she knew the answer. Just the fact that she wasn't taking the Princesses seriously, that she'd allowed her mind so freely to wander to him told her she was no better off than if she were peering up at his window. Here she was doing all of this to show him she could go somewhere and do something, and she was still standing outside his window in her mind. At that moment, it took Lorraine every shred of power she could muster not to drop the towel in her hand and run right back home and actually do just that.

What was she doing here? She asked herself that question over and over again. It seemed like a disconnect—the idea that she had to distance herself from Tommy to come closer to him. Did it even make sense in the first place? Lorraine felt suddenly alone, for the first time since she'd come to Manhattan. Did she really *know* any of these people? Did any of them *get* her? What was she doing folding *towels*? And in just a few minutes, she'd be forced to play slave girl to someone she already hated.

Lorraine had seen Mallory's face in the paper many times. And the one thing she always remembered seeing was a sour pucker at her lips, as if everything displeased her. Sure, Mallory was stunning, but that wasn't enough to make Lorraine admire her. Pictured with her friends on *Entertainment Tonight,* Mallory had often seemed like a running joke from where Lorraine sat—the very picture of the Manhattan frivolity that drove Lorraine nuts.

"Because I am so beautiful, it opens a lot of doors," she'd once heard Mallory say to an interviewer.

"*I'll* show you a door," she and Chrissy had howled it at the TV simultaneously. They both had walked around saying that to people that whole night, as if it were the most hysterical thing they'd ever heard. "Oh, Henry," one of them had said, when the guy at the delicatessen had asked what they'd been up to, "because I am so beautiful, it opens a lot of doors." He'd just laughed while he thinly sliced a half pound of provolone, the gentle hum of the slicer going all the while.

By the time she'd placed the last of at least one hundred towels (she'd lost count somewhere in the nineties) inside the cabinet above the sinks, Lorraine was being called over to Guido's chair. It had been announced that Mallory Meen, head Princess, was in the lobby. A nervous energy settled over the staff members in the color area. Guido whispered in her ear, "Don't be nervous," in a feathery version of his great voice that didn't hold the same power. But if he'd known her better, he'd have known he needn't have said anything. To Lorraine, Mallory was just another customer, when she would of course treat with respect, the same way she hoped to treat all customers.

"Oh, Miss Mallory, you *are* stunning today," Guido said in a voice that had come to remind Lorraine of royalty, in its affectedness and exacting pronunciation.

Lorraine thought she was pretty, but nothing spectacular. The only difference between Mallory and any other girl was about $20,000 a day's worth of fashion and beauty. "No. No. I'm a disgusting bloody wench. Have you *seen* this pimple on my chin? Two injections at Dr. Weiner and *still* it's ruining my day. How could *anyone* be expected to live like this?" Mallory couldn't string together a sentence that wouldn't be transcribed with at least one word in italics. She was everything you wanted to hate. But it was apparent that you couldn't take your eyes off her—she did have a fantastic allure. Not someone you'd want to meet your grandma, but *exactly* who you'd want at your party, in the car you make, the watch you crafted, at the destination you were promoting. Instant glamour.

Instant glamour didn't do much for Lorraine, who'd grown up at the Bay and treasured the real things in life over fantasies she could never attach herself to. They were just too far away to have any impact. In fact, it took every morsel of Lorraine's will to hold herself back from rolling her eyes. As far as she was concerned, this kind of girl was the picture of a City Bi-atch. No matter the preparation, the idea of kissing her ass quite possibly *could* kill Lorraine Machuchi. But no more than the idea of losing Tommy forever. She could eat crow for a little while in the name of love. Just look what her dad had put up with to be with her mother. *Mmmmm! Crow!*

"Mallory, I want you to meet our future star, here, Lorraine. Guido knows Lorraine is going to be his best colorist. And so he wanted Mallory to meet her first." He spoke of himself in the third person.

Thankfully, Mallory didn't have much interest in Lorraine. After she mustered the poorest excuse for a genuine smile Lorraine had ever seen (even from herself), Mallory turned back to looking at herself in the mirror while she talked at Guido, who should have been charging double for being her head shrinker.

"And *then*," she was saying as Guido painstakingly painted delicate highlights at her roots, which were only about a quarter of an inch long—a death-defying attempt for any colorist.

Lorraine was holding out dozens of square-cut foils like an automaton. Blocking out the Princess's speech she thought what she *would* do if given the chance—bring out the lemony pieces more around the face and crown, sprinkle a white-white blond in with them, keep the base really light, too, bring the eyebrows a touch lighter. It wasn't that she'd changed her opinion of Mallory, it was just that hair was a canvas to Lorraine. She never let her personal feelings get involved.

"You know how Tracey *never* really listens to anything you say, right?"

"Well, I . . ." Guido's big voice caught in his throat; he was understandably averse to getting in the middle of a Princess squabble and faltering quite endearingly, Lorraine thought.

It turned out it didn't matter one bit, because Mallory herself was guilty of the very same problem she was accusing her friend of. She just plowed ahead. "We were at the opening of that new *Chanel* store, and I said, 'I'm getting the new limited edition *jacket, skirt,* and *purse* they created for the event,' and so of course, I didn't want *her* to get them, because then I'd never be able to wear *any* of it. And I turn around and there she is with the f'ing shopping bag. And so I say, 'Umm, Tracey, what the *f* is in that *bag*?' and she's like, 'Well, duh, the new limited edition jacket, skirt, and purse, same as everyone else is buying,' like she hadn't a concern in the world about it."

While Mallory, without any hint of ceasing, shared stories defaming her friend Tracey, Lorraine busied herself looking over Mallory's preference card and thinking how she might get through the next couple of years trying to remember this kind of crap about people. Was it really worth it? The one common theme through all the stories Mallory told in her hour or so in Guido's chair was that she was above it all, that she didn't need any of them. Lorraine knew there wasn't a person in the world who truly felt that way. At least she could be honest enough with herself to admit that much.

When the time came to rinse Mallory's precious little head free of the bleach and dye, Lorraine escorted the Princess to the sink in silence as she "only prefers chatting when she initiates" (what a friggin' relief, Lorraine thought), she obediently doled out a "medium vigorous" shampooing and scalp massage, followed by a shea butter deep conditioning treatment (extra). Lorraine unwrapped the towel from Mallory's shoulder, replaced it with a fresh one from the supply she'd just replenished, and added her own little special touch to the treatment—one drop of citrus, two of peppermint essential oils right onto the towel. It was a little refresher to wake a client up before they met the outside world again. She'd started doing it at the Do Wop a few years ago, and the old ladies loved it. "Reminds me of that tub cleaner I used to use in the fifties!" one of her regular Silver Hairs had said over and over again with a smile, probably forgetting she'd ever said it before.

Lorraine began to run the water before it reached optimum hair washing temperature—warm, but not too warm—and switched to autopilot. It was the ultimate joy to see someone come in, to add your mark exactly as you saw you should, create an enjoyable experience and see a girl leave looking, to your tastes, perfect. But even now, when she didn't get to do things her way only, or put her small mark on it, the beauty in this simple thing always gave Lorraine pride and joy the way it often did.

The medium vigorous massage was halfway through when Mallory stirred. "Mmmm. That smells great. You're not bad, you know, Laurie."

"Oh, thanks Melanie," Lorraine said. You could take the girl out of Brooklyn, but you couldn't take *Brooklyn* out of the girl.

They both looked at each other with that difficultly-forced smile and exchanged what, from their separate worlds, boroughs aside, both could easily recognize, as mutual respect—from one Bi-atch to another.

Mallory's gaze seemed to float—through the back of Lorraine's head to some elegant thinking room in the sky. A smile came over her entire face, and then she focused on Lorraine again.

Lorraine didn't squirm. She wasn't going to begin to imagine what was going on inside a mind like that. Likely it had something to do with nothing important. As long as Mallory was happy enough to keep Don and Guido happy, Lorraine couldn't care less what else might happen. And she'd already expressed her approval on that end.

When Mallory spoke, though, it was with a remarkably changed tone—slow and exploratory. "Add it to my product purchase."

"Oh, actually, I can't. It's my own concoction." Lorraine was still massaging Mallory's scalp. Was she just being petty in an upstairs/downstairs way natural to a social setup like this, or did it genuinely feel good that Lorraine had something Mallory couldn't have? Whichever it was, it seemed a moral victory on the part of the whole world.

"Hmmmph," Mallory sighed, and shook her head in approval, her smile deepening as if Lorraine had just provided the answers to the mysteries of the universe. "Oh, okay. Well, then, you be my assistant when I come here from *now on*."

It was depressing to Lorraine that this crumb of approval put her in a good mood. "Laurie, you really are pathetic," she said to herself as soon as Mallory had disappeared from the salon.

As testament to her influence, after Mallory's invigorating shampooing experience, word spread around town and all the Princesses came in to have Lorraine give them the essential oil treatment. They also tipped $50 apiece, and so her mood wasn't bad, although her schedule was way, way behind. It didn't matter if you made other people wait—*they* would have to understand. But Princesses, you got *them* done right away, period.

Guido was strangely silent about the buzzing over Lorraine's treatment. After Don's powwow, she'd thought he'd be thrilled she'd not only kept her mouth shut, but actually *pleased* Mallory. But he hadn't mentioned it.

Lorraine questioned Don about it when they met in the mixing area.

All he said was, "You did a fabulous job Lorraine. It's just . . . well, Guido really doesn't like when people break the rules, color outside the lines, if you know what I mean." He was tearing a paper in half; folding it, tearing it again.

It was obvious Don himself was torn on the issue. And you didn't mess with family business. This Lorraine knew. She wasn't even going to ask what Guido had said about the essential oil treatment. It was obvious Don had a vested interest in hiring Lorraine. Her success would stand for a success of sorts for Don. Probably, it had something to do with him being unhappy coloring hair. However, she couldn't help but wonder—could it really be such a bad thing to go beyond the norm? To push things to the limit? Wasn't that what this opportunity was all about? Lorraine was confused, but she wasn't going to dwell on it. Life was more than a job. Life was about love and family . . . and most of all, she thought, despite the distance, life was about Tommy.

★   ★   ★

She was rushing as she pushed the apartment door open, hoping there would still *be* an apartment left. In the dash to just get there already, she forgot how big and forceful Pooh-Pooh could be. The dog had also apparently forgotten how easily she toppled over, so when he jumped for her, down she went.

"Pooh-Pooh! Oh, Pooh-Pooh!" she was screaming.

It only got worse when, finally, the horse/dog tired of pawing and licking her and ran back inside the apartment, presumably by way of instructing her to follow. She shook her head at herself as she willingly obeyed the dog. *Pathetic!* she said to herself before she was faced with the product of Pooh-Pooh's endeavors for the day.

Thank heavens for small miracles, there was no Pooh-Pooh pooh-pooh.

But, where there used to be a coffee table, Lorraine saw only a stick of wood, approximately the size of a jumbo toothpick. Miraculously, the lamp that had been resting on it was standing perfectly intact alongside the wreckage.

Her heart went into overdrive, beating at Metallica speed while she looked around the apartment.

"Okay, I get it." She poked her head in her bedroom, which had, thank god, been spared.

"I really do need to be on time for these feedings."

"Woof!" Pooh-Pooh agreed, apparently glad she spoke dog.

She filled the bowl twice—who knew what he would do overnight if she accidentally slept late—and watched the dog gobble up everything and then drink a gallon or so of water.

What the hell was she gonna tell Mrs. Romanelli about the table? How much did a table like that even cost? Worse than not having answers to any of those questions was not having Chrissy here to commiserate with her. *I'm so beautiful it opens a lot of doors.* Really, this was more difficult than she'd thought. *Had* she even thought? The end of the day seemed to bring out the regret and fear she'd been free from so far. Just the idea of going outside was creeping her out. And this was usually her favorite time. On top of all that, now she'd have to walk this horse/dog. How the hell was *that* gonna work?

Pooh-Pooh started clawing at the door and barking, and instinctively Lorraine jumped up on the sofa, half fearing for her life. At that point the dog started running crazy circles around the remains of the sitting area. *How did one make this stop? What would that Australian dude with the crocodiles do? Think! Think, Lorraine. Shit! So hard to think with a dog running circles around you and staring you down like that!*

She stood still for a moment (it was what you were supposed to do when sharks circled—she'd seen that traumatizing *Open Water* film), paralyzed. But when he opened his jaw wide and appeared to be going for the one remaining piece of woodwork in the room, she didn't think. Instead, out of nowhere, Lorraine heard herself scream.

"Hey!" she belted out.

The dog yelped, snapped his teeth shut, hung his head down, and walked in her general direction.

Okay, think. You got his attention. Now what?

She looked around for a clue. *Ah! The leash! Yes!*

As if she'd just been passed down an order from a government official, Lorraine swiped the leash from the side table where it was laid out and ran toward Pooh-Pooh like she meant business. She didn't like the way he was looking at her. She'd seen that look before. It was saying, "I dare you."

"Oh, you dare me? Do you, Pooh-Pooh? Well, we'll just see who's boss now, won't we. Don't mess with some Brooklyn-ite/City-bi-atch. You don't know who you're dealing with, Pooh-Pooh." She'd obviously lost her mind.

He continued to stare her down.

For all that talk, she didn't think this dog was going to cooperate. Still, she went in for it, holding the tiny latch of the chain leash open.

Pooh-Pooh jerked his head out of the way with the precision of a heavyweight boxer.

Lorraine had played Mike Tyson's Punch-Out!! too many times to give up after that. She came right back in on the left.

Pooh-Pooh outfoxed her by cocking his head the opposite way.

They went back and forth like that no less than ten times, during which time Lorraine was pretty sure that Pooh-Pooh had laughed.

"Come on, Pooh-Pooh!" She tried pleading, looking him right in the face in an effort to bring him around to her cause. "Don't you want to go outside with all the cute girl doggies out there?"

Pooh-Pooh held his stance, stone-faced.

"Oh, I get it, your tail don't swing that way, Pooh-Pooh? Okay . . ." She winked at him like she got where he was coming from. "They got those West Village doggie types out there in the park, too. You know, with their black leather and metal hardware. Pooh-Pooh, I'm not disappointed, I love you no matter what you are. You'll always be my Pooh-Pooh."

She shut up with a start. *What the fuck am I doing?* When a girl realizes she's been talking to a dog about his sexual preferences, after she's been babying a bunch of Princesses and sweeping loose hairs up all day and still hasn't eaten or sat down and has no friends to hang out with and no Tommy down the block, you can understandably expect a breakdown.

"Fine!" she screamed at Pooh-Pooh, which she'd already promised herself she would not do, and threw herself onto the couch, tossing the leash where there used to be a coffee table with a crash.

She closed her eyes and willed herself back in her room at home, with her mother screaming over the second-floor banister to her father, "If you don't stop leaving your rancid socks on the bathroom floor, I swear on the grave of my own mother, they will be tossed into the garbage disposal and shredded up like mozzarella cheese!"

Lorraine couldn't believe she'd ever *want* to hear a thing like that. She was never good with change. She hated change. And now that she was smack in the middle of it she could see why. What good could possibly come from this?

She was rubbing her tightly closed eyes with her palms with all of her might, with a faint hope that maybe when she reopened them she'd be in her cozy bed, ready for Tommy's call. And like her prayers had been answered, Lorraine felt something soft and warm at her foot. Her breathing came slower, quieter. She rubbed her eyes in a softer way, eventually stopping. When they opened, slowly, Lorraine was beyond shocked to see Pooh-Pooh licking her foot and looking at her with eyes that clearly begged for a cease-fire.

Never one to let anyone off the hook so easily, she softened her demeanor, but not all the way. "If I forgive you, will you let me put this leash on you?"

The dog yelped, blinked his eyes a few times—she thought he was laying it on a little thick, but didn't deny the meaning of the gesture.

"Will you be good on a walk and listen to everything I say?"

When Pooh-Pooh let out a heavy breath, she realized she'd pushed it too far and decided to be happy with the successful leashing. And out the door they went.

Even on a good day, in the daylight, Lorraine found Central Park difficult to navigate, with all its twists and turns and halfway indistinguishable greenery. With the sun nearly down and Pooh-Pooh clearly letting her know he'd negotiated enough by running at full speed God-knows-where, the halfway indistinguishable greenery had become completely indistinguishable. *Had she seen that tree with the acorn things before? Or was this* another *tree with acorn things?*

Sweating, swearing at herself for not changing into flats, for not paying more attention at botanically focused Girl Scout meetings, cursing at Pooh-Pooh for running too fast, swearing at passersby to get out of the way, Lorraine and her canine charge made their way deep into the middle of the park (west, she hoped). With his fur taken up by the power of it, leg followed leg followed leg, and never once did Pooh-Pooh slow down. As they reached a blacktop path, where runners and cyclists were making the rounds in iPod trances with song lyrics ruffling their lips, Lorraine gave into Pooh-Pooh's lead and tried to simply enjoy the scenery as it blew by her. Who knew? Maybe the dog actually knew where he was going. At least she was burning calories, right?

She could not get around the idea that Mrs. Romanelli had not made mention of Pooh-Pooh's size, nor given her any pointers for handling him. And here she thought the woman had really taken a liking to her, had truly cared for her situation. But no one who cared would stick someone with Pooh-Pooh. It was cruel and unusual. How would she ever get him back to the apartment? She was so tired already. It wasn't clear how long she'd be able to keep this up.

Maybe, if she could fall and break her ankle, then she wouldn't be able to go on and Pooh-Pooh would have to give in. Maybe amidst the police and the ambulance, Pooh-Pooh would get lost and then she wouldn't have to care for him anymore. *No, no!* Already she knew the pain in the ass was starting to grow on her. God, it really *must* run in the family, she said to herself.

At an opening in the chain-link fence that had run alongside the path for some time (hadn't she seen *that* already?), Pooh-Pooh slowed to a gallop, nearly tripping Lorraine, whose legs had gone on autopilot some time ago. When he finally slowed to an easy trot, he steered them into a small grassy field filled with dogs and their owners.

Whether by simply her own internal comparison or in reality, she couldn't be sure, but all the other pets and owners seemed to be following the natural order of things: The human setting the ground rules, the canine loyally following. There was a black Labrador pup with his goofy legs, clearly not all under his control yet, catching a chewed-up Nerf football thrown by his plaid shirt and khaki-clad twentyish male human. An older Silver Hair in a rather sharp Park Avenue ensemble of tan wool slacks and matching silk blouse with smart, patterned scarf (a far cry from the double-knit polyester of the Bay Ridge sixty-five-plus crowd) walked her obedient bichon frise in a sophisticated trot around the perimeter of the dog area. A group of teen *Ohmigod* girls (Princesses in training?) all highlighted in gorgeous honey shades watched their coordinating ribbon-topped poodles play delightfully on a cashmere Burberry blanket while they gossiped loudly. "*Ohmigod*, you should've seen what Miss Swenson was wearing in English class today. I'm writing a letter to the principal. It's a disgrace that instructors in our school should dress so poorly. How are we expected to show any respect for someone going around in last year's skirt length? *Ohmigod*."

A couple of beer-bellies in corporate casual kicked around a soccer ball while their retriever and pointer kicked around a worn ball of their own. The guys hardly had to glance at their independent, shining examples of well-behaved dogs. Everything seemed right in the human/dog kingdom except where Lorraine and Pooh-Pooh were concerned.

A look at Pooh-Pooh told her he'd seen the same thing. He seemed to want a belly rub, judging from the way he'd thrown himself down on his back and sprawled all fours out, revealing private parts which she really didn't think, at this early point in their relationship, she was ready to see. He was batting his lashes and holding his mouth straight in an attempt at sweetness for the benefit of those around them.

Instantly she knew he was putting her on. She was about to tell him where he could stick his kindness, somewhere involving a depravation of sunlight not far from her own private parts, when she saw something that abruptly brought about a change in her own demeanor.

Across the way, entering through the same fence opening she'd just been dragged through herself, was the cute guy with his jumpy Yorkie Maltese in pink rhinestones—the one she'd seen below Mrs. Romanelli's window. She barely had time to notice the same fidgety, flirty reaction from the *Ohmigods* and the Silver Hair before she decided to look sweet herself and take Pooh-Pooh up on his opportunistic offer. She might be obsessed, but she wasn't dead.

"Oh, that's a good Pooh-Pooh," she'd said, conscious of the cute guy's presence before she'd realized what that must sound like. Her face heated up with the embarrassment of the idea as she looked down at the dog, who was definitely smirking. Rather than get angry, she smiled big and batted her own lashes at him to show him she was on to him.

Lorraine thought she must be looking sweet to the cute guy and had just assured herself there was no way he'd heard her utter the words *Pooh-Pooh*, when he scooped the Yorkie up into his palm and took a seat not far from her, at the base of a big oak (at least she thought) tree. Here she was, being kind to animals (who, by the way, clearly didn't deserve it), at home in nature, being one with the earth—wasn't that all men wanted in a woman when it really came down to it?

By way of a nonchalant smile and nod, he acknowledged Lorraine and Pooh-Pooh, maybe recognizing Pooh-Pooh from the neighbor-hood. Meanwhile, Pooh-Pooh was starting to squirm a little bit on his back. He kicked a foot, and then another and before Lorraine knew what was happening, he was up and running those compulsive rings he'd made earlier in the sitting room, except this time around the entire dog field.

She could feel the eyes around her looking her way, wondering what would she do now? She didn't know! She just didn't know how to han-dle Pooh-Pooh! For lack of a better plan, Lorraine started running after him, never closing in closer than about fifteen yards behind him.

Two minutes later, and about to collapse, Lorraine gave in to the desperation of the whole situation, like a mother in a toy store at Christmas-time. "Pooh-Pooh! Pooh-Pooh! Get *ova* here right now, Pooh-Pooh, or you're gonna be in big trouble!"

Pooh-Pooh showed no reaction, but laughter rang out in tiny eruptions from the dog owners enjoying the free show. She wondered what the *Ohmigods* might have to say about her own outfit. Not that she cared, of course.

Sweat was running down into Lorraine's eye and stinging. If she'd believed in signs when she first agreed to this life change, should she believe in them now? Because they were all flashing "Mistake! Mistake!" bright as day. Here she was, still chasing after someone she'd never catch, while everyone watched, shaking their heads. Thinking of Tommy only made her angrier. She wouldn't even have come here, done any of this, if he'd just accepted her for who she was. With the fresh rush of anger, Lorraine ran faster, faster.

And then a branch, and a rock, feet stumbling, the *rrrripppp* of fabric tearing, a cold surge and then heat at her knee, the smell of torn grass and finally an unwelcome wet tongue at her face. From a ways off, she heard deep belly laughs. She was definitely going to kill the *Ohmigods*, whenever she could manage to stand again. Maybe with a stylish stiletto, so the crime would come across really ironic.

"Are you okay?"

She saw the jittery Yorkie before she saw him, the cute guy, hovering above Pooh-Pooh's enormous mass. Apparently the dog was sorry. It wasn't as clear, however, exactly where the guy stood, between the smile he was diligently attempting to hide between two fingers and the concern knitting in his furrowed brow.

"Oh, fine," she said, trying not to sour up at the smell of Pooh-Pooh's dog saliva all over her face.

"Your knee's bleeding." He reached in his pocket. "Here, take these napkins." He held a couple out to her. When she didn't move, he put the jerky dog down, patted her head gently, and applied the napkins to the bloody tear at Lorraine's knee.

Boy, Pooh-Pooh, are you lucky things turned out this way!

"I'm Lorraine," she said.

"Matt," he said, "and this is Lena . . . Horne, and we already know Pooh-Pooh from the building."

The same building!

They didn't say anything for a minute. Matt pressed a bit more firmly at her knee, and they both looked at their dogs, licking each other in the inappropriate places that were already becoming a permanent fixture in her city life.

Lorraine turned, looking rather green, to Matt, who seemed a bit more comfortable with the whole X-rated dog scene.

"They do that all the time," he said. "I don't know"—he shook his head and sighed—"but Romanelli thinks they're in love."

"Well, they're in something," she said, feeling conscious now in the gathering calm of Matt's hand on her knee. However, old feelings die hard, so she took over the napkin holding. Tommy's hand had been there the night before.

Not wanting things to get awkward, she tried to fill the space between them with friendly chitchat. "So, you got any Pooh-Pooh tips? The dog is a serious handful."

"Pooh-Pooh." He grabbed at his chin, looked up to the sky, a professor considering a philosophical question of epic proportions. "A lovable, if not totally insane dog."

The very pup in question had his head gently resting on Lena Horne, rubbing it up and down on her tiny, twittering stomach.

"He grew so quickly, Romanelli wasn't sure she could handle him. But she's something, that woman. Said she could take him, said she wasn't gonna waste her life running after another man. And after she said that, it was like, I don't know, Pooh-Pooh just started listening to her." He looked like he wished he had more advice to offer. "She did tell me this one thing, though. She said, if you stick your palm out flat, with all the fingers spread wide, he'll stop what he's doing immediately."

Would this not have come in handy only a few minutes earlier?

"I know," he said. "You wish I would have said that a little earlier."

"Yeah, well . . ." she answered, not disagreeing.

"So do I." He let out a deep sigh. "So do I," he repeated. "You know, sometimes it feels like you always think of exactly the perfect thing to do just after you've missed your opportunity."

Boy, did Lorraine know about that. She considered herself a master of missed opportunity, in fact. How many nights had she told her ceiling what Tommy could do with his Ping-Pong feelings he was always giving and then taking away!

"I know just what you mean," she said, her mind far off. And then she snapped back to the moment, thinking how nice it was to be chatting with someone normal, someone whose company she enjoyed, someone who gave her his full attention. "You're forgiven. *This time*, that is." She elbowed Matt, who was sitting beside her now. The pair tried to ignore their dogs as they continued to get entirely too familiar with each other—perhaps causing Matt and Lorraine to feel more intimate than they ought to have, having just met.

"So, how come you're watching Pooh-Pooh?" he said, his kind green eyes taking her in.

"Oh, you know, same way every Brooklyn girl winds up in a free Park Avenue sublet with a live-in horse."

"*That* old story." He sighed, shaking his head. "If only I had a nickel for every time I heard that one."

It was easy talking to Matt. Unbelievably easy. And so Lorraine gave into it completely. It had never been so easy to let her guard down. She hardly had a choice.

"It's not all that exciting, really," she said as a disclaimer.

"I'm sure that couldn't possibly be true, given the way we just met, you shooting around the park like Prefontaine."

He was so endearing. "Well, you see, I'm a hair colorist . . ." And so Lorraine let the negativity of the day go as she told him the whole, long story. Probably more than she normally would tell in her own environment, where everyone already knew enough to be the friend you needed—not to mention those nosy bodies you *didn't* need—and the common consensus was that you didn't need to make any new ones. Where attention was in excess, you never actively sought it. But if she wasn't mistaken, Matt was a great audience.

When she joked, "You know us Guidettes and our pizza boys," he gave into her lightness and let out a reflexive, "Ha!" She knew parts of her story looked bad. It was impossible to gloss over that aspect of it, but it was her lot and she accepted it. *Certainly, there had to be a dignity in that?*

His features quieted. He shook his head, as if he were realizing something for the first time, and said very quietly, "No. No, I don't think I had any idea."

She looked to him in silence and experienced the odd sensation of knowing exactly what he meant. But with no footing, no way of believing that she could possibly understand this virtual *stranger* so well, Lorraine convinced herself she couldn't possibly know what he was thinking.

He threw her a life preserver, handing the narrative back to her. "So he calls you at midnight every night?" Matt asked it softly when she was setting the stage for that terrible night—the night that had changed it all, or at least brought her to this, here, now.

She read his reactions, deciphered his thoughts. Could his concern, the way he bit at his lip, really mean what she supposed it to? How strange to wonder about things like that, which had always been so obvious to her in the familiarity of her friends, her life, her—if not exactly perfect, at least predictable—relationship with Tommy! Still, there was something intriguing, exciting even, about the unknown.

She went on and on, initiating him into the very thing she was both fighting for and trying to escape from. "Tommy and Lorraine. It's like you can't have one without the other. Peanut butter and jelly. Batman and Robin . . ."

Matt offered one, "Oil and water."

She knew what it must have sounded like to an outsider. In fact, from where *she* stood it didn't even sound all that convincing anymore. Maybe she was just tired, maybe it was something more. But she couldn't admit it, not yet. "I know, it's hard to explain. But . . ."

Again, he stopped her. This time more gently, with a hand close, but not touching hers, like maybe he'd wanted it to but thought better of it. "No, really. I understand these things can be difficult. It's just, you know, we only just met, but I, you . . ." He trailed off into silence and then laughed at himself—a good, real laugh—shaking his head out. "What I'm trying to say is, any guy would be crazy to treat you that way. And, just talking to you, it's hard to believe you would take that from someone. You just don't seem the type."

Perhaps she didn't know him that well, but she knew she could trust her instincts. It was strange, but she sensed he could see inside her. She knew he could really see who she was. It was strange and wonderful and refreshing beyond belief to be this open, to have someone be so open back. She wasn't going to waste the effort of trying to explain it further. Matt got it. There really was nothing more to explain. And at the moment, she wasn't sure she could even pull it off.

By the time a couple of hours had passed, and Pooh-Pooh and Lena Horne had relieved themselves (thankfully Matt had cleaned up the mountainous pile of poop), Lorraine was torn between excitement and fear. Maybe those feelings hadn't surfaced earlier at the hair salon because there she was a colorist, albeit not actually doing any coloring; but still, there was an accustomed stylist/client relationship that she fell into. But here, with Matt, there *were* no rules. Something was happening—she just wasn't sure what.

Lorraine thought Matt might have made some sweeping judgment about her stupidity, but he didn't. He just said, "Life is funny sometimes, isn't it?"

She shook her head in agreement. It seemed to mean both everything and nothing all at once. What had she been expecting him to do? It occurred to her that after only this short time she'd placed an unbelievable expectation on this man, with his miniature dog on a long leash, with a key looped around his neck on a long cord printed with the words "Honk if you love J. Edgar Hoover" over and over again. She'd expected him to provide, in a word, the answer to a problem she'd been trying to solve her whole life. It was ridiculous. Or maybe it was just the effect Matt had on her, a calming, soothing comfort—like she'd always known him.

Things had gotten a bit too serious for such an early meeting, so she tried to lighten the mood. "Like funny ha-ha?" which hadn't come out as funny as she'd hoped.

"I'll give you a funny ha-ha," he said, smirking all the same. "Princess Funny Ha-Ha, are you ready to take the dogs back to the palace?"

Was she? She'd been having such a nice time with Matt, and was glad when they took the walk slowly, allowing the dogs to stop at points of interest—fire hydrants, dandelion patches, lengths of stray toilet tissue—along the way.

"So what's *your* story?" Lorraine asked.

"Just your typical ex-con escapes the law, becomes Mr. Universe, spends his life fending off Guidettes with a stick story."

"I should've known. If I had a nickel for every ex-con Mr. Universe who had a miniature dog named Lena Horne. Jeez." If Matt had ever broken a single law—even a traffic one—she'd give him a million dollars. "I thought I saw you on the five o'clock news!"

They smiled easily at each other and she found herself saddened when the walk came to a close.

"As you may have also seen on the five o'clock news, I'm single."

"Girlfriend couldn't take all the attention you got? The weekends up at the joint . . ."

"Yeah. It's a real relationship killer. Nah. Honestly. It's just, I have a knack for finding all the women who have a handicap in caring about anything important."

"Give me an example," Lorraine said, trying to picture a girl who Matt might have a relationship with.

"An example. An example. Oh, the pressure." He breathed big. "Okay. Here's one. One of my girlfriends, you won't even believe this, Lorraine—she wouldn't go out with me one night because she had a pimple. It was our anniversary! I rang her bell, flowers, candy in hand—the whole she-bang—I can be a romantic, believe me, and pow! She dumps that on me. I'm like, 'You're kidding, right? I don't want to be callous or anything, but throw some cover-up over the thing. I'm in love with you, I don't care about a stupid zit! I'll kiss it!' You know? You couldn't even see the thing. But that wasn't the point. I'd been planning that night for months and the important thing was the *being* together, not what we looked like. I got reservations at this place that even turned away Brad Pitt! Because she loved that kind of garbage." He smiled, slowed the pace. "I'd been working out—I mean, I'm Mr. Universe, so I'm always working out—obviously . . ."

"Obviously," Lorraine rolled her eyes.

Lorraine thought of the Princesses she'd met earlier. "I think I know just what you mean. You wouldn't believe the *Princesses* actually came into the salon today. I was forced to kiss ass, and believe me, it's something I've a very short threshold for."

"You? I wouldn't have believed that. You look like a huge ass kisser to me. Not that I meant you look like you kiss huge asses . . . not that there's anything wrong with that . . . but . . ."

She jokingly elbowed Matt. Two elbows already! *Promise me you'll forget that pizza boy.*

He was quiet for a minute, and then said cautiously, "Well, remember those emotionally handicapped women I was just talking about?"

"No way!" She couldn't believe Matt—this Matt she'd just been talking to as if he were from the neighborhood—could *possibly* have been involved with any of the Princesses. "Which one?"

"Ahhhhh. Well, a name, what's a name really? Right?" He shook his head as if this would steer her to not want an answer.

But Lorraine held tight. "Oh, yeah, what's in a name? What's the difference. What are you kidding? I'm from the Bay—the town is literally built on gossip. I try my best to keep out of it, but there's only so much a girl can stand."

The dogs had stopped at a small pile of flattened cardboard boxes. Lorraine tugged on his "Honk if you love J. Edgar Hoover" key chain and said, "Just tell me quick, it hurts much less that way."

"Fine! Fine." He waved surrender and then took a deep breath. "Mallory. It was Mallory. And it was a long time ago, and it's ancient history. Like Mesopotamia ancient."

"I am shocked! I wouldn't think Mallory would date an ex-con!" She made light of it, but the idea of those two together did propose a disconnect for Lorraine. She couldn't think of someone she was less like than Mallory. And yet, here she was chumming around like she'd known Matt forever, possibly the same way he'd done with Mallory.

"You won't hold it against me, will you?" Matt was joking, too. But it seemed to be important to him that Lorraine didn't categorize him with the Princesses.

"Well, if you stop talking about huge asses, maybe I'll consider it."

By the time they reached their front door, Lorraine was giddy with the idea of acclimating to her new life and finding a new friend, so she extended the offer of future plans. "Same thing, same time tomorrow?" she asked, thinking it would also be less intimidating attempting this whole Pooh-Pooh thing if she had Matt's help.

"Wish I could, Lorraine, wish I could. Lena and I are off to Miami for a couple a weeks of sunshine. But we'll catch you on the flipside, for sure. I'm really glad you moved to the building, Lorraine. Really glad." He had a great smile, that Matt. It could say a million things at once. And you just knew they were all true.

He waited until Lorraine had Pooh-Pooh safely inside the apartment and unhooked from the leash to let the elevator doors close and take him up to his apartment on the sixth floor.

Lorraine thought about him up there all alone. She thought about some of the things he'd told her.

"Total 'old money,'" he'd said in a way that made the point anything but uncomfortable. "So where do I fit in to the whole thing, you're wondering? *Good question!*" He pointed at her like she'd just won a game-show round. Matt was a fabulous storyteller; he knew just how to bring you along for the ride, secure you inside his circle. "Basically, I manage my parents' investments. Stop, I know, so exciting! I'm lucky. I know, believe me I know. I'm so grateful sometimes it hurts. I'm so grateful that . . . well, you're gonna think this is the stupidest thing in the world," he said.

Lorraine was at the edge of her seat. She really wanted to know what someone like Matt really cared about, deep down. "Please, tell me!"

"All right, but not *one Trading Spaces* joke . . . and I mean that! I really love . . . carpentry."

"You know, some women might find that rather sexy . . . a guy in a log cabin somewhere, axing things, whittling, a long strand of hay between his teeth. I could definitely see you on *Trading Spaces!*"

"You promised!"

Lena Horne yelped, as if in defense of her owner.

"Sorry, sometimes I can't help myself. I blame my upbringing."

In her living room Lorraine tried to picture what Matt's parents must have said when he told them he'd fallen in love with carpentry during the "hard work" they'd forced him to commit to when he'd begged a semester off from college. She knew the pain of disappointing parents and all their hopes and dreams for you. She tasted her mother's disapproval every day. "My daughter wastes her life!" Mrs. Machuchi didn't beat around the bush. No. She cried to the Virgin Mother loud enough so the whole neighborhood could hear. *PLEASE pass the bread!*

"Boy, they regretted that!" He'd handled the serious topic with humor and ease that she saw came naturally to him. But she sensed the hurt went deeper than he let on.

At the window seat, looking out at the tiny lights in the apartments beyond—their televisions buzzing like they could have been anywhere in the world—Lorraine thought, no matter what you assumed about them, New Yorkers could surprise you. She pulled on her familiar comfy pajamas, told herself she could be anywhere in the world, and tried to make herself at home. No matter how hard this night might be, she was *not* going to run back to Brooklyn, she told herself in the mirror in her bedroom. But it couldn't hurt to have a little support.

So she affixed with a rolled-up piece of Scotch tape *just one* picture of herself, her Bobbsey Twin, and the man of her dreams. They were at graduation. Tommy had his hat slung backward, his eyes a hot cocoa, swirling with what might be. She loved the way he looked there. As for her and Chrissy, Tommy had them both in a headlock. Because she couldn't help but compare, she looked at Tommy's smile in the context of Matt's. After a moment she realized it was fruitless—Tommy's smile was indecipherable. It wouldn't tell you a damned thing. Backing out to the doorway, she glanced at the photo again before shutting the light and making her way to the living room. *Obviously it's a photo,* she thought. But gee, did she look small.

Back in the living room, Pooh-Pooh, unsurprisingly, was passed out and taking up the entire sofa.

Mallory Meen, Head Princess

Scalp Massage: medium vigorous

Conditioner: extra

Products: a light bodifier; NO shine product

Water: lemon AND lime, squeezed and mixed for one minute.

Lunch: Cobb salad from La Goulue (no bacon; chicken well done), with vinaigrette.

Conversation: prefers chatting when she initiates

Dog: Queenie

Queenie preferences: cinnamon flavor Doggie Do! biscuits (mini size); likes hair cut v. short and curled between ears; favorite bow color: orange.

eBay auction block #5
Description: Guido Salon "Preference Card" for Princess Mallory Meen. "When I first saw it, I nearly lost my lunch," says Princess Lorraine. "However," she adds—always her colorful self, "the Cobb salad from La Goulue happens to be delicious."

Opening bid: $425
Winning bid: $1225 by staceyprincess@princess.com

Comments: I *knew* she used a bodifier! But what kind. . . .

FIVE

♥

A COLORFUL TURN OF EVENTS

At home Lorraine normally drank whatever coffee her mother had gotten on sale at the Italian specialty food store. It was always fine, but to have landed in the discount bin, it was maybe ground improperly or a little on the old side, or maybe it was just a kind nobody ever bought. Lorraine and her father and brother had gotten used to it. Over the years the slightly irregular coffee had become the heart of their morning ritual: take a sip of coffee, make a joke ("Ah, gentle aroma of expired coffee beans, a special blend of stale and rotten . . ."). Her mother (depending on her mood), would laugh, joke in retaliation ("not unlike the scent of our bathroom, Eau de dad's dirty socks") or yell at her family to start making their own coffee, which they would gladly do if they didn't think the whole thing had become important to her and to all of them, this little thing they did together each day, them and no one else.

But in the weeks she'd been living in Manhattan, Lorraine got into the habit of frequenting a fancy coffee shop and treating herself while reading the paper. There were many choices, of which none looked old or stale. Lorraine tried first a vanilla cream latte, and then an Asian spiced latte. There were hundreds of other choices, so she hadn't had the same coffee twice. She hadn't yet created a routine. As Lorraine sat reading the *New York Post* and soaking in a patch of sun through the window, she thought about how much her life had changed in two weeks.

It wasn't a black or white kind of thing, changing your life. There were many components to consider, and when you hadn't been entirely unhappy with your life before, even when everyone thought you ought to be, you couldn't be sure you knew how to judge your own satisfaction.

For instance, this Alone Time everyone always talks about needing. Well, after a couple of days, it feels just plain lonely. Today marked her second full week of alone time, and Lorraine thought that must be long enough. And by long enough she meant the perfect amount of time away from the neighborhood. And by the perfect amount of time away, she meant long enough for everyone to think she'd made the right decision, and was comfortable with it, too.

Mrs. Machuchi had asked her daughter to come home for Sunday dinner last weekend, but Lorraine knew that was too soon. She'd spent the evening imagining the tastes of her mother's homemade gravy, the feel of the squished tomato between her own fingers. The smell of freshly torn basil. It had been difficult. But Lorraine felt it had been important to push herself through this separation from her home life and most of all, from Tommy. If she'd gone home then, Lorraine wasn't sure she'd have been able to come back to Park Avenue.

But today marked two weeks. And after this coffee, and a long day at the salon, Lorraine was going to pack her bags and take the R train out to the Bay. Pooh-Pooh was at the groomer's deluxe pet hotel for a weekend of man's best friend massage, pet pool, and canine playpen time. It would have been a pretty lonely weekend if she weren't heading home.

Lorraine finished the last sip of her peppermint cocoa latte and gathered herself for the final hours before she headed home. She couldn't help feeling her homecoming would be a test of sorts, a way to see if her plan was working. As a result, there was an edgy energy pulsing through her as she walked the couple of blocks to the salon.

Lorraine went through the main salon entrance, rather than through the store.

"Morning, Lorraine," said Rhonda, the receptionist. Rhonda always had a different hairstyle. It was good marketing. But sometimes it was bad for Rhonda's self-esteem, because often no one recognized her. Today the receptionist had bright red hair and fabulous winged layers, like Farrah Fawcett.

Lorraine took a stab and hoped she was right: "Morning, Rhonda! You look unbelievable!" Lorraine knew she was right when she got a smile in return.

"I know! It's fabulous! But I won't be able to keep it! In a week I'll be a brunette, or a blonde, or who knows?" It was a strange melancholy that could accompany a great but temporary hairstyle, and Rhonda's tone captured it even as she offered the elegant smile a receptionist must always offer.

Like most things, Lorraine thought, free hair care was a mixed blessing. "Whatcha got for me today?"

Rhonda passed her the long schedule everyone received in the mornings—lined with tiny boxes that accounted for each half hour of your day. Lorraine was paired with Guido, like she was most days. It was a mixed blessing in itself—it meant you were at the top of the assistants, but also that you were being closely watched. This didn't frighten Lorraine in the way it frightened most of her peers. But Guido had been strange with her since she'd started—exponentially since she'd assisted with Mallory—and so it was stressful to explore her boundaries with him. It was a stress to be unable to say, "Go shove it!" like she could with Carlo. And she was surprised to hear herself so much as think it, but it was a stress that Guido wouldn't just say "Go shove it!" back. At least that way you knew just where you stood.

Guido was dressed to the nines. He was head to toe in green crushed velvet—the haughty green giant. His loafers were tan with a tasteful buckle. Something had to be tasteful, Lorraine assumed.

"Good morning, *bella*," he said, kissing her on either cheek.

"Good morning, Guido." She kissed and greeted back.

He wanted coffee. "Lorraine, can you grab me a coffee from *Juan*?" He pronounced the name as if he were born in Old San *Huan*. You didn't ask how Guido took it. He liked it with extra milk and extra sugar—the fresh unbleached crystal kind—and a sprinkle of cinnamon. You were advised to memorize that information on your first day. It was told to you by whoever liked you, whoever hoped you made it. For Lorraine, that person had been Don.

"Don, what have you gotten me into here?" she'd asked. It was impossible sometimes to believe Don, with his pink mohawk, could conform with such gusto.

"Always so resistant, Lorraine. It's your best and worst quality, if you don't mind me saying," was how he'd put it.

He hadn't known how right he was.

Lucky for Lorraine, at least that time she'd taken Don's advice to heart. "Hey, Juan," she said to Juan's back. He clicked and clacked at his fancy Italian coffeemaker, with its mysterious compartments and tiny filters and shiny brass and silver. Lorraine thought even that was an art.

"What can I design for you, *chica*?" That was Juan's catchphrase for mixing up his coffees. It worked.

"One coffee—extra milk, extra unbleached crystal sugar, a sprinkle of cinnamon."

"Ahhh, the Guido." He winked. That was the other part of it. Juan wasn't allowed to tell you what Guido wanted if you asked. "Kills me when the kids get dhat drink wrong. I *chust* wwwwant to scream out, no, *chica! No!*"

They smiled at each other and Juan turned away from Lorraine to "design" Guido's coffee.

"What else?"

She had to order a drink for their first client, Mr. Markson: a black iced tea with mint infusion, as he liked to have it waiting when he arrived. Of course Guido hadn't told her this. He shouldn't have to. It was another test, but to Lorraine it was obvious. The art of detail came naturally to her, always had. If you did everything perfectly, but left a splodge of dye on a client's face, *that* would be what they remembered. You had to be one step ahead—always.

When Juan turned back around, there were three cups in front of Lorraine. One was Guido's and one was the iced tea. The mystery beverage was a soft caramel color and came in a tall glass with ice cubes at the bottom, hovering above an ornate silver base.

"What's that?" Lorraine wanted to know.

"That's the *Lorrainnnn-a*. Go ahead, *chica*. Try it." Juan made her name his own. He crossed his arms and stood back, confident.

Lorraine smiled at him and watched out of the corner of her eye as she took a sip from the old-fashioned candy-striped straw. She let the liquid swirl around her tongue, the back of her mouth, and finally down her throat. It was sweet, and a little spicy, too. There was a creamy texture to the drink, but it was light as air. "Delicious. Don't even tell me what's in it. It'll ruin the magic."

Juan smiled. "Any time, *chica*."

Guido was already walking Mr. Markson to his chair when Lorraine returned with the drinks.

The client took the drink wordlessly. That was Mr. Markson. He didn't like talking—it said so right on his card. He wanted his gray covered and he wanted it done fast. And then he wanted to leave. But he didn't want you to talk to him.

Lorraine wondered why. While she stood holding the bowl of purple dye for Guido, she made up fantastic stories about why Mr. Markson didn't like to talk. It could be he was just embarrassed by the idea of having his hair dyed. Or it could be more than that. It could be serious. Perhaps if he heard the world *dye* he would snap into a convulsion and begin grunting like a hyena, demanding bananas by the crateful. *Juan! The bananas for Mr. Markson, please.*

After a few minutes Lorraine handed Mr. Markson a cool towel for his forehead. He liked that as a refresher. And as Guido applied the final stroke, Lorraine propped the station's laptop computer (Guido's offered twenty complimentary laptops in all) up on the counter in front of Mr. Markson and set it up for him to check his e-mail. She walked away so he could enjoy privacy.

Mr. Markson was done quickly. After him there was a thirteen-year-old whose bat mitzvah was to be held the following day, then her mother, followed by a Brazilian princess, the ambassador to the Czech Republic, Eva Longoria, and at the end of her contract with L'Oreal—*Sarah Jessica Parker*. For each client, Lorraine did just the same thing. She paid careful attention to their preference cards, tried to treat them in the manner she'd want to be treated times ten, and offered a little something extra— whether it be an at-home care tip, the aromatherapy treatment, or a fun conversation.

Sarah Jessica was a talker. She'd always seemed on the level to Lorraine. And hey, it was unbelievably cool to hear about the great sweater she'd just bought on West Fourteenth Street.

"It was so expensive, though!" Sarah Jessica lamented.

"Oh my god! Tell me about it. I bought this shirt the other day downstairs, and I can't even tell my friends how much it cost. I'm embarrassed to say it!"

"I know just what you mean," Sarah Jessica said. "But when something is done so artfully, when it's such a perfect cut . . . I just think it's worth it. You can really appreciate that kind of stuff, you know?"

"I do. That's just what I said when my friend Chrissy commented on my $120 jeans the other night."

"A hundred and twenty! Don't tell Chrissy that these cost $300!"

They both got a laugh out of that.

"By the way, Lorraine, I really love your nails. Do they offer that style here?"

"*My* nails? Sarah Jessica, I'm sure they can do something like this for you here. Let me take you down to the cut girls so you can get those layers cleaned up a bit, and I'll come down and confirm. Sound good?"

"Perfect," Sarah Jessica said, pushing her hair away from her face in that sweet way she often did on *Sex and the City* with both palms out.

Lorraine was riding high on that conversation, but she was a little concerned about what Guido might think. Nails weren't even remotely in her job description.

She found Guido in the color room. He was looking over his schedule and reading the latest issue of *Us Weekly*. "What do you think of this whole Ashton and Demi thing? I mean, what do you *really* think?"

Lorraine wasn't positive, but she could have sworn his accent had lost some of its gilt, that it was more . . . ordinary, or something. "Ashton-Demi, huh? That's an easy one. She's in love. It's written on her face. Believe me, I know. And everyone's laughing and saying no, no, no, it could never work. But that's just making her want him more. Maybe she doesn't even know what she sees in him. But she's in love. I just know she's in love." Lorraine had taken the question to heart. Who was she talking about, really?

The ensuing silence was awkward, and Lorraine knew she'd possibly revealed too much. It wasn't like her. Guido changed the topic. "What can I do for you, Lorraine?"

"Well. You know how Sarah Jessica was just in here and it says right on her card that she really likes chatting?" She thought maybe if she could just show she was playing by the rules this would work in her favor.

"Yes, I do know what it says on her card. I created the cards, Lorraine." This was not going to be easy.

"Well, we were chatting, and we got to talking about my nails . . . and . . . well, she asked if we did them here. . . ."

Now he was looking at her with a pursed mouth and big eyes with deep lines sprouting from the corners. *A very unjolly green giant.*

"And I said I was sure we could do *something* like that, because of course, she's Sarah Jessica Parker, and we want to do whatever she wants us to do . . . and . . ."

"And so you want to do them?" he asked the question. As it hung there, she wasn't sure if she was supposed to answer it or not. He rapidly drummed his fingers on the counter.

But she knew the answer, and she'd come this far. If nothing else, Lorraine Machuchi had perserverance. "Yes, I want to do them. I just know they will look fabulous on her." She was waiting for him to disapprove, and she was ready, ready to argue her point. The words were already forming in her head.

"I would love for you to do them, Lorraine. You are right. They will look fabulous on her. In fact, Sarah Jessica isn't the only one who's inquired about your nails. I've been wanting to ask you if we could use your nail designs for a big campaign. It's hot, it's fresh. It's . . . Guido Nails. We've already scouted a vendor for the B charms, and you would just need to train the nail girls on the airbrush machine and the parameters of the over-all look. We'll start with three different options, and if you could just teach them on Tuesday morning, we'll add it to the *Guido Training Book C*."

That couldn't have gone better, right? This was just what she wanted, wasn't it? She was thrilled! (Wasn't she?) It was an honor that New York women—the most chic of New York women—wanted *her* look! So, why did something seem to be missing? Whatever it was, she couldn't turn back now. Something about this was big. And she wouldn't have any time to falter. She'd follow wherever it was this opportunity was going to take her. If there were any worries, she'd address them later.

Sarah Jessica stood back, not two hours later, and stared at her Guido Nails with the same grin she'd worn describing that great sweater she bought on West Fourteenth. "These are fabulous, Lorraine! Fabulous. Too bad *Sex and the City* is off the air because my character would have looked great in them! It would have been a real coup for your career. Still, this should be amazing for you. I'll call *Page Six* myself."

When Sarah Jessica Parker likes your product, you are one lucky girl. But when you get a call that the Princesses have just gotten wind of the new design and demanded that Page Six mention in the paragraph they got the Guido Nails *before* they mention Sarah Jessica Parker in them, well then, that is a winning-lottery-ticket moment.

Mallory came into Guido's nearly out of breath. She pushed her way through the golden doors with her very own hands—not something she *ever* did. And behind her there was an entourage even Diddy couldn't shake a stick at.

"Laurie! How *are* you?" She didn't give Lorraine a chance to answer before she continued. "The *nails*, darling! The *nails*! Do them! Please!"

Lorraine was squinting. She could barely see Mallory through the blinding light of a camera recording them, its gigantic lens hanging over their heads like a higher power, something bigger than all of them. There was a mass of people surrounding them, some snapping photos, some ask-ing questions of the Princesses. One of them popped out with a piece of paper and a pen, and said, "Lorraine, sign here, please." Guido nodded ex-pressionless that she should go ahead.

"*Entertainment Tonight* is filming me getting the Guido Nails. You're gonna be on *television*, Laurie, *television*! I'm sure the girls back home in the Bronx will be blown away by that."

Lorraine didn't like the way Mallory said that. It was condescending and it made Lorraine—or *Laurie*—seem like a turnip from the middle of nowhere waiting on line with a sign bubble lettered with "I love you, Al Roker."

Besides, it all seemed a little ridiculous. And already she saw herself drowning in the larger ocean of publicity for Guido's. It all left a bad taste in her mouth. But hey. This *could* make her famous. She hated to admit this, but she *was* going to be on *Entertainment Tonight*, and that *would* score big back home. *Especially*, she hoped, with Tommy. And wasn't that the *real* focus here?

Someone screamed from the crowd. "Get a close-up on Mallory's ring finger—right as Lorraine places the B on it. And then zoom out and back in again." Lorraine couldn't see beyond the halo of light around her and the Princess.

"Wow, some crazy lifestyle you've got," Lorraine said when Mallory hadn't spoken in a little while. The media racket seemed miles away in the quiet haze of their little patch of soft light.

"Think you can handle it?" Mallory challenged, a wild flicker in her eye.

"Me?" Lorraine asked. "What do I know about all this? I'm just a hairstylist from the Bay."

"Did you get that, Johnny?" the voice screamed again.

Lorraine didn't know if she loved the idea of that going on TV. It wasn't the way she wanted herself portrayed at all—in fact, it was the exact opposite of the way she wanted to be portrayed. She thought of that thing Matt had said: *Sometimes it feels like you always think of exactly the perfect thing to do, just after you've missed your opportunity.*

"Do you think you can get them to cut that part out?" Lorraine asked Mallory.

"Oh, but why?" Mallory asked. "It's so . . . wildly *colorful*!" The idea seemed to make her exhilarated, deliriously happy. It was weird.

When her nails were through, Mallory called Stacey to take her seat next. "Stacey, darling! Your turn."

Stacey watched every single thing Lorraine did, unlike Mallory, who was only interested in the final result. "Do it exactly the same way as you did Mallory's," she said. In case Lorraine didn't get it, she repeated, "Exactly."

The camera was getting hot in Lorraine's face, but even in this condition, she could do what she needed to do.

Stacey asked, "So what did you talk about with Mallory?"

"Oh, not too much," Lorraine said, thinking again of that stupid thing she'd said about being from the Bay.

"Are you excited to be on television?" Stacey asked.

"Sure, yeah." But now she wasn't so sure. In fact, she couldn't wait to go home.

Afterward, she put two different designs on Katharine—who asked every two seconds, "Are you *sure* you're doing everything right?" and in-between answered her cell phone and two-way pager, smushing Lorraine's work—and then Tracey, who informed Lorraine, "It's not *tawk,* it's *talk*," although Lorraine hadn't even said the word.

Lorraine wanted to tell Tracey where she could stick it, but the three of them handed her a $100 bill apiece as tip. Hell, she thought, maybe it *is* talk.

On the train Lorraine had started to think about Tommy, just maybe what he might think of the new jeans she bought that really *did* make her ass look unbelievably tight and her long legs stunningly slim. Even Lorraine couldn't believe she could ever in her life spend $100 on jeans, but without the discount, they would have been $200, and so obviously that was a huge savings, if still an extravagance. According to Sarah Jessica, they were a steal! Boy, that was a funny thing to think—that there was anything in her memory that had to do with Sarah Jessica. That Sarah Jessica was probably out at that moment telling someone where she got those nails.

Lorraine was wearing an off-the-shoulder, slouchy, long-sleeved body-conscious T-shirt that was sultry without being trashy, and she felt hot in it. There was nothing better to Lorraine than looking hot, because that's when Tommy gave her the most attention, when he was most able to overcome his hang-ups about saving her for when he was ready. And these new clothes, they gave her a new kind of hot you couldn't piece together from the shops on 86th Street. She felt herself give off an air of mystery, in the soft and lightweight fabric, in the unique melon hues, layered over a deep maroon, pointed heels with a precision she'd not seen before in a shoe, the delicate *klink-klink* of a pair of long hanging earrings, their crystals giving off light like mad. Lorraine had also been working on the wavy look in between clients, modifying it with hot rollers and some subtle layers around her face. The makeup girls played with her look, giving her heavily lined eye just a little softening touch that lent a refinement she admired.

All these things she put on like battle armor for a warrior. She'd laughed at the idea of that. Was it possible for her to do even the smallest thing for her own satisfaction, without that one goal in mind? Did anything matter, or exist even outside of its significance in bringing her closer to him? Had she come closer to her goal, or simply complicated the game of achieving it?

Still, she'd thought as she followed the familiar steps from the subway station to her home, she didn't appear that way to everyone else. She could at least take comfort in the success others would surely notice in her tonight. Couldn't she?

Placing her overnight bag in her old bedroom, the place that had been hers for so long, she realized it hadn't been all take and no give with Lorraine and the New Yorkers. She'd left them with her nails. She'd made her mark on the city. With that thought in mind, she left for the schoolyard.

"Bi-atch! You are f'ing gorgeous! A little slutty, but—"

"It's not slutty, Sister Theresa, it's fashion." Boy, it was good to see Chrissy.

"Fashion, shmashion, I can see your bra strap and that's not something the Virgin Mary would smile upon."

"Good to see some things never change," Lorraine said, watching the familiar cracks in the sidewalk pass under their feet. She wasn't going to explain the bra actually was made for that type of shirt, that it coordinated with the whole look. Not when Chrissy was already in a turtleneck.

"Yeah. Great." But she looked up at Lorraine and smiled, and it wasn't hard to tell how much she missed her best friend.

When Lorraine arrived at the schoolyard with Chrissy, Tommy was there already. He was doing his thing, acting like he didn't notice her. It was an effort for him, she knew, one that he wouldn't exert for just anyone. It was no easy feat, since Lorraine had gained the status of a local celebrity, leaving for a couple of weeks and then coming back looking different and surrounded by rumors of the wild success of her beauty career. *Just wait until you see me on* Entertainment Tonight! She thought of it with a mix of emotions.

"Damn Bobbsey Twin, Manhattan seems to be agreeing with you," Stevie said, kissing her cheek in the austere way everyone always did when greeting the girls in the group—you respected your girls.

Lorraine's cheek burned where Stevie kissed it, feeling Tommy's energy butterfly around everything she did.

Tommy tried his hardest to maintain interest on the three keys on his ring, which Lorraine knew belonged to his car, home, and Bay Pizza—in descending size order. He was wearing one of those button-neck shirts of his, this time with three buttons undone. And Lorraine tried her hardest not to notice the smooth muscle showing through, or the clean line where his shirt was tucked into his jeans, which held a flat stomach and, she knew, a tight rear end. She was gonna try and not think about the rest just then.

The electricity, the anger, the passion—all of it was palpable. You could see it in the just-loosening leaves dancing to their rhythm, in the sultry movements of the clouds. When people spoke, the words struggled, re-formed themselves through the energy between the two of them.

"Don't you think she looks hot?" Stevie asked Tommy, breaking the silence of it all, forcing Tommy and Lorraine to address each other directly.

He didn't answer right away. Instead, it felt to Lorraine that Tommy drank her in—all of her, in one long gulp of a stare that got her pulsing and twitching in all the places only he could.

God, it was hopeless, wasn't it?

And then he said, "She *is* hot."

Why? Why did that have to feel so good? Never, never did Tommy say anything like that in front of the group. Never.

He didn't move closer. He didn't attempt to start a conversation with her. Instead, he allowed the hour or so before they all went to the Blue Zoo lounge to serve as foreplay. Each twirl of his key ring, each lick of his lips was a calculated movement, and they added up to sexy. The way he considered Petey's words with a jump of his eyes—up and to the right— a quick glance at her, quickly pulled away. It thrilled her. She was so close to the finish line. To Lorraine, it seemed she had only to reach out her arm and she'd have everything she'd ever wanted.

The Blue Zoo normally hired a band on a Friday night, the kind of group that played songs by Pearl Jam and Nirvana that were popular when they were all young, that they would all know. The place was small and dark, and the band was jammed in by the front door with a low spotlight shining on them. In back there were a bunch of couches which no one was allowed to reserve except for them, because the owner, Rich, was part of the group. He would hang out with them all night, often adding a girl who was impressed by his power and probable wealth, to the mix—by candlelight, feeding her cocktails and lines like they were going out of style.

Chrissy and Big Bobby were just made up from a fight, and so they were lovey-dovey, Chrissy showing off some pair of earrings he'd bought her as consolation to the latest ho bag he'd crossed the line with. Which meant that Chrissy wasn't paying much attention to Lorraine except when Big Bobby went to the bathroom, or outside to smoke a cigarette. But that was all right. How many times over the years had Chrissy understood when Lorraine disappeared at the chance to spend time with Tommy? Thousands.

"We're so lame," Chrissy said at one of those in-between moments, both of them not really believing it, feeling deep down that this is the way of love. What else did they know?

And so Lorraine laughed, maybe too loud or too intensely for the unjoke. Stevie, Petey, Rich, and the dumb college girl he was hanging out with that evening looked up briefly. She answered style questions from the other girls in the group—Susan and Christina and Mary. All the while, she felt Tommy's eyes on her. She felt herself make the transition from never looking to stolen glances to naked stares: in the world of aphrodisi-acs, this one was lethal.

By the time they'd been there an hour and a half, or two Stoli Vanilla and ginger ales, Lorraine emerged from the ladies' room into a tiny hall-way in the back, separated from the rest of the bar by two swinging sa-loon doors. Tommy was leaning against a wall, one of his arms casually draped over the pay phone. And it felt only natural they slip through the back door into the storeroom.

"Oh, my god, Lorraine . . ." He whispered it at her hair, his face pressed hard there.

They didn't make it out the door before Tommy was kissing her, deep and hard and all tongue, the way she'd been dreaming on the train, all the weeks she hadn't seen him or spoken to him. And it wasn't the hurt or the way it could have been avoided that she thought of. *It must be true what they say,* she thought, *that absence makes the heart grow fonder. It really does.*

Lorraine imagined this is what those other girls of his must have got-ten, this first-time thirst Tommy was drinking her up with just then. His hands were all over her, inching down the back of her jeans, and then in the front, where she was all warmth and wetness, shivering. And this only seemed to make him hungrier for her, because he took her jeans down there and kissed her the whole time they had each other there in an of-fice they both knew like the backs of their hands.

And later, when she lay in his bed, and he stroked her hair, pulling his fingers through to the ends, his chest sweat pooling beneath her cheek, Lorraine thought maybe now things would be as she wished, that she could have this always. And everything he said only gave her more confi-dence. *And he parted the chocolate seas.*

He was interested in the city. "So what do you do at night there?" he wanted to know, letting down his guard the way he only did with her at times like this—after, when there was nothing left to hide.

Lorraine knew the importance of making him wonder, keeping him on his toes. But even as she spoke, she felt it wasn't . . . enough. "Oh, you know, there's always something going on." *I'm just a hairstylist from the Bay.*

He seemed to consider this answer as extremely meaningful, not saying anything for five minutes or so, stroking her hair and looking up at the glowing stars on the ceiling.

"Maybe I could come visit you next Friday?"

Lorraine's heart tugged with the sound of things she'd already heard in her head, in her heart. It was so much to have this now, after so long.

BROOKLYN QUEENS

Verse One
Real cool . . .
  "Brooklyn's in the house" (4X)
"Brook, Brook, Brooklyn New York!"
  "Brooklyn's in the house"
{*"Brooklyn"*}

Real cool . . . cause Brooklyn's cool!
Friday doin' the last day of school
Girls steppin' to the mall to swing
Settin' up dollars for their summer fling
Cars on the avenue create gridlock
And there's girls like MAD at the bus stop

eBay auction block #6
Description: Original song lyric notes by 3rd Bass. The song once again hit the charts during the B Back campaign (the other 9/10 of the song was cut by the FCC for explicit language).

Opening bid: $2500
Winning bid: $5900 by iruinsongs@americanidol.com

Comments: Ha! This song is popular, and you know what that means! We will turn it into a watered-down medley rescored by musical guest Kenny Loggins, sponsored by Ford, and Bo Bice will take the lead vocals. Maybe we'll get that William Hung guy to do a comeback appearance! Priceless! We'll beat that damned Princess show once and for all. . . . Maybe we can even get Lorraine to come and be a judge—she's a lot more colorful than that Paula. . . .

SIX

♥

COLORING OUTSIDE THE LINES

The anticipation of Tommy's visit filled Lorraine's mind as she sat, a few days later, in the coffee shop. This particular morning was sunny and she dipped her head back in the wing chair, and took a sip of her fancy Cinnamon Mist latte. The paper sat unread in her hands. Was she any better or worse here? Only time would tell.

When she was through, Lorraine rose and walked the few blocks to Guido's. Not two hours earlier, she'd made the same walk with Pooh-Pooh. Perhaps it would be better described as a run. Pooh-Pooh had been feeling energetic. It wasn't her first choice, but Lorraine had come to enjoy those jogs. After the initial pain, she'd started to like the way the muscles in her legs and her sides were tightening. Even Lorraine's butt was reaping the rewards of the Pooh-Pooh exercise system.

And the hand gesture Matt had taught her did lend a pinch of power to her relationship with the dog. At the very least, she had an emergency brake when things got insane. But the runs seemed to calm Pooh-Pooh, too. He enjoyed the exercise. Not surprising after a day in an apartment, she figured. She was far from mastering the situation, but she'd come along. It was all she could hope for, Lorraine guessed. Rome wasn't built in a day.

On the Pooh-Pooh pooh-pooh front, though, Lorraine could not quite get used to the idea that a balled-up plastic supermarket bag would be her only defense against the huge mounds of excrement that dog could produce. Worse, he always seemed to go right when people were looking their way, saying something about how cute Pooh-Pooh was, and asking his name.

Taking the walk slow and calm to the salon, she was just in the middle of thinking that she missed Pooh-Pooh, when she saw a store owner, one of Pooh-Pooh's many neighborhood admirers, emerge.

"Where's Monsieur Pooh-Pooh?" he wanted to know, scooping a dog biscuit from his pants pocket.

"Resting," she said. "We had a pretty vigorous run this morning."

"Ah, early risers," he said, winking and waving her off for the day.

At the salon Rhonda the receptionist wore a beachy blond color, with wild messy curls. It was a little too much, even for Rhonda. "I know, please don't say anything," she said earnestly, like she could barely hide her disapproval. Still she held her smile strong and passed Lorraine her daily schedule.

"Aw, Rhonda, you're all beauty," Lorraine said in reaction to her stiff upper lip.

Rhonda smiled like she meant it now. "Thanks, Lorraine. You're really something, you know. What's the word? Oh, yeah . . . you're *colorful.*"

"Never mind. I take back what I said," she joked.

"No, really. It's a fact. Says so, right here in the paper." Rhonda picked up the *Post,* open to *Page Six.* And there it was, the bit about "Colorful Brooklynite, Lorraine Machuchi," doing the Guido Nails on the Princesses and Sarah Jessica. "I'm just a hairstylist from the Bay," read the caption beneath her photo.

Great. Mixed blessings. They were beginning to be the story of her life. At least she looked hot in the photo.

Lorraine had to put the excitement aside to assist Guido, but he wouldn't come in until noon, when his first appointment was scheduled.

Lorraine had plenty of assignments to keep *a colorful hairstylist from the Bay* busy in the meantime.

1. Sweep and mop floor on second level.

2. Fold small- and medium-sized towels.

3. Stock color stations with foils, duck clips, combs.

4. Stock color closet with new shipment from L'Oréal.

Lorraine had to keep in mind that she was on the road to success. She knew this already from how the other colorists spoke about summer homes in the country and trips to Belize. But it was still difficult to come to grips with the everyday reality of sweeping floors when you knew you could be a top colorist, watching the Belize-trippers make mistakes and perform less than perfect color jobs out of boredom. Already, she wondered how long she could handle this track until she went begging her way back to the dead-end Do Wop—a quitter who'd presented herself poorly to the media when she'd had the chance.

She told herself that in time she could give that kind of Belize trip success to Tommy, and in return he could give himself to her free of all his hang-ups and they could have a couple of kids and live happily ever after, and she could cook him up great bowls of ziti with olive oil and a little tomato and he could laugh over how long it took to settle down. *When I was young!* he could say to his own kids, and the two of them would share the looks she saw between her own parents sometimes. Who knew? Maybe their whole crew would go to Belize one day.

Those kinds of dreams kept Lorraine company while she performed the mindless work she'd previously relied on neighborhood high school girls to do. And of course, there was Don.

"Ms. Finklestein would like to look more like Jennifer Aniston," he said in between clients an hour after Lorraine came in. "I hadn't the heart to tell her she's much more of a Bea Arthur, although it was hard not to, the way she kept telling me I was making her look old. 'Ms. Finklestein,'

I would like to say, 'Mother Nature has already taken care of that.' The woman's at least ninety-seven. By the way, Lorraine, you're looking so . . . what's the word? I know! You're looking so *colorful* today.'" He spoke softly, but apparently carried a big stick.

"Shut up." Boy, you give people a word. Lorraine could think of a couple herself.

"You know who's really colorful?" Don continued. "Ms. Finklestein."

Lorraine thought Finklestein was probably a little closer to crazy.

"Her card says she likes"—he cleared his throat—"to look just like Jennifer Aniston. To be told she looks just like Jennifer Aniston. To have all beverages and chitchat the way Jennifer Aniston likes them."

"Couldn't you just see Rhonda phoning Jennifer Aniston's assistant, asking, 'Yes, how does Jennifer like to have her dog's hair styled—straight, slightly wavy, or very wavy?' " Lorraine said and shoved a stack of towels in the cupboard behind.

But at least Finkelstein was nice, Lorraine thought after that conversation. On the whole, she'd noticed some pretty disgusting behavior from the clients at the salon. For the most part, they weren't friendly. They had nothing to talk about unless it was a complaint. They never remembered your name. They never said thank you when you ran twelve blocks and three avenues to get them a seared tuna salad from the only place they liked to eat at. They always looked you up and down. They always called the garments you wore against their tastes "cute." They wanted Internet access, telephone access, to watch soap operas on television. They had their dogs' hair styled just like their own ("Mini Me" was the name of the service and it went for $350 and included an assortment of Doggie Do! biscuits in a gift bag). They wanted things done quickly, or they didn't want you to rush. They screamed at people on their cell phones, and then they screamed at you when their battery died. They thought their color was too dark, too light, too brassy, not golden enough, not anything like J. Lo's at the Grammys in that picture from *InStyle* they'd showed you. They were a half hour late and not wanting to wait while you finished what you'd begun working on in the meanwhile. They would leave if you were more than twenty seconds late and tell you they were going to leak the bad service to DailyCandy so you'd be ruined.

They didn't like if you were pretty, they laughed behind your back if you were ugly.

Most of all, though, they wanted to see the Princesses. They wanted to know what the Princesses had done to their hair this week, wanted to know when they were scheduled to come in so they could catch a glimpse of what they were wearing. They wanted to talk about them and say how their sister's friend's cousin had seen one of them at a party for the Sims DVD computer game and her hair was frizzy and she was a huge bitch. Then they would smile and go back to wondering what the bitch was wearing and how quickly Scoop NYC could order one in their own size.

Some days Lorraine counted down the seconds until her lunch break so she could just get the hell out of there and walk over to a seedier side of town where people wore no-name denim and had no arches in their eyebrows. Most of all they didn't know she was only an assistant and therefore didn't treat her like one ("Have the girl run and get me a machiatto," "Send the girl to go return this to Bloomingdale's for me before it closes"). If the girl didn't get out of there for at least an hour a day, Lorraine was afraid she'd give one of those city bi-atches the what-for, which would hurt not only herself, but Guido, too. And she knew how quick a scandal like socking a Princess or even a Princess in Training in the jaw could spread and ruin everything for Guido. So she really tried to practice patience and focus on the future and the tips and even Pooh-Pooh, whom she was starting to really love.

When she came home at night, he was happy to see her. He wanted to lick her like crazy, which as disgusting as it smelled, started to become endearing. And he needed her. He wanted Lorraine to scratch right under his neck and say, "Good boy! You didn't eat any of the furniture today!" And then he wanted to spend some quality time dragging her fifty miles per hour around Central Park. He would look to her helplessly when she had to clean up his mountain of poop.

And he was starting to pay back, too. For instance, when Lorraine wanted to rent a movie and was really missing the idea of having someone to watch it with, Pooh-Pooh offered himself up with an understanding look, snuggled in with his enormous head on her lap, and watched a movie with absolutely no dogs in it whatsoever. It lessened the loneliness of the city skyline staring carelessly back outside the wall-to-wall windows, between the heavy velvet curtains.

Sure, she'd gone out with Don and his friends a few times. She'd even done dinner with a couple of assistants, but she was feeling a different kind of loneliness. It felt like something was missing. And it was more than the obvious fact that Manhattan was not the Bay.

Today the thought of lazy movie time seemed like a far-off dream to Lorraine, what with the hyperactivity of Guido running behind as soon as he arrived. This happened all the time, because all of his clients wanted to be seen early.

"Why they even make appointments, I'll never know," Guido said to Lorraine when reception rung with the news that three of his clients had arrived and wanted to be seen ASAP.

Lorraine shook her head, rolled her eyes, and said, "Listen, Guido, whatever you need, I'm your girl." He hadn't said a word about the *Page Six* write-up. That pissed her off. Was it against his religion to be happy for someone? Or was it just part of the Guido Method? Where she came from, you congratulated people on their successes, maybe even claimed a piece of it for yourself, just by knowing the person. But she shoved that aside.

The pair flew through two clients: a chestnut and a honey. But the queue for Guido was gaining strength. Lorraine eased things by taking drink orders, having a couple of women get washed, and extending deluxe complimentary conditioning treatments. But things were tense. These women didn't like to wait.

Normally, Lorraine knew Guido might give the ladies the option of having another colorist do their hair if they were in a huge rush, but everyone else was jammed. So, instead he did whatever he could to have Lorraine speed things up with the three women—he'd have her get sections ready while he was painting others, mix the colors, check when to rinse, apply the gloss.

"Guido, when do you think you'll be able to color my hair! I've got a meeting in an hour and a half!" None of this was a question. Ms. Stevensen wanted her hair colored an hour and a half before her appointment, and there was no negotiation. Colorists in New York City were magicians. There was no disputing that. They worked miracles every day.

Lorraine and Guido were halfway through a breathtaking young model—all legs and arms crunched in like a beetle—who'd been instructed to "get a new look," and was currently all red in the nose and eyes from crying. "And what if they let me go? And then my family back—een Rrrrrrussia will have no-*ting* and I'll lose my green card—and I'll have to work in the caviar farm and izz so cold zere! So cold!"

Lorraine and Guido were trying to calm her. "That will never happen to you. You are beautiful. They do this all the time. It's all cosmetic. *The look* has nothing to do with cosmetics—and you, my dear, have *the look*."

The model looked from Guido to Lorraine, teary. She let one leg extend gingerly, made small circles with her toes.

"He knows. He's seen it all, honey. You do. You have *the look*." Lorraine thought how nothing was what you would imagine. Maybe modeling really *was* hard. Boy, Lorraine would have to retract *a lot* of commentary if that were true—basically ninety-nine percent of what she'd said from 1994 to 1998.

They gave the model a fabulous look. The team hadn't spoken of what exactly should be done, but Lorraine had gone and mixed the colors she knew in one glance would be perfect for the gorgeous young Russian, and Guido had just started applying exactly where Lorraine was applying on the other side of the head, natural and quick and magically. Neither of them really noticed Lorraine was actually coloring the model's hair, or that it was she who had initiated the look they were applying. Instead, she soared through the hours. She was the President of the United States. She was Hayden Christensen on the cover of *GQ* (but smiling). She was on top of the world.

It was only later that she realized the implications. And when she did, Lorraine felt the way she imagined men and women did after they'd seen each other across a room and a half hour later realized they'd just lusted themselves into an affair that would ruin both of their marriages. They just got swept away in the moment.

But this was different—it was a Guido colorist rule that had been broken. And that was something you just didn't do. By the time they both realized it, Lorraine was already halfway through applying the color on Ms. Stevensen's crown, adding a little bit of auburn to the current mix, and Guido was finishing the third client who wanted her hair done five minutes ago.

Guido and Lorraine caught each other's eye in the mirror. Ms. Stevensen was yapping on her cell phone, "Sell! I said sell, you good for nothing bastard! We've already gone down ten points in the past twenty minutes!" She put her hand over the receiver and whispered sweet as could be, "Yes, can I have a water, Louise?"

"Sure," Lorraine was saying. The spell had been broken and she wasn't sure how Guido would react at all. On her way back from Juan's, Lorraine decided this must be a good thing. In fact, she should have thought of it before. It was exactly the sort of chance she needed. This was the first time in Lorraine's life she'd been permitted to color someone exactly as she thought she should. It was obvious from Guido's lack of attention to the error that she'd done a great job. Better than great. It had felt like the most natural thing in the world, Lorraine working side by side with one of the world's great colorists, deciding for him what should be done.

Everything was more vibrant—the water in her hand was colder than it normally was, the crystal glass more beautiful. She'd never noticed how fabulous the lighting in the salon was. Lorraine realized life could be so . . . alive! She smiled with the thought of it. Wow, she'd really done the right thing, coming here, giving up everything familiar. She could see that now.

"Oh, thanks, Louise," Ms. Stevensen was saying. Lorraine didn't even care about the name being wrong, about being *colorful,* or just a hairstylist from the Bay. She was so happy to have had this opportunity, which she felt would change her life forever. She'd read about how people got discovered. It was always something just like this, something out of the ordinary that happened and gave someone their chance to shine. And that's just what she had done.

She took Ms. Stevensen to the sink, and decided she'd blow out her hair herself. She wanted to show Ms. Stevensen how to optimize the look of the face-framing highlights she'd applied. And there was no mistaking the final effect. It was one of those moments in a salon that doesn't happen every day. One of those times when everyone gathers around and looks in awe at the dramatic change in a client's look.

"Oh, Guido, this is unbelievable. I don't even recognize myself, yet it's not anything that different. This is just exactly the way I should look. Oh, I love it!"

"Oh, Edie, I am so glad. You are gorgeous, stunning!" Guido held his chin so high, Lorraine wondered if he could see in front of him.

Ms. Stevensen left a hundred-dollar tip for Lorraine. When she passed through the gold doors, Lorraine asked to take a lunch break.

Guido told her that would be fine, why didn't she go down to the café and put it on his tab? She'd been so helpful he wanted to show his gratitude.

It was eerie, the way he hadn't said anything, the way he was treating her to lunch instead. She didn't know what to make of it, but she told herself what was done was done. Lorraine ordered herself a frisée salad with lardon croutons and Roquefort cheese and apple slices like half moons. For dessert she had a molton chocolate cake with a perfectly circular dollop of crème fraiche. She thought how she'd never even known these delightful treats existed a few weeks ago. If she and Chrissy thought fries and gravy were good, well, this was amazing! While she ate, Lorraine read a book one of the clients had recommended to her. She'd never really read any historical fiction before. Normally she just went for the paperback bestsellers. But this book was great. It was about a girl in a famous painting and how she'd come to sit for an artist.

When she'd finished her cake and took her first sip of yet another kind of coffee drink, Lorraine looked around at the neighboring diners and for the first time felt part of them.

"Goin' on Guido's tab?" Sandy, the waitress, asked her.

"Yeah, isn't that awesome?" Lorraine asked.

"I'd say it's a good deal. How's that book, by the way?"

Lorraine held up the back so the waitress could skim the summary. "It's really, really good," she answered while Sandy read.

"All right, doll, don't forget to leave me a fat tip." She smiled—from one employee to another—and winked before she turned to take Lorraine's dishes to the back for washing.

Back upstairs at the salon, Lorraine was really starting to feel good about her city life. She snapped her black assistant robe over her outfit, washed her hands, and went back to Guido's chair to find out who she'd be working on next.

"Lorraine, didn't Rhonda give you a list of things to do today?" He was twirling a brunette's hair up on one side with a large silver clip.

At first Lorraine didn't understand. Wasn't he booked solid? Weren't those tasks for downtime? Besides, she'd finished most of them this morning anyhow. She tried to make sense of his comment.

All she could come up with was that this was all a joke. Like he'd stick her back on those crappy assistant duties! She was Hayden Christensen, remember?

"Ha ha. Okay, really, who's next?" She looked at Guido, willing him to see things the way she hoped he would. As if she could make him do that by looking at him hard enough. She realized she was clenching her jaw.

"Lorraine, you know the rules," was all he said, his chin on the rise.

Folding towels while enduring mortifying demands from city bi-atches was bad enough when you thought it was the only way to reach your goal. But folding towels after you thought you were done folding towels and were now going to be coloring hair like nobody's business—well, that was nearly unbearable.

The rest of the day dragged on. Lorraine was in a terrible mood and tried to block the world out thinking about Tommy's arrival in just a couple of days' time. At five-thirty, when Lorraine had just one hour of torture left, her cell phone beeped to signal she had a message. And that message made her rotten mood even worse.

"Lorraine, Tommy." Her heart froze and then dropped down to her toes. She sat down in the color closet where she was listening and trying to hide from everything she couldn't stand just then. "Not gonna be able to come to the city after all. I'm sorry, beautiful."

She would not cry at work. There was no way she was giving in to this day like that. She would wait until fifty-five more minutes passed, and then she would leave and, with those nails they all loved so much, scratch the eyes out of anyone who so much as looked at her on the walk home.

```
PATTY POODLE: Can you describe the beginning of your
  relationship with Lorraine?

POOH-POOH: Roof, roof, roof, roof, roof, roof, roof,
  roof,roofffffffffffff. Roof, roof, roof, roof,
  roof, roof, roof, roof.
  Rrrrrroooof, roof, roof, roofffffffffffff, roof.

PATTY POODLE: And how about with Lena Horne?

POOH-POOH: Roof, roof, roof, roof, roof, roof, roof,
  roof, roofffffffffffffffffffffffffffffffffffffffff-
  ffffffffffffffffffffffffffffffffff
```

eBay auction block #7
Description: Transcript of interview with Pooh-Pooh on Pet TV, dated October 12, 2005, "Brooklyn Week."

Opening bid: $55
Winning bid: $250 by lenahorne@bgirl.com

Comments: Yelp! Yelp, yelp, yelp—yelp, yelp, yelp, yelp. Yelp!! Yelp, *yelp,* yelp. Yelp?

SEVEN

♥

TWO MEN TO NONE

Friday evening couldn't have come soon enough. With Tommy not coming to her, Lorraine convinced herself she was going back to Brooklyn for the purposes of keeping up the Sunday night dinner thing.

"What have you guys been doing this week?" She'd posed the question to Chrissy the night before, in the hopes of gaining some insight as to exactly why Tommy wasn't coming to visit her.

"Yes, I'm just gonna come out with it. He was dragging around some bimbo by the eyes last night at Petey's house. Everyone went there when it got too cold to hang out at the schoolyard."

She didn't want to hear it, but simultaneously had to know every excruciating detail. Before Chrissy even spoke, she'd conjured up the greenish wood paneling in Petey's basement, the old floral sofa that never looked quite clean despite the strong lemon scent that emanated from every surface of the room. She put Tommy all the way to the left, lazily draping an arm on some doe-eyed girl's arm, like it meant something he knew the poor idiot wanted it to mean. She knew the look on his face: smug, bored . . . the unattainable.

God, why did he need to do it? Again and again and again. Would there ever be enough evidence to prove to his fragile ego once and for all that he was good enough? It was only getting worse now. He barely had to muster any evidence of trying with the girls anymore. They just came to him—the young ones who'd heard the irresistible stories of their friends' best sex of their lives, the man they wanted to marry. The moves had a life force of their own; all he had to do was float with the current. At least Lorraine could take comfort in the idea that he was never like that with her. With them it was different. This she always knew.

"Did they leave together?" Lorraine could fill in the ho's face with a spectrum of Tommy's past conquests, not unlike those silly sepia photos you could pose for at Colonial Williamsburg with your head poking through a hole above frills of Queen Anne lace. She could even smell Petey's cigarette, hear Petey's mom yell down for him to stop smoking in the house. See Petey roll his eyes, tighten his jaw and feel his middle finger with his thumb, but never actually give it to her.

"I really don't know. I was gone already."

Lorraine knew this was untrue. There was only so much pain her friend could stand to dole out at once. And through this ancient code of omission they practiced, Chrissy could feel a teensy bit better about things. Lorraine, she knew, would ultimately ruin their plans of living next door, watching their children play in back, drawing chalk figures on the blacktop driveway. She hated to think her friend would never back down. It was her best quality and her worst. She'd told Lorraine as much more times than she cared to remember, because she knew Chrissy was right.

Lorraine really wanted to sneak Pooh-Pooh on the train, but even as she searched through duffel bags and carrying cases in the mega-closets Mrs. Romanelli kept of such things, she knew it was a ridiculous idea.

"Roof!" Pooh-Pooh said as she held a bag one-third his length alongside him.

"Yeah, roof to you! I have to go make a fool of myself in front of the man I love, and now I don't know how I'm gonna do that with you being so freakin' humungous. All right, all right. We'll just go for a walk, or I guess with you, a run, and then hopefully we'll figure something out."

Lorraine had purchased some of that outrageously priced workout wear from So-Low she'd sworn not two-weeks ago she would *never* spend

$150 on. When she pulled the super-soft stretchy cotton tank, low-rider bootleg pants, and matching zip-up hoodie over her newly muscular body, though, Lorraine could see the difference between these and her old high-school sweats.

She brushed her hair back into a ponytail that curled sweetly at the end, what with all the waves she'd worn in it that day, snapped the leash on Pooh-Pooh, who'd just downed a pound and a half of stinky doggie food that sounded like squishy mayonnaise as he gobbled it, and locked the door behind them.

The night was one of the crisper ones of the last few weeks, and the amber hue of the sky just seemed to suit her mood, all intricate and layered, changing as one looked higher, impossible to categorize.

She'd learned to keep up with Pooh-Pooh (he was even stopping at street corners now, if she gently said his name and tugged lightly on his leash) and running seemed like a do-able, if not exactly simple task. She ran, faster, faster around the reservoir twice, Pooh-Pooh galloping at full speed, his tail swaying to and fro, his tongue hanging out the side of his mouth in excitement. She was starting to recognize people—the guy on the old banana seat bicycle with the boom box blasting original rap songs, like he was stuck in another time; a girl who worked at Bendel's; a tall skinny guy who always wore fluorescent green; other dogs—a Chihuahua, a golden retriever, a Britney Spaniel, and their respective runner-owners. Lorraine waved to the hot dog vendors she'd made purchases from. Everyone recognized Pooh-Pooh. The dog was unforgettable.

When they'd finished the second loop, Pooh-Pooh led them to that tiny field he frequented every day. There she saw the *Ohmigods* and the Silver Hairs and the couple of jocks who made themselves permanent fixtures along with the random people who'd just wandered in. And then, as she slowed to a stop, unhooked Pooh-Pooh and rubbed under his neck, where he liked a medium-to-hard scratching, Lorraine heard her name called from behind a tree not far from where she was standing.

She saw a face a little more than familiar, and so welcome just then. She'd forgotten how welcome.

"Matt! You're back! So great to see you!" Why? Why was she sounding so desperate? She'd only met the guy once. It probably wasn't best to appear so lonesome and sad like that. And so she added, "Pooh-Pooh has missed Lena Horne so badly!"

On cue, Pooh-Pooh and Lena ran toward each other and met in a ca-cophony of barks, a dance of licks and gentle pawing and biting. Tiny tufts of hair lifted in the breeze and hung in a halo of sorts around the couple. Lorraine couldn't believe she felt jealous of the love between two dogs. She needed a drink. That would probably help.

"Hey there." He came and kissed her on the cheek like someone he hadn't seen in a while. Like someone he might have missed.

The guy was tan. And, Lorraine noticed, it looked great on him. So, apparently, did the posing *Ohmigods*, who were screaming, "*Yoohoo*, Matt, *yoooooooohooooooooo!*"

He waved at them and sat right with Lorraine, which, presented at least a sharp, happy spike in the line graph of the afternoon's misery, in the way only triumphing over a bunch of too-pretty *Ohmigods* could.

"Looks like you've got some fans," Lorraine said coolly, darting her eyes in the direction of the *Ohmigods*.

"Hey, no one said it's easy being this handsome and charming."

"Did you just say 'handsome'?" The word struck her as anachronistic, something Hugh Grant might say in a Jane Austen movie. She smiled with the images playing in her head—Matt in knickers and such.

"You got a problem wit da way I *tawk*, Miss *Brook*lyn?" Now Matt was smiling.

Lorraine returned with an elbow to the ribs.

"Don't shoot!" he screamed, mocking her with his hands over his face.

"Wha'd they feed you down in Florida to make your balls so big?"

He looked shocked, yet amused. He covered his mouth with his palm and then removed it and said, "Ah, you know, the wings of two dead flies, a couple of bat's ears . . ."

Lorraine rolled her eyes and felt the slow smile come over her, stretch-ing all the way at her scalp. It felt good. It really did.

"Looks like you've got your Pooh-Pooh under control."

Lorraine: Eye roll number two.

Matt: Extra exaggerated eye roll in response.

"No, really," he said, stretching his legs out long in front of him. "I saw you run in here. I don't even think Romanelli ever got Pooh-Pooh so well behaved. That was an expert unleashing. Top notch."

The dogs were once again trading elicit favors, to the disgust of the general public. Strangely, even that was growing on her. Pooh-Pooh was a ladies' man. Go figure—she'd fallen for another one. At least this one wasn't afraid to spend the whole night. He kept plans like a champ, too. And he was pretty cute, although of course, Lorraine knew looks weren't everything.

"So how was your trip, really?" Lorraine wanted to get back to Brooklyn, but this was nice, too, sitting here with someone she had instantly warmed to. Really, she felt closer to him than to some of the people in her group that she'd known for twenty years.

"It was nice. Really nice. Only rained a couple of times. Did a lot of fishing, you know—just me and Lena out on the boat, listening to the Allman Brothers."

"The Allman Brothers? Dude, what are you, some kind of hippie or something? Back where I come from we call people like yourself Stoners."

"Don't you technically need to be a pothead to be classified as a Stoner?"

"Nah. Tons of my friends are potheads, and they're still classified as Guidos."

"Takes one to know one, I guess . . ." He smiled, hooked his glance in with hers to show he meant it in a familiar, rather than judgmental way.

"I prefer the term 'Italian-American,' " she said, crossing her arms, pretending to be offended.

"Your wish is my command. Besides, I wouldn't want any of your cousins coming around and teaching me any lessons."

They sat in silence for a little while, taking in the sounds around them—the chattering girls, the random disciplining of dogs, far-off sirens, car horns, hoofbeats.

"Hey, you wanna see a movie tonight?" he asked after a little while.

Lorraine was surprisingly grateful for the invitation. She'd felt so solitary in a me-versus-them way throughout the day that his generosity hit her with a deeper pang than she was prepared for. She tried to think whether she should just accept and forget about Brooklyn. There was the idea, still forming itself, that she might like Matt as more than a friend. But in the past, these small victories over her obsession had never proven to be long-term wins. And since she really respected and liked him as a person, Lorraine tried to ignore her attraction, despite the obvious chemistry that existed between them. But there *was* that new Will Smith movie she was wanting to see. Plus, a *fun* weekend in the city was something she knew she *should* try.

However, try as she might, she couldn't get the idea of Tommy and some other girl out of her head. She needed to be with him. It was just something she had to do.

"You know," she said finally, touching his arm lightly, "I would love it, but I really need to find a way to get me and Pooh-Pooh back to Brooklyn tonight." Feeling surprisingly self-conscious about this fact, Lorraine grasped for a justification. "We've got family obligations, and . . . stuff." She looked to the ground, rather than at Matt as she said this, probably appearing far-off and maybe lost in thoughts. And she was. Aside from trying to figure out how the heck she was going to get the two of them home to the Bay, the idea popped into her head that her excuse didn't sound believable; that given what she'd told Matt about Tommy, he might be able to see right through her.

"Can't just shove Pooh-Pooh into a duffel bag, huh?"

"The thought had crossed my mind, but no, apparently you can't."

The dog looked up at them, as if he knew he was being spoken about and wouldn't stand for any shenanigans. Then he lay his head back onto Lena's belly to continue napping.

Lorraine wondered if dog's ears rang when someone was talking about them, too.

"Well, I've got a solution for you, but you can't tell anyone in the world that I let you do this because they'll all think I've gone soft."

"I promise."

"No, really, you have to perform the Matthew Richards family oath." He held his face in serious horizontal lines. His tanned hand smacked lightly at the grass.

"Ohhhhh-kayyyyyyyy," she said, lowering her lids suspiciously.

"Repeat after me."

"Well, aren't you gonna tell me what your solution is before I solemnly swear to keep it a secret?"

"You're a real tough cookie, aren't you?" He shook his head in mock frustration.

"Ah, well, you know us Guidettes, headstrong as the hairspray keeping our hairstyle up."

"That's a good one," he said.

"Are you gonna get on with it already?"

"All right, all right. First the oath, then I'll tell you. Raise your hand, and then put it over your chest, like so," Matt demonstrated, super gently and very teasingly, by placing a hand over Lorraine's wrist and smoothing her palm down over her chest.

Tingles erupted where the hand touched down. They quickly vibrated south.

"Now"—he cleared his throat—"I solemnly swear . . ." He winked at Lorraine's accurate prediction.

She repeated playfully, "Now," and then cleared her throat. "I solemnly swear," and then winked back at him.

Matt made slivers of his eyes, cocking his head. "Are you taking this seriously?" he wanted to know. And then softening, he reminded her that her hand was crossed over her heart. In case she'd forgotten, he again grazed his hand there.

They were silent for a second in the frisson of that connection, and then he got back to the unserious business of her oath.

"I solemnly swear that I will put the top down." He paused for her to follow, and she did, although unsure of what she was saying.

Matt continued, "Enjoy to the fullest, the godly power of a 360 horse-power 5.5 liter, 24-valve V-8 engine." He nodded his head for her refrain.

"I'll break all speed limits, and really try to concentrate on how awesome a Mercedes SLK AMG roadster is while Pooh-Pooh and myself drive to Brooklyn."

Lorraine's eyes widened to dollar-coin size. Instead of repeating the last line she shouted, "You're freakin' kidding me, right?"

"Lorraine, no, I am not *freakin'* kidding you, but I must point out that you haven't yet repeated the final portion of the oath." He said it stone-faced.

Oh, boy. She was developing a crush.

You've never driven if you've never driven a Mercedes. The traffic parted ways, the road was open, the night was clear. Lorraine was convinced it was one powerful vehicle. Pooh-Pooh was strapped in behind her. She figured he was only about two or three, which probably meant he wasn't old enough to be sitting in the front, much less without some sort of car seat she wasn't sure existed for our furry friends. He seemed to take to the car instantly. But, she mused, he was used to the privileged life and probably drove in a Mercedes all the time.

As soon as she started driving, the hopeless tone of the day just melted away like blown traffic lights—flickers she barely noticed somewhere far off in the periphery of her mind. In its place, warm thoughts about her city, the family she was about to see (if only for a minute or two before she drove off to see where everyone—everyone meaning Tommy—was for the night), the smile that would spread on her mother's face. Even if the car didn't belong to Lorraine, her mother would see her as making the kinds of connections that meant big things for her daughter, the variety of big things that had never crystallized for herself in the ten square miles she inhabited.

Most of all though, this car would resonate with Tommy. It wouldn't matter how many girls there had been since last weekend. This car would put Lorraine on par with his idea of success, with his ideas of what his life should be like, the people he deserved to be surrounded with. It was a desperate way to think, but she didn't want to concentrate on that part of it just then. However, it was impossible not to see the parallel—Tommy and her mother, Lorraine realized for the first time, weren't all that different. Perhaps that was why Lorraine's mother looked at Tommy with such disdain.

But none of that would darken the road ahead, the promise of the night. Lorraine always prided herself on seeing the larger scope of things, placing people not in black-and-white categories, but within the intricate web of happenstance and experience they came nestled in. She could look beyond weakness and mistakes and ignorance—hadn't she committed the same sins herself during the course of her life? Sure, and here she was, trying to correct some of those, though not sure exactly for whom. Lorraine tried to exercise the same forgiveness toward her own actions—tonight especially, when she was so confused about her intentions.

They looked pretty good, the pair of them—Lorraine freshly showered, her hair glittering with a few highlights she'd painted on herself in the wake of nothingness that had followed her few hours of falsely promising color work. Matt had noticed them right away. She wasn't so sure she could expect the same of Tommy, who seemed to perceive changes in a more obscure way. She had on a slinky silk camisole, beneath a deep green velvet blazer—cut so slim it could barely be buttoned, cut to create the illusion of length and a trim waist, according to the salesgirl, Tabby, who was pulling things aside on a weekly basis for Lorraine now. The girl had a knack for dressing, not unlike what Lorraine had for hair. And Lorriane knew—it was wise to let an expert ply their trade—the results would nearly always be surprisingly dramatic. The girl matched the blazer with a pair of grayed-out black denim with retro studs down the legs.

"Jesus," said Matt when they'd met at the garage around the corner.

"What?" Lorraine had been surprised to feel heat at her cheeks, and turned her head away.

"You're hot," he said. Matt shook his head like a towel on fire, and then plunged into mapping out the intricacies of the clutch and the tiny gearshift, the location of the E-break.

If she hadn't been sure of her transparency before, there was no mistaking it after he sent her off with a serious look. "If he doesn't want you, Lorraine, the guy's an ass." God, how did he know her so well?

Pooh-Pooh was still looking smart from his weekend of doggy pampering. Everyone in her family said so, when she pulled up to the house and honked the horn. Never had Lorraine seen her mother so ecstatic. The woman was glowing with pride. Lorraine had anticipated the warm feelings of self-satisfaction such long awaited praise would provide, and so she was surprised by her reaction to it. Her mother's kind words, her unfamiliarly warm hand on her shoulder, actually stung and incited an annoyance Lorraine wasn't prepared for. The car, in its gleaming silver beauty, with its buttery leather interior, felt like an insult to the depth of experience she'd been having lately—overshadowing the really important things. It also seemed to minimize the impact of Matt's introduction to her life, presenting him as a rich friend that only served to elevate Lorraine's status in the minds of her otherwise unimpressible mother and brother. In fact, this shiny car didn't remind Lorraine of Matt at all. He was old T-shirts and tiny dogs! She wanted to scream it. But what was the point?

Though her father smiled wide, she couldn't help thinking all this fuss must make him feel . . . well, not unlike how it made her feel. All she wanted to say to her mother was, *Stop! Shut it, Mom!* But you never said that.

"You should have seen everyone at the garage with your picture in the paper! I swear a couple of the guys cried." He winked at her. "So I says, 'What's the big deal—we always knew she was special. Don't need no paper to tell us that.'"

"Yeah, she's 'special' all right. Short bus special." This from her brother.

Her dad lowered his eyebrows, raised a tight palm, as if this might scare either of them. An empty threat he'd never follow through with.

"A Mercedes!" was all her mom could say, like there wasn't room for anything else in her head. She pressed her nose up against the leather seat.

"Please pass the bread!" her brother screamed.

Whether it was the trauma of trying to bridge two worlds, or simply the effect of long-awaited change on one Ms. Lorraine Machuchi, she couldn't be quite sure, but when she arrived at the schoolyard, Pooh-Pooh and the Mercedes revving, Lorraine had never felt so off-kilter. It was like something wasn't quite right in the city, and something wasn't quite right here. Plus, things here were starting to seem different.

Apparently Petey and Mary were a couple now, from the way they were holding hands and whispering, and as evidenced by Petey's high school ring, which Mary kept cupping in her fist as she dragged it, *chink-chink-chink*, across the chain she had it looped through. Climate-wise, it was cooler for sure, and a couple of the girls—Chrissy included—were wearing fleece jackets in variations of pink. Lorraine didn't like the look. Never before had she dressed in a way so indistinguishable from her peers, and now here she really disliked their biggest trend of the season. She thought the jackets lacked structure, did nothing to compliment their figures. Besides, you could tell from the haphazard seams they were poorly tailored. One of the seams on Chrissy's right sleeve appeared to be unraveling.

There could have been another reason for her disorientation. Amidst all the "Oh my gods!" and "Holy shits!" and "Look at Ms. Fancy Pants!" Tommy was painfully absent.

She tried—making her best efforts to smile, hold her back straight and blink away any trace of tears that were brewing—to appear as if she hadn't a care in the world. There was nothing in particular planned, so the car really became the center of the evening. Within ten minutes everyone was sitting on some part of it, adoring or fearing Pooh-Pooh who was hamming it up something awful—showing his white teeth, playfully bending his ears, wagging his tail, nuzzling into new hands.

Chrissy, who was on the more fearful side, was trying gingerly to pet Pooh-Pooh, but standing so far back, she had to stretch to get her fingertips to make the slightest contact with his fur. He stretched his neck to show her that little place under his neck that he loved people to scratch, and she freaked, screaming and jumping back. Big Bobby was nowhere to be seen, either. Chrissy didn't seem to mind, as he was due to meet up with her at ten-thirty.

"That is the biggest dog I have ever seen," she said, when she'd tugged at the hem of her pink fleece and smoothed the front down to regain composure.

"Look at the cutey-wooty," Mary crooned, performing her best cutesy speak for the benefit of her new boyfriend. Women understood these things to mean, *Look, I am June Cleaver; I am loved by animals and children alike. Can't you just see my eggs dropping down, blinking their eyelashes, waiting to be fertilized?*

Both Chrissy and Lorraine took it as a personal affront when Petey turned around and said, "Maybe *we* can get a dog like that."

Why hadn't anyone said that to them? How did Mary get so lucky? How did she fall for the only guy in the group who actually wanted to commit himself? They'd hung out with him just as long as she had, and hadn't ever found anything intriguing about him. The randomness of love seemed cruel to them. The sour mood made the two girls fall silent in the front seat while everyone continued to fuss over Pooh-Pooh, the leather interior, the tiny Mercedes icon embossed here and there.

"Whose car?" Chrissy finally asked. She wasn't ever bowled over by material things.

The idea of Matt and Lena, and the missed movie Matt was probably watching right now, made Lorraine think she'd made the wrong decision. Suddenly she regretted that she was sitting here in this car in front of the schoolyard. She was surprised by how much graffiti was on the wall at the handball courts, how much rust had collected on the chain-link fence, and the number of holes that had been cut in it. Had things always looked this way?

"It belongs to a friend of mine, Matt." It was a strange idea that Chrissy didn't know one of her friends and that one of her friends didn't know Chrissy. They were the Bobbsey Twins, for Christ's sake.

"Must be a pretty good friend to lend you this car."

Lorraine couldn't tell if Chrissy was jealous or snooping around for more information. Either way, she didn't want to get into it. She didn't like the way she was feeling, the way she didn't understand how she was feeling. So she changed the subject. "When did this place get so grody?" She posed the question to her friend, noticing a couple of kids she recognized as her brother's friends enter through a rather large cut in the fence.

"What the frig are you *talkin'* about? It's exactly the same as it always was. Everything's the same. Nothing friggin' changes." She grew silent again, and judging from the way she checked and then rechecked her watch, Big Bobby was already late.

"Are those the new jeans?" she asked Lorraine after a few minutes.

"Yeah, they just unpacked them yesterday. Aren't they hot?"

"Totally. How much?"

They always discussed how much. In fact, sometimes they negotiated price allowances and split the cost of clothes so they could share them. There was no reason Lorraine should feel so uncomfortable as she did just then sharing the fact that the jeans had cost $120—twenty bucks more than she swore she'd never spend on jeans last week, one hundred more than the week before. She lived in the City now. She worked at a Fifth Avenue salon. She had to dress the part. She had the money. She'd been hanging on to it forever. It was there for spending. There was absolutely nothing wrong with that.

Lie or tell the truth? She didn't know which way to go. But she'd never lied to her friend before, at least not when they weren't both aware of the lies, and she wasn't about to start then. Chrissy's ugly fleece depressed her. She lowered her voice to a whisper: "A hundred and twenty."

"I'm sorry. I surely didn't hear you correctly. Because I thought you said a hundred and twenty freakin' dollars. And there's no way you said that, right?"

Was Chrissy always this judgmental? Was Lorraine that way, too? She tried to appeal to her friend's more fashion-conscious side.

"Well, honestly, they sell for double that, so it was a steal, really. And they are like a whole new look in denim, forget for a second the amazing cut—which is the main reason they are so pricey—these studs are hand done. Just look at them! I've never seen anything like it. Just like when we were young, but the way they *should have* looked. You wouldn't believe the things these jeans can do for your thighs. Fantastic!"

"Whatever, Lorraine. That's ridiculous. Try to talk yourself into it all you want, but it's insane and you know it." Chrissy folded up tight and turned her gaze out the passenger window to a yellow car at the light.

Chrissy's temporary bouts of Big Bobby-induced coldness were normally easy for Lorraine to handle. You knew the reason, you ignored the behavior accordingly. But tonight she couldn't. Tonight the coldness between them only enhanced Lorraine's confusion about her current status in life.

Why had she come here? She knew the answer. Everyone knew the answer. And here she was sitting in a Mercedes, looking like a million bucks, and the only one having a good time was Pooh-Pooh, who apparently, could get used to anything. Ah, to be a big, dopey dog.

At eleven Lorraine called it a night and drove the Mercedes slowly home, past Tommy's house, because she just couldn't help herself. His blue Mustang wasn't there. She didn't think it would be, but it still put her in an even sourer mood.

When she arrived home, five twisty shrubs later, everyone was sleeping, except for her brother, who was probably out making the schoolyard look even worse, if he wasn't ruining some girl's life by making her fall in love with him and then stringing her along like a cat with a length of bright yarn.

Pooh-Pooh would have probably been a problem if Lorraine hadn't come home in the Mercedes. Her mother disliked dogs for the mess they come along with. *Big rats!* She'd once called them that.

The two of them went straight for the kitchen, where Lorraine emptied a can of smelly mush onto a paper plate (God help her if her mother came in and found a dog eating from one of her dishes). She allowed the tap to get nice and cold and then filled the collapsible dog bowl she'd bought for him the other day in Bendel's chichi travel shop, Flight 001. A designer dog bowl—maybe she had gone over the edge.

But she didn't think so when she saw him lapping out of it. God, that dog was happy. He had everything in the world and didn't even know it. All that punctuated his life was attention and food, exercise and excrement. Maybe, she thought, as the dog finished up with a major lick that reached to the tip of his head and *click-clacked* to Lorraine at the chair she'd sat in since she could sit, he isn't that different from me after all.

He was a good dog, that was for sure. He didn't judge her on how much money she could spend on a pair of jeans, didn't take his own personal problems out on her, and never made her feel lonely or out of place. She could even fart really loud right in front of him and he wouldn't make a peep. Pooh-Pooh snuggled up in bed with Lorraine the same way he'd gotten into the habit of back at Mrs. Romanelli's. They watched a couple of reruns of *Friends* and, with arms entwined, fell into a deep sleep.

When she first heard the noise, Lorraine thought maybe there *was* something to that ridiculous *Ghost Hunters* show. Perhaps her grandmother was coming back to tell her something. It seemed like a pretty suitable time for a haunting from her family's matriarch, what with living at her best friend's apartment, being wrapped in the warm, leathery paws of said friend's huge dog, and living out her grandmother's dreams the way her mother was constantly reminding her to do.

Also, she'd just appeared to Lorraine in a dream, wearing that flowery housecoat, with the red piping Lorraine always remembered her in toward the end, when all she wanted to do was sit in the patch of sunlight in the back and read Nora Roberts books without being bothered. In the dream, her hair was still thick and wild as a head of broccoli, and similarly styled in the same natural bunches of curls Lorraine had been born with. She'd scared Lorraine many times, waking her in the middle of the night to say that somebody named Stetson had just traveled back from the future to pick her up and she just wanted to say, *You can all go to hell—no, wait a minute, we are already here. Hell IS Brooklyn. Sayanora!* She'd always let Lorraine know this before rushing out to the front yard, at which point the whole family would have to chase her down the block.

In the dream, Lorraine's grandmother woke her in the same way, that thick coarse hair threatening with every one of its coils to scratch or tickle, but she said, "Lorraine, what the fuck are you doing?" (Her grandmother always loved to curse. She could tell it shocked people.) "You're sleeping with a dog in the same bed I left you in a year ago, and you're still pining over the same boy who's got you hanging on with a thread. And don't tell me I don't understand about love, because goddamn it, I do. I stayed here with your grandfather until the day he died, giving up all my dreams, and don't you think I didn't hear you and that spinster Romanelli talking about me like that. Now, get off your ass and make nice with that Mercedes boy."

So, Lorraine ignored the noise, thinking her grandmother wasn't done doling out lessons for the evening. It wasn't odd for an Italian grandmother to come back and haunt you in your dreams. And it wasn't odd for them to haunt you for real, either, if you listened to any of the women at church. But Lorraine hadn't ever had it happen to her before, so she was starting to get freaked out when twelve minutes later, Pooh-Pooh was up and barking like mad and the noise was still rattling every few seconds. It sounded like a slow typist at a computer keyboard. But her grandmother didn't know how to type, or use a computer for that matter.

Finally she opened her eyes and followed Pooh-Pooh to the window. Squeezing a fuzzy slipper tightly in her right hand (what the hell was she gonna do with that?), she put her free hand on Pooh-Pooh, who was standing upright with his paws at the window, and looked down to the street below.

To the delight of her nether regions, it was neither a ghost nor her grandmother. No, the figure was much more elusive than that—it was Tommy. And he was throwing rocks at her window as if she were some character in a Grimm's fairy tale. Surely this was not really happening.

She jerked back from the window to catch her breath. When she pulled herself together, she could see that Tommy was still dressed for the evening in a three-button open long-sleeved Henley tee. Even from there his eyes gleamed, lit the whole block. It was unbelievable what this boy could do to her.

"I gotta get outta here," he said. "Come on, take me, Lorraine."

Oh! To hear him say her name like that! To look up at her with need.

Lorraine did not waste time thinking what her grandmother's ghost might have to say about it. She grabbed Pooh-Pooh and her car keys and allowed the man she was mortifyingly in love with to drive her to her new home.

As they passed that view of forever broken New York skyline just before the bridge, Lorraine didn't try to put her feelings in a category or think too much what it might mean about her relationship to Manhattan, that her heart swelled with pride. They crossed one of the most beautiful, bold bridges in the world over to it.

They'd driven in silence, alone with their feelings, which were on both parts so big they filled up the whole car and the length of the road beyond. Lorraine and Tommy, driving in a Mercedes-Benz, with a dog so enormous in personality, it outsized his body by a mile. It was something.

The things we do for love. You could fill all the pages in all the journals in all the world with those things, and still not have enough room to fit everything in. You could tear yourself inside out, forget everything you ever were, start over and then start over again, and still that might not get you what you wanted, but it wouldn't stop you from trying. The world could be watching you and directing, "Wake up! Snap out of it!" and you wouldn't hear because the look on someone's face when he was driving was so all-encompassing there was no other room in your head for anything else. And the reflection of a streetlamp glittering off his eye could hold your attention indefinitely. What else could you do but give into it all?

"Lorraine, look at you." He was whispering and burying his head in her hair, breathing in loud. "You smell so good." It seemed Tommy was living out some kind of dream of his own as he said these things so slow, and so thought out, like they were coming from somewhere familiar and yet untapped.

They were on the bed Lorraine had called her own for a little while now, and which, after her Brooklyn trip, seemed more inviting than she'd remembered leaving it. He stayed there, at the underside of her hair for a while, kissing and crying and holding on to her tighter than she remembered him capable of. From there, he traveled down to her neck, up to her chin, found her mouth, danced around it with breathy, feathery kisses and then plunged in deep, finding her tongue with apparent pleasure.

At finding her Cosabella thong and matching pink lace bra, Tommy seemed to be living out a fantasy of his own. Rather than pull the outfit from her body as she'd remembered him doing before, he kept it on, stretching the elasticized material out of the way here and there, and finally, teasingly, stretching her panties to the side to make room for him. With a groan, they were joined, hungrily.

Later, when they lay in Lorraine's bed, Tommy did that finger combing thing she loved through her hair and finally spoke. "This is the most comfortable bed I've ever laid in, Lorraine. My god. Where do you get a bed like this?"

Lorraine didn't know. It had been a case of sheer luck for this one to fall into her hands—for the whole thing to fall into her hands. And now, finally, she could appreciate the luck of it, enjoy the blessings of it, with less confusion about her feelings.

She excused herself to slip on a minuscule black negligee Tabby had put aside for her, and the garment had the desired effect. Again, they took all they could from each other.

"You've done it, Lorraine. You really have."

When Tommy said this, wrapped in a silk Chinese throw blanket, the crimson hue so contrasted to his tanned arms propped on Mrs. Romanelli's kitchen table, Lorraine saw everything done, complete. Finally, she thought, the chase is over. Finally, we are where we should be. She didn't get into the logistics, the who, what, when's, and even worse, what might happen when Mrs. Romanelli came back and all of this good fortune slipped through her fingers. There was tomorrow for that.

They looked out the window beyond and saw with a smile a billboard that resonated with both of them. But more so with Lorraine, whose smile was more of an appreciation for the significance those nails and the girl who they belonged to might have on the city that had impacted her life so greatly.

"Guido Nails," it said. "Only at Guido's, Park Avenue." And there it was, a picture of Lorraine's very own hands, standing high over Park Avenue, one palm open and one closed, an elegant Van Gogh-like blossom, in an autumnal burnt orange on the pointer finger, a golden B on the left pinkie. She was reminded, then, of what a fortune-teller had once said to her—*your right hand shows your fate, your left hand, what you do with it*. And she looked from the hands, so perfect—airbrushed to a painstaking milky flawlessness—to Tommy, who thought probably of what he'd seen in the paper. Though her face flushed, she told herself it wasn't so important *why* she was here. She was here, right?

Lorraine,

The most beautiful girl in all of Brooklyn.
The girl I'd waited for until the time was
  right.
I could've had a different woman every night
and oftentimes I did, although it was a sin.
I don't know why I do what I do,
But you always know, right on cue.
Lorraine, I love you.

                                                    —Tommy

eBay auction block #8
Description: Poem written on Sept. 21, 2004, at 4:30 A.M., after Tommy spent the night at all the bars on Third Avenue. The poem was never given to Lorraine.

Opening bid: $50
Winning bid: $4500 by Tommy1@aol.com

Comments: Dude, that is a very touching poem, and I am planning on having it published. I LOVE YOU LORRAINE!!!!!!!!!

EIGHT

♥

CLASSES

When she was younger, Lorraine hated school. The classroom setup, the confining desks, the teacher-student relationship—none of it had ever quite worked for her. Listening to someone drone on endlessly about topics they'd quite obviously bored of years before never afforded much of an education for Lorraine, who preferred the hands-on approach. And now that she was being forced to take the "Guido Method" courses once a week, following an eight-hour shift, her aversion to the idea was understandable. Unlike the color class that had landed her here, this class was strictly for assistants at Guido's.

Basically, people who wanted their hair colored for free would sign up at the front desk as models (you wouldn't believe the waiting list), and the assistants would perform whichever hair color technique was being taught that evening. Lorraine thought she should be teaching the class, not taking it. The whole idea was ridiculous to her.

Lorraine would have been in a rotten mood at color class on Tuesday night if it weren't for the glow of the weekend still lighting her from the inside out. Nothing could smolder the fire she'd walked around with since Friday evening. And a few things had tried, for sure they had. First there was Saturday afternoon. Lorraine and Tommy and Pooh-Pooh had all been starving. All the sex and wine and sex and wine had taken its toll on the couple attached by the eyes, hands, and pelvic regions. The dog had suffered from being forgotten amidst all of that. Lorraine never thought she could forget about something as enormous as Pooh-Pooh, but when she was around Tommy, there was nothing else. She'd even forgotten about food for herself during all the long hours they'd been together. Something she normally reverted to in any situation, any mood, had just slipped out of her head.

And so they decided to indulge in an overpriced brunch at a bistro by the name of 92, which, though not as delicious as neighboring Sarabeth's, offered outdoor seating and advertised itself as being pet-friendly. The showering portion of the procedure set them back another couple of hours, as one thing very sexily led to another, and then another.

Finally, though, with freshly washed and air-dried waves cascading over her shoulders, secured back from her forehead with oversize plastic sunglasses, and a form-fitting So-Low stretchy outfit complimenting her every curve, Lorraine took Tommy's hand with her left, and Pooh-Pooh's leash with her right. And when they turned at Eighty-ninth to make their way to Madison, Pooh-Pooh went wild with delight. He was a one-dog show of barks and curvy leaps, his groomed coat shining in the sunlight as he pulled Lorraine as quickly as possible toward the object of his affections.

For right there in their path was his very own Lena Horne. Lorraine was less embarrassed by the dogs' overt sexuality than she was at Tommy and Matt meeting. She was taken aback by her discomfort. Why should she care?

An older woman with elegantly up-twisted white hair and a gold-buttoned cardigan walked by, a purse dangling at her elbow, her palm turned down as it swung to and fro in coordinated rhythm with her hips.

As he shifted his posture up toward the hand-holding pair, visibly readying himself to speak, Lorraine noticed Matt drew out more famil-iarity from her than he had the evening before at the park. He was easy and gracious in his Saturday afternoon Adidas pants and wash-weary Yale T-shirt, his J. Edgar Hoover key chain in its regular place. It certainly didn't seem like he was adding to the group's discomfort. With ease, he waved and winked at the gold-buttoned woman and she smiled wide in return, bending her fingers into a dainty wave.

The exchange did not go unnoticed by Tommy. His eyes followed in a series of twists and turns, stops and starts, seldom blinking along the way.

"Can't take these dogs anywhere," Matt said, shaking his head with an easy hint of a smile.

It broke the glacier Lorraine imagined between the two men, if not the pieces of ice floating about herself. The men laughed. And when that sound faded away to silence, Lorraine found herself floundering for words.

"Tommy, this is Matt," she said. The sound seemed to emerge from outside herself. The inside of her mouth was a wad of cotton. The thing was, she wasn't Lorraine when she was with Tommy. She was drunk and gorged, making up for all the time he'd starved her. There wasn't room for anything else, especially the confusion she'd felt all the times she'd been with Matt, the dizzyingly rapid familiarity she was faced with in his presence, the odd idea she had his car keys on her kitchen table, the strange presence he'd had in her mind as she drove his car to a place that had become increasingly alien to her.

There was silence while, presumably, Tommy matched the face with the car, sized up the situation, and assessed possible risk. He dragged a finger along the inside of Lorraine's palm and even amidst the confusion, she felt joined to him—one finger could do this to her.

"Ah, Mr. Mercedes," he said, with a tinge of what could be interpreted as either jealousy or condescension—neither of which, put Tommy in a good light.

She could excuse him of anything. She was the one who'd told him Matt's father had given him the car. But she hated to think Matt had negative feelings for Tommy—the most important man in her life. Conflict seemed to meet her at every mental turn. She wanted to scream out and defend him, saying, "You don't understand!" She longed to cover him with her body and protect him from anything, everything—even Matt, who she felt . . . well, whatever she felt about him wasn't going to stop that instinct just then.

But at the other end of her brain, there was a new, contradictory thought tugging at her conscience. She didn't want anyone to see Matt in a negative light. Of anyone she currently counted as a friend, Matt was the most generous, the most intuitive and understanding. She hated the idea of any tension involving him. But, she did feel tension, and Lorraine was nearly positive it wasn't merely in her head.

Still, the confusion that hazed around that chance encounter melted away in the sun-flooded delight of brunch—Bloody Marys and three-egg omelets and sides of bacon, generous bistro napkins and plates with sailor stripe rims. Every word spoken was broken ground, as far as Lorraine could see. The pair had been in new territory in Manhattan, with so many of Tommy's feelings coming to his tongue, with so many pretty things surrounding them. He had pulled aside the deep velvet curtain normally separating his heart from her. Not only that, he was someone else entirely, it seemed—someone who tried an omelet stuffed plump with feta cheese, ignoring the admittedly daunting hints of green vegetables woven through. He sipped at Lorraine's mimosa she'd ordered after her spicy Bloody Mary.

"It's champagne and orange juice," she'd said.

And when he'd tasted the liquid on his tongue, at his lips, at the back of his throat, she'd barely recognized him and his childlike contemplation mixing fear and unbridled excitement. He'd thrown her for a loop with compliments and public displays of affection, his mouth at her ear, his hand down the back of her stretched waistband.

"Let's go back upstairs, Lorraine," he'd whispered soundlessly on her ear, each movement of his mouth tickling, telling the story of what was to come.

Sixty hours of bliss followed—a movie they didn't watch. Art, critically praised by the pair ("The Kandinsky is painted on two sides," he sent them laughing, repeating a line from one of the thousands of movies they'd watched together in their shared histories) in a hushed museum of echoed whispers and the occasional cough. His cool scent—the same cologne he'd been wearing since high school—trailed around them, changing the museum forever for Lorraine, making his impression there. At the Met they attached their own rose-colored meaning onto Impressionists of the American and French varieties before boring of the indoors and the finer things. A shopping spree with Lorraine's discount at Bendel's, where she noticed her now familiar arc of shock, disdain, and eventual pleasure at unfamiliar quality, all building in Tommy's own City Transformation. He had the salesgirl snip the tags right off a shirt, there in his dressing room, and walked out wearing it. A walk/run/scream/walk with Pooh-Pooh around Central Park and beyond. Contemplation of the zoo's population of sea otters and the proper treatment required of a tiger. Lorraine could barely remember her own little lion then, why she'd torn his insides out, how she'd felt. She lost all that in . . . a throwaway camera, a smile meant for only one woman who'd waited so long for it, and then the silence at the window, looking out, with those hands now appearing almost God-like above on the billboard, with all that had changed beneath them.

Now, what were two hours of needless color class to Lorraine in the face of all that? Here she had everything she'd ever thought she'd been missing in her life. So what if Guido had her sweeping floors and folding towels? She took her now familiar seat, next to the girls who looked half her age, probably were—who swiveled their stares around competitively to see who was better, thinner, had clearer skin and nicer clothing, tonguing their teeth in the face of someone with a more perfect smile. The boys who took care to get to know everyone, adding levity with their friendly, overly accommodating way.

Lorraine watched Guido as he came in, walked directly to the chair he always used, the one where Lorraine had enjoyed one day of independence since she'd moved to Manhattan, given up the routine she'd enjoyed for nearly thirty years as if it were nothing.

She was far off in a corner by the window. She'd be glad to look out over the lights, the sliver of visible moon, when she finished the assignment too quickly and didn't feel like chatting with the hair model here only for a free dye job—who'd be thrilled she wouldn't have to complain or make any adjustments to a dye job from Lorraine, who could do this all with one hand tied behind her back.

All through the day, her disappointment with last week's experience had stung her. Lorraine had been, if not unfriendly, tight-lipped with Guido. She didn't trust herself to say more than "yes" or "no," or at the very most, "I'll be right back with that." She wasn't used to holding her tongue, having to suck up her feelings and step down graciously. By this late hour the effort required had her exhausted.

Normally, a run like the one she'd taken with Pooh-Pooh before returning to the salon for class would have her energized. But tonight it seemed to have the opposite effect. She was drained beyond belief. The soothing hot shower had only made it more difficult to leave the comfort and unconditional love from Pooh-Pooh, who watched her draw lines around her eyes and deposit powder on her cheek as if she were one of the models in a Degas.

"Tonight, we're practicing color correction, people," Guido said, some of his royal affectedness visibly deflated from his customer-oriented day voice. Lorraine noticed Guido rarely looked her way as he addressed the group, continued on to explain the complexities of fixing botched bleach jobs, what to do if a color was too cool, too warm, or just bleached out. He tried to find words for ideas Lorraine knew must come to an artist instinctually, the way she'd heard so many other instructors attempt before. At the end of the day, either you had an eye or you didn't. And she did. And she was attempting with her last shred of energy not to care that this talent of hers was going unused. She credited whatever patience she was exhibiting to Tommy. He was all she'd ever wanted, wasn't he? He was the reason she was here in the first place, wasn't he?

Instantly Lorraine had assessed the problem areas of the model sitting in her chair. The girl's hair was entirely too cool for her complexion. It had lent a green cast to her skin, so Lorraine warmed up the whole look, painting chestnuts and honeys and beige-blondes to offset the brass. She instructed the girl to use shampoo and conditioner designed for color-treated hair, so the color would not fade back right away. There would be a bit of fading, she warned her, but overall, she'd love her color. Lorraine lifted the color of the model's brows a few shades, although this was not a necessary part of the lesson, or a specific request of the model.

While the girl's color was processing under the bonnet dryer, Lorraine scanned the room and noticed the others were just starting to apply color, clumsily messing with unnecessary foils, many still mixing at the color bar. She let out a long sigh and set herself to pass the time at the window, as she'd expected to do.

Perched high above, she saw that same Guido Nails billboard that had affected her so deeply at her own apartment the other night with Tommy. She wrung her hands, and then ran a finger over the lines of one and then the other, never looking down away from the sign. She'd been gazing so intently that the pair of hands looking back at her from across the way had started to fuzz into a sort of bridge-shaped mass when she was startled to feel anger again pierce at her chest.

Really! Those were her very own hands! That was her very own style Guido was advertising, making money from. The least he could do was to allow her to color hair. Although she hated to think poorly of him, Lorraine couldn't help but think of Don, and how middle-of-the-road his work was. And yet, because he'd finished his training, he could have his own clients, his independence. It seemed contrary to the natural order of things. Still, she had to keep reminding herself that this was the way of the world. There were rules, steps, and you had to take the time to follow them. Why did she imagine herself to be different, somehow absolved from these duties?

Because she was good. That's why. No, she was better than good. She was freakin' awesome and everyone knew it. And the hands—the one with the fate and the one requiring her own will—seemed to become more meaningful with the weight of that fact. Hadn't she already altered her fate by coming here, by influencing people like Guido, by having her own hands perched way up high over Park Avenue and Fifth? And in turn, by training the manicurists to make those skinny rounded tips, to carefully apply the *B*, by watching fabulous New York society girls walk out of the salon with nails fashioned after her own personal style, in her color, with her trademark bud on the right pointer?

She worked these ideas through the mill of her mind, grinding them down, polishing them, and then going through it all again as she rinsed the client into a crisp array of color, taking time to massage her scalp, scratch with her Guido Nails around the ears and above the forehead, where clients always got itchy from bleach. And then, like a sign all its own, her musings were disturbed by none other than Guido himself.

"Lorraine," he said, in an off-putting mix of haughty and exhausted, more commonplace intonations.

"Yes," she said, not yet looking up to see the worried look on his face.

"Lorraine, would you mind covering the class for me?"

At that unexpected question, Lorraine took a second to fit all the pieces together before popping her head up, not unlike that old game of Concentration she used to play as a child—racing to get everything where it should be so you avoided a cataclysmic shakedown.

The urge to answer sarcastically, the way she would have responded if she had been *Shove It Lorraine* and it had been her uncle who had played three such unfair hands one after the other—giving, taking away, giving with no frame of reference as to why—was overwhelming and seeping like poison all the way to the autumn-inspired yellow ochre leaf on her Guido Nails. But she resisted it. In the game of playing by the rules, you needed to hold your tongue, especially where possible advancements were concerned. She was learning this now. *Do not pass Go, do not collect $200.* Okay, it wasn't the ideal way, but you take it. You just go and scrape up whatever you've been given and you don't ask questions. You can reconfigure your strategy later.

"Sure," she said, as if this were the most natural request in the world, as if the rest of the students hadn't suddenly been pushed far, far outside the tiny circle she was standing in with Guido.

Her model's face was smug with pride. Lorraine saw it when she turned her head back down, not wanting to give a thing away from her expressions. The effect of her ecstatic model did not go unnoticed by Guido, who suddenly felt the need to qualify his statement.

"I see you have done a fabulous job on our model—" he said more grandly than he'd spoken throughout the evening, turning his head up to grab the name from a soundless prompting at Lorraine's quick lips, "Rowena, here."

In this business—even for those models coming in for freebies—Lorraine knew the importance of lip service, of making a girl feel important. She could be the secretary of an *Elle* editor, on staff at the *Today* show, one day she might be someone herself. And that's the way you wanted them to remember you—as the one who treated them as if they were special all along. We all think we're destined for greatness, but when someone else agrees without any prompting from your end, well, that's something you can't put a price on—unless that price is $350 for a full head of highlights, $400 plus for corrective color.

It's how you make her feel, it's the myth of beauty—the world women create so the real one can be more tolerable. A woman can wake to the grayest of days, without a leaf left in sight, nothing but crackly brown branches and mottled patches of ice as far as the eye can see. And with a spritz of citrus Miller Harris and a luxurious shea butter cream, she can bring to the moment the warmth and delicacy she requires. And if today's savvy girl can do all that by herself, well then, at the salon she wants the goods delivered by the bushel. All she wants in a stylist's chair—all any of us want when we rush over during lunch hour or at the crack of dawn before the office opens—is to be beautiful, to be the Princess we are in our own minds, whether of Park or any other avenue. A girl wants to look at herself in the mirror and think, wow, I see how unique the shape of my eye is. Just look at how my cheekbone juts out like that. And so what if Tommy or Davey or Jimmy or Jack didn't notice? It's there and someone else will see it.

But there was more to it. There was the need to be unique. The way Lorraine saw the beauty of each client in the salon, the way she knew how to bring that beauty to the forefront, highlight and gloss it, make it more obvious. That was her talent. And for a moment she knew Guido saw. Maybe he'd even seen how she'd done the same for herself since she moved here.

The students were terrible—each color job worse than the next, messy sections, overprocessing, underprocessing, general lack of matching a person's features with the proper tones. Lorraine was deeply frustrated to be thrown in with such novices, to appear indistinguishable from them to the senior staff and clients. But she didn't show it. Lorraine could be all business—she always could. Even back in high school, she'd go home, close her bedroom door, read her assignments, outline and write out essays in neat cursive, efficiently considering what questions might be asked of her on a final exam.

With as much "before/after" and "do this/because that" as was possible, Lorraine demonstrated to each student, and the class following along, where they could have improved upon their work and exactly how that could be achieved. But she knew even that could only take a student so far. You could give them the skills, but if they didn't have the talent to put them to use, it would never work out.

"You have a very good way of explaining yourself, Lorraine," one of the more junior girls, Stacey, noted to her after the class was through.

"Well, I should," Lorraine said, pulling the button-up nylon robe from her body with a *snap, snap, snap.* "I've only been doing this for thirteen years." She balled up the robe and tossed it in the designated basket.

The girl's shock flew over her like a tidal wave. "Thirteen years! And you're only at the same level as *I* am?"

On the walk home, a man was singing "Oh, Sherry" at the top of his lungs about two feet in front of her for five blocks and two avenues. She could have taken another route, but she wasn't in that type of mood. As far as patience went, Lorraine was plum out.

When the singer finally turned off her route, she promised herself that the next person who so much as smelled offensively was going to get it from her. The safest bet, feeling so sour, would have been to go home. Go home, get into your old sweats, and watch the super-deluxe cable lineup you were not paying one cent for (sixteen HBO channels alone!). She knew, she knew she should have done it. But she also knew she shouldn't care about this class and this salon and all that crap, since she'd already achieved the goal she'd come here to achieve—Tommy! But none of that was stopping her from feeling like an angry bull charging toward that little red cape.

So she walked east to the only place one really could go to at a time like that, Cold Stone Creamery, for a mix of coffee ice cream, freshly crushed M&M's, marshmallow, almonds, a heart attack's worth of hot fudge, and five turns of whipped cream (no cherry, please). And as she did,

Lorraine shot nasty looks at anyone who passed by, especially skinny little *Ohmigods* (she knew eventually they would grow up and sprout hips and more padding, but she couldn't help herself), and lovebirds (why hadn't Tommy called her yet today?).

Everyone probably hated her, but she didn't care. In fact, she felt like encouraging more people to hate her. The tall high school girl in the twisty ponytail behind the counter reminded Lorraine of herself, and she piled up all her own self-hatred on her, imagining she, too, would become obsessed with a boy who'd eventually drive her to insanity and a thankless position at a posh hair salon. She watched, with growing frustration, as the girl piled ingredients over the mound of cream and sugar, crushed them with the efficiency she herself would have wasted on such a no-end job, and when the girl passed her over the most perfect sundae she'd ever in her life seen, she couldn't bring herself to reach out and grab for it, to take this girl further down her wasteful journey, down the road to Nowhereseville.

"Miss, do you want your sundae?" she said, with the very same edge of sarcasm Lorraine herself would have used, the girl's own Brooklyn accent highlighting the question.

When Lorraine didn't answer, she tried once more, "Miss? Triple fudge, crushed almond, M&M's, marshmallow, super coffee sundae?"

"Uh, he*llo*," a man's voice probed sarcastically, somewhere from the serpentine line behind her, its population of pleading children driving everyone to the edge of insanity. There was no room for a Guidette having a nervous breakdown without pushing everyone off the edge.

And then the floodgates opened and her tears stung and the girl went to grab for a bunch of napkins (so resourceful!) and Lorraine turned to make a run for it.

```
              BARNES  &  NOBLE
              BOOKSELLERS


      October 13, 2004

      History of Old Brooklyn      $49.99

      The Business of             $25.99
         Hairstyling

      Your Little Dog—            $14.99
         What Is She Thinking?

      Pamela Anderson             $12.99
         "On Cars, Wet"
         Calendar
                                 ─────────
                                  $103.96
```

eBay auction block #9
Description: Matthew Richards's Barnes & Noble receipt from the day he spoke with her in the park about her predicament at Guido's.

Opening bid: $42
Winning bid: $598 by <u>Ohmigod!@netzero.com</u>

Comments: I still think Matt and I would have been perfect together. Lorraine, Schmorraine, *Ohmigod*!

NINE

♥

BROOKLYN'S IN THE HOUSE

The freezer-burnt Häagen-Dazs in the only flavor she didn't want, vanilla, sold to her in a crushed-in pint, was conspicuous in last year's festive holiday packaging. It was rung up by a man who didn't look away from a soccer match on his snowy television, screaming loudly in a Middle-Eastern tongue, while palming to her the improper change and a plastic bag with a hole along one of the seams. And none of it did much to soothe Lorraine's mood. Neither did a night of snuggling with Pooh-Pooh, nor the three unreturned messages she'd left for Tommy.

But the morning run did. The winter weather was edging in, if it hadn't fully arrived yet. Despite the depression this normally brought on, Lorraine was able to buy herself some sense of thrill, at least for the time being, at discovering New York City this way for the first time. The birds were getting on their way, but a few lingered loudly—maybe calling for other stragglers to get together. The chilly twigs snapped brightly underfoot. The slightly burnt sweetness of roasting chestnuts already joined the cloud of scent that hung over Manhattan's busier sections. At this time between summer and the holiday season, there seemed to be fewer tourists and thus more room to move, which Pooh-

Pooh gladly claimed, running on one side of a path and then the other, married to none.

Stores changed their window displays: autumn-toned pottery in pumpkin hues, inviting smatterings of red and deep greens and browns, glittering jewels shown in ruby and emerald—perfect for a holiday gift if only you started saving now. Police officers wore their jackets, zipped only halfway, their walkie-talkies echoing louder in the barren trees and sparse grass.

She could almost forget everything in the world running this way, noticing life this way. Feeling part of something new did have its advantages, as did the warmth and blind comfort of the familiar. The spirit of conquering, achieving had rewards of its own. You could feel more strength coming to the table with more knowledge, more that you didn't have before.

And so it was a little confusing when she was shaken out of her own thoughts and her own morning journey by a voice that rang both new and comforting at the same time.

"Hey there."

She realized it was Matt who'd spoken, and she allowed herself to drift back from her dreamy state to the rhythm of human interaction. "How's it going?"

"Well, you've got me out of breath for the moment. I could barely catch up with you," he heaved the words out, his chest rapidly rising and falling.

"Let's sit," Lorraine suggested at a coffee vendor parked next to a bench.

"Deal."

"Can I buy you a coffee?" Lorraine asked, pulling a couple of folded dollars from a zip pocket in her sweatshirt. Digging her hand in there, the same way she had that morning with Tommy brought back the awkwardness she'd felt. She knew she needed to say something about it, but that wasn't Lorraine's way. She didn't need to talk over every detail. You just moved on, right? Wasn't that the best way? Then nobody could tell if you were just being insecure—or a little neurotic.

"Definitely. Milk, two sugars, please."

After the exchange with the wordless coffee vendor, Lorraine and Matt unhooked their animals, which of course started a frantic lovemaking session. They looked away at the same time, which brought them face to face with each other.

For a minute they looked at each other the way people are normally too self-conscious to.

"I'm sorry," they both said at the same time.

"For what?" they both asked at the same time.

And then the easy laughter comforted them both.

"It *was* awkward wasn't it?" His face crinkled up like a ball of Saran wrap.

Lorraine was thrilled that Matt addressed the Tommy incident first. "But why?" she asked.

Matt looked at her for a second, and then said in his friendliest voice, "Silly, isn't it?"

Either he'd never really felt the things Lorraine had imagined or he'd just come to terms with the idea that her heart was somewhere else.

She didn't think she'd ever know which, but for the moment, a swell of quick regret was swallowed up by an even larger tide of relief. Lorraine had too much to think about just then to add another, possibly more confusing, element to the mix.

"How's your work going?" she asked when it seemed time to change the subject.

"Same old. Not too much ever changes. Pay the bills, buy a new shopping center on Rodeo Drive, charter a plane, you know." He smiled easily. "But as for my real work, you've got to see what I built out in Florida. It's due to arrive tomorrow by FedEx."

"What? What is it?" Lorraine saw the way he became energized at the mention of his furniture design—the quickened pace of words, the widened eye, the extra blinks. It was a boyish, unbridled excitement. She could see that. He loved what he did. Knowing he could get out to Miami and do what he really wanted a couple times a month made the daily grind endurable.

She found herself trying to settle on an image of his work space there, placing him at a picture window, with the waves gently rushing on the shore beyond, rays of sunlight illuminating his face. Matt was good people. That's what her father would say. He always said that of people he respected. It was one of the few things he ever said. He said it of a few guys he worked with, and of Tim Specker who patrolled their neighborhood, who had brought her grandmother home (often naked as a babe and screaming, "Prude! Just a little longer!") more times than Lorraine could remember. She knew he would say the same of Matt.

"You're good people." She hadn't even realized she'd said it aloud.

Matt's eyes silently questioned her. His mouth formed a pleased, but confounded smile. What did she mean?

"Oh, no, you're not going to make me an offer I can't refuse?" he asked.

Lorraine punched him playfully. "That's original," she taunted.

"What's going on at the swanky salon? Got your hands full with those Princesses?"

Given the opportunity, the words just spilled out. Why was it, Lorraine wondered, you could have the best intentions of appearing impenetrable, a Terminator of emotions, and then go on and ruin everything?

"I just hate this anger I feel toward Guido. Why am I so impatient?" She fiddled with the plastic cover on her coffee.

"Well, Lorraine, if you really want to hear my opinion, sounds like Guido needs you more than you need him. I can't *believe* he's used your nail design without giving you any credit. Believe me, he knows you should have got a cut of those profits."

Lorraine didn't see herself as a business tycoon. She wanted to rule the nursery, not the boardroom. There were no visions of Armani suits dancing in her head. It had just never seemed important.

"Ah, that's not really my thing," she said, instinctively wiping the idea away with a palm.

"I know, I know you're not the cutthroat type, Lorraine." As he said this, Lena Horne came galloping up into his lap and he stroked her back.

Lorraine couldn't help but point out the obvious. "Oh, you mean, as opposed to you?"

He looked down at his lap and shrugged his shoulders in surrender. "I can be in touch with my feminine side without feeling like my masculinity is threatened. I learned it from Oprah."

Lena snuggled her bow-tied fluff of hair into his sweatshirt, marking her territory.

Lorraine thought she knew just where Lena was coming from.

"Seriously, though, Lorraine. That's why he's afraid to let you go so fast with all the clients. He thinks you'll stage a coup."

Her head was shaking in disbelief even before the words were at her lips. "That's ridiculous! You should see this guy. Couldn't hurt a fly! He's just following the rules. He thinks if he lets *me* break them by moving too quickly up the ranks, then everyone will be bugging him for the same thing." She didn't know why she was defending Guido so vehemently, or why her voice had gotten so loud. Wasn't she feeling suspicious and angry at him herself? Still she didn't want to get involved in a battle of wills— or any battle at all. Too many other things in her life felt like a war. Hair coloring—that was supposed to be peaceful, enjoyable, the haven she escaped to when other things were pushing down on her too forcefully, not something she had to work so hard at. But hadn't that been exactly the case since she'd started at Guido's? Hadn't she been fighting to get through every day, save for those couple of hours that had seemed so natural and wonderfully fulfilling when she got to do what she did best?

"I totally appreciate the advice, Matt. But the difference is, you're a businessman, and I'm a hairstylist. You just don't know the beauty industry," she said, trying her best to convince him, and herself.

The two o'clock slot was the worst lunch you could get. Not only was it the latest, it also meant you'd be stuck with all the clients rushing you through their own lunch hour color appointments, juggling food-delivery orders onto silver trays with one hand, washing hair and holding foils with another, mixing colors, basically running around like Pooh-Pooh when he got to circling.

Her stomach was so empty, she'd just about imagined what every item on the menu would taste like. Don was putting it on his tab. And she was feeling a little embittered after towel-folding, hair-sweeping, and anything and everything but what she wanted to do; all the while glancing out at those billboard size hands of hers, telling her maybe Matt was right. So, Lorraine decided she'd make Guido pay, if only for an overindulgent lunch of four entrées and two appetizers, plus one slice of chocolate blackout cake and a ricotta cheese cannoli for dessert.

"Hungry?" Don asked sarcastically.

"Why do you ask?" She smoothed the linen tablecloth in front of her, then started fidgeting with the sugar packets.

"Hey, Lorraine, you just gotta hang in there. You know the way things go. Believe me. It kills me to see you sweeping up like Cinderella. I know you're worth more. You know you're worth more. Even Guido does. He told me about class the other night. I swear to God, he's never done that before with a student. Never."

She didn't know if she liked the idea of Guido talking about her with Don, or vice versa—but maybe Don had been trying to get Guido to move things along with her a little more quickly. Who knew how that conversation had come up?

"I don't know, Don. It's really hard to be treated like a novice. A lot more difficult than I imagined. I thought the promise of money in the future would help me tough it out, but it just doesn't seem worth it. I never cared much about being rich. I'm not sure I'd even know what to do with rich. I don't know how much more of this I've got in me." It was true. Tommy was the one who cared about rich, or thought he did anyway.

She slurped her Diet Coke with abandon, turning over in her mind the fact that she'd just lied. True, work did suck—but she *did* have it in her. She would tough it out. She always did. That was who Lorraine was. She wasn't about to go changing that now. Sure, she was exaggerating the truth a little, but she was freakin' frustrated and couldn't help it. A little goodwill from Don wouldn't have hurt; that's all she was looking for.

"Lorraine, Lorraine, I know. You are . . . I don't even know how to say it. You're one of the greats—a van Gogh, a Renoir. You are. Anyone can see it."

That helped. She could listen to those kind of comments all afternoon. It might help get her through the week. "Go on," she said, smiling.

"Seriously. You are fantastic. Guido confirmed that for me, although I didn't need him to, not by a long shot. And that chance he gave you, to teach last night, that was *huge* for him. The Guido System was created over fifteen years ago, and it has never been broken—not even for me, his own brother. You, Lorraine, have already done color on two clients—who, by the way, have already requested you for a rebooking. And you've taught a color class you were meant to be a student in. Just hang in there a little longer. I promise it will be worth it."

Lorraine let out a breath that could have blown out all the candles on a hundred-year-old's birthday cake, then leaned back in her chair. She couldn't believe how bad work was getting to her. Never in her life had she experienced this before. Things were so bad here she hadn't even thought about Tommy that day, and she'd not heard from him since Monday.

Their appetizers arrived and Lorraine ordered five dipping sauces, just because she was in that kind of mood. She wanted it all and she didn't want to be told that there were rules—this goes with that. She picked up a tempura zucchini and tossed the whole thing in her mouth, reached for a stuffed mushroom, and simultaneously forked her Waldorf salad.

Don shook his head. "Women."

"Yeah," she said with a full mouth, lifting more in its general direction. "You should see me and Chrissy when we tuck into the food like this. We could really eat, I tell you. We're the van Goghs of eating, you could say."

Don smiled. "How is Chrissy?" he asked a few seconds after. "You should have her come down, do her color or something. Then we can all go to lunch or something."

"Or something, or something, or something. What's this all about, Don? You sweet on Miss Chrissy?"

Don became fascinated with his own soda, dragging lines around the frosted side of his glass with a finger. "No," he said, pouty.

Aha, Lorraine thought. Something interesting. "You'd consider falling for a Brooklyn chick?" she asked, swiping the last tempura zucchini and dipping it in the newly arrived horseradish sauce, which she thought with pleasure was truly meant for the onion rings. The taste of the two together—her own deliciously fattening concoction—was nearly too much. She could barely remember what they were talking about, much less notice the way Don's voice had taken on a sort of hostile edge (as close to hostile as Don's voice could get); or the way he wasn't eating anything, just sitting with his arms crossed in front of his chest.

"All right, Lorraine, you wanna know the truth? We're *from* Brooklyn!" He caught the volume of his own voice and then leaned in and switched over to a thunderous whisper. "Our parents still *live* there." Don let out his own enormous breath, threw himself back in his own chair, like he'd just been exorcised—the demonic bridge-and-tunnel part of him somehow lightened by merely admitting to it.

Surely this couldn't be right. Guido was a . . . *guido*? Sure, anyone could tell the haughty accent was a fake, but she hadn't realized how hard it was working to cover up another, stronger accent!

"Let me get this straight. Guido is so ashamed of where you guys came from that he covers up his accent with a fake royal family voice that nobody buys anyway?"

Don was shaking his head. "I know, I know. He takes voice lessons. He makes *me* take voice lessons. I don't even know how to sound like myself anymore, I'm so mixed up."

"But why? I *love* Brooklyn! You should be proud to be from there!" The whole episode was making her homesick. Or maybe she was just—nauseated; she had just eaten quite a bit, and getting upset on top of all that fried food was probably not ideal. But there was more. This was about Guido, but it wasn't about Guido. To Lorraine, it seemed like all the problems in her life had to do with people's opinions of Brooklyn. She was feeling caught in the middle of a major borough war. Couldn't everyone just unite under the title of "New Yorkers" and leave it at that?

"I am, I know, but Guido, he took this seminar from a 'life coach,' back when he wanted to get out of Supercuts and start his own sa—"

"Guido came from SUPERCUTS?????!!!!!!!" Lorraine screamed and sent half a mouthful of cheeseburger across the table. "Ew. Sorry."

"First off," Don continued in the super-strength whisper, "*stop* screaming. He'd kill me if he knew I told you—which leads me to the oath you must make never to tell a soul."

Again with the oaths? What the hell was with these Manhattan guys?

"I solemnly swear on the Verrazano Bridge"—she bopped her head up and down, droned through a formal oath—"never to tell anyone that Guido is a guido."

Even Don spit out a laugh (and some of his own cheeseburger) at that.

". . . unless, of course, I drink too much and have no control over myself."

Don rolled his eyes. "Seriously, Lorraine. The reason I told you is because we are all the same people. You're good people, Lorraine. So is Guido, although a bit of a mixed-up one at that. But he sees himself in you. He's so proud of you, feels connected to you. Maybe even—"

"What? What?" Don had gotten her attention, using her father's words like that, invoking that type of neighborhood jargon that meant so much to so few.

"Maybe even he wishes you were related to him, so *I* wouldn't be such a huge disappointment."

"Oh, Don. C'mon! You're a success. You went through all the steps of Guido's Method, you come to work every day. You're completely reliable, wonderful, compassionate. Have you ever even been on a vacation since you started working here?"

"Yeah, Lorraine, I know all that. I *have* to do all that because I'm a crap colorist and you know it." His serious gaze forced Lorraine to pull remnants of a smile on her face down toward the floor.

Some people got up from a nearby table, with a racket of chairs screeching on the tile floor, jackets zipping and purses readjusting, a light rattle of loose change. Lorraine's cake arrived along with two small dessert forks.

They dug into the fluffy chocolate as Don explained to Lorraine how he wanted to be a business manager, a talent scout for his brother. "I'm the Mark Burnett of beauty. I want to put together the right cast for the ultimate reality experience—a beauty parlor." His face was forlorn. As absurd as it may have sounded, it was his dream and Lorraine could tell it meant the world to him.

Don said he'd always felt he could recognize greatness. "Look, I found you," he said to the tablecloth, "and now I . . ." He swallowed the end of his sentence.

"Don't cry!" Lorraine soothed.

He didn't cry, but he didn't acknowledge her, either. He kept on talking: "But that wasn't enough! *Nooooo.* Nothing is *ever* enough for *Guido.* . . . *Guido* doesn't like change, *Guido* doesn't want to mess with the clients he'd always worked with, the methods he'd always used. . . ."

She wondered why now all of this was coming to the surface. And it made her realize something strange about her own predicament— Lorraine and Don, two people on opposite sides of the table, were also on opposite sides of the same problem. She was a talented colorist without the means to do her thing. And on the other hand, though he was in an enviable position—coincidentally, exactly the one Lorraine wished for herself—he didn't really want or have what it takes to run with it. Ironically enough, he wanted something else altogether! Why did it seem that what everyone sought most was the one thing they couldn't have? And was there a way to ever make peace with the prospect of not having it? And if there was, should you? The predicament didn't merely plague her own family, as she'd always thought. Here was someone else with the very same problem. The same problem and no answer.

She had to fight off the initial frustration this boring old, seemingly answerless predicament ignited in her before answering. "First off, Don, I'm sorry I've been so frickin' self-involved I hadn't even thought about your own problems and feelings. I really feel like a dick about that. Second, I want to say that if it hadn't occurred to me before, boy, you and I, Don—we are so alike it's not even funny. And third, Mr. Seeker of Talent, Mr. I Know Who's Got It and Who Hasn't, I'm sure you know you've got what it takes to get all that together for yourself—isn't that supposed to be your specialty? And besides, you found me, so *obviously* you're fantastic."

Later that night, snuggling in bed with Pooh-Pooh, Lorraine didn't quite know what to do or how to feel about the information she'd gathered. But she was letting it all soak in, allowing it to course through her veins, flow through her arteries, make a place for itself within the existing ideas she already held. And for once, she wasn't in a rush to tell everyone what she thought about it. There were some elements of the Guido Method that had proved useful to Lorraine Machuchi, whether or not they were intentional. Patience was one of them.

> I don't say "yeah." I say "yes."
>
> I don't say "wouldja." I say "would you."
>
> I don't say "gimmie." I say "I'll have."
>
> I don't say "hey." I say "hello."

eBay auction block #10
Description: In this, Guido's voice lesson assignment #1, he practiced the fundamentals of removing his Brooklyn accent.

Opening bid: $150
Winning bid: $1250 by guido@bboy.com

Comments: I think it atrocious that your company would slander my reputation with such nonsense. And besides, everyone has to learn to become comfortable with who they are, and for some people this can take longer than it does with others. As you can see from my new e-mail address, I am now ready to show I am a B Boy. However, you will be hearing from my attorney.

TEN

♥

GUIDO IS OVERBOOKED

When Lorraine was in high school, hair two feet wide by four feet long, she'd become obsessed with the story of Marilyn Monroe. She'd had to choose a biography to report on for English class, and that was who she'd decided to read about. But the story pissed her off. Here was a woman who had what everyone in the world hoped for—success, riches, the attention of the masses, not to mention the kind of beauty only rarely seen. And yet, she was never happy. Always, Marilyn was looking for something else, the one thing that would make her feel complete. Lorraine knew before she read the book that Marilyn had committed suicide. She'd seen the TV movie with Chrissy and her mom, the three of them using up a box of Kleenex between them. Still, the ending of the book shocked Lorraine like she'd never been shocked before. She couldn't finish. She couldn't write the paper. In the end, she'd decided to switch to Ben Franklin. At least he'd done what he set out to do without much complication, and stuck around to enjoy it.

The thing was, after wanting and wanting, the idea that finally having that coveted ideal for yourself wouldn't ever be enough, that it wouldn't ever be all you thought it would be, was too much to bear. If there was one comforting aspect of Lorraine's ongoing disappointing obsession with Tommy, it was that she still had the hope of Someday to look forward to.

This idea comforted Lorraine when finally she got a call from him to say, Hey, he was sorry he'd gotten so carried away last weekend, but he just wasn't ready for that kind of commitment. He wasn't gonna say "it's not you, it's me," he told her. He wouldn't do that to his Lorraine. All week long he'd thought about the right words. That's why he didn't want to call her right away. No, he wanted to work it all out into the proper words before he told Lorraine that they should just put the brakes on, because everything was moving too fast.

I am NOT going to find out if there was a girl to go along with all that "working out." I am NOT. I am NOT!

"You know how I feel about you, Quichy." He only ever called her that when he wanted something.

But what the fuck did he want NOW?

"I just need a little time to work things out in my head, Lorraine."

Yeah, because fifteen years hasn't been long enough. She knew not to push it, though. He didn't respond well to pressure—over seventy-five women could testify to that. She knew that he'd get to feeling blue and call her, or just show up late one night, and then she'd have another shot to win him over for good. That was just the way things were. A lot had happened—he needed time to work it all out. She would wait. How could she stand this? She didn't have a choice. How do you explain how the river runs or how the seasons just keep flowing one into the next? Some things are just bigger than any of us.

The weekend had been sort of lonely, sitting and stewing about Tommy, forcing herself not to go to Brooklyn. Because it was The Right Thing To Do. Throwing herself into Tommy's weekend would just have made her look jealous, insecure, and desperate. She didn't go to the family dinner on Sunday for the same reason—she didn't want to look out the kitchen window over to Tommy's house. She didn't want to see him reading the sports section with a steaming cup of black coffee, two sugars, as if he hadn't a problem in the world, as if it hadn't even crossed his mind that he hadn't seen Lorraine in six whole days.

There was always Pooh-Pooh. And food. Brunch was a fabulous New

York City institution. They didn't do "brunch" in Brooklyn. They didn't do eggs Benedict with gooey poached eggs and rich hollandaise, or a Cobb salad the size of a football stadium with tangy blue cheese and crunchy bacon. The Guidos never thought of smoked salmon over a generous layer of cream cheese on black bread, topped with sour capers and freshly ground black pepper, perfect rings of purple onion overlapped with precision.

And if you don't believe brunch is an institution, just look at the line at Sarabeth's on a Saturday or Sunday, when the sun is bright. Lorraine still preferred 92, because she could sit outside with Pooh-Pooh, taking in the people of her neighborhood, their perfect casual attire—jeans made to look thirty years old, sweaters cut to slim a waist or an arm, in the perfect shade of sky blue, makeup made to look natural, a pair of giant plastic sunglasses pulled high atop a glossy slick of hair.

Elegance was the thing here. There was elegance in the facade of the buildings, in the step of a gentleman walking home with the newspaper rolled perfectly under his arm, his white pants freshly laundered with the creases ironed in, in the shop window signs advertising "Pre-Holiday Special, 30% reduction in seasonal merchandise," small and without fluorescent colors and outsize bursts like you saw littering Eighty-sixth Street in the Bay. Even Lorraine was more elegant in Manhattan, even her loneliness had a certain grace to it, in the way it spiraled around her, in the way it traveled through her straw as she sucked a bit of Bloody Mary up into her mouth.

She could have called Matt—should have, probably. But she didn't want to use him to ask for his company only when Tommy's was an impossibility. It didn't seem right. There was a lightness to his tone that you didn't want to quash. You wanted to protect it, stroke it softly with your palm, care for it, and not let it go. And since she'd thought all the week long she'd be having a repeat performance this weekend of all the things that had thrilled her so much the weekend before, she thought Saturday, Sunday, and Monday were off limits for hanging out with Matt.

But Tuesday—when she went back to work—should be fine. She would be able to dial his number and suggest that movie without any complicated feelings of guilt. That's just what Lorraine was thinking as she passed through the giant gold doors of Guido's salon Tuesday morning. Those doors were 14 karat through and through. A publicist had dreamed up the idea, promising Guido that if he invested the $500,000 into the doors, they would land him in every single daily paper and monthly magazine in the country, if not the world. And she'd been correct.

But the gold didn't do very well in the wet weather. It would stain and lose its luster. It would wear thin where people pushed at it. Plus, there was the security issue. When you flaunted something like that, people wanted it. And often, they'd stop at nothing to try and get it. Five years back someone had succeeded in stealing one whole door. It was a big coup involving a jewel thief and a whole *Ocean's Eleven*-style team of elegant burglars.

Even that didn't stop the force that was Guido's. The heist brought Guido more success. His was named the number one salon in the world after that, and the Princesses became permanent fixtures. It was the image he'd gained, not the fancy doors, that had brought them. Golden doors were nothing where they came from. Maybe, Lorraine thought, they even sat on golden toilets, brushed with golden toothbrushes, rinsed with water from golden cups.

And besides, the doors were insured. Even while the one was missing, it didn't hurt business one bit. If anything, the clientele increased. Curiosity brought people to come take a look. A Japanese magazine did a story on the stolen door, which brought a whole new source of clientele—Japanese tourists. They snapped up photos and stylish cuts all at the same time.

Lorraine was expecting a methodical day—Tuesdays were notoriously slow and marked by lots of mindless chores. There would be the towels, the foils, and plenty of opportunity to sit with her thoughts, wonder for the thousandth time what she was doing here, if there would ever be an end to her ongoing struggle with Tommy. And also about Matt, about whether she could have a friendship with him, or whether the risk of hurting him would be too great.

But no sooner had the golden doors come to a perfect *whooshing* close behind her than she heard voices calling her here, there, and everywhere.

She heard her name in three pitches, from three directions. Being the logical, unflappable sort she was, Lorraine went directly to the closest person who'd invoked it, Jacqueline. Jacqueline was as tall as Lorraine, but French, which for some reason lent her an air of being taller and older. She was more willowy, that was certain, and without exception she wore black, head to toe, with an expensive-looking floral print scarf tied and wrapped all different ways—in her hair, about her neck, pinned over her shoulder, at her waist. She wasn't pretty exactly, but the Frenchness seemed to make up for that, too. There was a mystery about the way her almond brown eyes blinked slowly, closing for many seconds at a time, the false eyelashes she wore meeting and then opening up like a butterfly's wings. She was a bitch, and really just run-of-the-mill at coloring hair— but Jacqueline's claim to fame was being fast. And that, Lorraine respected. She admired people who knew what they had to do and did it. So few people she knew were that way—most folks would labor over something until it just about drove them crazy, or until the decision was made for them, whichever came first.

For that reason, the two of them, they worked well as a team. She knew that must be why Jacqueline had chosen Lorraine as her assistant for the day. What she didn't know was what everyone was freaking out about.

"What's everyone so damned crazy about?" she asked Jacqueline on the way to her station, where Jacqueline needed her help "*tout de suite.*"

"Someone fucked up royally, darling. The annual benefit for the Association for Poor Girls Who Want Bigger Boobs—*deeeee* APGBB—is at the Met this week, and nobo*dy* at reception put it in *deeee booooook.*" Her hips swayed exaggeratedly as Lorraine followed behind her.

Lorraine was caught between stifling a laugh and having absolutely no idea what the oversight had to do with the hyper-rushed mood about the salon—it's not like there wasn't some benefit going off every night of the week that kept them booked solid. But Jacqueline answered the unanswered question for her anyway.

"Zee fucking Princesses. Zey'll all want zeir *rrrrroots* done today. And of course none of zem has made zee appoint-*te*-ment."

Jacqueline already had twelve clients on her schedule. "You believe diz *sheet*?" she said to Lorraine as she passed a copy of the schedule to Lorraine. As quick as lightning, she approached the client waiting in her chair and switched to a singsongy, effusive manner that Lorraine supposed Jacqueline thought Americans expected of the French.

"*Alors, alors!*" She was double air kissing to the delight of her client.

"Bon-JOUR!" the woman for whom no jewel was too big or too bold exclaimed with an equally bold accent—Texan perhaps.

"*Ma petite! Comment vas-tu?*"

The client thought for a second, working out words in the air with a Guido Nailed pointer finger adorned with a purple flower, holding up the largest green stone Lorraine had ever seen. Finally she smiled proudly and replied, "Tray BI-ennn, MERCY!"

"Ah! You have been practic*ing*, Katharine! Now, darling, what have you used on your hair? Eeet looks kind of *green*." Jacqueline was a master of the smile that meant *moron!* but that others took as a kind understanding. It was another reason Lorraine liked her. And Lorraine understood why it sprung to Jacqueline's face just then—it killed a colorist when her clients didn't listen to care instructions. It meant more work and more time and, well, just think of someone storing a Whistler in their moldy basement.

"Oh, dear! You are right! Well, we were away in Hawa-eeeee and I'm afraid I just swam and swam in that pool all day long."

You could easily believe this explanation by looking at her fleshy facial skin which looked sort of well done, if not completely overcooked, except for a small area around her eyes, which must have been covered by sunglasses.

"Ah, dear, you must use sunscreen on your tresses. Lorraine, please have reception add the entire Kerastase Soleil line to Katharine's tab."

In that time, Lorraine had been grabbing sections, passing them to Jacqueline to paint purplish mud-looking bleach onto, and in that short time, Jacqueline had finished. She didn't have to tell Lorraine how long to set the dryer for. Nobody had to tell Lorraine anything. If she had her way, she would have told Jacqueline to convince her client to go one shade darker, especially with the tan. The white blond color didn't sit right on Katharine's build or face shape. Instead, she pressed some buttons, and with a quiet beep, Katharine had a halo hovering around her head, distributing heat as it went.

"Could I get you some cappuccino with one Sweet 'n Low, Katharine?" Lorraine asked, remembering the detail from her card.

"Why, that would be just wonderful. You're all so wonderful here! MERCY!"

Lorraine passed a stack of brand-new magazines to the client before leaving to retrieve the cappuccino order.

Juan, beverage master, was whirling around, zipping up espressos, steeping hand-tied bags of Indian teas in mugs of hot water. "What you need, *chica*?" he asked, his back to her, passing two beverages to another assistant, James, on the other side of his circular sunken beverage bar.

"Cappuccino, one Sweet 'n Low on the side."

Even Juan was happy doing what he was good at. You could tell that. Maybe he was saving to open his own chain of cappuccino bars. Everyone knew he made the best. It wouldn't be hard to branch out. He'd already been featured in *New York* magazine for the Best Cappuccino in the city, with a smiling photo to boot.

When she brought the beverage back to the Texan, Lorraine chatted her up while preparing sections at a neighboring seat for Jacqueline's next client. And when it was time, she brought Katharine to the sink to rinse her off; she followed Jacqueline's instructions to a T. She'd have done differently, but this was Jacqueline's art, and she respected that. Although, increasingly, through the day, she realized no one respected hers. Watching Jacqueline's Guido Nails in bold red brush their way over one head after another, her gold *B* catching the light every once and again, while Lorraine held sections out for her, tried to make an art of predicting just what Jacqueline would want before she could ask, the fact became more than clear to Lorraine.

There wasn't time for lunch. Lorraine had to use that hour to fold the towels and cut the squares of foils, organize the duck clips Jacqueline would need throughout the rest of the day. Her stomach was grumbling, but she always kept a few sucking candies in a drawer to keep from getting dizzy or slowed down by hunger. She tossed one to Jacqueline, who gave her a look like she'd just read her mind. *Good,* Lorraine thought, *at least I can be good at being underused. At least that's something.*

At around two-thirty, anyone who was really paying attention could see the energy at Guido's had reached the Code Orange level. Assistants' ponytails were looking disheveled, there were splodges of dye on hands and along cheekbones, dotted on chins. The stylists were cutting corners, sticking clients under the dryers when they didn't really need to, buying time to finish someone else without appearing neglectful.

At three forty-five, the first dissatisfied client surfaced with a rather loud expression of her disapproval. "Excuse me, Jacqueline, but this is unacceptable."

Lorraine looked up to see what the *Ohmigod* might be referring to. Probably she thought she needed more light pieces around her face. This girl—holding a little dog Lorraine recognized from the park—was a master client. She'd been having her hair colored since she was six years old, and she knew exactly what looked best on her. If that was what she was referring to, Lorraine would have to agree. She looked a little washed out. Over time the highlights had come to look almost all one color, which can happen sometimes. Lorraine would have thrown in a shock of chunky nearly-white blonde and a few real dark pieces in—about five minutes work—and then recommended a heavy fringe of bang before passing the *Ohmigod* off to the cut girls.

The *Ohmigod* confirmed Lorraine's hunch. And then Lorraine saw the dissatisfaction on Jacqueline's face, the pure disdain for her client, which was probably more personal than anything—because, really, the girl was right.

"You know what, darling Little Miss Money Bags? You need to trust your styl*eest*." Jacqueline employed the tone a nursery school teacher would to a little boy caught tucking into the class snack on the sly.

Lorraine tried not to show her shock, but she knew this was a potentially explosive situation, with the fuse already ignited. The client was always right—not only in the Guido Method, but in all methods. If she wanted her hair purple with a touch of green, then by God, that's what she should have! You could gently guide your client to the most optimal style for her, but in the end, the choice was hers. It took time to build a level of trust where the client understood that letting the stylist make the big choices would result in the best possible style, and sometimes it never happened.

Never, though, did you call your client the names you thought up for them in your head. Jacqueline had already dug her grave by treating a client that way. It was grounds for immediate dismissal, and she knew it. So she didn't hold back. "Oh, and by dee way, you have a crooked nose, and everyone knows you throw up in zee bathroom after you make us order your stup*eeed* Happy Meal from McDonald's. Lorraine will finish you off; she's a better colorist than I am anyway." Jacqueline turned to Lorraine, and she could see the sad glaze over her eyes.

She'd just cracked. That was all. Who knew why? She could have merely been hungry. Lorraine felt sorry for Jacqueline. She knew what it was like to work for so long for something, only to see it slip through the teeth on your rattail comb. She was surprised by the hug from her French colleague. It was rather strong, maybe because Lorraine was the only one around; or maybe because Jacqueline didn't want anyone to see the tear Lorraine felt soaking into her neck. At her ear she felt more than heard the words, "You are wonderful, Lorraine, really wonderful. Don't waste it."

Jacqueline tossed Lorraine one last look before fanning all her Guido Nails over her chest, like two Chinese paper fans in a finale dance. She looked down at them with a smile, and turned with a wink to go—who knows where.

As her hips swayed in that too-obvious way and the ends of her silky rose-printed scarf picked up in the wind of her rapid step, she didn't pay any mind to the *Ohmigod*.

"Do you know who I AM, for fuck's sake? My daddy is, like, the biggest publisher in the world! He, like, discovered that Henry Potter guy!"

When Jacqueline had disappeared between the golden doors, the *Ohmigod* turned to Lorraine for approval. "Well, he is," her voice trailed off.

Lorraine smiled, just as Jacqueline would have, saying *moron!* on the inside, while appearing sweet on the outside. she dried the *Ohmigod*'s hair while asking a neighboring assistant to bring Ms. Wilkes a nice cup of chamomile tea with honey. "It's her favorite," she said loud enough for the *Ohmigod* to hear, placed a reassuring hand at her shoulder, squeezed, and then passed her the latest issue of *People*. Her card said she loved to read it. Then Lorraine plunged into coloring her hair.

Back inside the color room a few minutes later, Lorraine took a second to breathe and think about what had just happened. She was ecstatic, but worry was starting to cloud over her happiness. She'd ignored the Guido Method—again. Just then she felt a vibration coming from her back jeans pocket. *What now?*

The strange, long string of numbers looked like a mistake to Lorraine. Still, she answered. "Hello?"

"Oh, darling Lorraine! So great to hear an *Americano*! How are you dear?" Mrs. Romanelli asked.

"Oh! Mrs. Romanelli, I'm doing great!" To add to the worry of what had just happened, Lorraine remembered the missing table Pooh-Pooh had destroyed. How was she going to fix that?

"Lorraine, you can't lie to an old Italian woman! Surely you know that!"

Lorraine had the instinct to grab on to the counter behind her, shrink into it. The idea of someone "watching" her was a teensy bit off-putting. Then she let it all spill out.

Mrs. Romanelli only let Lorraine talk for a couple of minutes before cutting her off. "First of all, don't worry about the table. It's the fourth one poor Pooh-Pooh has gone through! The store keeps a stock of them for me, so just call up ABC Carpet and Home over on Broadway and speak to Len. Now, as for the real important issue, don't you dare doubt what you just did with that spoiled girl! Sometimes you have to break the rules, darling, to get where you need to be." Then Mrs. Romanelli got distracted by someone else on her end. "Thomaso! How *are* you darling? Oh, my, your muscles have become so pronounced, dear! Please, let me rub some sunscreen on your chest! You don't want to burn."

Lorraine was glad to let Mrs. Romanelli go. She did not want to imagine her rubbing sunscreen on Thomaso—already her mind had conjured up too much. After she'd placed her phone back in her pocket, though, Lorraine did think about her words. It was true, wasn't it? You were always hearing about movie stars and all kinds of successful people who didn't listen to the way you're "supposed to" do things. She hadn't meant to break the rules. It was her instinct that had told Lorraine to take over where Jacqueline had left off. And something about Mrs. Romanelli's call—although odd as hell—made Lorraine more confident in what she'd done. There was a wisdom she'd always felt in her grandmother, and somehow Mrs. Romanelli's presence communicated that same sensation now. Boy, did she miss her grandmother. At a time like this, it hurt to breathe she missed her so much.

When she'd had a chance to rinse the *Ohmigod*, Lorraine was happy with her work. She'd fixed the color just as she'd imagined it. The *Ohmigod* loved it, and when she went down to the cut girls, she did exactly as Lorraine had suggested with her bangs. In the spirit of efficiency, and because it felt so damn wonderful (and because in the tornado of activity, nobody had noticed), Lorraine took over Jacqueline's client list for the rest of the day.

The next two hours were a blissful flurry of activity. Lorraine didn't even notice she hadn't eaten anything since her raspberry scone with breakfast. In shades of that other day, when Guido had unwittingly let her do just this same thing, Lorraine was flying, operating on a different level of being. She was a colorist again! And boy, did it feel freaking awesome. Each client looked better than the next. The hours moved along lyrically, one movement flowing into the next, and then the next . . . until all things came to a screeching halt.

All the blow-drying, the chatter, the patter of assistants' feet running here and there, the *squish-squish* of shampoo and conditioner pumping, the *sssssshhhhhh* of mousse foaming in a palm, all seemed to fade out to a gentle hum. Suddenly all there was in the world was Guido. He appeared in her mirror towering over her and the client she was standing over, Mrs. Tinnerson.

Because she knew the importance of such things instinctively, Lorraine smiled, rather than let her jaw drop to the floor at the instant realization of the situation's severity. She politely excused herself for a moment and followed Guido to the color closet, where he closed them both inside with a gently shut door.

She looked right at Guido, pretty sure she was about to be sacked, already thinking about her uncle, who would be forced to take her back by her mother. He'd want to take her back anyway, if only for the I-told-you-so quality such a gesture would afford to their already tempestuous relationship. And for the first time, Lorraine was surprised by the fact that the idea resonated with unmistakable disappointment.

Guido looked right back at Lorraine and then shifted his gaze up and around, taking in all the bottles of color and all the mixing bowls and brushes and the color swatches and books—the whole Guido kingdom had been built essentially from this room. And then, as if reminding her who she was standing in there with, he stared her down, with waved brows and bulging eyes, never once blinking, never fidgeting. "You know what's happened here today, Lorraine. You know what you've done. I don't need to remind you that you've broken the rules again. That's two times now. I tried, Lorraine, I tried to appease you by handing over the class. Never in my career have I done that for another junior colorist. But apparently, that wasn't enough for you."

She felt all the *buts* forming in her head, only they sounded silly. Sure she'd acted swiftly, done a good job, but she knew it wasn't what Guido wanted. Even though she'd been happy, in some ways she'd felt like a thief, stealing something that wasn't hers, wearing jewels that didn't belong to her. But all of the other sensations had been so intense, she couldn't listen to those nagging doubts. Lorraine was in a zone then, and it hadn't mattered that she wasn't good enough for Tommy, or that she'd been stressing over Matt. None of it mattered. The whole world was what Lorraine was doing, the precise movement of her fingers, the vision of color in her mind. Was she going to have to pay for that? She pressed her finger pads into her nails, and a thought popped into her head. The Guido Nails. They were Lorraine Nails. Matt's words came back to her: "He needs you more than you need him."

Suddenly she felt bold. "Guido, you and I both know I am an exception." And then bolder. "You and I, we come from the same place." This could have meant Brooklyn, this could have meant talent, anything really. But it seemed she had gotten his attention. "I am a star stylist, Guido, and if you don't recognize that, I think we both know that someone else will." Lorraine knew how to play hardball—now it seemed all the tactics were flying back to her.

Guido breathed deeply, and sighed. Was there regret in that sigh, regret that he'd taken advantage with the nails, robbing her of any credit she was really due? If there was, she wouldn't bring it up, wouldn't push the issue. The most important thing to her was simply to color hair freely.

"All right, Lorraine. You've got your wish. Ms. Wilkes has a big mouth. She stayed here for an extra hour just staring at herself in the mirror and telling all the clients what a magician you are, and of course, adding how important her 'daddy' is."

Lorraine smiled. Maybe hard work does pay off.

"Yeah, and?" Lorraine wanted to know, her old fire coming back to her. Her days as a fish out of water in Manhattan were officially, instantly, behind her. In fact, she couldn't see why she'd ever felt like that in the first place. No matter where she was, she knew what she was good at, and she knew who she was. Maybe she'd just forgotten for a minute.

Guido gave Lorraine a careful look. "And, Lorraine, the Princesses were sitting right there when she said it. And Mallory herself was sitting in my chair. I'd just come back from mixing her color and she screamed, like the little spoiled bitch she is, 'Stop!' Like I was her stupid little puppy Anna was coloring next to her. 'I want Lorraine to color my hair,' she said. And now, Lorraine, the fate of my entire business rests in your hands."

Lorraine stood stock-still. Guido sighed once more, turned, and left the color room. "I expect you on the floor in two minutes," he called over his shoulder. For a moment, Lorraine felt rooted to the ground. But her trepidation soon passed. Lorraine wasn't worried—she had confidence in herself. And besides, the Princesses didn't scare her. A head of hair was a head of hair. Sure, you'd up the ass-kissing a couple thousand notches. *You look like a huge ass kisser to me.* But even on that she only had a certain threshold. Lorraine didn't fear being herself—people respected her for it. Jacqueline had respected her for it, and that was precisely how she'd landed this unique opportunity.

Lorraine was ready for the Princesses.

Page Six

October 15, 2004
Onetime Brooklynite **Lorraine Machuchi** of **Guido's** salon in the swanky **Bendel's** department store on Fifth Avenue wowed all present yesterday, after Froggy stylist **Jacqueline Lefronge** suffered a nervous breakdown at the head of client **Ms. Wilkes**, who reminds the *Post* that her father is "the biggest publisher in the world, and is responsible for that Henry Potter dude." While **Ms. Lefronge** drowned her sorrow in twenty croissants beurres at Payard, **Ms. Machuchi** took over her seat and made **Ms. Wilkes** look "just like that mean woman on *Desperate Housewives*" according to **Ms. Wilkes** who could not stop looking at herself in her hand mirror during our interview. However, more important, **Ms. Machuchi** proceeded to color **Mallory Meen** and all the Princesses. Appointments with **Machuchi** are currently booked until 2015, according to sources at the salon.

When **Machuchi** was questioned, she simply stated, "Fuhgedabboudit!"

Just kidding. She didn't really say that. But we couldn't help ourselves.

eBay auction block #11
Description: Framed clipping of *Page Six* mention of Lorraine Machuchi's first hands-on coloring experience with the Princesses. Arguably the day everything started happening for her. In fact, a lot more than she knew . . .

Opening bid: $250
Winning bid: $1250 by mswilkes@mydaddyrich.com

Comments: I will be keeping this, as it was ME ME ME who spread the word about Lorraine. I am the one who told those Princesses, who think they are just too good for someone like me, even though it was MY daddy who found that Henry Potter dude!

ELEVEN

♥

A PRINCESS IS BORN

Princess, princess, princess. Lorraine thought she'd heard the word so often associated with Mallory of late, she could barely remember what it was supposed to mean in the first place. Before she'd come to Manhattan, before she'd given more than a second's glance to Mallory's picture in the paper, she'd really only thought of one Princess in her life. Like every other woman in their neighborhood, Lorraine's mother had a sort of mystical fascination with Princess Diana.

They watched her whenever she was on *Extra!* or *60 Minutes.* They saved, in protective plastic covers, the special issues of *Time* and *People* that featured Princess Di—as everyone referred to her—as if she were already a friend, as if they knew in their hearts that if ever they did meet her, she would treat them as an equal. They discussed—on woven chairs out on Lorraine's driveway—the sapphire earrings she'd worn, the icy blue satin blouse she'd chosen, as if they were intimately acquainted with all of the contents of her closet. They always had an idea of what they would have done differently with her hair.

But one thing her mother always said stuck out in Lorraine's memory more than anything else. Lorraine's mother was sure that Diana was in love with Charles, that the beautiful life they were pictured to have was absolutely perfect. It was impossible for her to believe otherwise. In fact, after the divorce, she stopped following Diana altogether. Mrs. Machuchi could not stand to accept that all that perfection could possibly be imperfect.

Being a young girl, Lorraine had mimicked her mother's thoughts on the topic, Scotch-taping carefully cut magazine pictures onto her wall, mounted in construction-paper frames, until it became impossible to do so. The word was out—they were divorcing. And soon after, there was Dodi, and the accident. And when Lorraine's mother mourned the death of everyone's precious Princess, Lorraine couldn't help but wonder if her mother was mourning more than that, if it weren't possible that her mother was giving up on the idea of perfection and everything she'd hoped it to be.

Lorraine wasn't sure if that was such a bad thing. At least it was more realistic. She'd kept one picture all these years, of Diana in her sapphire earrings, a perfect silk chiffon bow tied at her neck, to remind her that despite how things might appear, nobody's life was perfect. And she'd always taken solace in the idea of that. Most of all, the grace and poise that very beautiful princess had maintained, no matter the hardship, was what Lorraine was inspired by just then, as she went to face—head-on—a very different sort of princess.

Despite the fact that Lorraine had utter confidence in her abilities, she was a tinge nervous as she strode—with her own most princesslike grace—over to Jacqueline's old chair, now apparently Lorraine's chair. There sat Mallory Meen, the other three Princesses in armchairs behind her, a personal assistant chatting on a telephone while mopping excess oil from Mallory's face with a French blotting paper, the dog barking rather loudly, still with a few foils on his head from the stylist Mallory had snatched her puppy from only moments earlier. The camera crew didn't help lessen the lump in her throat.

"You're my new colorist," Mallory said, holding her hand up gingerly.

"So I've heard," Lorraine said, shaking Mallory's hand firmly, although she knew the Princess hadn't intended for that to be done.

Mallory shot a gaze up to Lorraine to express her displeasure with the sassy tone. "Laurie," she said, using the same intentional voice she had last time, "I hear you're the best. I only get the best. So show me what you've got. And then do my dog. Queenie's roots are absolutely horrendous."

Queenie let out a low, squeaky moan, like she couldn't go on looking like that for one more second.

The camera swiveled Lorraine's way.

"Sorry, Melanie, but I don't do dogs. Why don't you have Anna finish her up so we can concentrate on you, sweetie? You don't become a top stylist by coloring a pup, now do ya?" Lorraine let out a *huh*, disguising itself as a laugh. It wasn't rude. It was marketing. And marketing was something a Princess, if not all New York girls, responded to. You wanted the best, and if someone had a good argument to support why it was them, well then, you fell for it all—hook, line, and sinker. And nothing was more convincing than someone with an attitude of unwavering confidence. Shit, you could sell a tub of Pooh-Pooh's pooh-pooh if you threw it in a provincial jelly jar and labeled it with a pretty Italian-looking font.

Lorraine watched Mallory assess the situation, taking in her Citizens of Humanity Jeans and James Perse off-the-shoulder top Lorraine had just bought downstairs, and then rapidly readjust her attitude. Mallory's face softened; she looked at Lorraine through the mirror and said to her assistant, "Bring Queenie back down to Anna, would you, Ceecee?"

"Of course, uh, Meessss Mallory."

The dog and the assistant were gone in the blink of an eye, cameras following them to the door.

The other Princesses' eyes bounced around in syncopated jumps— following Lorraine's every move, memorizing them so they could be sure Lorraine would copy for them exactly what she did on Mallory.

Have you ever been on a plane when turbulence kept everyone anxious throughout the flight? The pilot will feed bits of information to the passengers to ensure they feel secure about what the issues are and that able hands are on the control panel, guiding the way to safety. By the time everyone's strapped in for the landing, there's a hushed air throughout the cabin, all eyes looking down at the wheels, the wings, minding what they consider to be the significance of a slightly rotated flap, a bit of cloud cover to the right. The responsibility, the expectation, the idea that everyone has in their head, that they are somehow qualified to judge the performance of the pilot based on watching season one of *LAX*, a holiday screening of *Airplane!*, or having flown to Europe four times on the redeye adds tension to an environment already as thick with it as a Sunday night meat sauce in the Machuchi residence.

You might not think a Princess's hair color as important as a safe 747 landing . . . but you'd be wrong. You'd be ignoring Guido in the security room, standing over the shoulder of the guard, watching from three different angles Lorraine's swift, precise color application, hoping she brought it all home safely. You'd be disregarding the hushed crowd around Lorraine watching her use that five-color method of hers, the one that looks different in all different lights, the one she knew would blow any girl's mind when she took a look in the mirror and felt like a million bucks—even *before* she applied her makeup.

Her movements were rapid, detailed. The crowd continued to gather behind the crew. Juan was passing out beverages, trying to slide in front of the camera announcing each one in his elegant Latin accent, "A *mocha* swirl cap*puccino*—iced." A media op was a media op. Everyone knew Mallory, everyone understood the importance of what was happening. Stylists passed the word, and one by one they moved in close—a cluster of shiny black nylon robes. Those who'd arrived first brought the newcomers up to speed, and with the growing group, the chatter began to rise.

You might think a girl would get nervous at such a moment, with so much pressure mounting. But after everything Lorraine had been through—changing her life, slaving for Guido while keeping her tongue, acclimating to the City life—this was nothing. *This* was what came natural to Lorraine. It was the same thing she'd always done—or knew should be done, whether or not she actually had the chance to see it through. Even when she wasn't allowed to be creative, even when she had to keep herself happy with imagining the process while mindlessly holding out foil squares for the senior colorist, she was still paying close attention, being mindful of whether the client's roots were too "hot," or if they would benefit from a shine-boosting conditioning treatment to seal the cuticles, etc.

In fact, Lorraine fed off the energy in the room, ate it up, become bolder with each new pair of eyes, each "Ooooh" and "Did you see what she did there?" and "I wonder how that will come out."

As she applied the last stroke of her brush, she turned her head to see those giant hands of hers staring down from the billboard. And she realized this was the happiest she'd ever been in her life. There were other things in her life besides Tommy, other things that she could do to change her fate, to find her happiness. And this was it—and it was spectacular! Now that she had this attitude, who knew what might happen?

Emboldened, Lorraine dropped the brush with a *clink* into the bowl that her favorite co-assistant Damian was holding out for her. He didn't at all seem surprised to see her in her new role.

"Damian, take Princess Mallory to the sink, use the essential oil mix to massage her temples and shoulders, and grab her a half-caf, no foam with two Splenda."

And then she turned to Mallory, getting in the last word herself before Mallory had the chance. It was the way she'd always handled fights in the schoolyard, with the gangster girls she shared classrooms with. Sum it up, walk away, always get the last word. "Miss Mallory, it's been a pleasure coloring your hair. You have fabulous hair, and it was a dream to work on." She stuck her hand out for Mallory again.

This time the Princess took it, Guido Nails to Guido Nails, smiling in that unstoppable way women do only at this very moment, when they are nearing the end of their primping session and know they look hot.

"I'll come show you when I've been dried," Mallory said unwaveringly.

That was something a stylist normally asked, not something they were offered. It was an honor. It meant you'd done a good job. It meant the client looked to you for approval, considered you the master of their hair's fate. Damian put a fresh towel around Mallory's shoulders and started steering her toward the sink; a parade of Queenie, Ceecee, the other three Princesses, a bunch of stylists, and the camera crew trailed behind.

Mallory turned back, Lorraine's giant billboard hands eerily making a frame up over her head. "Oh, and Lorraine," she said, using the correct name for the first time, "I'd like you to be my guest at the APGBB benefit. They've done some poor girl from Brooklyn. I think you'd appreciate the transformation."

It wasn't the kindest invitation, but not even the President of the United States (they'd done a "Revitalize New York!" commercial together), could expect that from Mallory.

"That's a wrap!" the cameraman yelled. Lorraine was surprised Guido had allowed the cameras to witness the days events.

But now, it *was* a wrap—and the final seal on the fabulous new fate of Lorraine Machuchi—stylist to the Princesses. And that was no small deal.

Lorraine,

The pain!!!!!!
You do what you want.
I am a pizza boy/man.
I hurt.
I bleed.
I do bad things.
But, you, I need.

eBay auction block #12
Description: In this never-mailed poem, Tommy attempted—if somewhat poorly—to explain his feelings to Lorraine.

Opening bid: $38
Winning bid: $356.35 by <u>Pattyfromthediner@hotmail.com</u>

Comments: Ha-ha! Tommy, I will show the world what a weenie you really are, how could you lie and say you would come down to FL, when you were in love with someone else! I thought that night in the meat freezer really *meant* something!

TWELVE

♥

GETTING THE HANG OF POOH-POOH

If a run with Pooh-Pooh was wonderful when you were in a pissy mood, it was doubly wonderful when you were on top of the world. Three hours after Lorraine's coup, and she wasn't thinking about tomorrow or what might result from all her good fortune. All she was thinking was how much smaller Madison Avenue looked, how much more familiar the milky stone facades, how much friendlier the faces, how much brighter the sky.

Lorraine was riding such an adrenaline rush, even Pooh-Pooh was struggling to keep up with her. "What's the problem, Pooh-Pooh? You pooped or something?" She would apparently never tire of joking about doodoo. That was another new thing she'd discovered about herself recently.

"Me, nah!"

Lorraine turned around in surprise. If her dog had really just spoken to her, he had a very soothing, sexy way about him. *Wait, wait!* That was no dog . . . that was Matt, and he was laughing so loud as to border on obnoxious.

"Hahaha! So funny! Isn't it hysterical to watch your friends crack up, imagine their dogs are shooting the shit with them!"

"*Are* we friends, Lorraine?" Instantly his voice softened, his smile straightened. It was as authentic a display of desire as she'd seen. He petted Pooh-Pooh on the belly and stood, close.

Could she give in and be romantic with Matt? She'd tried so hard not to, but he was not making it easy! Didn't she deserve it after all the hard work she'd been putting in—a *reward* so to speak? But would it be rewarding to hurt a friend? She knew the answer was no. She silently cursed her conscience (why did it have to show up just then????) and made an effort to be good.

"Of course!" she patted his back like a chum.

"Woah there, killer. Lotta energy today, huh?"

Maybe she was trying too hard to be friendly.

"Woof! Woof!" Pooh-Pooh broke the silence.

Lena was trying to get "things" going with Pooh-Pooh, who apparently had a "headache."

Matt gave a mini shrug. "Women," he said, shaking his head.

"Guess what happened to me today?"

"What's that? Told Guido that he needs you more than you need him?"

"In not so many words, yes."

Lorraine told him about Mallory, how she'd done her hair and been invited to the benefit.

Matt was quiet, punctuating with "hmmms" and "aha," rather than his usual rich commentary.

Lorraine told herself she wouldn't care one bit if he was thinking of Mallory in a romantic way. *Not one bit, not one bit.* She repeated it over and over, hoping to make it true. Besides, he could be thinking *anything!* About those trees swaying over there, or maybe how that woman's shirt doesn't match her skirt at all, or how sometimes fast food isn't so fast. Or maybe even about Lorraine. Not that she cared.

"And then I did all the Princesses. It was unbelievable, really."

"So how do you feel?" He finally perked up, although he didn't look exactly comfortable.

"Well, that's the thing. I'm not really sure. I mean, I know Guido was using me pretty badly by giving me no credit for the nails. But he wasn't awful. He did *ask* if he could use my nail design for the salon. And he did give me an opportunity. I mean, look, I wouldn't be here right now if it weren't for him. And Don . . . How's Don gonna feel that I ignored everything he told me? He was busy with his clients all day, but I got the feeling he was avoiding me. He was the only one who wasn't clustered around watching. Just last week he'd taken me to lunch, begged me to be patient with the Guido Method, told me how much Guido had already bent the rules for me, and here I went doing just what he asked me not to."

"Okay, okay, hold on a second." He put a gentle hand at Lorraine's back and guided her toward an empty bench. They both sat down and let their leashes go. (Pooh-Pooh had apparently been persuaded out of his "headache".) "First things first. Rock on for making it, Lorraine. Take a second and step back and be proud of yourself. There are tons of great stylists out there who never make it because they don't know how to meander the jungles of New York City business. It's a dog-eat-dog world— no offense guys—and you didn't get eaten alive. Congratulations. And as for Guido, don't you dare waste a second feeling bad, Lorraine. He held you back for as long as he could; that's the truth. He's already made tons off your nails without passing any of that on to you, and even if you wind up coloring every client who comes to the salon for the rest of your life, it doesn't hurt anything but his ego—the money still goes in his pocket. And as a good businessman, he realizes that if you're that good, he *has* to step aside and let you take the top clients. That's a hard move, but knowing your limits is the name of the game. If he doesn't treat you right, there's nothing stopping you from going elsewhere and taking the Princesses with you."

"But doesn't that seem, I don't know, *wrong,* to you? I mean, I don't want to hurt anyone's ego. I don't want to hurt anyone, period."

Matt was shaking his head, sighing. "Lorraine, it's not your fault you're good. It's not your fault you had the sense to step in when Jacqueline left."

"Yeah, but I wasn't really supposed to do that, and I knew it."

"But you saved the client for the business by doing a great job with her and sending her out addicted to Ms. Lorraine's style."

He picked up her hand then, softly. With his pointer under her palm, he gently raised each of her fingers up, looking down at her nails.

Lorraine felt something in her chest go hot, then cold. *Be a good girl, be a good girl*. But why? Why did she always have to be such a good girl? Look at Tommy. He never cared a lick for being good. What was this *curse*?

"Go on a date with me, Lorraine. Forget that jerk."

She was officially numb. Yup. Couldn't move one limb. Which was good. Because it stopped her from saying, *Yes, okay! And I'd love to show you this little pink thong I'm wearing, too!*

The thing about Matt was, not only did he listen to her—really *listen* to her—he also didn't push things. He wasn't going to force her into a date if she wasn't ready. Lorraine could see him force a change in his demeanor, put that romantic part away for the time being. And she was surprised at how sad she was to see it go.

After a few moments of silence he asked "How 'bout coffee, then?" He was back to friend Matt, just like that.

It feels like you always think of exactly the perfect thing to do, just after you've missed your opportunity. "Okay, sounds wonderful." *But didn't the other thing sound so much better?*

Lorraine and Matt snapped the leashes back onto their pets, because according to the signs, you had to in the park. They walked so close that every now and then, their elbows touched, or forearms grazed, or a tendril of Lorraine's waves tickled Matt's shoulder or arm. Lena and Pooh-Pooh played a twisty, cross-over leash game that had them zigzagging, which wasn't helping Lorraine much in the self-control area—bringing her closer to Matt then farther, and just when she was breathing normal, too close again.

They spoke of everything they had been up to and what they would be up to, and then how things looked around them and above them and through the eyes of their dogs.

"You have really gotten the hang of Pooh-Pooh, Lorraine. It's unbelievable," Matt said in between sips of a frothy cappuccino. They were at a tiny little Italian café, outside at a marble table with the two dogs at their feet.

She looked down at her dog, the whole weight of him miraculously leaning on tiny Lena, and she could swear the line of his mouth stretched into a smile. She looked up at Matt. "You didn't happen to see that, did you?"

"He just smiled at you."

Lorraine smiled at herself. She hadn't really thought about her progress with Pooh-Pooh. It struck her how rewarding the relationship was. Pooh-Pooh had fallen for her just as quickly as she'd fallen for him. Sure he'd eaten the table, but didn't everyone do crazy things for love? Just look what she'd done herself. The idea of the table, though, struck her. Maybe she could surprise Romanelli and offer Matt a fabulous opportunity, too.

"Hey, Matt, you know, I was thinking . . . I need a table, you need some furniture clients. How 'bout you make a replacement coffee table for Mrs. Romanelli? I'd love to buy a piece from you."

He sat back for a moment, stroking his chin where a beard might have been. His gaze was focused right into the organic unbleached-sugar bowl.

When it had been a minute or two, Lorraine wanted to make sure he hadn't checked out permanently. She waved a hand in front of his face. "He-lloooooooo."

Matt's gaze continued for a millisecond and then he shook himself out of the tiny coma he'd lapsed into. "Sorry. I was just designing the piece in my head. I'd love to, by the way. But I was thinking, you could use a vacation, I could use your opinion as I progress on the table . . ."

He was obviously thinking he'd revealed enough for Lorraine to know what he was proposing, but Lorraine wasn't going to let him off the hook so easily. So she raised her shoulder, turned out her palm, gesturing for him to clue her in. "And . . ."

He switched from friend to sexy and made a tiny smirk. Immediately he switched right back.

Oh, he was good! Panties—stay!

"And I want you to come hang with me in Miami."

This could put her in some serious trouble, she knew that for a fact. It was one thing to be strong and protect him from her romantic whimsy otherwise known as Tommy when she was going back to her place and locking the door four or five times. But when there were no shirts and those board shorts that hung really low on his hipbones, and only a hallway separating them, well, she could not be responsible for what might happen then! Still, she really could use a vacation. It would probably be good for her! Also, she could take Pooh-Pooh, and when else would she ever get a chance to do that? Lorraine acted on impulse, rather than sticking with the safe and comfortable. "I'd love that," she said.

They couldn't go for a while. Matt couldn't get away from work before the new year, at least—maybe a couple of months after that. At first Lorraine was disappointed. She could really use a break right at that moment. Five months was going to be hard to get through now. However, she tried not to let her disappointment show. Besides, it was probably for the best. The way she was feeling about Matt now, it could only lead to disaster. Maybe by then Lorraine would be settled with Tommy, and there wouldn't be an issue. Or who knew, maybe she'd even be over him. How many times had she said that?

"You'll love F-L," he said. "Our house is way off the main drag. There's nothing around for miles. Just sand and water. Completely secluded." Matt told her more about the place and the closest restaurants and what the dogs could do and how they'd take his family's private jet so the dogs wouldn't have to be stowed away like luggage.

Lorraine had never thought about it before, but that sounded very cruel to her. Pooh-Pooh, she commented, would probably gnaw his way into the main cabin anyhow. Not that she would know; she'd never been on a plane before.

"You've never been on a plane?" Matt's voice was soft.

"Never. Anytime my dad said 'Let's go to Disney World or Las Vegas,' my mom would say, 'What's the point? It's not Italy.' " She smiled, but it wasn't really funny.

Matt got it. "Well, I'm so glad your first time will be with me, then."

He didn't make her feel dumb or inexperienced like most people did when she told them she'd never been on a plane. He made it seem like something he was thrilled to present her with—like a beautiful gold bracelet.

Something broke between the two of them that evening. As far as Lorraine was concerned, whatever it was that had been hanging in the air, complicating things between them, had dissipated. And though she'd have to wait awhile for her first air travel journey, there were plenty of other firsts Lorraine shared with Matt over the next few days.

Always they met in the park after Lorraine and Pooh-Pooh's run, and always they ate dinner, somewhere new, somewhere Matt suggested. After the first three times, it became less of a spur-of-the-moment idea and more of a routine. At the end of the third evening at Brasserie on Park, Matt lingered at Lorraine's door a moment, looked at her like maybe he'd kiss her—or maybe he'd let her just think he would. After he turned, he said, "Tomorrow, Sushi Hana." And that had been just what Lorraine was thinking—not just that they'd get together again, but that she wanted to try that spot. She'd passed by and mentioned it to Matt once before.

They went to a spot famous for casual steaks—BLT Steak, and then the newer sister spot, BLT Fish; they sampled the Palm and the Oak Room in the Plaza and the Oyster Bar in Grand Central Station. They dined at David Burke & Donatella, had lunches at La Goulue, and ate dessert at DTUT.

It was wonderful, going with Matt to those spots. To Lorraine, it seemed he knew everything about New York—at least in terms of the architecture and the design. And now, no matter where she might be, Lorraine would find herself wondering whether something was Rococo or influenced more by the Art Deco movement; she'd admire the Federal-style row houses when she had a chance to visit the West Village. This was a New York she'd never envisioned—a world away from shopping and fashion, rushing to catch subways and fighting feisty old men for a taxi-cab. After Matt noticed Lorraine's growing interest, he invited her over to view the eight-DVD documentary series *New York* by Ric Burns, which had run on public television a few years back.

"The last time I watched something on public television," Lorraine said, "it was *Sesame Street.*"

Matt laughed his deep, warm laugh. He loved that Lorraine was "so real." He said that after some quiet contemplation, with the straight posture of his that made you feel he was giving you all of his attention—everything he was. And she knew that he didn't mean she was dumb, or unsophisticated. It was a compliment—one, she realized, that wasn't so different from being "good people." In fact, it was just the same. It meant a lot to her that he'd seen this in her. She cared a great deal what Matt thought of her in general. Which got her thinking, what did she think about herself?

Lorraine thought about her relationship with Tommy—with all the hiding acceptance letters and acting differently in public she hadn't always been "so real." Just now . . . just now was "real" really becoming a trait of hers. And only when Matt pointed it out did Lorraine realize it was something that made a difference. If she really thought about it, Lorraine *felt* different. She wasn't one half of a set of Bobbsey Twins. She wasn't Tommy's girl. She was finding things that interested her, and her alone—things she wanted to read about, research, experience. There was more room in her mind and heart now that she hadn't spoken to Tommy in a while.

But the question remained: Was she merely filling time until he called, or would this new Lorraine stick? She wasn't sure. However, for the first time in history, she hadn't sat home waiting for him to call, hadn't run out at the first rumor she'd heard of him with some other girl. For the first time, Lorraine was just being Lorraine.

And so, when the day of the gala for the Association for Poor Girls Who Want Bigger Boobs drew near, the new Lorraine didn't approach it with the same cynicism and condescension she normally would have. In fact, the new Lorraine was surprised to find herself rather excited.

MEMORANDUM

To: J to the L.O.

From: Samantha (S to the Amantha?)

September 31, 2004

Dear J to the L.O.,

I found this in my in-box this morning. It is a review of a colorist that is due to appear in the February edition of *Allure*. I know you were looking for a new colorist and so I went and had her do my hair and she was the best! So nice, too—real neighborhood girl just like you! And she treated me like a queen, even though she had no idea who I was! Everyone was gathered around watching her like she was a real star.

Your faithful assistant,
Samantha

eBay auction block #13
Description: Memo from J. Lo's assistant Samantha, informing her employer of a brand-new stylist in town—the one and only Lorraine Machuchi.

Opening bid: $550
Winning bid: $3500 by Jtothelo@jtothelo.com

Comments: My hair has never looked as good as it does now that Lorraine is my stylist. I will save this forever.

THIRTEEN

♥

THE BEAUTY OF BORROWING

The only time Lorraine had ever heard of personal shoppers was when she'd watched *Lifestyles of the Rich and Famous* with Chrissy. They'd watch it in the summer, hair semi-damp, forming crunchy S-waves over their shoulders, after hours in the pool in Petey's yard, their skin too tanned and flaking at the surface. They were high school freshmen then (or "fresh*women*" as they often corrected), so freakin' bold with the idea of everything lying out before them—the fresh denim binders they'd just bought, the paper lined with the slim rows for writing. They thought it looked nicer with their bubbly print and script, hearts topping *i*'s wherever possible, new shiny locker mirrors and folders in rainbow colors.

Robin Leach was telling the audience, as the camera squeezed in on an elegant department store with pink carpets, that Wonder Woman, Lynda Carter, had a personal shopper. She was too busy to buy her own gifts, to choose her own wardrobe, and besides, she wasn't great at it. "After all," she joked, "I'm no Wonder Woman." Of course Robin Leach laughed. It was his job to laugh. But the girls had said what they thought he couldn't: *Obnoxious.* That was the word they'd used to describe the idea. *Too good to choose your own clothes?* The whole idea smacked of snobbery and supremacy to the both of them. After that, when they'd see old reruns of *Wonder Woman* on TV, they'd sing in unison, "Bitch!" and then they'd laugh as if it were the funniest idea in the world.

What would Chrissy and that girl say of Lorraine now? By the end of September, Tabby in the junior's department had become Lorraine's own personal shopper of sorts. They worked on barter. Tabby was one of those change addicts, and she would alter her hair color the way someone else might switch shoes. Lorraine had colored Tabby's hair four times by then, free of charge, and now that Lorraine was actually an official senior stylist with a top clientele, Tabby was treating her with even more importance. She'd say Lorraine's name loudly when she arrived so everyone would know the stylist written up in *Page Six* that very morning depended on Bendel's very own Tabby for her wardrobe decisions. The girl had a dollar sign tattooed to her arm. Literally.

"Lorraine Machuchi!" she boomed with a big voice, throwing herself on Lorraine in a deluge of kisses and hugs. "Have I got a dress for you! You know I don't really work in the formal department, but when I told the manager it was for you, she said, 'Go right ahead!'"

Lorraine didn't know just how she felt about the heads turning her way, ostensibly wondering who she was, assessing whether or not they should emulate her long nails or laugh at them, love the way she wore her hair or imagine their own style a better choice. On the one hand, she'd never been much for the spotlight, but on the other hand, she now understood the importance of fame. The more visibility you got, the more people who knew about you, the more business you got.

It was a lesson that came easily. Ever since that fateful Princess day, Lorraine's life was barely recognizable as a direct result of the publicity the event had afforded her.

"Just wait until the monthly magazine articles come out in a few months," Don had said to her over lunch the previous day. "*Allure*'s Most Wanted fetches the best results. You'll be booked for the next millennium straight." Don had been quiet, much more reserved toward her for the past week.

In fact, she was thrilled he was going to lunch with her at all. She missed him. Sure, there were other assistants and stylists she could lunch with, but Don was her friend. And she hated to think she'd damaged that. A few days away from him really cemented that fact for her. Still, she'd understood and wanted to give him space to work through whatever he had to.

Probably, she'd thought, he'd taken some slack from Guido about Lorraine's audacious behavior, since he'd been the one to find her. But she guessed now that Matt was probably right to a certain extent—that after the reality settled in, Guido had likely reassessed his business plan to include Lorraine. One thing was clear—whatever had happened, Guido now had a calmer, if not rosier, outlook on the whole thing. And Lorraine guessed that had eased Don's situation somewhat.

"You should ask for a raise," Matt had advised her after she'd shared with him Don's warming trend. She might have known Matt would have some idea like that tucked in his head—he was always looking toward the next step, looking for more. She could see how his family would find him indispensable to their business. Still, she wasn't quite ready for another jump, and for the moment, she was happy just to be doing what she wanted, to have the Florida trip to look forward to, even a television spot lined up with *Today* in a few weeks' time. There was a lot to be happy about.

Besides, she still had to get used to all this attention. That reality hit her once again as she and Tabby made their way to the dress department. They passed the rounders and the wall racks, paillettes and lace, silk chiffon and organza, like the most stylish labyrinth in all the world—all the way to a secret room, done up in marble and blond wood, a leather wing chair with nail heads to one side.

"Ta-da!" Tabby said so loud the two syllables echoed in the room, smacking Lorraine repeatedly in the face, making her wince.

She didn't judge Tabby's overexuberance, her theatrical display. Though they had different manners, Lorraine could understand wanting to be part of something, feeling blindsided by the desire, not knowing how to act. She'd been there before. "Tabby, it is gorgeous. Oh my god, is it gorgeous." And it was. Silk. The most tiny bodice that could lend anyone a miniature China doll look. Strapless, and from the waist, the floorlength skirt feathered out in thousands of chiffon layers, or rather leaves, fluttering weightlessly with each step. She gingerly touched a finger to one, afraid she might damage this beautiful dress that was surely meant for someone else—some Princess or a Queen.

The dress hugged Lorraine perfectly. Her new, light musculature gave her tall frame a delicate precision that offset the softness of the dress beautifully. But the gown's most outstanding characteristic was the color. Never had Lorraine seen a color like this—a bold Caribbean Sea blue. It was everywhere, all you could see. It made her dark hair brilliant in the light, her dark eyes intense. It wasn't the kind of thing the old Lorraine would have chosen, waiting in the background for Tommy to finish whatever, or whomever, he was doing at the moment. But now, here, for the new Lorraine, it was perfect.

They both stood staring at her in the mirror for a moment. Even Tabby was speechless. "How much?" Lorraine asked as soon as the question popped in her head. It was the Band-Aid theory: get the pain over with as quickly as possible so you can move on.

"Do you really want to know?"

"Is it that bad?"

"Yeah."

"Are you gonna tell me, or do I have to read your mind, Tabby?"

Tabby's face was all puckered up, like she was about to give a deadly prognosis to her patient.

"Just rip off the Band-Aid, Tabby. Go ahead, tell me." Lorraine's eyes softened. Already, she was bracing for disappointment. She couldn't have a dress like that. Sure, she'd never cared or even dreamed up any gown like that before. But now she was here, and knew the reality, the potential of things, and wanting could hurt her. It could hurt her to realize that in a Princess's world, she wasn't really a Princess. She was just Lorraine Machuchi, Guidette who happened to be a good colorist.

She barely even heard Tabby read from a piece of paper a number that could pay for the state of Massachusetts. Twice.

The illusion had been ruined. Who did Lorraine think she was going to a ball, anyway? Wearing these clothes? Living on Park Avenue? Freakin' Cinderella? *Please.* She started to unzip the dress, awkwardly positioning her elbows behind her waist, watching herself as the material around her loosened, fell to the ground, revealing the real Lorraine—a medley of stretch marks and scars that told the story of her life. She even noticed a small tear in her Cosabella bra.

Apparently, Tabby saw the desperation in her face, because her own screwed up sadly. She opened her mouth to say something and then stopped, cupped one hand over her mouth, and with the other smacked herself in the forehead. "Wait a fucking minute! Lorraine, I think I have a way to get you in this dress!"

"Paging Caroline Simons! Paging Caroline Simons!" Tabby's voice boomed out over the P.A. system before she hung up the receiver with a bang. "Caroline's the formal department manager! She can let you *borrow* the dress if she wants to, if we explain to her how important it will be for Bendel's that you look fabulous at the event. That you get photographed in the hottest dress of the season!"

Boy, Tabby was smart. That sounded like a great idea to Lorraine, who, grabbing at the dress like a couture life preserver, made a silent prayer to her grandmother to help her out this one time. *I know, Grandma. I swear, I am not wearing it for Tommy. It's for me.* She wasn't sure if it was true or not, but she hoped there was a chance it might be. It was a wonderful thought, anyhow.

Caroline, however, didn't see quite the same novelty in the idea that the girls did. To her it must have sounded a lot like something she was asked to do about nine million times a day because without looking up from a pile of paperwork she was paging through, she said, "Girls, I get asked the very same thing about nine million times a day."

"But but this is Lorraine Machuchi! You know, Lorraine!"

Caroline yawned, closed her eyes for a stretch, and then said, unimpressed, "And what exactly does that mean to me?"

"She can do your hair for free!"

"You gotta do better than that. I haven't paid for a haircut or dye job since 1982."

"She can do your nails!"

"Those Guido Nails are kinda cute, but still, a *manicure* isn't getting anyone in that dress." She flipped a page soundlessly.

Just when it seemed the most hopeless and the girls were exchanging glances of disappointment, Lorraine saw Tabby's whole face light up, like a Christmas tree plugged in for the first time. She had something. She had something that was going to get Lorraine in the dress. You just knew she did. "She was personally invited by the Princesses. She's sitting at their table."

Caroline stood, turned, and started making her way to the door. Without so much as a lilt to her voice she said, "Well, why didn't you say that in the first place? Have it back the next day, with no stains, or it's your bank account. I'll call shoes and fine jewelry and tell them to expect you."

If you've never had your foot in a two thousand dollar pair of shoes, you might as well skip this paragraph. Instead of reading, just go right out to the closest Barney's or Jeffrey's and do yourself a favor and try one on. Because if you don't you'll never *really* know. You just won't believe what happens to you. There is a shoe and then there is A SHOE. One is something with a function that could, on occasion, look cute or sexy or professional, pull together an otherwise drab outfit instantly with the right belt or brooch—which are all, undoubtedly, wonderful assets. The other, though. *Marona Mia!* The other is a work of art. It's what makes women hide credit card statements from their husbands. It's what makes women hide credit card statements from themselves.

Lorraine of "What, this shirt? I got it at H&M for $8.99" fame didn't know. So, when she slipped her foot into the Jimmy Choo sandal, with its enormous white crystal topped thong, she was utterly unprepared for the flutter that shot through her.

Shit, she was hot. She knew it. She felt it. And she tried, desperately, not to think what Tommy would say if he saw her like this.

The necklace Tabby chose for her was tiny, fragile—a woven choker of diamond-encrusted golden leafy vines.

That night, in front of the wall of mirrors in Mrs. Romanelli's dressing room, Lorraine sat with her legs flung over the side of a dainty wood chair with its spindly arms and legs in her beautiful, expensive dress and her beautiful, expensive shoes and scary expensive necklace, and really looked at herself. And while she continued to force all Tommy thoughts from her mind, Lorraine asked herself a frightening question. If he ever finally did leave, once and for all, what would she fill all that empty space with?

With all those uncomfortable thoughts swirling in her head, Lorraine took a nap in a very pricey ensemble in a very uncomfortable position.

When she woke, and saw herself thus, she panicked—she saw in the mirror a girl she didn't recognize. A girl who was changing. The shock of the realization rumbled through her system, and she leapt up, suddenly desperate to take all the glamorous items from her body. She needed to get herself on the first train to Brooklyn for a dose of the familiar.

As soon as she'd made the decision, Lorraine felt more like herself. She recognized the thoughts swimming around her head with more conviction. She pulled on an old pair of jeans, the ones that used to be her favorites. And then, realizing they just didn't look as good, she tossed them aside and jumped her way into the Citizen jeans. *You're allowed to change a little. Aren't you?*

Lorraine grabbed her purse from the side table near the couch, went to the door, and tried to make a run for it before Pooh-Pooh noticed. But no sooner had she locked the door than the barks began—loud, then even louder. It was a desperate cry, and it seemed to Lorraine to say, *Don't leave me! Don't leave me!*

She knew that feeling. She hated to be left behind herself. She pressed the elevator button, but when the door opened and showed the porter's smiling face, Lorraine couldn't bring herself to ignore Pooh-Pooh's cries.

"Never mind," she whispered, fingering that Trump-worthy necklace she realized she'd left on.

As much as she might try to deny it, Lorraine had a life here in Manhattan now. She wasn't just a Brooklyn girl. Not that there was anything wrong with that—but there was someone new emerging inside of her. Or, she thought as she walked back, perhaps not so much new as rediscovered. This particular Lorraine had always been there somewhere, just hadn't had a chance to come out and see the Art Deco architecture in Rockefeller Center.

Lorraine clipped the leash onto Pooh-Pooh and said, in the spirit of her old summer joke, "Let's get the hell outta Dodge." But it wasn't summer anymore. And Pooh-Pooh didn't get the joke. But Lorraine and her furry friend had a hell of a run anyhow, and enjoyed the night in the way they'd come to do together.

Dear Lorraine,

I love you. I love you. I love you. I love you. I love you. But I must know HOW COULD YOU DO THIS DO ME? How could you leave me for that LOSER, Tommy? I know you warned me, but when you kissed me like that behind the bowling alley, I never would have guessed in a million years that you actually meant it. And then I saw you there at the prom, by yourself, and it nearly broke my heart to see you like that—staring at him with that college girl, who was nothing compared to you. You have broken my heart, Lorraine, and all for nothing. You know we could have been great together.

Love and hate 4-eva,
Ryan Levy

eBay auction block #14
Description: Love letter from Lorraine's high-school peer, Ryan Levy. In her official biography, *B Girl,* Lorraine claims it was the experience with Ryan that made her so cautious about starting anything with Matt.

Opening bid: $120
Winning bid: $2500 by tommyl@aol.com

Comments: Yeah, sucka! That's right! It happened once; it will happen again!!!!!!!

FOURTEEN

♥

SHE'S A PRINCESS, ALL RIGHT

Prom night hadn't been all that wonderful for Lorraine. Sure, her hair looked fabulous. It always did. And she'd made a couple of bucks styling some of the other girls' updos, using her mother's kitchen sink, table and chairs as style central. At twenty-five bucks a pop, she'd pulled in nearly $200. Her mother had screamed her head off in Italian the whole time. "*Santo Giovanni! Santo Giovanni!*" But Lorraine was careful to have the hair cleaned up constantly. She'd paid her brother a couple of bucks to do it. And it hadn't been hard to convince him, what with all those girls there for him to ogle. Lorraine wasn't sure he'd even thought about anything else between the years of 1984–2000. He'd zipped that broom around so fast, you thought he might take off.

But she'd planned poorly. She'd thought for sure Tommy would ask her based on a comment he'd made two years prior. "I can't wait for our prom. It's going to be so awesome to be able to get the fuck outta here. Ya know? You'll look all pretty with your strapless dress and heels and your hair up. And we'll be saying goodbye for good to this place." They'd been in the schoolyard, drinking off-brand beers with blue-and-white labels you could peel off in one piece, when he said it. Lorraine remembered clearly that it had been a steamy summer day, and Tommy had his shirt off. All the guidos did. Lorraine and Chrissy had been wearing those tiny bandeau tops under cotton one-piece short outfits, belted with a stretchy cotton band—bright as can be in Day-Glo colors. The day had grown hotter and more uncomfortable to Lorraine then—another far-off date to feel impatient for.

Sure. It hadn't been a proposal exactly. But somewhere in her mind, she'd settled on the idea that they would go together. And each morning when she woke to face another day of disappointment—Tommy not saying or doing anything to indicate Lorraine was anything more than a friend—she could grab on to that image of herself in the strapless gown, Tommy swinging the limousine door open to escort her inside the backseat, tiny glittering lights all over the ceiling, changing colors from pink to blue and then green.

A month before, she'd reserved a limo with Chrissy and Big Bobby— it would be just the four of them. The day was getting closer and closer, but Lorraine still hadn't faced reality. Standing on a footstool in her kitchen, watching her mom with a rare smile on her face, singing an old Frank Sinatra song while she pinned the hem of Lorraine's dress for shortening—iridescent chiffon and lace overlay—she still refused to think about it. Tommy hadn't mentioned the prom, and Lorraine had been too afraid to bring it up. She'd started to hear rumors that Tommy was bringing some college girl from Staten Island.

Lorraine lived that final week leading up to prom the way she lived a lot of her life—in her head. Dreaming up scenarios about how she would be kissed, and what posture she would hold before the camera, and how Tommy might brush a curl from her face when the band played "Hold Onto the Night."

But Tommy did go with that girl from Staten Island. And Lorraine watched from her bedroom window, biting that stuffed lion from the Bronx Zoo, mushing its fur. She was paralyzed. They must have spent forty-five minutes out there, Tommy's mother snapping photos on their yellowed lawn, sometimes stepping back onto their neighbor's perfectly green one to get the right angle, the proper distance.

All she could think, standing there, the sun just beginning to sink and send rays of pink and orange over their street and the five twisty shrubs between them, was how unbelievable he looked in a tuxedo. She noticed how his hair looked so dark against the crisp white of his collar, how nicely his jacket fit. She calmed herself thinking of Tommy, enjoying him like that. And although the night would be a torturous series of disappointments, one leading into the next until she was numb to it all, Lorraine knew she at least had enjoyed that much. And no college girl from Staten Island could take that away from her.

Tonight, eleven years later, in a borough that felt more like a world away, was Lorraine so far from that girl at her bedroom window? That girl alone in the back of a stretch Cadillac limousine? She tried to make this night about herself. She tried to make it not about Tommy. But, all dressed up this way, looking so glamorous, it was impossible not to think of him and what he would say and what he might think and whether she met his expectations.

Lorraine took one final look at herself in the mirror, her diamonds sparkling in the light along with the shimmery pigments of her charcoal eyeshadow. Lorraine had the palest pink lipcolor on, with a high-shine clear gloss over it. Her blush was a natural rosy hue that mimicked her true blush. High in color, she looked alive and vibrant. Lorraine gently placed the essentials in her evening bag—a hard, golden shell she'd borrowed from Mrs. Romanelli. The woman had told her she could use anything she liked. "My God! Someone should! This crap cost me a fortune!"

In the taxi Lorraine saw Manhattan in a hushed, glittery blur flashing past. It was right after Fashion Week, and the ball was being thrown in the same tents in which the shows had been held. Lorraine had actually been allowed to style and color some of the extensions they'd used in the Peter Som and Oscar de la Renta shows—she'd been requested. The excitement buzzed as people zipped back and forth preparing what she could feel would be something extraordinary. Right away Lorraine noticed the tents had been reconfigured to make one grand ballroom.

They'd added boatloads of tiny white lights, suspended like twisty branches all around the perimeter of the room and from each corner, meeting all the way up at the very top of the tent. Each table had a centerpiece of white roses. Everything was white—white linen tablecloths, two white candles beside the flowers. There were tiny white boxes with tiny white bows at each place setting of white china—rimmed in an elegant weave. And most important to the paparazzi and the television crews with their microphones and cameras, was the white catwalk where, one by one, each perfect looking attendee entered.

The pomp accompanying each entrance forced Lorraine to wait for a good fifteen minutes on a queue before actually entering the party. Looking up and down the line of tuxedos and ball gowns, Lorraine couldn't believe she was part of this, rather than looking in from the outside, wondering what all the fuss was over. It had never been her goal to get here, but then again, she hadn't ever had many goals aside from the one that was becoming increasingly clear to her would never materialize.

Now that she was here, though, it was clear to Lorraine why the rush of it all could be so alluring, and she couldn't help but get swept away. The whole scene was exactly as she'd seen it pictured in movies—the moments that would make you grin so big you couldn't wipe it off if you tried, the scenes where Lorraine and Chrissy always sighed and knocked their heads together, dreaming of what their own most wonderful moments would be like.

Looking with a more discerning eye, she noticed the Hilton sisters, that wacky magician guy she couldn't remember the name of, Cybil Shepard, Tyra Banks, that Avril Lavigne chick. There was Diddy and Kanye West and Ben Affleck with Jennifer Garner and Matt Damon. She saw Steven Baldwin and that daughter from the Osbournes—Kitty or Katie or something.

Lorraine's heart was racing as she started to realize that she was where everyone in the world wanted to be. She was at the party the E! Channel would be featuring the following day. She knew this because they were right there—filming everyone, with that annoying woman with the raspy voice helming it all. This was cool. Seriously cool. Wait a minute! Just one minute! Was that Jennifer Lopez? She LOVED Jenny from the Block!

"Jennifer! Hi, Jennifer! I'm a huge fan! Huge!" The second it came from her mouth, Lorraine wanted to grab the words with her fist and stuff them back down her throat. That was not the kind of girl she was—another starstruck rookie! How? How could she be such a moron? And then it occurred to her that she'd never been afraid to tell people what she thought. Why should it be any different with a star like Jennifer Lopez? Hell, she was from the block!

Jennifer took one look at Lorraine's nails and whispered something to her bodyguard before coming over to her.

"Are those Guido Nails?" Jennifer asked, her skin just as creamy as it looked on television. She really did have great skin!

Lorraine thought she had such a sweet way about her. Every time she'd watched those specials about her, she'd thought she would be someone Lorraine would really get on with. She couldn't believe J. Lo knew about Guido Nails, and in a roundabout way, knew about her! "Why, yes, they are! In fact, I'm Lorraine Machuchi—the inspiration for the Guido Nails." Okay, so that was a little lame, she thought after she'd nearly screamed it.

But J. Lo didn't seem to think so. "Lorraine? You're Lorraine? Get out!" And then Jennifer Lopez proceeded to push Lorraine back with both hands—*Seinfeld* style—until she nearly fell on the floor. Her voice reached a squeal as she exclaimed, "Lorraine, the stylist at Guido's in Bendel's?"

"Yup, that's me," Lorraine said, hardly believing it herself. Surely, this was a dream. Surely, her grandmother would appear indecently clad—laughing and cursing—at any moment now.

"Please give my assistant here your information. She told me all about you! I'll be off shooting a movie for a while, but when I get back I would love to have you do my hair. I know you've done the Princesses, and they look fabulous! Just fabulous!" Then she winked at Lorraine and said, "Stay cool, girl. See you soon." And like that, Jennifer Lopez was gone.

Holy cow! Shit! *#$%!! She was stunned, barely noticing Christy Brinkley getting interviewed at the head of the line. The scene was slowly imprinting itself onto Lorraine's mind. But as soon as it sank in, Lorraine felt the overwhelming need to tell someone about it. Jennifer Lopez wanted Lorraine to style her hair. Jennifer Lopez. But who would she tell?

This opportunity, like everything lately, had its ups and downs. She could come to this fabulous event—but only had one ticket. She rubbed her forearms up and down, her lack of a companion suddenly stinging.

She'd never been alone so much in her life, but she rarely felt it as severely as she did just then. Of course, Chrissy was the obvious choice. But Lorraine had let things go between them. So had Chrissy. Would her friend see it that way? Or did she feel deserted, plain and simple? They hadn't spoken in so long, Lorraine was sure there would be a fog of tension between them when they finally did. How long had it been since they'd spoken? Lorraine tried to think back. Could it possibly have been a whole entire month since she'd uttered a single word to the person she'd seen every day of her life up until August?

That last conversation had left such a sour taste in Lorraine's mouth. Now, though, Lorraine was growing increasingly aware of the fact that Chrissy had just been acting in the same manner she always had. It was Lorraine who'd changed, and she'd been strangely intolerant of anyone who hadn't. Still, how would she mend things? The longer she left things, the worse it would be. She thought about that fact about twenty-seven times a day, but Lorraine hadn't been able to bring herself to phone her friend. And as a result, Chrissy didn't even know about Lorraine's weekend with Tommy. She didn't know the disappointment that had followed. It was all just part of the widening rift between them. It seemed Lorraine would need a year to catch her friend up on everything that had led her to this point.

But, maybe, just maybe, she was taking this all too seriously. Maybe it was easier than that. Maybe friends were always friends, no matter what changes forced a gap between them. On the off-chance that might be true, Lorraine tried her friend's own Teen Line. "Hey, peeps. Miss Chris isn't here right now. You know what to do."

When the long beep gave way to silence, Lorraine found herself in a predicament that seemed familiar these days: she didn't know what to say. But, in the seconds before she spoke, in the familiar lilt of Chrissy's voice, the tone of which she knew so well, in the room and all its belongings that echoed in each word, she did know one thing for sure. She loved her friend, and although things were strained between them just then, they would work it out. And so she spoke. "Hey, there, Miss Chris. It's your other Bobbsey Twin here. And guess who she just saw? Jennifer Freakin' Lopez!!!!!!"

There was a fair amount of crackling and then a beep, a click, and finally, like a warm sweater on a freezing cold day, Chrissy's voice. "Get the fuck out of here!!!!!!!!"

"Seriously." Lorraine could feel her smile broadening uncontrollably.

"Where are you?"

"I'm at this ball for the Association for Poor Girls Who Want Bigger Boobs."

There was silence that Lorraine took as Chrissy's consideration of this idea.

"You're kidding, right?"

"Totally serious."

Finally, wonderfully, the laughter they'd always shared was there, bridging their gap, at least for the moment.

"They should have picked you."

"Hey, I've got plenty."

"For a thirteen-year-old boy, sure."

"Chris?" In her rows and rows of hand-sewn silk chiffon feathers, her smoky eyes, and perfectly rosy cheeks, Lorraine felt the comfortable rush of familiarity with her oldest, closest friend—and that same torn feeling she had in her Mercedes that night. She wanted to run all the way home to Seventy-seventh Street, but at the same time she couldn't be happier just where she was standing. But this time, she felt the Brooklyn in her rise up, fill her so densely it expanded over the whole line and the tent beyond. Finally she was able to recognize it for what it was: pride. Sure she'd made plenty of mistakes. But there were some good choices, too. Either way, she'd missed her best friend. She hadn't realized how much until then.

"What?"

"I miss you. Will you come in and hang with me soon?"

"Sure," Chrissy said.

It didn't sound necessarily certain that she would. But it was a start. They would find their way, navigating the new landscape of their friendship. Of that, Lorraine was certain.

★   ★   ★

When she clicked her phone shut, Lorraine fixed her eyes on the entrance, just a few feet ahead. Soon she'd be entering the party. The media—a cartoonish cloud of mikes and booms, cameras and gossip show hosts, now busy with that redheaded woman from *The X-Files*—would either recognize her or not. She wasn't sure, with the fluttering in her chest, which she would prefer. Lorraine fidgeted at the clasp of her purse, feeling not exactly self-conscious, but maybe a little lonely—maybe a little conscious of her solitude. Maybe a little lone-*lier* now she remembered her friend and felt so far from her, both in distance and experience.

But she didn't have much time to consider the idea. In a series of *click-clacks*, one leading, three behind, the Princesses came upon her, cutting the whole line, celebrities and all, to join her for the grand entrance by the paparazzi. Mallory, Stacey Reed, Tracey Levin, and Katharine James were dressed all in pink. They'd decided to do it that way. "For Breast Cancer," the three secondary Princesses clarified Mallory's statement.

"Oh, you're raising funds for the pink ribbon campaign?"

They looked dumbfounded. A couple of mumbles told Lorraine they were just wearing pink, and thought maybe they should associate it with a reason.

"You must always have a purpose, or the press will forget about you." That's what Katharine said, with obviously no concern over the morality of the statement, her eyes darting around to see who there was to be seen by, her lips rubbing her gloss over her mouth, pouting up in preparation for the camera.

"And who are you wearing?" Katharine asked Lorraine.

"Oscar de la Renta," Lorraine said, though Katharine barely paid mind to her answer, smoothing her hair down and fluffing up the bottom.

The next few minutes ran by so quickly, Lorraine barely knew what transpired. Mallory grabbed her hand, squeezed it. The redhead from the *X-Files* moved past the flashbulbs, exclamations of "Just one last question!," quickly scribbling pencils, microphones and Joan Rivers and her ever-thinning daughter, whom Lorraine recognized from that show she'd grown addicted to a few years back, *I'm a Celebrity, Now Get Me Out of Here*. Lorraine and Chrissy had enjoyed a good run with that line. They could be at the bowling alley, and out of boredom scream, "*I'm a celebrity, now get me out of here!"* The guys didn't get it. "Where the hell you wanna go?" they'd ask.

"Oh, Mallory Meen! And the Princesses! All in pink? Tell me darling, why are you in pink?" Joan asked, her familiar rasp extremely endearing in person.

"Yeah! Why pink?" and "What's with the pink!" "Over here!" And "Who's that girl in the turquoise?" From farther off, Lorraine heard her name on someone's lips. She couldn't tell who, with the glare from the lights, and the music blaring in the background, and so much movement overall, but she distinctly heard, "The colorist! She's doing the Princesses, and Jennifer Lopez, too!"

"And . . ." Mallory grabbed the microphone, cleared her throat. She squeezed Lorraine's hand then, too. "She's the newest Princess. We all took a vote. We decided we needed a representative who was more, shall we say . . . *colorful.* Colorful is the new black this year. Everyone knows it. Nobody wants to be wasp-y. It's all about edge. And Lorraine is the best colorist in the city. She has a hell of an edge. Lorraine Machuchi is the newest Princess."

"Ohmigod!" "Hhhhuuuuuuuuu!!!!!" There were so many gasps, you could swear you were in a hospital room, having just received some terrible news. *"Your baby has two heads,"* a doctor might have said, his voice slightly muffled behind the scrubs. Lorraine didn't think even that would incite as much chaos and upheaval.

For her part, Lorraine felt not unlike how Frankenstein's monster must have when people saw him for the first time. She could just picture Mallory, Katharine, Stacey, and the other one all sitting around in a laboratory, in matching pink lab coats, deciding on their newest project, how they would affect the trends this month. How they would present their pet project to the public. *For immediate release: Strange strain of society actually comes from Brooklyn . . . of all places.*

"And we are presenting Lorraine with this honorary ribbon for breast cancer, the cause we are all dressed for tonight." With an icy touch, Mallory pinned Lorraine's dress with the ribbon, right at the very top of the bodice, to the applause of many—Lorraine couldn't tell just who. How was she supposed to feel? What did this mean, exactly? In a way it was wonderful. It was obvious this was big—but big success or big disaster? It wasn't exactly clear.

In a blinding series of photo snaps, questions, a microphone in her hand, and a video light illuminating her diamond necklace, Lorraine was presented to New York society.

"Lorraine, your dress, tell us who you're wearing, darling. All those feathers, it's *gawgous*!" Joan Rivers approved.

"Oh, it's too beautiful for me! I feel like . . . like I'm impersonating a person who would wear this dress! Someone like, I don't know maybe—"

Joan interrupted with a shriek. "Sarah Jessica Parker, ladies and gentlemen!" She handled the introduction as if the girl were a miracle she'd just witnessed.

But Sarah Jessica, even before she acknowledged Joan, tapped Lorraine's shoulder from behind. When Lorraine turned around, Sarah Jessica was right in front of her. And she was wearing the very same dress!

"Holy shit!" Lorraine screamed it and then cupped her mouth. "Oops."

"I knew you had good taste!" Sarah Jessica exclaimed. She wasn't even phased by having a dress twin.

"See, Joan, now *this* is the kind of person who should really be wearing this kind of dress."

"Sarah Jessica, did you hear that Lorraine here is the newest Princess?"

"Wow! That's so cool!"

A different microphone was stuck in Lorraine's face as Joan moved onto Sarah Jessica's interview.

"Lorraine, what about the cause? The APGBB? What do you think of the *cause*?"

She thought of her friend, Chrissy, just then, and how comfortable she'd instantly felt, just knowing Chrissy existed—that somewhere, no matter where, she was in Lorraine's corner. "They should have picked me," she said, pulling at the bodice of her dress with a Guido Nail to emphasize the point.

It was a funny bit. Lorraine didn't know it then, but it had sealed her fate. She *was* the colorful Princess. And tomorrow it would say so wherever it mattered.

Her gut told her the whole thing was a bit ridiculous. Still, she couldn't mistake the rush coursing through her, the pride she walked with, hand in hand with Mallory Meen, head Princess. A couple of girls in jeans were leaning over the rope that held back the onlookers. Lorraine smiled at them. A few minutes ago she *was* them. But who was she *now?*

Her mother would be proud. That was for sure. Her grandmother, too. Her next trip home would probably be the proudest moment of her mother's life. Who knew what Tommy would make of it. When he saw her in the paper, on television, he'd probably be right back at her doorstep. And sick as it was, the thought excited her. Wasn't he the reason for all this, if you really thought about it?

One thing Lorraine hadn't considered, still hadn't really zeroed in on during all of it, though, was how *she* felt. Would she even know how to figure that out?

"Lorraine, you have to meet Senator Lieberman, and Hillary." She was pulled one way. "Oh, Lorraine, you *must* try the caviar. It's delightful." A tiny pancake filled with a mound of black fish eggs and fresh cream was passed into her palm. She had to admit it was delightful—salty and sweet, not at all what she would have imagined. "Have you met our newest Princess?" Mallory said to one man, and then three women, another man, a couple, a woman, another couple, and then, finally, someone with a voice that registered with her like cozy pajamas after a long day in heels even before she looked up to see his face.

"Why, yes, we have met," Matt said.

In the disorientation of seeing someone out of context, of being so out of context yourself, it took Lorraine a good minute or two to recognize Matt. He was wearing a tuxedo, the kind with a vest and an old-fashioned necktie. His hair was freshly gelled and he smelled of aftershave. He looked, unwavering, until his blink brought them both to a sharp breath. He was hot, with a hint of tan to his complexion, like a ripened fruit. Still, knowing what he looked like outside of this room was so comforting. He'd been able to do the one thing she hadn't managed to do herself, despite J. Lo's recognition and the fact that she'd just been announced as part of the most well-known group in the room, the city, the world—he made her feel like she *belonged.*

"I didn't know you'd be here. How come you didn't mention it?" Lorraine asked, unable to wipe the smile from her face.

"Of course I'm here. I can recognize a good cause when I see one." He lifted his eyebrows twice like Groucho Marx. "I thought it'd be more fun to surprise you. And boy, was I right."

"I've always been a supporter of the poor, formerly underserved, flatchested population of America, myself." And then, more serious than she'd imagined it in her head, "And as for seeing you here. I'm definitely surprised. Pleasantly so."

"Oh, *Matty-Pooh!*" Mallory rushed over to where they were both standing, embracing Matt with a real hug, the sort Mallory hadn't given to anyone the whole night—in fact it was the opposite of the feathery touch she tried to pull off as a hug. "Have you met our newest Princess? Lorraine is just so *colorful*, don't you think? Say *New Yawk,* Lorraine, would you?"

Lorraine did not appreciate this new description of herself. She hadn't a desire to be the token anyone. In fact, this was just the sort of thing she couldn't stand in City Bi-atches. She was just about to open her mouth and tell Mallory where to stick it when Matt gently squeezed her side, urging her to let it slide. He whispered in her ear, "Remember your career, Lorraine."

Her jaw was aching from the pressure of retaining a smile. She wasn't sure she was keeping quiet just for her career, or merely because she couldn't care less what the members of this circus thought of her. In some greater sense, she nearly understood that it didn't matter at all what description they lent her, that she would become well-known just the same. Cases in point: Paris Hilton, Anna Nicole Smith. She wasn't even sure how she felt about the possibility of celebrity. For the moment, Lorraine was coasting on autopilot, just letting everything happen, seeing where it might take her. People's opinions had never bothered her in the past, and maybe they wouldn't now, now when it really mattered to keep a stiff upper lip.

The one thing that did bother her, though, was keeping her opinion to herself. Lorraine decided that though she might be able to appear gracious and tolerant, she still had to be true to herself. If you let someone think they could do whatever they wanted to you, they would walk all over you. And Lorraine never let that happen to her. Except, of course, with Tommy, which she guessed made her all the more intolerant of it elsewhere. There were ways to say things so people knew where you stood.

"Oh, *Melanie*, you're so silly." She smiled that bitchy-sweet smile.

Mallory looked thoughtful, then smirked. "Laurie, you're just so colorful. Isn't she colorful, *Matty-Pooh*?"

"Colorful. Definitely, Melanie."

Mallory's face experienced a severe gravity pull, her color racing toward a fiery boiling point. Then, catching herself, forcing her smile to return, Mallory went to pull Lorraine away from Matt. As she did, Matt leaned in and said softly at Lorraine's ear, "Promise me a dance."

"I solemnly swear."

And she was off, their intimacy hanging about her like a halo, strengthening her.

In the ladies' room, Lorraine knew there was a stylist on hand, "refreshing" everyone's hair. It was her salon who'd been assigned this honor, after a bidding war had been conducted by all of the top salons in the city. "We'll put full-size shampoos and conditioners in the gift bag!" "Well, we'll put full-size shampoos and conditioners *and* curling irons!" It had been one up and one up until Guido won—and it was kept secret exactly what he'd donated, only to be revealed the night of.

When Lorraine came out of the stall and washed her hands, a woman in a tuxedo thrust a cotton towel in her hands. Out of the corner of her eye, the way she was used to doing at work, she saw in the mirror, just who had been assigned the duty of working this party, making a presence on behalf of the salon. The funny thing was, when the selection process had been conducted a few weeks back, Lorraine hadn't even been considered. No assistants were allowed to bid on the job—only senior stylists. And now, the way things worked out, she'd gotten an even better ticket into the party.

"Hey, Heather," she said.

"Hey, Lorraine. You look amazing," Heather was fluffing up a woman's bangs with a tiny round brush. Her smile was genuine—she was rooting for someone on her team.

"Thanks," Lorraine answered, glad again to meet someone she had a connection to.

"So how is it on the other side?" It was an interesting question. One she would have been dying to ask herself, had tables been turned. But now she was on this side, she wasn't sure how to answer. It was weird, that was for sure. It was nothing you could have imagined. And, Lorraine considered, it wasn't one that had a black or white, good or bad, answer. It was much more complicated than that, each step requiring forethought, each decision sprouting dozens of possible repercussions. But that wasn't what someone wanted to hear. "It's beautiful," she nearly whispered, deciding that was definitely true—or part of a larger truth than she'd known to exist before, anyway.

Back at the ballroom, Lorraine reentered unnoticed. From this vantage point, she could see everything and everyone. She could watch, from a distance. The idea soothed her. Maybe, she considered, that was something Lorraine ought to pay more attention to about herself. Being at the center didn't excite her, didn't get her going the way it would Tommy, or her mother, or grandmother. She ought to remember that.

From there, underneath the boughs of twinkling lights, the wall of heat against the tent's inner wall and the coolness from outside meeting right at her feet, Lorraine scanned the hairstyles, considered what she might do to alter or improve upon them. She saw a woman tuck a bowl of caviar into her purse, and she couldn't help but let out a laugh as the woman strained to pull the buckle tight. There was a couple kissing softly, the man's arm draped over the back of the woman's chair, tracing endless circles at her bare shoulder. Her black hair was piled prettily up on the very top of her head; her diamond studs glittered smartly. He whispered a single syllable into her ear and she tossed her head back and laughed. Lorraine could appreciate that kind of intimacy in a couple. She knew how hard it was to find it, to reach that place. If she hadn't felt that same way with Tommy, hadn't tasted it and felt it, Lorraine would have given up hope long ago.

Her mind flashed to a time early last summer, before she'd moved here. Nothing much had been happening. They were sitting in his car, the familiar feel of the leather seat warming her bare shoulders. They were parked across from the beach, and though they couldn't see the waves, they could hear them. The flaws that cracked the veneer of their relationship were invisible then. He'd just looked at her—looked and looked, holding on to her hand.

Sure she'd tried to attain that with other men, men who wouldn't give intimacy and then take it away, just like the ocean tide. But after the initial thrill—an unfamiliar kiss, a fancy get-to-know you ceremony, dinner, dancing, a hint of desire, a front-door moment, no other man had ever kept her feeling that way. It was a lonely way to live, she knew. But she knew she could wait for the payoff. In the meanwhile, she could find joy in simply watching someone else feel it, in knowing how to recognize it. She'd learned to do that.

"Penny for your thoughts." It was Matt, who, she was beginning to notice, brought his own tide of emotion with him. He handed her a glass of champagne with a strawberry stuck onto the rim.

Growing a bit conscious, Lorraine got the feeling he'd been standing there for some time, that maybe he knew what she was thinking. She felt her skin warm at the possibility.

As if justifying her concerns, he looked right at the couple she had been staring at. "Can I have that dance now, Miss Colorful?"

Lorraine punched him playfully on the arm.

He wiped at it like she'd hurt him and winced.

She rolled her eyes.

And with that same rhythm, he placed the glasses onto a side table, and they made their way around the dance floor. There were doubtless a lot of questions he could have posed to Lorraine. But he remained silent.

He was looking at her; intently, seriously—as if she'd just been discovered, gold in his backyard. Lorraine realized she might not be able to protect him from her capriciousness much longer. She said what was on her mind without thinking. "You don't want to get involved with me."

"Yes, I do."

"But—"

He didn't let her finish. He placed his finger on her lips, which by then were already opening to him, and shook his head. He knew, and he didn't need to hear it. The finger rested there, in place of his mouth, while the string quartet plucked out a timeless tune.

Oh, he was good.

When the music stopped, they kept going, swaying back and forth. His finger, along with the rest of his hand, was exploring Lorraine's own hand, fingers. He said nothing. She said nothing. When the band announced the dinner was being served, he held on to her fingertips a few seconds, before letting them fall with a *swoosh*, back into the depths of the feathery leaves of her dress.

Matt turned slowly, and without looking back, took his seat way across the ballroom, where she lost him among the identical black tuxedos and dark patches of hair flickering and waving in the candlelight. Wobbly from the dance and all that had been exchanged between them there, Lorraine went back to the table, where she felt as out of place as she would at a chicken farm in South Dakota.

Mallory wasn't there, but the other three were. And they wore bitchy looks on their faces—even bitchier than usual. *Bitchy in Pink*, Lorraine thought with a smirk. When they didn't speak, she finally did. "What's wrong, girls?"

Stacey crossed her hands over her chest. "Oh, only that you're having an affair with the love of Mallory's life."

"Who? Matt?"

"*Who? Matt?*" Tracey mocked her.

"What the frig is the problem here? Matt and I are friends. He lives in my building. He watches me clean up my dog's poop in the park." She wasn't sure if she believed that, or even why she was defending herself.

"Ewww, gross," Katharine said.

The soured faces of the other girls reflected a similar sentiment.

"Don't you have someone to do that for you?" Tracey asked. "That's just disgusting. Princesses do not clean up pooh."

"But I'm the *colorful* one." Lorraine used her own mockery to defend herself.

"That's true." Stacey shook her head in consideration. "Well, good thing you're not *going out* with Matt or anything. Because Mallory would have a fit. And you *do not* want to see her have a fit."

"I don't believe her," Tracey said.

"Yeah," Katharine said, although it appeared she was hardly paying attention.

"Yeah," Stacey asserted with a nasty look to her eyes.

"Girls, what do I have to say to prove it to you?"

"I don't know," Tracey shrugged. "But it better be something good."

If Lorraine wasn't going to enjoy having Matt, a fact she thought she'd settled on, she was surely not going to take the rap for it. And so, whether she was just wanting to go over it all again for the sake of having him *somehow,* or she just missed the idea of girlfriends to bounce these things off of, Lorraine told every single detail of her history with Tommy to the girls.

Apparently, there was something about it that struck a note with each of them, or so one could assume from the tears quickly fingered away before they could do damage to foundation and powder and eyeliner, the patting of each other's backs, and the looks of mutual recognition.

And something happened to Lorraine, too, when she let these girls into her life—her real life, she softened toward them. She could see good things beyond the bad (and there was plenty of bad). Katharine obviously had selfishness induced ADD. To even listen attentively for longer than five minutes appeared to present a challenge to the pretty blonde, whose heels bounced up and down, up and down, incessantly. Lorraine wondered what exactly she was so consumed with. And Stacey, sure she was judgmental—and basically an obedient pup on Mallory's taut leash—but you could see the struggle that fact posed for her. You could see how badly she wanted to break out, without any idea of exactly how to do it. And Tracey, with her constant corrections ("it's Zag-ot, not Zagat,") obviously had something to prove.

By the time Mallory returned to their table from flirting with Prince William, the girls were so smitten with Lorraine, they were nearly sitting in her lap.

"Looks like a regular love fest here. Tell me, what's been the subject?"

"Well, Mallory, we were just thinking," said Stacey, second-in-command. "Wouldn't it be fun to give Lorraine a crash course on being a Princess?"

"It wouldn't really be a 'crash course' unless it was a last-minute preparation for a test," Tracey corrected.

"Well," Mallory said with a wicked laugh. "It is sort of a test, isn't it?"

Lorraine wasn't frightened. Not one bit.

Mallory ~~Heen~~ Meen

Diet Prescription

Breakfast: 2 (two) large celery sticks with fat-free cream cheese or low carbohydrate peanut butter OR two egg white omelet with spinach

Lunch: 1 (one) large tomato halved and grilled with fat-free mozzarella

Snack: 1/2 (half) large cucumber, sliced and dipped into low-fat goat cheese spread

Dinner: Arugula leaves in lemon and drizzle of olive oil with grilled chicken and Parmesan cheese

Drinks: mint tea with lemon; water with lemon (repeat as desired)

Sweetener: unlimited Splenda

---

eBay auction block #15

Description: Mallory Meen's diet prescription, derived by Dr. Stephanopolis, the celebrity diet doctor responsible for the Veg and Protein for Life!® Diet. Reportedly, Mallory lost ten pounds in two weeks on this diet, and then proceeded to gain it all back at a greasy diner, where whe ate a quarter-pound bacon cheeseburger and extra French fries with barbecue sauce on the side before Lorraine arrived to meet her a reported four times. While Mallory continues to deny the claim to this day, waitress Sally Langin testifies, "Oh, she ate it. It was like the girl hadn't seen food in a year! She even licked the plate when no one was looking and asked for an extra order of fries to take home. Slipped the take-out container into her purse! In her defense, we do have the best fries this side of the Brooklyn Bridge."

Opening bid: $550
Winning bid: $2500 by weightwatchersdevotee@weightwatchers.com

Comments: Dear Mr. Ebay (interesting name, by the way), we here at Weight Watchers® are thrilled to hang this specimen in our Middletown, CT offices. You see, it has been our pledge for over forty years to teach the citizens of the world that a healthy, balanced diet is the best way to live. Unfortunately, the media and Hollywood, for that matter, continue to perpetuate a body type that is simply unattainable to the majority of the populace. This wonderful, rarely found piece of evidence will serve as a reminder that even those women you think look so damn perfect and skinny, not to mention pretty and stylish, with money coming out of their asses, are maintaining unhealthy diets, not to mention those that are impossible to maintain over a lifetime (unlike our flexible *POINTS*® plan or No Counting® plans; now 10 weeks for $89.50!).

FIFTEEN

EDUCATING LORRAINE

But maybe she should have been just a little bit concerned. One week later Lorraine found herself at Fred's, the high-profile restaurant on the ninth floor of Barney's New York. It had been sort of a hectic seven days, and she was exhausted—she had even tried to back out on the day's scheduled events.

"But it's going to be relaxing," Mallory assured her, without giving her a chance to object. She was immaculate in dark denim, mint green loafers and matching form-fitting, but not tight, Ralph Lauren cabled cashmere. Her purse was from Tod's—a midsize calfskin tote that even on sale cost more than most people paid in rent each year. There was a Red Dress Campaign pin secured on the strap, carefully placed to show how committed the Princesses were to heart disease prevention for women.

"If anyone asks, we eat, sleep, and breathe heart disease. Do you hear me, girls?" She'd said this the other day at an event for Agua-thin-a, a fat-burning water. They'd all been drinking fat-burning skinitinis, composed of fat-burning water with tons of Italian olives and freshly pressed olive juice, which was currently being touted as a weight-loss miracle (not to mention being in keeping with the whole "Tuscan" trend sweeping the nation via a well-orchestrated marketing campaign by Tuscany's tourist board. (The ad goes "Come-a. We-*a* are-*a* more-*a* than-*a oooo*olives." This from a guy with just the kind of pasta belly you would imagine an Italian to have if you took Super Mario Brothers at face value. And then he's interrupted by a kid in one of those one-piece jumpers any Brooklyn kid would catch a beating for wearing, who bites into a big green olive, juice spraying all over, and says, "But the olives are *squisito*!").

"Have you heard about the new genetic typing being done for heart disease now?" Lorraine had asked, chewing on a particularly tangy olive. She'd just read about it in *The Times* and had found the idea fascinating.

"Uch! Lorraine, don't speak about such horrible things at a cocktail party. It's rude. We wear our pins as often as possible, show visible emblems of support, and speak our devotion to the cause. But don't become a dullard by actually *talking* about it."

Lorraine had never thought this would be the world she'd exist in. She didn't spend those hours poring over *Vogue* with the intention of shedding her accent and gruff exterior for a chicer, more refined model that might use words like *charming* and *delightful* and *dullard*. She wasn't stupid, though. She knew what Manhattanites thought of bridge-and-tunnel girls like herself. Even people who visited the up-and-coming Brooklyn neighborhoods like "Bococa" still did so with the idea that it was "cute," like candy sticks and birch beer in Old Mystick Village, or a tiny lost puppy with one eye. Never was it to be taken seriously, and *never* was it actually to be taken into your home.

Sure, a friend might move there if they ran out of cash or wanted a better environment for an unborn child, but they never *talked* about it, and they never expected anyone to actually *visit*. She wasn't naive enough to consider she could ever emigrate from Brooklyn to Park Avenue—not in status anyway. And while she could appreciate a hot new trend, fabulous tailoring, and a huge advancement in liquid-to-powder foundation, she never wanted to actually change who she was to fit in with the other people who were into such things. Still, here she was. How could she explain that?

The other girls fidgeted with the Red Dress Campaign pins at their purse straps, apparently either showing pride in their commitment or trying to remember what the little dresses stood for, until they were seated at a table by the window.

Mallory pinned one at Lorraine's purse strap and made a face. "First stop, new purse." Her voice was serious and without a hint of sarcasm. And without skipping a beat, she told the waiter without looking at him, "Mint tea, two lemon wedges, ten Splenda, and one ice cube."

The rest of the girls said in unison, "Same."

"And you, mademoiselle?"

"Coke, please."

There was an appalled hush at the table as all eyes landed on Lorraine.

"That's poison, you know," Mallory said, pouring the contents of a Splenda packet down her throat.

"That's why it tastes so sweet." Lorraine said.

"I heard you've got an affinity for poison," Mallory said.

Lorraine didn't look up at the girls. She wasn't going to ask if they'd said anything about Tommy . . . or Matt for that matter. Even if they did tell Mallory, they'd never admit to it. She could tell that right off the bat. Very little actually *meant* anything to them, and loyalty didn't make the cut.

"Always have." She met Mallory's eye.

"We'll all be detoxing next week, so you might as well enjoy it now."

Lorraine didn't even want to know.

In the meanwhile, she needed the caffeine jolt. She'd been up for nearly one week straight. Ever since the ball, which had ended early for Lorraine. In fact, it had ended the second Lorraine's cell phone rang. And to this moment, as she sipped at her controversial Coke, that 99 Civic worths of a dress was still lying on her floor, the airy skirt a perfect circle. Pooh-Pooh was afraid of it, so he steered clear.

She'd been out the door, paparazzi bulbs and camera lights glowing around her, as soon as she'd seen his number on her caller ID. She'd gathered her things and run out, hoping no one was looking. Lorraine hadn't wanted to catch Matt's eye; she hadn't wanted the cheerleading of the Princesses. Hadn't wanted to hear any more of Billie Holiday's "My Man," that had been playing while the string quartet took a break. When the door closed behind her—the cold air already smacking her bare shoulders, shutting that twisty lighted tent world away—she couldn't hear the song, the noise or the laughter anymore.

When she thought about it this morning, it seemed like a blur. What had she felt? What had gone through her head? The truth was, absolutely nothing. Nothing ever mattered in the face of Tommy.

"I saw you on TV, Lorraine!" he'd been screaming as she rode to meet him. Lorraine had thought the taxi driver could probably hear his voice beaming through her cell phone into the front seat. "How did you *get there*, Lorraine? How did you *do it*? You're so *far*. And I'm *here*. I'm HERE. But I'm catching up to you, Lorraine. I'm waiting here for you and your *fucking* door bitch won't let me in. Tell him to let me in, Lorraine. Please."

She'd wanted to reach through the phone, hold him, suck the poison out of Tommy. She'd never heard him this way before. He'd been drinking, that was for sure. She'd heard rumblings of his problem through the grapevine—Tommy's mother told Mrs. Sussman when she was at the Do-Wop; Uncle Carlos told Lorraine's mother, who told Lorraine's brother, who told Lorraine. Lorraine had sucked up her pride and even called Tommy to see if he was okay. Was it Tommy she'd wanted to check on? Or was she worried about how she might recover if something happened to him? It didn't matter either way. He hadn't returned her call.

She'd listened twice to his outgoing message. "Do it." That's what it said.

The first time it seemed to indicate to Lorraine that she should maybe come and see for herself. But when she'd hung up and listened again, her sense of it had changed. The second time it felt like he was telling her to move on with her life, to do what she should to go to the top. But hearing him like that in the taxi, she knew her first reaction had been right.

The porter was on the line. "Ms. Machuchi, what shall I do with Mr. Lupo?"

She'd hated to hear his name handled that way. *He's not a bad person!* she wanted to scream. She calmed herself enough to say, "Please let him into the apartment. I'll be there in a minute." But even Lorraine could hear the shaky, wavering tone in her voice. Her heart felt squeezed like a lemon.

But it wasn't going to be a minute, Lorraine could tell from the standstill she was sitting in. Lights were going from red to green to yellow and back again and no one was moving. You could hear fire trucks and ambulances racing by. Cars did their best to squeeze over to one side and let them pass. The long, angry beeping ahead was not helping.

"Can't you get off onto Third Avenue or something?" Lorraine had heard blame in her voice. If she wasn't going to blame herself for where she sat right now, she had to blame someone. In the stark difference of her surroundings—the ugly vinyl of the backseat, the scratched Plexiglas divider ahead, the peeling sticker with the taxi's information—it had become clear to Lorraine she'd just left something extraordinary behind. She already felt the freeze of regret creeping into the already complex mix of emotions.

"What do you think? Traffic is gonna just magically part ways for you, honey? You think you're a princess or something?"

It was a good question. Who did she think she was? One second she'd been in there, letting herself relax into the life, and the next second she was right back to the edge of what could be, her mouth already going dry at the idea of his lips on hers. She had learned to make a feast of these crumbs—they always filled her up. But the problem was she wanted more. "Therein lies the rub," Chrissy always said. Lorraine had found the phrase irritating, though it rang true. If she could just break that cycle. But then she would have to give him up completely, and she wasn't ready for that. She wanted him.

And she'd gotten him, all right. She'd barely slipped through the door when he was at her, like he, too, had been starving. Her chest puffed with the idea that only she could satiate him. She could tell everyone, "See, I told you. You just didn't know. You weren't there to see it. You couldn't understand." She'd practiced those things, had them memorized. She knew she'd never actually use them.

The salt from his tears had lent a savory element to their kisses. It had felt like they were feeding, tearing into each other. Each time their encounters grew in intensity, and at the same time, more elusive. He'd pulled her into him, digging his fingers into the base of her back. Her dress—possibly torn from overanxious unhooking—lay on the floor. All

$8,000 of it. It meant nothing then. Lorraine had been amazed—how importance could transfer from one thing to another, just like that, as if that first thing didn't ever matter at all. How could you ever know what was important if the importance was so transient?

An hour or so later Lorraine had found herself thinking: If Tommy had drunk this much, how had he driven here? Had something specific thrown him into such heavy drinking or was this merely a natural progression from the road he'd been traveling his entire life? She'd wanted to see him for all his desperation. When she tilted her chin down to look at his face, resting on her chest, fluffy feather comforter all around, all she'd wanted to see was something pathetic that would let her finally rid herself of him once and for all. She'd ached for the opportunity to say those things she had rehearsed hundreds, thousands of times before—the things that showed her self-confidence and independence and strength. They were just the sort of thing you'd want to say at sunset, an orangey haze lowering around you as your ponytail swayed back and forth; things you wanted to say as you walked farther and farther from your old life and deeper and deeper into your new one—the one everyone had always hoped you'd realize.

But she hadn't see that at all. She saw Tommy as more real, more exposed than he'd ever been. He couldn't keep it up any longer, the life he'd been performing for the benefit of all eyes following along. Of all the women in all the world, he'd chosen Lorraine to be the one he shared this with. At that moment it had seemed to her there was no other couple in the world who knew each other so well as they did.

"Lorraine"—his voice was meek and nearly unrecognizable—"you do know that I love you, don't you?"

The light had still been on; the clock read 12:30 A.M. in a neon green digital display. Outside the window there was honking and someone screaming about the whereabouts of his shopping cart. Above it all had been Lorraine's hands—the one that held fate, and the one that could change it. But none of it registered with Lorraine.

No, she'd been was busy trying to think whether Tommy had just said "I love you" or if she'd dreamed it into being. For a second there, it had seemed completely real. He did have a strange tone she never could have imagined—wavering somewhere between a cry and a song. But she couldn't be sure enough to settle comfortably into it. She'd let the idea wash over her as she moved her hand gently over his hair, back and forth, back and forth.

"I found it!" the shopping-cart owner had screamed. "I found my shopping cart! Thank you, God, for showing me the way to it! Hallelujah!"

The rolling sound had grown lighter and lighter. And then there'd been quiet again. Tommy's hair felt silky soft at Lorraine's fingers, thick and safe—like a child's blanket.

And then that tiny voice had come from Tommy again. This time there was no mistaking it. He shifted, his red eyes looking blearily up at her. "Lorraine. I said I love you."

It should have hit her harder. But the disappointments had left a mark on her. She knew the danger of elation—it only ever dissipated into nothing. And besides, despite how it might have looked to an outsider, Lorraine already knew he loved her. She'd always known. There was no mistaking the way he looked at her, touched her. The thing was, he just didn't love himself. And somehow, he'd grown to blame her for it.

"I know you do, Tommy. I do." She hadn't recognized the sound of her own voice. It sounded so brave, self-assured.

And as his breath grew slower, the feel of it warmer and heavier on her breast, Lorraine had briefly remembered herself at that party. It was with relief that she thought how narrowly she'd escaped kissing Matt. She'd hate to hurt someone the way she'd been hurt by Tommy. And the way Matt had been looking at her—well, let's just say she was an expert at that look; she'd practically invented it. The memory of the event, of the celebrities she'd been introduced to, the people she'd mixed with—those things still lingered in the background. It was impossible to deny that she was part of something now, that she was decidedly woven into the framework of something bigger. For the first time in her life, Lorraine felt like she hadn't any idea where the future would take her.

The bell had startled both of them. Lorraine hushed Tommy back to sleep after she'd slipped out from beneath him, wrapped and tied a robe around her. Pooh-Pooh was looking sort of hurt, curled in a half moon in front of the door. Another innocent bystander in the pileup that was Tommy.

She hadn't thought who it might be. Now, sitting across from Mallory, fingering her own Red Dress Campaign pin, she replayed it in her head, feeling positive she wouldn't have answered the door if she really had. Of course, she should have known it would be Matt. Who else could it have been?

As it stood, though, he'd taken her off guard, standing there in his tuxedo, so black against the white hallway. "Where'd you run off to, Cinderella?" He'd said it slowly, softly, just the way you'd want someone to show they'd missed you. "You left your present behind. It looks like you didn't even open it." He held it out to her, gently touched it to her hand.

Lorraine had wanted to let him in. Her heart warmed over with the sound of his voice, the brightness of his smile lighting up the air around them. But she couldn't have let him. Nor could she have stood there and tried to and figure out why he was affecting her this way.

Pooh-Pooh had poked his head around the open door, probably looking for Lena Horne, halfheartedly accepting Matt in her place with a series of long, wet licks.

The box grew warm in her hand, her body heat radiating like mad. The energy of the evening, of her lovemaking, the tension of Tommy lying not twenty feet away—it had all culminated at the surface of her skin.

Matt had bent down to gave Pooh-Pooh some attention, petting and scratching and whispering the kind of soft praises dogs seemed to go for. The dog appeared to be making a point to Lorraine, who'd ignored him all evening, by extending extra tenderness to Matt. He rubbed his head up and down at Matt's knee.

"You gonna open it or what?" He finally looked up to ask her.

She'd fingered the silky white bow before pulling at one end of the ribbon, untying the loose knot and lifting the lid of the box to reveal multiple layers of tissue paper. Lorraine had pulled the paper back with a light rustle to reveal a brown-and-white striped envelope. She'd recognized it instantly. The envelope was from Bendel's. Turning it over to tear open the seal of the envelope, Lorraine looked up at Matt. He'd obviously known what was inside.

Strange, was how she'd describe the feeling of looking back at her own hands—her own nails featured on a gift certificate for a complimentary set of Guido Nails. What with her coming out that evening as the newest Princess, it had seemed nearly too coincidental. Had she missed something? Had Guido already known Lorraine was being crowned? Or was this merely a coincidence? Either way, Lorraine got the sense that the stakes had been raised, that without her meaning for it to happen, the tension had risen. The complication of success was biting at her ankles like a pit of hungry snakes. And it was time for the left hand to do something about it. But what?

"Lorraine, *you* stole the show tonight. It wasn't about that newly C-cupped girl from Brooklyn. I, for one, hardly even noticed her chest." He sighed at the missed opportunity. Even in the most serious of times, he could make Lorraine laugh. "It was about a *naturally* C-cupped girl from Brooklyn." He did a hand gesture that she assumed was designed to invoke the Beastie Boys.

Lorraine had fixed her eyes into an angry line, but her smile gave her away. There was such an easy way between them.

"Well, Princess Lorraine, I just wanted to show you that." But he had looked at her like there was more . . . so much more.

She wanted to say something, but didn't know what. And that quickly, the left hand missed its chance.

Tommy had padded in, with a haze of sleep around him, the feather blanket draped about his waist, dragging behind on the polished wood. "Hey," he said to Matt. He must have vaguely recognized him from that chance meeting after brunch so many weeks ago.

Lorraine had been struck by the irony of the situation. She'd spent so much more time with Matt than Tommy since that day. Matt knew everything happening to her; Tommy knew nothing. But she did nothing to prevent fate from taking its course. She'd stood paralyzed, her feet glued to the wood planks, her hands helpless at her chest, as Matt looked to her with heavy eyes that hurt deep in her belly. They moved for the first time to her dress, still on the floor where it had been torn from her.

"I guess, that's my final cue."

★   ★   ★

She hadn't seen Matt since then. Tommy had stayed all the next day and then left early in the evening—just when she would have wanted to cozy up with him against the coming week and all the unknowns it might bring. The night had been long, filled with questions she couldn't answer. The only thing she seemed to feel for sure was that everything meant more now; at each crossroads, there was more at stake. And it wasn't clear she'd be able to let things roll along anymore. Lorraine would have to take control of her fate, and that would mean answering lots of questions she'd been putting off for years. For the first time in her life, Lorraine seemed to have what she wanted. And she was terrified.

The Coke went down quickly. It wasn't nearly enough. She ordered another to the disgust of her fellow Princesses. After, they ordered their meals: spinach and egg white omelets, well done, for Mallory, Stacey, Tracey, and Katharine. A cheeseburger and fries for Lorraine.

"I'm colorful," she said, shaking her head when it arrived with a dainty ketchup bottle accompanying it and two bright green pickle disks. Cheeseburgers had never let her down over the years. They had been wonderful friends, always meeting her expectations. And now, when Tommy had given her more than he ever had before and she could still see, burned in her head, an image of him at her window seat, pulling her toward him—she needed some comfort. Because she was learning to see that the more you got, the more you had to fear for its absence.

Tracey stifled a laugh. "Can I have a fry?"

"Of course," Lorraine said.

Mallory rolled her eyes.

Tracey tried not to notice.

Directly following Fred's, Lorraine was taken to Ralph Lauren, where a two-ply cashmere cable-knit sweater was chosen for her in a salmon hue, along with a chocolatey purse that could carry a small child with plenty of room to spare.

"The purse is awesome. But the shirt is a little too loose. And way too pink." She knew the color was in. In fact, it had just been declared "New York City's newest black." But Lorraine wasn't a pink kind of girl. She tried on the black in a smaller size. "Perfect." She had to admit it was a great sweater.

"Nobody said this would be easy," Mallory said.

High tea was at Takashamaya. They had an adorable tearoom down in the basement. Lorraine had worked so close to that store all this time and never known about it, as if she'd been holding on to an oyster shell for years without realizing a pearl was nestled inside. All the cool stone and warm woods and fragrant teas, the tiny portions of pudding and sushi and colorful salad shining in a delicate dressing, all served in their own bento box squares, seemed like wonderful secrets to Lorraine.

Maybe even they didn't exist for everyone, just for the people who knew about them. And now that Lorraine was here, they came to life, just for her. Each vibrant bite tasted delicious in her mouth—not just greasy or salty like the foods she normally treated herself to. The smells were different from the simple blend of tomato and oregano, salt and pepper of her mother's cooking; the tea leaves' aroma enveloped her like the sweetest perfume. And yet, with all the luxury came the awareness at the perimeter of her mind that all this might come crashing down.

Facials were next. There was a woman up on Eighty-seventh Street who had been the private facialist of Gwyneth Paltrow (apparently, she's never had a pimple in the time they've worked together) and had gone on to build an entire clientele based on just that one fact. "She needs the works," Mallory said to the facialist. "Microdermabrasion, deep pore cleansing, laser, fruit acid peel."

Lorraine didn't think her skin looked bad. In fact, she was shocked to see the difference when the miniature woman with the prematurely gray hair was through. She was glowing. After a couple of hot towels, lots of aromatherapy (nice to be on the other side of things for once!), and a good amount of shoulder massage (medium to vigorous, they wrote on Lorraine's card), she felt like a million bucks.

"Wow, you are awesome," Lorraine said to tiny Tanya when she looked in the hand mirror, heady incense burning and low light offsetting the new-age music. "Where did you study?" Beauty industry people were beauty industry people—and they shared a mutual respect for a job well done.

"I went to Christine Valmay," tiny Tanya said.

"Oh, they're great," Lorraine said. "And how long have you been working at Breathe?"

"For about one year."

"Do you like it?"

"You know, you're the first client ever to ask me that."

"Are you serious?"

"Totally. I do, though. I love it. The products are great."

"What is that you were using?"

"Oh, it's Yon-ka, a little soft-gel peel, followed by a micro-peeling exfoliation. I mixed this bit myself."

"How do you know how to do that?"

"My darling, my grandfather was a medicine man. I studied at the top beauty school, and I run a lab in my free time. I can look right at your face and tell you exactly what you've been eating, what mistakes you've been making in your cleaning regimen, and fix it for you in one session."

"A woman after my own heart."

"A Princess with a heart. The first I think." Both women got a laugh out of that.

Tiny Tanya's hearty laugh was bigger than she was. Like she'd been storing it up and needed to let it out.

"I'm the colorful one," Lorraine said by way of explanation.

"I know." Tanya smiled and pointed to the *New York Post*, which Lorraine had seen earlier.

"Colorful New Princess is B&T all the way." *Could Brooklyn be cool?* The lead sentence asked.

Lorraine screwed up her face.

They'd interviewed one of the socialites who'd served on the board for the gala. "What do you think of the new Princess?" they'd begged. "Oh, you mean the one from Queens or Brooklyn or wherever?" If it wasn't Park Avenue, much less Manhattan, it was nothing, as far as an Upper East Sider was concerned. What could the world possibly be coming to if a Brooklynite had become the center of the universe? It was an interesting question.

Tiny Tanya put together about eight products for Lorraine, wrote out a "skincare prescription" that was sure to add an extra hour and a half, at least, to her toilet. They were chatting in a bubbly manner when Lorraine joined the rest of the Princesses in the lobby. And somewhere between the Ralph Lauren compliments of Mallory and the free facial card Lorraine was presented with for use whenever she wished, something strange happened to Colorful Princess Lorraine.

She really began to get excited and have fun.

The Princesses were different, that was for sure. But they were there. They didn't have to work, so they were around on a Monday, which was rare for Lorraine. They had a ticket to the entire city, and they wanted to share it with her. Sure, her inkling that they had chosen her for more than just her cool factor was turning into a major suspicion. It seemed the paparazzi and the video crew were equally suspicious, staking out at every single place they went. But what could be the harm? Half the world, if not more, would kill to be spending a day this way. Now she could see why.

After the facial it was time for nails, and then laser hair removal and a private shopping appointment at Bergdorf. "Lorraine, how do you like Manhattan?" "Lorraine, how has your life changed since you became a Princess?" She laughed her way through the microphones, tape recorders, and swirling pencils, wondering where the road would take her, feeling how funny it was that people suddenly cared about what she was thinking. But it was the last question that finally made Lorraine start, that stirred her from the carefree mood she was settling into. "Lorraine! Do you have A BOYFRIEND?"

The question dragged out, as if in slow motion, while it made its way to her ears and through to her brain, where it processed into something really, really important. The thought connected to other, more familiar thoughts and memories. They were on her new bed, on his old bed; there she was at her window, watching him take that Staten Island girl to the prom, watching him drive around with one girl, another, and yet another. But she wasn't standing at that window anymore. And she could do something about it.

This was her chance. This was how she could help Tommy.

She wasn't dumb. She didn't think, la-dee-da, I'll just do this, make him famous, he'll be perfect and then we'll live happily ever after, no risk involved. Sure, it lurked somewhere in her mind that there was danger in bringing him into all this celebrity. She wasn't sure exactly how, but she

felt it, sure as can be, with a dull pressure in the base of her skull. By bringing Tommy in, she was somehow putting herself at risk.

But the microphone was in her face, and he'd been so desperate. All
those times she'd wanted to help him—wished he'd gotten into NYU,
prayed he would feel better about himself, finally reach that elusive place
he longed to go—they all came back to Lorraine in that moment. She felt
her mind switch, as it often did, to that alternate mode with only one all-
consuming goal in mind. And that's when the answer came to her.

"Yes. Yes, I have a boyfriend. His name is Tommy Lupo. And he's from
Bay Ridge, Brooklyn."

A wave of horrified sighs swept through the crowd of media folks. A
Princess went across the bridge for love. First a "colorful" princess, and
now this. This was the reason you had to keep tabs on things, make sure
only the really elite people were involved in the really elite things. Because if you didn't, this was the kind of thing that could happen. Soon
there'd be people from Queens, and the Bronx in the City . . . who *knew*
what might happen next? The whole world could only be consumed in
flames following something so apocalyptic. The whispers were growing to
shouts. "This is outrageous!"

Lorraine surprised herself by loving every second of it. It seemed to
her, people could really get lost in meaningless causes.

The yoga class was a wonderful—and quirky—escape from the
media circus. And what's better, the experience inspired an impromptu
trip across the bridge.

"We all go to yoga for Alex," said Stacey as they were changing into
the yoga gear they'd just purchased in the lobby shop for ten times the
suggested retail price.

"We all go to yoga *class* to *see* Alex," Tracey corrected.

Eyes rolled.

"Who's Alex?" Lorraine was facing her locker, pulling a pink sports
bra over her head. She had to wear pink. She thought of quizzing the
group to see who remembered what the pink symbolized, but reined herself in just in time.

"Ahhhh," Tracey and Katharine sang in unison. "Only the sexiest guy in all of New York."

Lorraine had been sort of against yoga. Wasn't that the exercise of choice for crunchy hippies who never took showers and grew their armpit hair until it could be braided? But now that she saw the sort of "enlightenment" available to her, Lorraine thought maybe yoga was looking more promising.

However, that idea was quickly quashed. Compared to the Bay Ridge Guidos, Alex was a skinny, wiry zero. Sure he had some arm muscles, and a rather high sweat factor. But those things alone would never get Lorraine's blood pumping. This was one area where Brooklyn had Manhattan beat—big, muscular hands down. Nonetheless, Alex tried.

There were strictly women in the class, save for one man in the far front corner, who—judging from his pink unitard—was probably gay.

Alex was sitting in front with legs crossed in a variation of what Lorraine had always referred to as "Indian Style," completely unaware of any un-PC connotation. "It's nicer to call it *Lotus*," Tracey corrected.

Alex's eyes were closed, and quite self-consciously, he was ignoring them in a way that begged to be noticed. Every so often he would roll his head, deliberately and slowly to one side, let it travel in a long, sensuous journey to one shoulder, then fall with a deep sigh onto his back, the other shoulder; then he would hang his chin onto his chest, breathing deeply. He reversed this movement a couple of times, while through the hidden Bose speakers, a string instrument plucked out a light song that seemed from another era, if not another world altogether.

The Princesses sat smack in the middle of the class. They wanted Alex to notice them, but they didn't want to appear desperate, Lorraine deduced. Each had a pink mat (everyone else's was peach, blue, or purple), with a tastefully small Princess logo (an elegant tiara), embossed with silk thread at the front right corner. Lorraine was presented hers with a loud smacking roll-out by Mallory.

"Here you go, Lorraine. It's your very own Princess yoga mat. Sure, we're selling them on our Web site with half of the proceeds going to Connecticut upper-middle-class children's exposure to ethnic diversity organization, but we want you to *have* this one." She smoothed it out for Lorraine, looked to her for a response.

Lorraine had a growing respect for this girl who literally thought of everything. She left no stone unturned. Sure, Lorraine had never wanted to practice yoga, but so what? She was open to trying at least. "I adore it," Lorraine said, wondering how that word had made its way into her vernacular. She'd never noticed it there before.

Even before he opened his eyes, Alex lowered the lights in the room to a super-dim setting via remote control. He seemed to be showing everyone how great he was with his fingers; how he could do anything with his eyes closed.

Judging from the collective readjusting, smoothing, spine straightening, and tummy tightening, his efforts achieved the desired results.

"Good afternoon, lovely women of New York. And Bob." He tucked his head down until you could only see the top of it, joined his hands in prayer, and said in a whisper following a lip lick, "Na-*ma*-ste." He waited to hear the class repeat the gesture and phrase, and then slowly opened his eyes again, lifting his head. A slow, wicked smile crept to his face, building gradually until there was nowhere else to go.

"And let me guess. This is Princess Lorraine in the pink." He walked over to Lorraine's mat, where she was sitting with her knees to her chest, hugging them with her arms. The shirt she was wearing was a belly shirt. She wasn't really used to wearing that sort of thing.

Alex crouched down until his knees were nearly touching Lorraine's. He lifted her right hand from where it was digging in her thigh, and kissed the palm slowly with closed eyes. "Namaste, darling."

Lorraine felt like she was having sex in front of the class. And although it was wonderful to taste the jealousy of the twelve other students who remembered with joy the first day they'd come to class and received the very first palm kiss from Alex, male escort serving as yoga instructor, she found him unattractive, and his advances unwanted.

Lorraine forced a smile to her face.

"Have you ever taken yoga before?"

She was literally inching away from him now. "Um, no. Normally I just run about four miles a day with my dog, Pooh-Pooh."

Everyone laughed, apparently picturing Lorraine running with her own stock of dog doo. Except of course, Alex, who could not be stirred from his sexy mood, no matter how many scatological references she made.

"I mean, I don't run with dog pooh-pooh, no. That would just be gross. My dog's *name* is Pooh-Pooh."

The whole class shook their heads in understanding.

As if she hadn't just been talking about poop, Alex said, "Oh, that explains your musculature." He said it with a look that seemed to take in the entirety of her "musculature."

Lorraine tightened her grip on her thighs, holding on for dear life. She wasn't sure what might happen to them.

Finally he got up, but not before rubbing her shoulder as if they were old friends, sharing some secret no one else in the class knew of.

Despite the case of the heebie-geebies Alex had incited, it was easy to fall into the slow wave of his voice, accompanied by the string instrument plucking softly. With her eyes closed, she melted into all the postures, laying and stretching legs, shoulders and arms. The grace of the flow moved her. At one point she was lying flat on her back; her legs were spread wide, bent at the knees with the feet touching, making a diamond over her mat. She felt a pair of hands press down on each thigh, just below her pelvis. His hands were forceful, yet gentle. She thought that must be what a yoga instructor was supposed to do. But when his fingers began butter-flying around a bit too close for comfort, Lorraine sat up with a start. What the hell was this guy trying to pull?

Not even that stirred him. He was going to speak, and, she hoped, explain the benefit of touching her so near her crotch.

"Great top," was all he said, smoothing his hand over the exposed sliver of belly she was already feeling uncomfortable with.

"Now, walk or hop up to the front of your mat," Alex was saying from the back of the room, where doubtless, you got the best view of such a move.

Lorraine chose to walk.

All the other girls hopped as if onstage, shaking bangs and stylish layers of hair back from eyelashes, and pursing glossed, sultry lips.

During a balance pose, Alex came up from behind and stuck his face in the space between Lorraine's shoulder and head, his arms again at that exposed part of her waist. She burned with mortification where his hands touched; his too-sexed-up whisper gave her a chill of displeasure.

From time to time, he would egg them on with his own version of an encouraging cheer. "Do it hard."

Each time Lorraine looked around for someone to exchange expressions of nausea with. But from the looks of it, no one found this the slightest bit off-putting.

At the end of the class Lorraine enjoyed the lying down pose where you got to drape a blanket over yourself, away from the inquisitive eye of Alex.

"So, didn't you just *love* him?" Mallory wanted to know back in the locker room.

"Are you kidding?" Lorraine's face was so screwed up, there was no misjudging her distaste.

"Well, he definitely liked you. He'd probably go out with you."

"Again, are you freakin' kidding? The guy's a skinny little perv."

The girls looked at one another, shocked. How could anyone not like Alex? That's what their stares begged to know.

"Lorraine, Alex is a New York woman's best friend. He gives her just what she needs to feel like a woman. That's what *New York* magazine says. And if *New York* magazine says it, then it is so."

"Whatever. You wanna see hot guys in a sexy workout environment, you just let me know. I know the best place there is." Lorraine was thinking about the Sweat Box, the gym in Bay Ridge where every hot guido in Brooklyn worked out. The place was sex. It was better than sex. A girl could orgasm just watching a guy slide the weight disks onto the bar.

"Yeah, but will they hit on us?"

Lorraine could only laugh at the absurdity of the question. There was no way to stop them from doing so—not even the signs above the treadmills that read in big block letters DO NOT HIT ON THE LADIES!

Five minutes later they were piled in the limo that had been patiently waiting for them during the yoga class, and made their way toward the Brooklyn Bridge with cameras rolling.

"I *cannot* even believe we are going to Brooklyn. And not even Brooklyn Heights or Park Slope or anywhere cool. We are going to Bay Ridge.

Ha!" Mallory seemed delighted with the idea of herself doing something so wacky, so—as she might say—colorful.

"Yeah, it's just what NBC would want!" Stacey screamed.

Mallory's eyes grew stormy and black in a matter of seconds, and she looked as if she could burn a hole through the Stupid Princess with the intensity of her gaze. Just as quickly, she recomposed herself and said, "NBC! What *are* you talking about, darling?" Instead of waiting for an answer, Mallory swept the foolishness off her like a stray hair and asked Lorraine, "So, what does one do at the Sweat Box?" She handled the words as if they were slimy raw meat hunks.

Lorraine didn't know what Mallory was up to, but honestly, she didn't care. After worrying and wanting, she was having a good time. And here she was going home as a Princess. She wasn't sure what would come of it, but even that felt okay. She was sick of worrying about consequences. Besides, she didn't think she'd see Tommy, as he was working the dinner shift already, and so there wasn't the worry of that to muddy up the experience. She was already worrying about what she'd said to that reporter earlier.

"Lorraine! Hey, Miss Fancy, how *you* doin'? And who are your gorgeous friends?" Sal behind the front desk wanted to know. He was wearing a Sweat Box muscle tank that had armholes cut all the way down to the top of his shorts.

Mallory pinched Lorraine painfully on the fleshy part of one arm, and Stacey on the other. Apparently, they approved already.

As they made their way from one sweaty weight room to another, took their places on treadmills, sipped suggestively from sport bottles of Evian, the Princesses gained the attention of every ripped guido in the Sweat Box. They pretended to watch the soap operas on the televisions hanging above, but it was obvious to anyone who looked that they, like every other girl who worked out at the Sweat Box, weren't paying a lick of attention to the screen. The real entertainment was the flexing and squatting, pushing and pulling going on just beyond, greased up in a way people might poke fun at in a ritzier borough, but only because they hadn't experienced it firsthand. The cameras seemed to find them, even there.

"Friggin' unreal," Stacey said of the place.

Lorraine laughed. "You are so colorful!" she teased, tossing her pony-tail behind her shoulder.

Effortlessly the girls walked out with two dates apiece. Mallory got three and made out with the head trainer in the steam room.

And, Lorraine thought, *she* was the colorful one?

That wasn't the only time during Lorraine's Education that she taught the Princesses a thing or two about her neck of the woods. She reciprocated her private shopping experience at Barney's with a private appointment at Benny's warehouse of merchandise that "fell off a truck." Everyone went home with some variation of mixed-material Gucci and a couple of Juicy track suits for under a hundred dollars apiece. "I never knew a bargain could be so much fun!" Mallory said. "Here I was always saying 'you get what you pay for.' "

After that, she took them to the Dollar Store, Dollar Tree, and Everything's 99 Cents! Lorraine gave up on trying to explain the subtle differences between them. Then they headed to TJ Maxx and Amazing Savings, where Katharine found just the vase she was looking for to sit atop the table in her front hall—for only $25!

The girls were snapped by the photogs and documented by the videographers at every step along the way, and pretty soon Katharine's was the most popular vase of the season. Amazing Savings announced they were taking over all the Odd Lots in Manhattan—by 2010 they were planning on twenty-five locations citywide. "And I'd never even heard of them before!" Katharine had said. The chain asked the Princesses to act as buyers for their own branded housewares division . . . for a handsome profit, of course.

Lorraine's presence was proving quite profitable for the Princesses all around. After the vase phenomenon, no less than five home accessories companies approached the group with proposals. Three morning shows offered room makeover slot proposals. A new magazine, *Spend!,* asked them to style "Princess Pages." TJ Maxx asked them to do makeovers once a month as a promotion—a well compensated promotion of course.

For her part, Lorraine's life had done a complete 180. Her familiar days, the ones she could walk through with her eyes closed, had been replaced by unpredictable, twenty-four-hour whirlwinds, where anything and everything could and did happen without the slightest warning. The man she'd been pining over her entire life had declared his love for her, and it looked like—in this world where you could be famously celebrated for absolutely nothing—finally she might be able to save him from the problems that had always stood between them and happiness.

Running with Pooh-Pooh, with the darkness all around them like a cozy blanket, she thought, despite the complications, life was good.

MEMORANDUM

To: Princesses Mallory, Tracey, Stacey, and Katharine
From: NBC
Re: The Royal Life Goes to Brooklyn

After substantial testing, it has been found that the Brooklyn-location episodes of *The Royal Life* tested quite well in the Midwest as well as the North Atlantic states. We would like you to plan an evening outing including bars and multiple hook-ups, etc. Also, please do something intriguing with that sexy guido of Lorraine's—Tommy. He has tested extremely high on the West Coast, so that will have us covered nationally by sweeps when we reveal the truth to Lorraine for our finale.

eBay auction block #16
Description: Memorandum from NBC top executives to the Princesses that sparked the beginning of Tommy and Mallory as a couple, as told to E! Channel's Brooke Burke.

Opening bid: $650
Winning bid: $3,580 by anonymous@NBC.com

Comments: We would like it to be known that NBC does not and would not administer this type of direction to any of its staff or cast members of its programming. And furthermore, if we did, we would not have to disclose it and are legally absolved from any complications that may ensue as a result.

SIXTEEN

♥

SIX MONTHS LATER

The first warm day was a welcome one, with its sporadic tweeting and its prematurely shed clothing layers. Not that Lorraine had had more than a second to even notice the weather since she'd become a Princess. Her career, though quite unchanged in theory—she hadn't learned any new coloring techniques or had any kind of drastic alteration in style—was completely unrecognizable. Lorraine was the top colorist at Guido's. There was no disputing it.

Even Guido had stepped aside for her, as Matt had predicted he would. It did bother him, though, a fact that was apparent from the transformation in his demeanor and his look. The normally flamboyant, grandiose Guido had taken a silent turn. When he moved Lorraine to the window seat he'd always occupied, the one where shoppers peered in to see the newest styles, to check out what was being invented today, it took something out of him. And he in turn, took it out on Lorraine.

"Lorraine," he would say, "we do *not* make it a habit to leave our personal belongings out on the floor!" That on her birthday, when she'd had a flower delivery.

He was always angry at her for something. If it had been her uncle

Carlo, she would have given it right back. But this anger of Guido's, it was different—he was angry in the way Lorraine had been angry at life before, for not panning out the way you planned. She knew it took a while to get used to such a big change. Apologizing, she knew, would have been fruitless. He had choices, but he had to get ready to exercise them. And that was something you had to learn for yourself.

The saving grace was that he was gone a lot. "Catching up on vacation time," Don had explained—without really explaining—to Lorraine at a rare lunch, when she asked where his brother was off to. The relationship between the two fast friends had become completely strained. But that fact wasn't as surprising to Lorraine as the natural way in which she accepted it. Her friends had always been so important to her. She had nearly forgotten about the fun she and Don had looking for apartments, over-ordering lunch on Guido's tab to make up for a frustrating shift upstairs. When you were out of things to complain about, you had far less allies, Lorraine was learning . . . and a lot more enemies.

The Princesses were not exactly enemies, not exactly friends. Mallory had asked her to a one-on-one lunch a month or so ago, which had become a habit for them exactly three times a week. Monday to Barneys, Tuesday to Sarabeth's, and Wednesday at a greasy diner Lorraine was forbidden from mentioning to anyone.

"How's Tommy?" Mallory wanted to know. She was picking at a well-done egg-white omelet with spinach and mushrooms at the diner.

How was Tommy? Well, currently, he was passed out on her bed. He'd probably get up in an hour or so and eat some of her food, ignore her dog, and then call her to complain there weren't any cold cuts left in the fridge. Lorraine wasn't even sure her boyfriend *was* Tommy. She'd get home, and he'd be angry at her for no good reason; they'd race in a private car to an event, where he would impatiently wait for his chance with the cameras while cursing the unworthiness of those being interviewed instead of him, all the while complaining of a paltry gift bag. Then the sex monster would come out, and he would try to take everything he hadn't gotten that evening from Lorraine. She was feeling as if her boyfriend were a vampire. But she wasn't going to admit failure to Mallory—she wasn't ready to say that now that she finally had what she wanted, she wasn't happy with it—the very trait she'd mocked in other people her whole life. Besides, another thought was poking through and muddying everything—could it possibly be *her* that was different? Was it possible that Tommy hadn't changed at all?

"Oh, wonderful," she lied. Words like that only pulled you further away from people, Lorraine knew. But she couldn't help it. Especially with Mallory—the more she hung out with her, the more it became clear that *nobody* knew Mallory. Lorraine wondered if even Mallory knew Mallory. "Mallory, is that grease on your purse?" Lorraine grabbed at it, sitting atop the table between them. She thought she could smell French fries coming from the supple leather bag. "Are those French—"

She didn't get to finish before Mallory ripped the bag from her hand, snuggled it onto her lap, and straightened herself out, as if erasing that moment from time. "You should bring him to the McQueen opening tonight," Mallory said without blinking, her face impenetrable.

What had she been up to? Lorraine still didn't know, all these months later. But the words sat poorly with her, and after that, they came back whenever she saw Mallory in the coming weeks. By the ghost of Lorraine's dead grandmother, she swore something weird was going on.

The Princesses were at Guido's no less than twice a week. They were getting their still perfect nails filled in with fresh acrylic, indiscernible trims in their hair, the never before attempted two-centimeter root highlight refreshers from their fellow Princess, Lorraine. She hardly noticed the cameras anymore.

Don mentioned as much over jumbo Caesar salads with grilled shrimp (Lorraine had asked for hers well done). "And how does Princess Lorraine like her friends?"

Lorraine thought it a strange question. If she were to be candid with Don, who she'd not so long ago been candid about everything with, she would tell him some funny stories, some dirty little secrets: that Mallory secretly battled bad breath, that Katharine couldn't pay attention to anything for more than two seconds, that Tracey hired someone whose sole job was to zipper her Seven Jeans up while Tracey held her stomach in on the floor. That kind of thing. But she couldn't. She couldn't be open with Don, and she couldn't be open with Guido, couldn't just say, "I'm sorry this happened! Why don't you just fire me if it's so bad? I am so sorry I have made you feel this way. I didn't mean for any of it to happen!" She couldn't be frank with the Princesses, although they were growing increasingly frank with her, letting her into their lives, scheduling one-on-one lunches during which they bashed the other girls with abandon. She couldn't say anything to anyone, it seemed.

"Everything's wonderful." She softened her features when she said so, to make such a hollow-sounding appraisal appear true.

"Great. With me, too." Don had nothing to add. He went on eating his French fries, busying his hands with dipping them in ketchup and adding more salt.

She could see Don wasn't great. His pink hair had been dyed black and it looked terrible, especially with the light blond roots starting to show. In contrast, his eyebrows nearly disappeared, making him look in turns expressionless or wildly excited. But it was more than cosmetic. He was likely being blamed for the way things had worked out with Lorraine; he likely blamed her for his brother's sadness, for his brother's misdirected anger. She tried to convince herself, again, that all this pain would take her somewhere. Obviously, something was working—if not perfectly, then at least in a survivalist way. Anyone could see, her life was greatly improved. Right?

To all appearances, she was doing wonderfully. Lorraine worked quickly—always had—and so it was easy for her to color thirty clients in a day. That meant a lot of money for Lorraine, and a lot of money for Guido. There was also the Guido Nail design. She created three new varieties each month. This month the Spring Guido, white on hot pink, the Gilded Guido, gold on white, and the Frilly Guido, which featured an actual cutout of old Italian white lace over a baby pink nail. Of course, she had to teach the manicurists to create them. And then there were the television appearances. She had a regular spot on *Good Day New York: Hair, now!* Every Friday she'd wake up at five A.M., a car would pick her up at six A.M., and she'd head upstairs to the studio where the makeup artist would apply, the stylist would futz and spritz a little, she'd be walked through one door, into another, told with a finger to a mouth not to speak, get a microphone threaded up her shirt and secured onto her collar, be handed a glass of water, led to a seat under a very hot row of lights and do just what she did at work—color someone's hair.

Throughout the show they'd check in with her and she'd explain what she was doing, and why; she'd have to mention L'Oreal at least three times during the spot. At the end they'd show the glowing girl, who was, without exception, thrilled at the makeover results. Someone would declare Lorraine a genius, Jim Ryan would crack a joke about getting highlights—no, not on his head—and in a flash it was over and she was shuttled back out again and up to Guido's. There must have been sunlight/snow/rain/clouds. But if there were, Lorraine didn't know about any of it.

She'd always loved the changing of the seasons, watching the colors change, filtering it all through and spitting it back out as a subtle alteration in a client's color, in the way Lorraine herself applied her own makeup, the way she dressed in the mornings.

One day she realized that the winter had passed into spring without her ever taking note of it. Suddenly she missed that aspect of her old, slow-paced lifestyle—sitting back and watching.

Lifting her face to drink in the sun, Lorraine picked her cell phone from the handy Velcro pouch on her Ralph Lauren purse and dialed Chrissy. But, as was more frequently the trend, Chrissy wasn't home. Lorraine thought of the weather and guessed her old group was probably out in the schoolyard, minus herself—and Tommy, too. Part of Lorraine still missed that routine. She missed shaking her head at the younger delinquents her brother hung out with, missed the feel of the sun-warmed cement under her palm and the familiar jokes of her friends.

But when she pictured her old life, it was impossible to put herself there, to remember what she looked like there, the things she'd thought, the ideas she'd had. Now, everything was run, run, run. Lorraine knew she couldn't picture herself as that old girl, quietly watching Tommy crush her hopes by putting his hand around some other girl's arm. And even if Chrissy had been home, what would Lorraine have said to her?

Lorraine's new social dance card didn't leave her much time for anything. From Guido's there was always some event to attend, whether it be for a new designer down in NoLiTa or an old designer in a new store in

the Meatpacking District, or even a restaurant launch party. Manhattanites celebrated the launch of just about anything—a new toothbrush, a
magazine, a pair of underwear that had a pocket for holding a condom,
a purse collection made from recycled trash, a dog shoe collection, perfume for your vagina, diamond-encrusted flip-flops, all-weather jackets,
a newer, better Botox. But why was Lorraine invited? Because she was
a Princess. They wanted to be able to type her name onto a list of people who used this perfume or wore those big, fat hundred-dollar boots
that you couldn't actually wear in the snow. In fact, she was obligated to
go. They all were. If you didn't go, you weren't going to get your facials
for free anymore, you wouldn't be on the all-access list at the hottest
lounges and bars in town, and you could forget what the inside of a VIP
room looked like. And then, you'd be just like everybody else. That was
the one thing they all avoided like the plague.

"Katharine, you aren't seriously going to wear your UGG boots again
this winter, are you? You'll look just like everybody else. If you want to be
ahead, it's back to skinny boots again this year." Mallory knew all of these
things. She dedicated her life to knowing all of these things. Never in her
worst nightmare could she fathom being like anyone else. Never would
she wear black when everyone was doing it. She'd go ahead to the next
season and do turquoise and bohemian just to make a splash. The moment
she saw someone wearing anything she had, she donated it directly to
Cancer Care, the vintage clothing boutique—unless of course, everyone
else was donating their own ubiquitous clothing to Cancer Care at the
time. Then Mallory's was off to Housing Works.

When you walked in to these events, after checking around to make
sure you weren't wearing the same thing as anyone else, a tray of champagne would be shoved right at your face by some sexy, young would-be
model doing the catering thing at night. They didn't do the catering as
much for the money as for the opportunity to be discovered. If the server
happened to be female, she would be pretty, but not be allowed to wear
much makeup—foundation was fine, but skip the blush and absolutely *no*
mascara. And also she had to be—and if necessary, act—completely va-
cant, so the guests who were less attractive could at least make themselves
feel better by saying, "She might be pretty, but so dumb." When you

stepped back, you saw a lot of tall blond waitresses forgetting drinks and the guests complaining about how awful the service sucked. And that was a good party.

There was always a tray of tiny open-faced sandwiches smothered with smoked salmon and crème fraîche. If you stood by the door, you always got the best shot at the hors d'oeuvres. Lines and clipboards and cameras; gift bags and town cars home. And there was always Tommy. Lorraine's prediction about his becoming famous by association had been spot on.

He'd been waiting there for her after another day of yoga and tea and shopping—a Saturday routine she'd really taken to. Even Alex was growing on her now that there were other new girls for him to manhandle.

"Gonna have my picture in the paper tomorrow, Lorraine."

"Why? Sexiest man in America?" Lorraine teased outside her building, leaning into him, out of the slight chill still lingering. She was taking what she could of this time with him, when he came to her, needed her. Already she was trying not to think about how it was diminishing.

"No. Because I'm Lorraine Machuchi, Princess's boyfriend." The idea didn't seem to thrill him.

They were quiet for a second, each recognizing the disappointment of realizing what you want never turns out as you expected.

"From Brooklyn, no less." He said it as if he were embarrassed by it, as if he hated it. He said it in a way familiar to her—in a way she'd heard from her mother and grandmother before that, a way plenty of people could fall into using if they got to judging their lives by their old wood paneling or outdated upholstery alone.

Lorraine hated to see him like this. If anything, his drinking problem was worse. She smelled scotch on him again—a pungent cloud surrounding him, fogging him up so he was nearly unrecognizable. She didn't want to think she'd seen his car parked right across the street. How was she excusing not saying anything about this? Not even asking? If there was one thing she was not going to think about, it was that filmstrip she'd watched as a high school freshman: the young son heard his dad pulling into the driveway, and ran out holding his freshly-carved pumpkin only to be run over by his drunken father, who didn't even notice.

She knew that, in some cases, right was right and wrong was wrong, but her life was so covered in a veil of gray she couldn't tell black from white. Everything Tommy did had a complicated but real excuse that, God help her, she could still buy into. It was as if she could see inside Tommy, how much he hurt, how all of Lorraine's success was eating at him, making his own failures that much more pungent. Yet she convinced herself that if she could bring him in, make the world part his, he would be fine; *they* would be fine. Everything she'd ever wanted was right there, and she wasn't going to let it go, no matter how much it twisted and squirmed as she tightened her grip. Just *look* at them. Her breath caught in the back of her throat, as she did just that in the lobby mirror. How could *this* be wrong?

"He's not that smart, is he?" Mallory whispered to Stacey. They were toasting the opening of a bar memorializing the nineties—with a load of kitschy items, like a huge 90210 sign in neon, fuzzy couches formed to spell out "Yada yada yada," and a bar shaped like the *Titanic* with a huge blue heart-shaped disco ball swirling above. They were sitting atop a bench against a wall with the song title "Hip Hop Hooray" written in graffiti style when she said it. She had to speak pretty loud to talk over Naughty by Nature, who were signing autographs and trying to nab a re-ality show deal with some MTV producer at "their wall."

It had been loud enough for Lorraine to hear. Mallory knew it, too. Lorraine had a boyfriend—she was the only Princess who did. How could this be acceptable to Mallory, the head Princess?

But Lorraine had already become used to jealousy where Tommy was concerned. Every girl wanted him, no matter what she said or how she might act. Many had gone out of their way to show him that. But they all got nowhere. Lorraine tried to calm herself with this fact.

Just the week before, Tommy had offered to get a drink for her and had come back with a model-caterer's number tucked into his pants pocket. She'd watched him from across the room. It had been some time since she'd played that part—felt the familiar twist at her stomach, the dryness of her tongue as her eye followed over the corners of the girl's clearly glossed mouth, first pinching in at a pout, and then slowly spread-ing into a teasing smile. Finally, her eyes lowering suggestively, she pulled out the pen, looping a number Tommy would never call more than once. At least, he *would have* called it once. But what about now? She couldn't bring herself to ask. If she said it out loud, she would have to admit what she'd just seen was real. And that would be the first crack of many to come, which would eventually spread and shatter their relationship into too many shards to put back together.

She hated that she was barely speaking with Chrissy, her friggin' Bobbsey Twin, save for a phone message every now and then. Sure, she still loved her—the sound of her voice was enough to remind Lorraine of that. But when you didn't speak and you didn't see each other, you became removed from each others' lives. Just then when it seemed too big of a burden to bring someone up to speed, all you had were "just fines." And two "fines" made for a very short conversation. But the bittersweet taste in her mouth seemed commonplace to her now. For everything you got, you had to give something up.

She wasn't even taken aback by Matt's disappearance from her life. At least that one she had predicted. Even now she felt ashamed, thinking of that night of the ball—Matt's midnight appearance, the way Tommy's sleepy body emerged in nothing more than a feather quilt. She'd tried to warn him to stay away from her! Not hard enough, though. That Lorraine knew. She'd been attracted to him, hard as she tried not to be. He had a sexy way about him, but beyond that, there was the way he *knew* her, *listened* to her. That connection had made her relationship to Matt different from anything else in her life. Now, gone were their nightly tête-à-têtes, their movie nights, the talks of that Florida trip, the long hours in the crisp evening at the dog run. The couple of times she'd seen Matt out at the park and gone for coffee with him, their conversation had been strained.

"Pooh-Pooh looks well," Matt said at their last meeting.

"Yeah," Lorraine agreed, desperately searching for something to say. She felt the loss of his friendship intensely. He had been a positive presence in her life, and she knew it. She was dying to say something to him then, to tell him how worried she was about Tommy, that he called in sick to work most days and would probably be fired. She wanted to see what Matt would say about it all—Tommy's staying with her most nights, barely going to Brooklyn at all, skipping out on work. Most of all, she wanted to explain how crushing it felt, after so many years, to be disappointed with her dream.

But she'd let their friendship slip between her fingers. And besides, there were just so many free hours in a day. And lately, Tommy was taking each and every one up. When he wasn't sullen or angry, he would want to take everything she was for his own. It was as though he thought the harder he made love to her, the tighter he gripped her hip, the more her success could become his. And the press wasn't helping matters. Nobody wanted to see a Brooklyn invasion succeed, so the reporters were looking for something bad to say about Tommy at every turn. "Lorraine's guido gets drunk," one headline would say over a picture of him with his eyelids at half-mast, sloshing a cocktail over the side of a glass. "Lorraine's guido joins the unemployment lines," it said over a picture of him eating at McDonald's in the middle of the afternoon.

It was true, he felt too good for his pizza job. He always had, but now that he saw the alternative, it was unbearable for him to drive around delivering chicken cutlet parmigiana subs to families he felt "hadn't a clue."

Lorraine didn't mention that one of those was her own family. His sour mood was so thick, there was no point in trying to reason with him, much less suggest that he consider anyone else's feelings.

Tonight proved no exception to his blue mood. "Which event are we going to tonight?" Tommy asked when Lorraine got back to the apartment, finding him in exactly the same spot she had left him. There were a good four feet between him and Pooh-Pooh. The two hadn't exactly become friends.

Lorraine plopped down between them, a hand at each one's head, scratching like mad. She'd wanted to suggest staying home. She'd wanted to rent a movie, maybe have a talk about what was going on. But she saw the look in his eye—it said he'd stayed in all day and couldn't bear to be there one more second. So she gave him what he wanted. "Helicopter to the new Mercedes SUV launch in the Hamptons."

His mind was racing. Could he get a Mercedes? Might they give one in a gift bag? Did they make gift bags that large?

As she had been so many times in the past month, Lorraine was turned off by his greed, his shallow side. But you couldn't leave someone when they needed you most. She knew that. It was the kind of thing her father had said to her so many times in her life. He hadn't needed to say it, either—his life personified the idea. There wasn't one person her father hadn't helped: drunks who slept in front of the abandoned factories, her angry mother, her "colorful" grandmother. Her father was always there for people he loved, and even those he didn't.

She'd just go run with Pooh-Pooh for a little while and cool off.

The heat hung in the orange-purple air and smacked her in the face when she left the air-conditioned lobby with a wink at the doorman. Lorraine had grown to need her runs; this night she needed it more than ever. The pressures of her life were weighing down heavy on her, making her tighten her shoulders and clench her jaw. She crossed Park and turned on Seventy-fifth Street toward Madison Avenue. Where had she been while the green leaves had been growing back on the winter-beaten trees? Pooh-Pooh tried to stop at a friendly cockapoo, but Lorraine tugged at his leash. She was going to do what *she* wanted to do for a little while— even if it was only during a run through the park.

As they entered the park, and one familiar curve gave way to another, Lorraine loosened a bit, and surprised herself when a couple of tears burned down her face. Crying wasn't normally part of her agenda. It didn't get you anywhere. Crying was the territory of soap opera players— the ones she and Chrissy used to roll their eyes at religiously, every weekday at three o'clock. But who knew if Chrissy even did that anymore? Maybe Chrissy had taken up crying herself.

Moisture was beading up at her forehead and over her bare arms. It seemed she couldn't run hard enough, fast enough. She ran until she came to the same place Pooh-Pooh had dragged her that very first day, where she'd spoken to Matt for the first time. She unhooked him and sat at the base of that very tree, allowing Pooh-Pooh to go flirt with the other dogs clustered at a bush across the field.

Lorraine watched without really focusing, her attention somewhere inside.

"Excuse me. Just wondering if I can sit here. Or is this spot reserved for royalty?"

The sound of Matt's voice sent calm waves rushing over her, perking up her demeanor.

"Royalty only. Sorry. There's a nice spot over by the *Ohmigods*." She turned her head up to see him. It was the first time she'd really looked at him in a while. His dark hair was longer, touched with some lighter spots—she guessed a result of sunshine. His skin was beautifully tanned.

"Oh, but then I'll have to deal with all that flattery and adoration, and I'd so much rather get ripped on over here."

"Oh, all right." Lorraine pat the ground next to her, smoothed away a couple of stones.

"How ya been, Princess Lorraine?"

She was getting sick of avoiding that question with empty responses and so she turned it around instead. "How you doin'?"

"I've been all right, generally. But you know what? Something's been bothering me."

Lorraine was just thinking how refreshing it was to hear some honesty for once when her phone rang. She resisted the urge to throw it on the ground and stomp on it. Instead, she flipped it open, and noticing the number as her own apartment's she excused her rudeness, surprised herself by rolling her eyes, and then answered, "Hello?"

"Lorraine, are you aware the helicopter leaves in twenty minutes from the West Side?"

She was and she wasn't. The idea that she should've turned back kept popping up, but she kept telling herself, just four more lampposts, just three more, until she'd forgotten she had anywhere to be. "Oh, so sorry." Without realizing, Lorraine rolled her eyes a second time and pointed to the phone. Without realizing, she pulled at the charms of the Brooklyn Bridge and the Statue of Liberty on her "Princess" name necklace, the one she'd designed and had made. H. Stern had licensed the design from her and sold out the first five hundred in two days.

Without realizing, Matt smiled at her the way he had before their relationship had become so strained.

The gestures brought them closer, softened the stiffness between them. And it didn't seem awkward at all when curiosity brought him to finger the charms himself, to look at her, his cheek very close to her own, and smile his approval of the pieces.

Tommy's frustration came through the line. "You know what, Lorraine, I'm just gonna go. I don't want to miss it, and honestly, it's really selfish that you completely forgot about me here."

Lorraine didn't even consider whether she'd been selfish. That was just ridiculous. Anyway, she felt twenty pounds lighter just thinking she could have the night off.

"Are you in trouble, Lorraine?" There was a little string tying that smile of Matt's to her own—each sparking the other's, like circuits along a current.

"Just the opposite, actually. I think I'm avoiding trouble." She looked over at Pooh-Pooh and Lena, feeling embarrassed by their passion, which obviously even distance couldn't diminish. She sighed deeply as she turned back to Matt. "What was that you wanted to talk about?"

"I just wanted to say I'm *sorry* for putting you in that position the night of the ball—you know, surprising you like that. And I didn't mean to get angry at you. It's not your fault. It's just, I must have imagined it, but I thought there was something between us. I really was surprised to see you with that guy. But I'm completely over it. I will not try to be anything more than friends, Lorraine. I get it. You tried to tell me, and I guess I thought I could be the one to change the way you felt about him. That was just dumb. So I thought if I owned up to it, we could go back to the way we were."

Lorraine waited for the rush of relief to wash over her. She could be with Tommy, and have Matt as a friend! Wasn't that just what she wanted? Of course it was. It was, it was . . . exactly *not* what she wanted.

Lorraine felt a sadness well up in her heart. Was he really ready to give up on her, just when she was really starting to think the opposite about him? She steeled herself to meet his gaze. But then she noticed his actions weren't exactly matching his words.

As Matt was telling her he'd completely given up on her, he was brushing her hair back from her ear, inching closer, kissing the apple of her cheek, causing spidery waves of heat to rush out to every corner of her face and neck.

For once, Lorraine didn't think about what it meant. She didn't try to protect anyone, least of all herself. She didn't worry what this might do to her tenuous reign as Princess.

Her phone buzzed again in her pocket surprising them both.

"Hi, Mrs. Romanelli! How is Italy?"

"Oh, Italy. It is just the picture of elegance, dear. Your poor grandmother, if only she could be here with me! But no, she has to continue haunting everyone in Brooklyn. Anyway, I'm thinking of taking a lover."

Lorraine screwed her face up. She knew Mrs. Romanelli was a romantic, but envisioning her and a lover was just a bit more than Lorraine could stomach. Still, she was delighted to hear she was having a good time.

"Well, isn't that exciting?"

"Not as exciting as what you're doing now, Sweetheart."

Lorraine looked up instinctively at the tree she was sitting under. She could not tell you exactly what she expected to find there. "And what is *that*, Mrs. Romanelli?"

A deep belly laugh came across the transcontinental phone call. And when Mrs. Romanelli again caught her breath and got the last few hiccups of laughter out of her system, she turned unmistakably serious. "Oh, Lorraine, you know it's impossible to fool an old Italian woman. You are in love, and not with that guido from the Bay. It's all so wonderful. Please put Pooh-Pooh on."

Lorraine carefully said the words back to Mrs. Romanelli. "You want me to put *Pooh-Pooh* on?" Her eyebrows were way up in her hairline.

Matt was twirling the crazy person sign and smiling wide, but he pulled Lena Horne from atop Pooh-Pooh all the same, and encouraged the enormous dog toward the phone with a pat on the rear.

Pooh-Pooh took a seat and put his left ear up to the phone. His eyes danced back and forth as muffled, incomprehensible words came out of the earpiece. When the words came to an end, Pooh-Pooh barked once and then ran back to Lena Horne.

Matt and Lorraine looked at each other in disbelief for a few seconds before looking toward the dogs.

Lorraine spoke first. "You don't think the dogs can—"

Matt cut her off. "You know, I think we're better off not going there. Some things, you just have to accept at face value and move on."

Conspiring dogs and psychic old Italian ladies, but there was one thing Lorraine was not going to just accept (both dead and alive) were one thing, but after all the time she'd been coasting along, just letting things unfold as they may, Lorraine made a decision about something really important: She was going to do *exactly* what she wanted to tonight.

He whispered her name, his lips dancing at her ear. Chills crept up her spine. Matt tucked a stray hair behind Lorraine's ear before turning her face gently in his direction. The attraction between them was unmistakable. His gaze flitted from her eyes to her mouth. She heard a twig snap as he shifted his position completely toward Lorraine; his knees were bent at her waist and she could feel the warmth of his thighs there. Lorraine's breath came heavy, jerky as his lips alighted on hers. They took a long, tender time like that, their arms embraced each other. And then the passion—pent up for so long—overtook them and their kisses grew in intensity. It seemed their connection deepened with each moment they were joined that way.

"Let's get out of here," he said, after. His key loop jingled around his neck as he stood, and extended a hand out for Lorraine to follow.

One hour later, in the glow of a first kiss that was extremely long in coming, the pair were driving in Matt's Mercedes over the Brooklyn Bridge. His hand was covering hers, and they both looked on in silence as they curved around and made their way onto the BQE, glancing out at the most beautiful view of the city.

Lorraine thought they'd be free of speculation back in Bay Ridge, no paparazzi or *Entertainment Tonight* or E! Channel documentary. Also, she loved the fried calamari at 101 at Third Avenue and 101st Street, a stone's throw from the base of the Verrazzano Bridge.

"You know, I can get in big trouble for going on a date with you, Matt." They were sipping some delicious red wine when she said it.

"Oh, yeah, Miss Mallory getting a little jealous of everyone's favorite Princess?"

"Well, who wouldn't?" Lorraine teased, poked at a ring of calamari, dipped it in the spicy marinara, and tossed it in her mouth. "Mmmmm. Now, that is good." You just couldn't get calamari like that outside of Brooklyn. Lorraine was certain of that.

"Let me be the judge of that," Matt said and skewered and dipped his own. After a second, he shook his head nonchalantly. "Yup. Best fried octopus I've ever tried."

"Lorraine, you like?" the waiter, Jimmy, came over and asked.

"Perfect," she said with a wink.

"Well, we want you to know this meal is on the house, Princess Lorraine."

"Oh, you don't have to do that, Jimmy." Lorraine still felt humbled at all the generosity she'd been granted as of late.

"Nonsense. We'll make millions off your visit tonight."

"Well, when you put it that way . . ."

"Boy, crazy life you're leading these days, Princess Lorraine," Matt said when the waiter retreated.

"Yeah, you know, it's so weird. I don't know if I'll ever get used to it. Before, I never thought there was anything wrong with my life. I loved my home, my friends. But now, I see the benefits of this, too. To be honest, I don't love either. I feel like I'm stuck somewhere in between, like there's no way out." It felt amazing to say that to someone, to let out the weight she'd been dragging around.

"That's not weird at all, Lorraine. That's growing, which is the hardest thing we ever do in our lives. It's taking me a lifetime to get there myself. In fact, Lorraine, you and I might win medals for the oldest people to come of age in history. Actually, I think you've just realized your rite of passage. Me, on the other hand—I still haven't been able to tell my father I want a different life."

"Matt, don't be so hard on yourself. You've put in all these years for your father—not because you were afraid, but because you were grateful. And I think it was the honorable thing to do. My own father would be proud, and that's no small thing." As she said it, she knew it would be true.

"I never really thought I had a choice. If you saw his face, if you knew how proud he was of the work I did for him, you'd see why there was no other choice. My dad built his fortune from nothing, Lorraine. And in five years I quadrupled it." He was looking far off then, into the face of someone he loved, but also feared confronting.

Lorraine thought again how refreshing his honesty was, how it made her want to be more honest and drew her to him with such force.

"But you *did* have a choice. You could have just done what you wanted. Lots of people do, you know."

"Yeah, but I had it easy. I could still go down to Florida and work on my furniture."

"Give yourself some credit, Matt. You woke up every day, gave your dad ten hours, made him millions, even when your heart wasn't in it."

"I've been thinking a lot, Lorraine. I've been thinking it's time. I *have* made my dad millions. I can sell off his assets now and make him millions more, and he'll never have to worry a day in his life. And then I can really do this furniture thing. I've got so many ideas, so much I want to do. I have a deadline. The end of the month. June is gonna be my last month in finance. After that, I'm out." From the way he spoke, you knew he was serious about it. And he made you respect him for his commitment, for not throwing in the towel, for deciding he'd help his dad the best he could, and wait to chase after his own dreams. It was the noblest thing Lorraine had heard since, well, since her own father had committed his life to making money for her mother, to making a plan to get her retired in Italy, no matter how hard he had to work to achieve it.

"You know what, Matt? I've got someone I want you to meet."

And they drove down to 79th Street, past the traces of hopscotch chalked on the sidewalk, past the Do Wop Shop for hair, which, sleepy and dark, seemed to be a metaphor of itself. Home again. Lorraine realized she was more at home here than she'd thought. The thing was, she just needed to make room for the new Lorraine here in the Bay. She loved the hum of the familiar, the lyrical quality life could have when you flowed right through it, dictating your own pace. The only thing she hadn't dictated before was the direction of the path. Now she needed to write her own music, her own lyrics—finally sing her own song.

"Dad."

He hugged her so strong, Lorraine could feel her rib cage contract and the breath get knocked out of her. And it was wonderful.

"My little Princess. You know you were always *my* little princess."

Lorraine smiled big. "Dad, I want you to meet Matt."

"Matt, huh?" Mr. Machuchi smoothed his tongue over his teeth, made some exaggerated sucking noise. This was all part of his intimidation scheme. Only, he wasn't all that intimidating.

"A pleasure to meet you, Mr. Machuchi, Lorraine's always talking about you." Matt was so easy with people, it was impossible for others not to warm up to him. Eyes twinkling, he extended his hand. When Mr. Machuchi reached out his own palm, Matt gently placed the other palm over his. It was a greeting someone really meant.

"Why don't we all sit in the kitchen?" Lorraine had never seen her father ease up on the dangerous father act so quickly. He still barely grunted at Tommy when he came in the house. And they'd lived down the block from him for twenty-eight years.

Matt didn't know it, but an invitation into the kitchen was a compliment. The kitchen was for family. Guests stayed in the dining room or the living room, but never the kitchen.

Lorraine smiled big at her dad, who looked back at her like maybe his age and experience meant he knew something more about this situation than she did. But Lorraine had aged and experienced a lot herself in the last six months. She knew just what her dad was getting at.

"Where's Mom?" Lorraine asked as they made their way behind the sofa and through the doorway that led to the kitchen.

"At the movies. *Under the Tuscan Sun* is playing . . . again."

They smiled a knowing smile in the soft glow of the range light that dimly lit the room, giving it a cozy feel.

In the kitchen he took the coffee out of the freezer and asked Matt and Lorraine if they would like a cup.

They both said they would.

And while he went through his own routine, one he could perform in his sleep, Lorraine could see the beauty in it—the way his hands swiftly measured out the right amount of coffee, filled the carafe, poured it out, the way he frothed up the milk into a light, airy cloud. Her father knew how to make an Italian coffee. From looking at his calloused hands and the black half moons that doubled as his fingernails, you'd never guess such a thing. But in the soft light of the range lamp, his familiarity was stunning, elegant. His daughter looked over to Matt.

He was also looking on, his features soft, the shadows of her father's movements dancing over his face. She imagined that Matt, with his own surprising stockpile of beauty, saw her father's preparations in a similar light. When he sensed Lorraine looking his way, he turned to her and took her hand in his own, moving his thumb back and forth over her fingers. They both turned their attention back to Mr. Machuchi; just like that, they were all joined. It was the most peaceful Lorraine had ever felt. It was everything she loved about her old life, and everything she loved about her new life, together and illuminated.

On the way home Lorraine watched the buildings of her hometown shrink smaller and smaller in the side-view mirror—so many brownstones and restaurants of every ethnicity, Irish pubs and proud firemen in their respective firehouses, a few high-rise buildings, with their balconies built to look out at the Verrazano, the water beyond. But, shrink from view as they might, she didn't feel they were small in the least. If anything, her hometown was bigger inside her than it had been before. And she imagined she brought that strength and the pride that accompanied it back with her to the other place she now called home.

As they crossed the Bridge and turned onto the crowded avenue, with all the street signs in Chinese, the city bustling with life, Lorraine's phone rang.

"Princess L, Katharine was just proposed to by her father's partner's son. They will be the richest couple in the world. Ha!" It was Mallory. "How are you, darling." It wasn't a question, and Mallory left no pause in which Lorraine could answer it. You could just hear her white smile glistening. "We want to have a kitschy bachelorette party at those guido bars you're always talking about; we'll have this writer from *Elle* follow us. Tommy told me everything I wanted to know tonight. You plan it for next month, okay."

"Okay." Lorraine sensed something overly tense in Mallory's voice. Or maybe she was only getting paranoid because of the company she was currently keeping. Of course, she would never stay away from Matt just because he'd gone out with Mallory a million years ago. All's fair in love and war. You couldn't keep people away from each other. Lorraine had suffered hard and long enough at the hands of that reality. Sure, it sucked. But people had to do what was right for them—that was life. And she was starting to realize that, in the end, things had a way of working out the way they should.

"And one more thing, Princess L." She spat out the name with spite and anger, paused and finally went on. "You know, you live by the sword, you die by the sword." Mallory laughed sweetly, then bitterly, in tiny little tinkles. She was silent for a second. "I made you, Lorraine, and I can break you." And then, as if possessed by the spirit of June Cleaver, she said five octaves higher, "See you at brunch Saturday, darling."

"Which keeper was it this time?" Matt joked. Lorraine just smiled.

Mallory calling like that while they were together, acting sort of threateningly, got Lorraine thinking. She'd known from the outset how Mallory felt about Matt, and vice versa, but the idea that they'd once been together always struck her. It seemed impossible to Lorraine that someone like Matt could be interested in someone like Mallory.

"Mallory," Lorraine said her name, hoping maybe he might say something about her.

"Ah, yes. She's something else, isn't she?"

"Yeah. She sure is."

They were silent for a second, and then Lorraine realized, if she was curious, why shouldn't she ask him? Honesty was the theme of the evening anyhow—wasn't it? She took a deep breath and thought of the best way to phrase it. She didn't want to seem jealous. "How did the two of you get together, anyhow? It seems like a very odd pairing."

"Aaaaaah, the great question—how could it happen? Well, you see, I was abducted by aliens. They came down in this great big spaceship with all these flashing red lights and . . ."

Lorraine socked him in the shoulder. "Aliens? Come on."

"Really, though, I don't think it was much different than your story. We grew up together. We went to school together. We lived on the same block when we were kids. The only difference between our stories, though, Lorraine, is that Mallory and I were never serious. I knew I could never be serious about someone like Mallory . . . not in the way I could be about someone like you."

Well, she thought, *how's* that *for an answer?*

> "Oh, *Lorraine*, our love holds on, holds on.
> Oh, *Lorraine*, our love holds on, holds on, holds
> *onnnnnnnnn.*"
>
> "Woof!"
>
> Oh, *Lorraine*, our love holds on, holds on, holds
> *onnnnnnnnnnn.*"

eBay auction block #17
Description: Spy cam audiotape transcript of Matt after his evening in Brooklyn with Lorraine, singing a "Lorraine version" of Steve Perry's "Oh Sherry" in the shower, his dog Lena Horne barking in the background.

Opening bid: $375
Winning bid: $2565 by Mattswood@mattswoodworks.com

Comments: Lorraine, if you thought I would let you win this, you were sadly mistaken! Ha-ha! Now, my image as hot, impenetrable stud remains intact. Where did you put that video of me painting your toes in Florida? Damnit!

SEVENTEEN

♥

THE PROPOSAL

Despite the occasional ambiguously nasty comment from the Princesses, the next few days went by rather quietly for Lorraine. Tommy had not come back to Lorraine's apartment after the Mercedes event. At the time, full of the positive energy of her evening with Matt, Lorraine had been relieved to have the place and her thoughts to herself. Still, lurking somewhere behind all the pleasant ideas she was playing with, there was something troublesome about Tommy's sudden disappearance. She was beginning to wonder if there wasn't a connection between Tommy's departure and the cryptic warning Lorraine had gotten from Mallory earlier.

The following morning she saw his picture in the paper, chummy with Mallory and two champagne flutes behind the wheel of a brand-new Mercedes SUV, looking as if he'd been born there. Lorraine had looked long and hard at his face before her discomfort took a concrete form. Every pixel that made up his dark eyes, his now whiter-than-ever teeth, all came together into one whopping realization that hit her like front-page news: Tommy was not a nice person.

The more she stared at that picture, nestled between a photo of Paris Hilton and "friend" and a photo of a dog wearing a cat costume, the more she saw. He was transforming right before her eyes: She saw now he wouldn't ever make sacrifices for others. He would never take responsibility for his own mistakes. And most important, he would never be able to love anyone else, because he was entirely too much in love with himself.

It wasn't that he was deep and hurting, as she'd always thought; it was that he was shallow and too lazy to accomplish anything for himself. When he'd been tossed into this new world, with opportunity, success, and even temptation all around him, all his shallowness had become all-too illuminated. And with each negative she attached to him, Tommy became that much less good looking. There was an unevenness to his eyes. His smile lifted more on the left. But the worst feature of all were his eyes. They reminded Lorraine of vacuums—not the cleaning kind, but the ones you learned about in space, the ones that could suck you in for good, pull you in and erase you for eternity. For once, that didn't seem like a good thing to her.

Lorraine knew there was more than just the smug look on Tommy's face as he sat behind the wheel of a $46,000 car that brought about the change—something magical that involved not one, but two boroughs, some delicious calamari, an English-comprehending conspiratorial canine with a funny name, an eccentric old Italian millionairess, and coincidentally enough, another Mercedes. But whatever the reasons, she knew she was done being obsessed with Tommy. The spell was broken. And now the sight of him made her sick. So sick she went to the bathroom behind the color room and she threw up eighteen times—once for every year she had been in love with him.

The next day, when Guido asked Lorraine to lunch, she ordered only a peppermint tea and two slices of rye toast. She wasn't taking any chances. On top of her existing nausea and nervous stomach, a lunch invitation from Guido only proved additionally aggravating. Everyone at Guido's knew a lunch invitation from Guido meant only one thing: You were getting fired.

They sat in silence until their beverages came. Lorraine thought that a pretty cruel firing tactic—let the poor sap squirm a bit first—but she couldn't think of a thing to say to alleviate things. She wasn't yet sure if she should be angry, or sweet and understanding. Looking around the room to get her thoughts together, she noticed a girl in the far corner wearing her very own highlights. She turned her head and saw another, on whom she'd used a softer version of the five-color technique. She turned to look behind her and there were one, two, three, four more women eating lunch there at Bendel's with her highlights, glimmering five different ways in the lights. Some of the girls started to look at her.

She turned to Guido to see if he'd noticed.

From the expressionless glance he gave her before turning to the iced tea the waiter placed before him, Lorraine guessed he had. But if there was a possibility he'd missed it, the waiter, who knew Lorraine well after all this time—in fact, she'd covered his gray with a beautiful chestnut just two weeks ago in exchange for to-go dinners on demand—made sure there wasn't a person in the restaurant who didn't miss the impact Lorraine had made on the clientele of Bendel's.

"You like?" he asked with his lyrical voice. This waiter's name was Wayne, and Lorraine thought it a good fit, though she couldn't tell exactly why. But it definitely suited his medium build, his lighthearted way, easy mannerisms—he was a guy whose entire presence seemed to say, "Everything's all right," and the name seemed to reflect that.

She looked to Guido, who was performing surgery on his iced tea—remove lemon and mint sprig, place both on napkin, extract straw, stir one teaspoon of sugar around with extra-long spoon—and then back up to Wayne. "What's that, Wayne?" she asked.

"Oh, you mean you didn't notice these wonderful new lights? Mr. Bendel installed them himself when we told him about all the Lorraine Highlights eating here. He thought enhancing how great the girls looked for a longer period of time would just make them that much more eager to rebook, come back, spend more money. You know how *that* all goes. In fact, he's licensing the Bendel's lighting out to restaurants, bars, shops all over the city." He looked around and smiled, obviously proud of his friend.

Lorraine thought again what a nice guy he was. His comments almost made her overlook how angry they had probably made Guido. With a cold sting in her rib cage, she thought maybe those lights were why she was being fired.

Wayne put an easy hand on Guido's shoulder and spoke again. "Hope I didn't ruin the surprise Guido was about to spring on you. He penned the whole deal with Mr. Bendel." Wayne smiled big before leaving, completely oblivious to the anger bubbling up inside both of them.

Oh, okay, so she didn't get anything out of the Guido Nails, but this was *way* too much. Everyone was making money off her talent except for her. Now she was just angry. The idea of waiting for Guido to talk first flew out the window as the new fired-up Guidette plan took effect. "What the hell, Guido?" She waited long enough for him to open his mouth, but not so long for sound to come out before she continued. She was going to give him a piece of her mind. In fact, she was going to give him all the pieces she'd been saving up for a whole bunch of friggin' people. *Bad timing, Guido,* she thought before the Bay-style anger started firing off. "First, you hold me back for no damn reason. Then you steal my nails and give me *no* credit for it, not to mention any money, which I could totally sue you for, if I wanted to. Then you make me think I've been promoted only to take it away. Until, *of course*, it's convenient for you to leave a class. And then I save your ass again when one of your stylists has a meltdown. Then you hate me for being talented—hate me for something *you* hired me for in the first place. That is totally *not* my fault, and you make me pay for it, never once congratulate me, nothing! God, Guido, I mean, I know everyone's got an ego, but you are the most successful stylist in the city, can't you make room for someone else? Jeez!" The force of all that anger backed Lorraine up against her chair.

She was going to ignore the fact that she was starting to feel bad about what she said—that underneath all the anger, she knew it hurt him to have to give Lorraine top billing over himself. She kept reminding herself over and over that his hurt feelings didn't give him the right to treat her so poorly, that she still had to stick up for herself. If she didn't, Lorraine would have jumped up over to Guido and taken it all back. She was forcing herself not to be too nice. She dug her Guido—make that *Lorraine*—Nails—into the pink linen of the tablecloth by way of forcing herself to stay put. And then waited for him to speak.

Guido was a massive man. It was something to see his features get so hardened, to see the lines deepen and make sweeping gestures from his mouth to his ears, eyes to hairline.

It scared the shit out of Lorraine. But, despite the steam from her tea warming her face, she forced herself to stay cool.

And then, slowly, like the descent of a sun on a summer evening, the lines softened, became shallower, until they nearly disappeared. She thought she saw the beginnings of a smile sprouting from his giant mouth. And when it blossomed, she saw the Guido she remembered from that first day, the one who gave her a chance, recognized her ability, and took a chance on a girl who came from the same place he did—in whom he might have recognized his old self.

"Oh, Lorraine." He shook his head and sighed a great big sigh. "What can I say? You're right. When you're right, you're right. You can't pull one over on a Brooklyn girl, can you?" He let his perfected accent relax a little. Shades of the original Guido softened the edges of his words.

Lorraine was still on the defensive . . . but she was certainly interested in seeing where he was going with all this.

"No. You can't." Her words were short punches. Her swiftly shaking head emphasized their impact.

"So you probably want to know why exactly I invited you to lunch, when everyone knows the only reason I invite any of the staff to lunch is to fire them."

Lorraine's stomach dipped and she instinctively grabbed on to her teacup, as if merely touching it could put her nausea at bay.

Smiling big, Wayne brought Guido's cheeseburger and fries, and placed that adorable ketchup bottle alongside.

Guido picked up a golden fry, crunched it in one bite. "Oh, god, sometimes you just have to. So good."

Lorraine wanted to smile, but she forced herself not to. This was business. She still had no idea if she should be mad or not!

"So, let me get right down to it, because there is nothing worse in this world than cold French fries."

That was seriously true, Lorraine thought. She made herself sit still, one hand still on the teacup.

"Lorraine, you are the best colorist at Guido's. Better than Guido. In fact, right now, I'd say you're the best colorist in Manhattan. I've had a hard time dealing with that. And you've given me a lot of space and understanding in that department—I know that. If the tables were turned, I don't know that I would have been as gracious, that's for sure." He tossed in another fry. Held one out to Lorraine.

She was feeling surprisingly less nauseated. The fry seemed like a peace offering she shouldn't refuse, so she took it. "Oh, so *good.*" She couldn't help herself from softening a bit. It was that good. But she straightened up again quickly, drew her shoulders way down onto her back, the way Alex taught her in yoga.

"And the truth is, it's decision time. I know the world is your oyster now. You can go anywhere you want, open your own salon. And the reality of the situation is, the entire clientele is going to follow you, Princess Lorraine—you've got the talent, the right image, everything. So what I'm offering you is a partnership of sorts. Sixty-forty for you of course—and you can call it Princess of Park Avenue, a Guido Salon." He pulled out a folder from somewhere inside his blazer, opened it to reveal some legal-size documents with tiny notes typed up in the margins. "It's all been drawn up, copyrighted in your name. If you say so, construction starts tomorrow and the place opens in a month. Your own salon, Lorraine. It's everything you deserve." He lowered his voice to a raspy whisper, brought his face close. "I wanted to make you an offer you can't refuse."

They both laughed a hearty laugh at a line every Brooklynite knew by heart. Then they shook on it, the soft glow of multi-tonal highlights glowing all around them.

```
Love Spell

1 set of fly's wings
1 drop lavender
2 drops vanilla
3 crushed-up leaves
10 bits red paper
7 Pop Rock's kernels
```

eBay auction block #18
Description: Love spell used by Lorraine Machuchi to gain the attentions of Tommy Lupo in the 7th grade.

Opening bid: $85
Winning bid: $274 by LorraineBKLYN@Bgirl.com

Comments: That's just embarrassing. Where did you guys get this? Gino? You are in serious trouble, brother. . . .

EIGHTEEN

♥

LORRAINE'S GOT A LOT TO LOSE

Initially Lorraine was ecstatic at the news. God, who would have ever thought it would happen to her? She was going to have her own salon. No one would be able to tell her what she could and couldn't do. She could make her own rules, take credit for her own ideas . . . *really* do what she wanted.

The rest of the day Lorraine daydreamed about the style of the interior design, trying to list all of the tiny details she'd found helpful or irritating over the years. Each time she went to reach for a color brush, she considered whether it was kept in the ideal spot; whether her clients had the proper space to stow their things. She wanted comfort levels optimized. The sky was the limit as far as the luxuries she might provide at the Princess of Park Avenue salon. Details were constantly popping into her mind—drawers to stow your purse (she'd seen that done at Butterfly Studio), that five-way lighting, a magazine library at each station, personal shoppers on call to grab items from Bendel's while you wait!

Her mind was spinning when she got home that night—she still hadn't told anyone about the news. Lorraine wanted to tell Matt first. For one thing, he'd been the one to push her to expect more from the very beginning, to be stern with Guido, who he knew had recognized Lorraine's abilities from the start.

But there was more. Matt had seeped into her, overtaken the part of Lorraine that had been occupied by Tommy. Now, it was Matt who was always on her mind. Whatever it was that happened to her, she wanted to share it with him.

She laughed at herself. It was such a youthful way to feel. That was it exactly—Lorraine felt like a teenager. Anxiety-ridden until she could see him, talk to him; giddy when she did. Of course, she tried her best to hide it from him.

"I've got news." They were in their regular spot, under the big oak. Flowers were in full bloom all around—had that just happened overnight? Did they just stick those things already blossomed right into the ground? She didn't know. The idea of possibly not having noticed those flowers until just then made her think more about her own situation. Could she really miss Tommy so little that, like those flowers, she was barely noticing his presence or the lack thereof?

Matt had a softness to his features that made you absolutely positive he understood and empathized with every single word you said even before you said it. And he could look at you with those green ocean eyes so intensely that, for that moment, there was no one else in the world, only you. The idea made Lorraine feel shy. Never had she been someone's whole world, not someone that she'd cared to notice, anyway. It was a strange idea to think someone might know you that well, and empowering to know they wanted to. As she felt her cheeks grow warm, she felt his hand graze her rosy skin.

"What is it, beautiful?"

She gave Pooh-Pooh a slow, soft palming on his back, then looked up at Matt. "You are looking at the sixty percent owner of Princess of Park Avenue, a Guido Salon, copyright Lorraine Machuchi."

He grabbed for her hand, gave it a squeeze, and firmly placed his free hand at the base of her neck. "Lorraine, that is wonderful. You are wonderful. Shit. I am so happy."

That was just it, she thought, as he came in and kissed her softly on her lips. He wasn't just happy for her—it was more than that. Her happiness actually made *him* happy. Like her happiness and his happiness were one in the same. She could barely believe the idea of it, that Matt cared that much about her.

Lorraine knew not everyone felt the same. She felt the now-familiar fear crash into her—take your success, but give something else up! But she knew now that fate wasn't just a cruel plot against her; and whatever it tossed her, it didn't mean she couldn't enjoy the good with the bad! She was coming to realize that quite the opposite was true: The trick of it all was to learn how to take the good with the bad. And the funny thing about coming to understand that fact was she already knew just how to do it! She'd suffered because of Tommy during her whole life, but she'd been disciplined enough to let the simple things soothe her—enjoying a game of hopscotch with her little cousin's friends underneath a beautiful sunset, making small talk with the owner of the German deli, the rush of comfort from her oldest friend, Chrissy. She'd just never recognized that skill as a strength before.

So, given the pattern that good and bad always traveled in—hand in hand—she wasn't all that surprised to find a hysterical Chrissy outside her front door when she arrived hand-in-hand with Matt, their respective pet's leashes crisscrossed at least six times, red and green braided up like a Christmas decoration.

"Chrissy!" Lorraine didn't know the extent of loss she'd been suffering without her friend until she saw her there, so obviously sad, so obviously needing her.

They came together in a hug so tight Lorraine could feel every tiny hiccup of Chrissy's chest, every short attempt at dragging her tears to a halt. After a few minutes, her friend had been soothed to at least a normal breath pattern and Matt had untwisted the leashes. The friends parted.

Matt held out a hand for Chrissy and, instinctively, clamped the other one on top of hers. Without Lorraine telling him who she was, Matt already knew. "Chrissy," he said, smiling like he'd fit the last puzzle piece in.

Lorraine thought again what a fantastic listener he was. In fact, she couldn't even be sure she would realize the same thing if the tables were turned.

"Ahhh, Chrissy. It is so great to finally meet you. I'm Matt." When he excused himself, Lorraine thought it was because he sensed her friend's need to talk with her alone. He didn't pressure Lorraine by kissing her there, making her choose to go public with their relationship. It was a gesture of understanding, of knowing Lorraine wanted to tell her friend about her new relationship in her own way.

He turned to go, then remembered one last thing. "Lorraine, I'll have these papers for you later."

In the elevator Chrissy sniffled. "What papers?"

When Lorraine got through sharing the wonderful story, with all its twists and turns, Chrissy was playing with the fringe on Lorraine's cashmere throw, her feet curled up underneath her on the sofa.

"Lorraine, I am not surprised in the least," Chrissy said. She was shaking her head with satisfaction. It was true—she'd always seen her friend's potential.

If memory served, Chrissy had even advised Lorraine to open up her own salon in the past.

"I always knew the sky was the limit for you . . . if you could forget about Tommy, that is. At least you always had that to fall back on. But look at *me*." Her chest was pulsing again, her shoulders jerking. Chrissy was hysterical.

"What? Chrissy tell me . . . what's happened?" She rubbed her hand over her friend's arm. She knew how much all of this hurt. It had always been the meat of their friendship—this hurt they shared.

"That's just it, Lorraine. Nothing happened. He cheated on me again. This time he didn't even bother spraying his car with an air freshener. He let her perfume just hang there for me to walk into, choke on. It almost felt like he *wanted* me to know, like he thought it would be an easy out." She threw her head back over the top of the cushions, closed her eyes. "I'm fucking pathetic, Lorraine. I just didn't say anything. I was just too scared to say anything."

"You're not pathet—" She didn't get the chance to finish before Chrissy continued.

"And you know what I was thinking the whole time? I was thinking of you. I was thinking how you made all this for yourself, and how you've stayed so strong, even when Tommy is with someone else—"

Up until that moment, Lorraine was thinking of calm, soothing ways to advise her friend. But at the sound of his name, she froze. She couldn't make sense of what she thought she'd heard. His name was hanging somewhere in a cloud of incomprehensible words. What could Tommy have to do with this? Now it was Lorraine's turn to cut her friend off. "Excuse me. What the frig did you just say?" She was shouting, as if it was Chrissy who'd done something wrong.

"You know, Tommy being with that Melanie or Mallory or whoever."

It was her heart that ached the worst. In light of all she'd realized about him the idea that he could always find more ways to hurt her brought that icy hollow spreading into her core.

Even being over him, even now, being in love with someone else, Lorraine felt ashen, as if she'd been burned until she was nothing but the shell of herself—like you could crumble her, grayed beyond recognition, between two fingers. She'd done everything for him, and now he was just trying to hurt her. Part of her pain, she knew, was based just on that fact. How could she have loved someone so selfish? How could she have blinded herself to his faults?

She certainly wasn't blind now. And one thing she could see was that he had *no* idea what he was messing with when it came to Mallory Meen. Lorraine didn't know exactly what the girl was up to, either, but she was going to find out. First, though, she had to help her friend. There were some things that trumped others in importance. The funny thing was, Chrissy was recovering from the loss of Big Bobby the same way Lorraine had recovered from the loss of Tommy. So she knew exactly what they needed.

When Wayne placed the two cheeseburger-deluxe platters and the matching mini ketchups in front of the girls with the urgency such an order deserved, Lorraine said to her friend, "Something is missing. Seriously missing."

Chrissy looked around, a questioning look hanging over her brow etching lines in her forehead. Suddenly, the lines and brows straightened. "Of course."

Then they said in unison, "Two chocolate shakes, please, Wayne!" Laughter felt good. They were easy friends again. But things weren't completely the same between them. Lorraine sensed, and she knew Chrissy also felt it, that she had become a sort of leader to the two of them—at least at present. She'd had the kind of experiences that could help the pair fix their long-standing history of mistakes.

When the two curvy glasses arrived, their frothy, frozen contents rippled to overflowing heights, the girls shouted, "Cheers!"

"To Park Avenue!" Chrissy said.

And Lorraine agreed, "To Park Avenue!"

Two women in pink cashmere *shushed* them.

They laughed and held up their large chocolate shakes. After all, they were Brooklyn girls.

"So good," Chrissy said, working her way through a monstrous cheeseburger bite, waving the burger around for extra emphasis. A few sesame seeds went flying, which again got them laughing. Chrissy was acting like she was overcome with the experience, coming at it with all she was—not just the parts Bobby left over. It was something beautiful to watch, Lorraine thought.

Amidst all the pain the two girls had just worked through, Lorraine realized she was having . . . *fun*. She hadn't come so far as she thought—not so far that her best friend wasn't her best friend anymore, as she had feared. And that thought comforted her in a tangible way.

When dessert time came around, Chrissy stopped her fork midway from chocolate cake to mouth. She screwed up her eyes and cocked her head before asking, "Isn't that your friend, Don?"

Lorraine turned in her seat. Yes, it was Don and he looked as if he'd noticed them. Actually, it looked like he'd wanted them to notice *him*, but couldn't quite bring himself to do anything about it. Seeing him there, Lorraine thought it was high time they clear the air between them, too. After all, hadn't his brother already cleared the way for them? Lorraine had missed Don sorely, and she was more than a bit hurt by his absence in the past few months. But she understood. Don needed to work through his own problems until he could be the person he wanted to be.

"Let's ask him over! Can we?" Chrissy was puffy chested and fluttering her hands over hair and clothes with smoothing actions that could only be categorized as instinctive.

"You totally love him! I knew it!"

"Don't say anything!"

"Should I not say that he asked about you? That he obviously likes you, too?"

"Are you f'ing with me, Lorraine?" Chrissy could never believe a compliment about herself.

Lorraine knew the cause of that weakness, and his name started with Big and ended with Bobby. "I would never F with you, Chrissy. I love you."

"Don!" Lorraine waved him over.

The pink cashmeres *shushed*.

Don waved back.

"Come over!" she said, palming him in their direction like mad. Two people she had thought she'd lost—and here they were, just like that. She'd nearly forgotten what friendship *felt* like. She swore then and there never to let that happen again. Sure, things could get awkward, but you had to push where it mattered. If there ever was a next time, it would be more than likely she wouldn't get so lucky with the second chances.

The pink cashmeres *shushed*.

"Celebrating your wonderful new salon?" Don asked when finally resettled at their table, his Greek salad and iced tea placed in front of him.

Lorraine couldn't get over the way he was talking to *her*, but smiling at Chrissy while he did so. Don had such a youthful openness to him, he might as well have been wearing a sandwich board printed with the words "I love Chrissy." It was that easy to tell how he felt about everything. And as obvious as it was that he was happy right now, it was equally as clear that he was unhappy about coloring hair. He'd covered his roots, but they didn't exactly match the lengths of the deep blond he was currently wearing. But even that small fault made him approachable, not too perfect and untouchable like some people could be.

"Actually, yes! We were!" Chrissy answered for Lorraine, obviously not wanting any of her bad news littering the path that might carry her to a date with Don. "I'm just trying to get Lorraine to let me do the accounting for her. I'd love to get a job in the city."

Lorraine was surprised. This was the first she'd heard of Chrissy's feelings on the matter. Could she even picture Chrissy outside of the Bay? Well, they were supposed to be twins, weren't they? "I would love it if you would!"

The idea of working with your friends, the people closest to you, was a wonderful concept to Lorraine, so she started thinking of all the other people she might ask to join the salon. She'd already started hand-picking the stylists in her head, even making a couple of phone calls. They were the best around—some from the top beauty spots in the city. Those were the obvious choices. But others she was planning on stealing from tiny salons that no one had ever heard of. She knew firsthand that there were plenty of people who wound up in spots like that for reasons that had nothing to do with lack of talent. After all, she was one of those people herself, wasn't she? And the reason she'd come to Guido had everything to do with the boy across from her with the slightly off-color roots. It was because of Don.

"You know, Don, I've got a lot of stylists to hire. As a matter of fact, I've only got colorists in mind as of right now. And after that, there will be a lot of business decisions to make. You know, creatively, I'm your girl, but as far as the rest goes, I haven't got a clue. You think you'd ever stop coloring hair to be my business manager?"

From the frisson that went right from his eyes to the tips of his fingers, Lorraine imagined he would. "Well, shit! From one Guido to another one!"

"Hey, we're Guid*ettes*!" They each took a punch at one of his arms.

The weeks flew by in a blur. Lorraine barely had time to sneak make-out sessions in with Matt. He was *such* an amazing kisser. Lorraine could sit there and kiss him all day, if only she had a chance to do it. But she hadn't had much time between, "Lorraine, do you want eggshell or beige?" and "Lorraine, would you like gold or copper tassels on the curtains?" Not to mention all the undercover work she had to do, hand-selecting her colorists.

She wasn't complaining. It was awesome taking control of every creative aspect of her own salon—the style of which was completely her own. The decorator she'd chosen, a woman named Helen, really let her bring her own tastes through, while working with resources and options only an expert in the design field would be capable of unearthing. Don had found her, of course. And from the start, it was an epic partnership. For starters, Helen was "secretly" from Brooklyn. Over fabric swatches and dainty china cups of chamomile tea in a Lexington Avenue showroom after hours of the same, Helen added this caveat: "But I'm gettin' tired of acting all hoighty-toighty, ya know? Sometimes a Brooklyn girl just wants to be a Brooklyn girl." Lorraine knew just what she meant.

However limited, it was, even more awesome to spend time with Matt. As potent as her pain had been all these years in the face of Tommy's semirejection, this—her desire, their mutual desire—was more, everywhere, in every part of her body, with her all day, even when she wasn't here, on his cozy sofa, his toned stomach leaning against the curve of her waist. Warm on cool, that ocean smell of his was everywhere, or at least so it seemed to Lorraine.

Her cell phone rang, and Lorraine ignored it.

"Do you think it might be important?" Matt asked, his finger trailing its way up from her middle.

"Sure. But not as important as this."

"Well. Nothing could be as important as this." He said it in a joking tone, but when Lorraine giggled her response, his face turned up to her own, his expression serious. He kissed her hard, a kiss that proved his point.

"I love you, Lorraine."

Tears came when she responded, "I love you, Matt." She cried because it was true—she loved him. And she didn't even need any fly's wings to make him love her back.

Again, her cell phone chirped.

"Frig it," she said when Matt raised his eyebrows. She knew he wouldn't take it personally, make a big deal about Lorraine taking a call while they were together. He didn't worry over the little things. That wasn't his style. But it made her want to give him her undivided attention all the more.

Lorraine was completely naked by the time the ringing picked up once more.

"I think you should get it, Lorraine. Someone really wants to talk to you."

The number was unavailable, so when Lorraine picked up, she was mildly fearing the worst—hospitals, firemen, Tommy, who knew? "Hello?"

"Princess Lorraine, we had a lunch date today. Remember?"

No, she had never heard of this before.

"No, I don't remember that, Mallory."

"Well, we do. I'll see you in five minutes at the diner."

She wasn't going to be bullied by Mallory. Her frenemy had been in a rotten mood since Lorraine had started spending time with Matt. And although she never advertised it, the paparazzi had gotten involved. There she was every morning after she'd been with him, drinking a coffee, walking Pooh-Pooh alongside Matt and Lena Horne (never mind the fun the press had with the antics of those two), their pictures front and center in the paper. Lorraine inspected every millimeter of the pictures. She couldn't tell if their enchantment with each other was as clear to everyone, or just to her.

And now that Mallory and Tommy were so obviously an item, it mattered to her even less what Mallory thought. That was so clearly a pointed gesture, meant to hurt her, and her alone—that she could barely look Mallory in the face. Lorraine and Tommy had still been together for all Mallory had known when she'd "canoodled up with him at the Mercedes event," according to one gossip hound. "Tongues everywhere" had been the caption below their photo. They deserved each other.

"You should just let her sit there, Lorraine. But you're too nice for that, aren't you?" He was shaking his head. "If that wasn't the trait I loved about you the most, I'd tell you you're a fool."

It hurt Lorraine to pull herself from his warmth, his couch. His hands had come to mean comfort. They were elegant in their own way—

calloused and cut from all his woodwork into a pattern uniquely his own. She ran one of her fingers over a particularly rough bit on his thumb. She could linger there all day. But, she thought, maybe Mallory needed her. And she knew her success was in part a product of Mallory's efforts— albeit under somewhat questionable motives—in taking her on as a Princess.

The diner was packed with Silver Hairs eating chicken salad clubs on rye toast, giant lettuce leaves sticking out below the crusts, pretending the meal was in accordance with their medically prescribed diets, or else pretending to forget about it altogether.

"What did you eat for lunch, Grams?" She'd posed the question to her own grandmother not so long ago. "Oh, just a sandwich," she'd say. The idea brought a smile to her face as she walked past them all, dressed for business with their oversized necklaces and eyeglass chains hanging, pickles and golden French fries piled high onto speckled ceramic plates.

Lorraine guessed Mallory hadn't noticed any of them from the way her rhinestone Baby Phat cell phone was attached to her lightly Paula Dorf-blushed cheek, her two-way pager between her Guido-Nailed thumbs. Lorraine strained to see some shred of feeling underneath that clay exterior. But all she could sense was the mysterious smell of French fries and leather. "Mallory." She smiled, and slid in the booth opposite her. She soon realized there wasn't time for pleasantries.

"Lorraine, you've really been slacking on your responsibilities. I haven't seen you at one event this week. There were Maybelline, Caudalie, and Megu events, Clinton's biography launch . . ." She crossed her hands over her chest slowly, deliberately. If you looked closely, you could see her eyes had spidery red veins over them. Her straightened hair (Matrix had asked her to bring the trend back for their new hair-care line) was dented toward the top right. They were small things—but Mallory was all about the small things.

As if she read Lorraine's mind, she said, "You mustn't forget the small things."

Ignore her. Just ignore her. "I've just been busy, Mallory. You know, the salon is opening in just a couple of weeks. I was thinking maybe we could all wear something by Rebecca Taylor. I always loved her stuff, and she's designed these awesome wrap-robes for the salon. I thought it would be great."

"You know, Lorraine, you are entirely too wrapped up in your salon. It's like nothing else matters to you anymore."

For a second, Lorraine thought Mallory really did miss her and was hurt by her absence. She thought she could see it in the way she sat up a bit too straight, held her chin a bit too high. "You miss me, don't you?" Lorraine smiled, attempted to soften the mood. Hey, if she was going to let this thing with Tommy slide, then the least Mallory could do was smile, right?

But, even if it were true, Mallory refused to let anyone see it. "I don't miss anyone, Lorraine. We're here to discuss responsibilities. I trust you haven't forgotten about Katharine's bachelorette party next weekend. The *Elle* writer needs the itinerary faxed to her this afternoon."

Lorraine effortlessly rolled out a restaurant name and three bars, as if she hadn't just wrangled them up on the spot. She still had her street smarts, after all. Lorraine picked at a souvlaki platter; Mallory swallowed three half spoonfuls of vegetable soup. They both knew it was bad news for Lorraine to come to the greasy diner and not have anything greasy. But instead of mentioning any bad news, it just hung there between them. They didn't mention Tommy. They didn't mention Matt. Mallory took two calls on her cell phone, answered five text messages with the speed of a career secretary. Even as Lorraine waited for Mallory to finish with her various distractions, she still didn't think she hated her. Though maybe she should have.

When the waitress, Sally, brought their bill, Lorraine handed her an invitation to the salon opening party. She'd been so nice to her all these months Lorraine had been coming here. She never gave attitude, even that day when Mallory sent her coffee back three times for being cold, when really it had *gotten* cold just waiting there for her to drink—which she never would, since she never drank caffeine, only liked to smell it. "Caffeine, Princess Lorraine, *will* kill you. Never mind what it does to the enamel on your *teeth.*"

Whenever she said that kind of thing, the listener (Lorraine included) couldn't help but swipe her tongue across her own teeth and then button her lips. It was just the type of reaction Mallory incited. If there was an available corner, you'd have the urge to walk yourself to it and sit there for twenty minutes or so. In her presence, you couldn't help yourself.

Before she rose without excusing herself or saying goodbye, Mallory put on her patented air of insincerity—the same she used to thank the waitress for bringing a third new coffee—smiled big and said to Lorraine, who'd only been searching for good things to think of her, "Looks like you've got a lot to lose now, Lorraine, don't you?" She hung her Kelly bag over the shoulder of her nautical striped shirt (accessorized with strands and strands of multisized navy crystal beads like something out of *Bazaar*), pulled her shield sunglasses down over her eyes, and looked challengingly at her companion.

Lorraine wondered for the thousandth time why she was still friendly with Mallory. For all her morals and everything she'd ever held dear, she hoped the real reason wasn't because she wanted her salon to succeed. That would make her no better than the rest of them.

Dear Lorraine,

I can't believe I am doing this, but I must tell you the truth!

Mallory is out to get you! We are all cast members of a reality show, and the joke is on you! It's all been staged-very high drama-to shock you, and make you have a nervous break-down. I want to tell you because you are such a good person, Lorraine, and I know how much Tommy has always meant to you. It's all too awful to think about! If only those Hilton girls didn't get so famous, then maybe Mallory wouldn't have gone so far! But I'm not making any excuses for her. I only want to warn you, darling Lorraine.

Best,
Stacey

eBay auction block #19

Description: Found by Curtis ("not Bert!" he says), this note, written by Stacey, was brought into the limousine the night of the staged bachelorette party. For reasons unknown, Stacey never gave it to Lorraine, and so Curtis, the limousine driver, found it while he was cleaning the limousine ("We keep our cars perfect with a twenty-point cleaning!" he asks we add). Because he wanted everyone to know the truth (and not because of the cash), he has placed this item up for auction.

Opening bid: $125
Winning bid: $722 by Staceyprincess@princess.com

Comments: I would never try to hurt my best friend, Mallory, this way. She is perfect and I would never think anything less. I did not write this letter, never would write this letter, and plan to bring legal action up Bert, the limousine driver.

NINETEEN

♥

BACHELORETTE NIGHT

The sticky summer moisture clung to Lorraine's skin on the night of the bachelorette party. Rather than allow her hair to frizz, she styled it the wavy way. Rather than let her face look sweaty, she wore her makeup dewy to begin with. The sun was still up when they set out in a Hummer limousine, and picked up each of the Princesses at her doorstep. Katharine's stop was last in order for her to unveil her six-karat ring to the widest audience.

Lorraine had been picked up first. She had left Matt at the new salon space. He was building the most beautiful mirror stations and a grand reception desk, rich and warm at the same time—the kind of thing you didn't see at any of these modern, cold salons. The place was nearly done. And Matt had thrown himself into it, his first project for his full-time furniture business. It had definitely softened the blow to his dad when he told him he already had a contract worth a ton of money from the most influential woman in Manhattan. That's what he told Lorraine. Reflexively she asked, "Who?" *Lorraine,* he'd said, *When will you realize how special you are?*

She watched a muted Manhattan flash by in streams of smooth light, inside the warm, safe back of the car. Had she conquered Manhattan, like everyone was always hoping to do? The idea of her own salon thrilled her—the freedom of it, anyway. The business, she really could do without. Not only did the number crunching and jargon exhaust her, it also bored her to tears, not to mention scared the crap out of her. But that was the great part: She had people she loved to do those things for her: Don and Chrissy.

They came to a halt in front of Mallory's. Lorraine got out to hug her and plant a kiss at the air surrounding her cheek. That's when she first noticed the camera crew following the limo. Suddenly her cozy ride was transformed—she felt naked, violated. It seemed everywhere she went these days, her privacy was infringed upon. More than once she'd caught those camera guys in the bushes across the way. Sometimes you couldn't see them, but you knew they were there. She guessed it was the price you paid. She could use all the publicity she could get with the salon opening so soon. But, tonight, with the mood she was in, the last thing Lorraine wanted was to be filmed so obviously, so intrusively.

"Princess Mallory, you look stunning." And she did. She'd gone all out. She was wearing one of the new circle skirts—the ones only the rich girls will look great in, because the more affordable imitations won't be cut so trim at the waist, won't have that amazing weightless lift of a 1950s Hollywood glamazon. It was done in a neutral color, and printed with huge crimson blossoms, some of which were delicately embellished with jet beading, crystals and sequins. At the top she had the world's most slim-cut tank that hung perfectly at her tastefully sized chest, and an equally shrunken Chanel blazer over that. Truth was, she would stick out like a sore thumb in Brooklyn. But it would work *for* her. Brooklyn boys were amazed by the glamour of Manhattan women. At least in Lorraine's experience.

Lorraine was wearing slim white pants, a tiny Chloé jacket with sailor stripes, and a sparkly tank with her grandmother's faux-Chanel chain link pearls. She may have had a certain allure herself. But she didn't want any of those boys. And she hoped to GOD that the one she'd always been scanning the crowds for in the past wouldn't show up. Not when everything was going so well. It had been one thing to be in love with Matt when she hadn't seen Tommy in a while. But would she fall back to her old ways when she did? Sick as she was when the idea struck her, she wouldn't put anything past herself, in light of her history. What about if she saw him with Mallory? The idea of it was too terrible even to consider.

"Oh, this old thing . . ." Before coming two inches from Lorraine's cheek with her own, she added, "You look pretty amazing yourself."

The two of them stood face-to-face, perhaps a second too long. The respect, if not love, they shared for each other was obvious. The women were both leaders—they merely led in two different directions. The catch was, neither trusted the other as far as she could throw her.

Lorraine caught the van pull out behind them. The E! crew was always followed Mallory, but something about this gave Lorraine a bad feeling.

They picked up, in order, Tracey, Stacey, and Katharine. Each time Curtis, the driver, came around, walked up to their doorway, took the girls' hands, and introduced himself cordially, with an Old-World charm you didn't often see today. "Good evening, mademoiselle, I am Curtis, your driver. Please let me know if there is anything I can do to enhance your experience tonight."

With the exception of Lorraine, the girls didn't so much as acknowledge him. Each was wearing a version of Mallory's circle skirt, slim tank, and jacket, and as soon as the door opened and the rest of them came into sight, their attention was swept away in comparing outfits.

It hadn't occurred to Lorraine before how they never let her in on their dressing decisions. She'd never been much for dressing just like someone else, never mind three someone else's. But now it did seem odd to her. If she was a Princess, wasn't she supposed to act just like the rest of them? She knew she never had, anyway. Did that have something to do with what Mallory was getting at the other day at the diner with her ice-queen routine? And if so, what was she trying to say exactly? *You've got a lot to lose now, don't you?*

Katharine had that look about her. You know, that look that says, *Ah-hhhh, I'm done now. I can sit back and relax because I have done it.* But it also said something else: *I've done it first.*

The other girls settled on their looks in response. Their too-big smiles and too-crinkly eyes said *And we absolutely hate you for it. Plus, over sixty percent of marriages end in divorce.*

Lorraine glanced at the rearview mirror and their driver, Curtis, grimaced at her as if they were players on the same team. Was she that different? The one you would pick out and say, I can most easily approach her? As Curtis's grimace turned into a smile with a matching head shake, she thought, *yes, I am.* That said something about who Lorraine was, no matter where she may have gone.

"Well, guys, Curtis put some fabulous champagne in here for us!" Lorraine said, trying to relieve the tension pushing them all back into the cool leather seats.

"Who's Curtis?" Stacey asked, inspecting her Guido Nails, probably thinking about how she didn't find Katherine's fiancé attractive, and besides, Europeans were so much more desirable to her.

"The driver who just introduced himself to you two seconds ago."

"Whatever." Then she turned to face him. "Bert, can you turn up the music back here?"

The *Elle* writer was short. Next to the five Princesses, she was somewhere between a Munchkin and Mini Me. She was also dressed flashier—and as if she'd gone through all the samples in her closet and couldn't get any of the improperly sized, but free garments to work with any of the other improperly sized, but free garments. Lorraine thought again about the idea of getting what everyone else wanted and not being happy with it. More and more, she saw the syndrome around her. The result for the *Elle* writer was a studded black velvet shirt so low cut and so blousy that she had to keep sliding it back into position every two minutes so that her chest wouldn't show entirely. Paired with a circle skirt, the reporter looked like she was playing prima ballerina. At least, Lorraine thought, the girl could feel good about getting the circle skirt right. Maybe she didn't notice the rest.

"I'm Ashley," she said, holding her short-nailed hand out for Lorraine. Apparently she'd met the rest of them. *But when?* Lorraine wondered.

"Lorraine." Ashley's hand was cold. She was nervous. How could anyone be nervous to meet Lorraine? The idea was too absurd even to consider. "I'm so thrilled to meet the famous Lorraine Machuchi, right on the eve of her new salon opening."

"Well ..." She didn't get to say anything before Ashley cut her off directly.

"You know," she said, "I cover beauty, too. Do you think you could get me one of those cards?"

"Which cards do you mean?" Lorraine asked, stumped.

"You know, the free-service cards for editors?"

Oh, those cards, Lorraine thought. Secretly, the request had delighted her. Sure, Ashley had gone about it all wrong, and with no tact whatsoever, but she went about it—and that was something Lorraine could admire in someone. "Yours will be the first. You should come to the party, too. We open next week."

"Oh, thanks! I'm already coming to the party, though."

Things could really get bigger than you, couldn't they? A publicist was handling the launch. Lorraine didn't have any idea what was going on with that. She got that odd sensation that everything was growing, growing, inflating like one of those Snoopy Thanksgiving Day parade floats, and Lorraine herself was holding the string one hundred feet below. And tiny in her skinny white pants—chic as they might be—she didn't know where to pull the plug.

"So, girls, just act like I'm not here!" Ashley said, as if that were going to be a possibility, as if she were the kind of girl who blended right in. And then, as if she'd never suggested it in the first place, she said, "So can I get some champagne around here, or what?!"

Mallory offered her fake flattery face. Lorraine smiled at the familiar recognition of this look—a smile constructed from two lips so strong they could crush you between them. She reached for the champagne and poured it into a Princess-monogrammed flute ($49.99 on www.princess.com, genuine full-lead Tiffany crystal 6 oz. capacity), which Tracey held out for her. A bit of champagne dripped onto Tracey's fabulous circle skirt.

"Oh!" She looked at the quickly spreading dark circle in horror. "Look what you did, Mallory! I'll look like a sloppy drunk on television for all the world to see!" As soon as the words spilt out—like a champagne overflow themselves—her face turned red as a ripened strawberry, her eyes bulging as if they just might pop right out and smack the window across.

There it was again, Lorraine thought, making sure to smile on the outside as if she hadn't noticed Mallory flip out about that *television* reference! But it was obvious that van was following them. What could all the secrecy be about?

"Tracey! What in heavens are you talking about? I'm sure there won't be television crews following us to *Brooklyn* of all places! No offense, Lorraine." Mallory, fake as ever, smiled the largest smile she could muster and tried to blot at Tracey's skirt. The smile couldn't hide the facts: The crews had followed them all there before.

"But, Mallory," Tracey was flustered. "Anyone can see the crew, clear as day, following us!" As if emphasizing the point, the van now had someone's head sticking out the top. He waved their way when they turned around to look.

Mallory was about to speak, her mouth poised, her eyes daggers, when she was cut off by Ashley the Invisible, who appeared stumped.

"But didn't you say NBC—"

Whether by accident or accidentally on purpose, Mallory spilled even more champagne on Tracey's skirt. "Ooooh!" everyone exclaimed. Ashley wadded up some Princess-embossed napkin squares (available at www.princess.com for $12.95 a dozen) and scooched closer to the girls to help clean up the accident.

Lorraine saw right through Mallory's thin excuse for a distraction. The question was, why?

The restaurant, 101, had reserved the best seat in the house—the one by the window in the back. "I cannot believe you all ordered so many carbs!" Ashley the Invisible exclaimed, her renegade nipple coming a little too close to the low-cut neckline for comfort.

"Haven't you heard, dear?" Tracey answered. "By the way, your nipple is showing, again. Carbs are back. It's the Mario diet. You up the carbs, go veggie all the way, and super low on the fats. Julia Roberts lost her twins' fat in *two weeks*."

Ashley the Invisible scribbled away madly, turning a shade of purple that was off the charts.

As for Lorraine, she enjoyed the hum of 101. The regulars, the wait staff. Petey and Mary even came over for a moment before going back to their table, just a few feet away. "Lorraine! Look at you, Miss Famous! How *you* doin'?"

Surprisingly, fine, she wanted to say, *despite the fact that there are at least a dozen photographers and videographers behind me, and there is some type of plot brewing here that can only be bad—make that very bad.* And despite the fact that she did indeed smell trouble more than ever, she *was* fine. When you'd already faced your worst fears, you didn't worry so much anymore. But even better than that, she didn't feel uncomfortable being in Brooklyn with the Princesses. Maybe, she thought, she wasn't exactly a Princess, and wasn't exactly a Brooklyn girl. Or maybe, she thought, she was both. "I'm great! You guys should meet up with us later at the Blue Zoo!" And she meant it. Why shouldn't she? She couldn't remember why she'd ever felt so out of place when she'd visited home before.

"Sure, we were planning on going there anyway," Mary said. She used the dual pronoun so comfortably, like she'd been doing it forever. Lorraine was happy for her friend. She deserved it. For once, Lorraine noticed she wasn't seeing everyone else's happiness through the filter of her own experience. It was rather a weightless feeling.

When the fried calamari came out, so delicately breaded, weightless in their own golden brown way, whisked straight from the fragrant oil they were crisped in, only she and Ashley the Invisible dug into the tiny hollow disks. Lorraine watched the streetlight outside turn from red to green, the cars lightly rolling forward beyond a few couples walking hand-in-hand toward the promenade just a few blocks beyond. She even liked the flow of traffic better over here, as she watched it from her seat. It was better to be looking out than concentrating on the whole restaurant staring at you on account of the cameramen making no attempt at inconspicuousness.

A guy Lorraine knew from high school approached the table slowly, but deliberately. A tight gray polyester-blend shirt strained a bit at the buttons concealing his perfectly developed pecs, as he tried to pick Mallory up. "Anyone ever told you you're the most beautiful woman on the planet?" He crouched down soon after he said that to Mallory, close enough for her to smell his cologne—which honestly she could have smelled from across the room.

"Why, no." Mallory was playing the shy role. She loved the attention—she lived for it. You could see her eyes grow really serious, her lids coming together slightly, her focus tightening. She wanted him to fall hopelessly in love with her so she could add him to the list of millions of others. That way she could count them up when she got bored.

Lorraine wondered something she often had about Tommy—when would it ever be enough?

"So when can I take you out?" These guys didn't beat around the bush. They went right in for it. Subtlety wasn't part of the game.

"Why don't I just give you my number?" Mallory grabbed for her purse, pulled out her sterling silver Princess pen ($42.99 on www.princess.com) and French-milled calling cards from Papivore, and wrote a private number beneath her printed name and e-mail address in tasteful, delicate handwriting, feminine without a hint of froth or frill.

"Have a wonderful evening, beautiful," he said, and then strode away from their table.

"Oh, how authentic!" Mallory exclaimed.

"If you thought he was simply 'authentic,' then why'd you give him your number?" Tracey wanted to know.

"For kicks," Mallory said, as if there were no mystery as to why, as if her friend had just asked the most obvious question in the world.

"Aren't you afraid that Tom—" Tracey didn't get to finish.

Instead she was hit with an iron stare from Mallory.

Stacey inspected the lighting above.

"He's just adorable. Like a big floppy-eared dog. I'll make his century," Mallory said, checking in with Lorraine with a Cheshire-cat grin.

Lorraine was no moron. And she'd already known, although she'd somehow convinced herself it was mainly in Tommy's head and that he'd spread it around to feel important.

Ashley the Invisible didn't pick up on any of the controversy. "You were going to ask about Tommy, weren't you?"

No, she wasn't surprised so much as sick to her stomach. No, if she was honest with herself, she had to admit she already knew exactly what was going on. And she had to admit, she shouldn't care. Hey, wasn't this the answer for both of them? Those two deserved each other. They could make each other miserable for eternity. It was so obvious, anyone would see it. Why else would he have disappeared? Where did she think he had been? Why else would they have been photographed together so many times while Lorraine had fallen off the party-circuit radar?

But Lorraine knew there was a difference between knowing something, and *knowing something*. Now she *knew* it, she didn't know what to do with it. And now she felt herself going through the familiar reaction—the stabbing feeling at her stomach, the ice that went to her heart. The worst part was, when this happened to Lorraine, everything she had on felt like it didn't fit—she felt like Ashley the Invisible looked. Then there was her hair—she was sure it didn't suit her like that. It was surely sprouting from her head, pieces twisting and twirling like Medusa. There were no words in her mouth. Just dryness, catching at her throat.

Could this be happening? Could she be regressing, going backward? Could it be that everything that had happened to her was just a dream? Could she wake and find that none of this had happened? Could she still be just the colorist from the Do Wop, the one who'd thrown her life away for a boy she'd never have? The one the old Italian women in the pork store shook their heads at wiping tears from beneath their Coke-bottle eyeglasses at the sadness of her life?

Everyone was looking at her. They knew Lorraine didn't take crap; you could not pull one over on Lorraine and get away with it. That, she knew, was the reason she'd gotten this far. She felt eyes boring into her, a hundred unspoken pleas to, if not for her own sake, right some wrong Mallory had bestowed on each of them. Tracey was even *smiling*. But in the midst of the noisiest silence she could ever recall, Lorraine could only manage, "Excuse me. I have to go to the ladies' room."

Chrissy, Chrissy, please pick up. She was saying it out loud, hoping it would somehow help. "Hey, peeps. Miss Chris isn't here right now. You know what to do." *Chrissy, Chrissy, where are you? Oh!* She remembered. *You're with Don!*

"What the hell is going on in there? Can't a girl take a pee in peace?"

Now, that was the kind of attitude Lorraine needed! But she couldn't even bring herself to respond to the stranger. She'd curled up into a little ball, and didn't know how to unwind herself. She furiously dialed Don's number.

"Lorraine, how are you?" His voice was strong, happy. It was a Don she barely recognized. He had that same humor he'd had when they'd first met, but there was a confidence, an edge she'd never known him to possess.

She couldn't speak properly yet, so she attempted to convey her need in the most efficient manner possible. "Chrissy," she whispered.

"Girl, are you okay?" her bathroom mate inquired.

"Chrissy!" she whispered again when she heard her friend's voice on the line. The tears were coming now, and she could barely even get that name out. It must have sounded frightening because she got the question echoed from the woman in the next stall: "Are you okay?"

"I-I don't know. . . ." Now she was just hysterical. Everything felt as if it were crashing in on her, and there she was, sitting on a toilet seat in white pants, watching mascara-blackened tears rain small stains over her thighs. As if feeding off of the strength Lorraine couldn't locate inside herself, the neighbor punched Lorraine's stall door in with one swift thump of her fist. The girl was no one Lorraine recognized. But she still came up and held Lorraine to her, rubbed her hands over Lorraine's head as she pushed it into her bosom, comforting her like a life-long friend. "Oh, shusssssshhhhhhh. It's okay. It's okay."

It was just what she needed. Somehow, this stranger comforted her completely. Through the phone Chrissy was saying, "I'll meet you at the Blue Zoo. And Lorraine, don't forget who you are! We are *not* the Bobbsey Twins anymore! We are grown-ups and we don't have to take that kind of crap! *You* are the one who taught that to *me!* Lorraine, don't let this happen. Don't let him hurt you."

In that bathroom, the familiar smell of cleanser wafting around her—it was the same one her mother used in their own bathroom—Lorraine knew she was at a crossroads in her life. Sure, she'd accomplished a lot already. She'd come so far in the way other people expected of her, but Lorraine knew *this* night—*this* night was the real test for her. She was that figure she always had pictured in that Robert Frost poem, caught at the diverging road, being forced to choose one. It hadn't hit her before how difficult it might be to make a choice, to truly say goodbye to the familiar. You could say goodbye but still hold on, so that you never really let it go. And this pain made her realize she was still clinging to her old relationship somewhere in her heart.

"Lorraine, isn't it?" the girl said, lifting Lorraine's head gently.

"How'd you know?" Lorraine whispered, pulling herself from the thoughts she'd been swimming in for God knows how long.

"You're famous around here, Lorraine. Everyone knows you. You know that Hanukkah song from that guy, what's his name?"

"Adam Sandler?" Lorraine sniffled. This woman's face was getting sweeter and sweeter.

"Yes! Adam Sandler! That is a funny one, isn't it?"

Lorraine shook her head. She wasn't sure where this woman was going. As far as she knew, Adam Sandler wasn't from Bay Ridge, and she wasn't Jewish. Pulling her face further from her bosom, she noticed she'd soaked the woman's blouse.

"Well, the same way he's proud of all the great Jewish people, we're proud of you for being from our town."

If only people knew the truth, that she was no better off now!

"What's the problem, honey?"

Lorraine just shook her head.

"Aw. That's okay. I know it's hard to tell people sometimes. But, you know, I always say, you can't go wrong, Lorraine, if you just remember who you are. Think back to that, and you'll never go wrong."

The words were bringing the tears back. Lorraine could feel them stinging, and then glossing up over her eyes. They hadn't yet dropped, but they were making the woman all wavy, like a dream.

"So nice to meet you. I know you'll be okay." The woman stuffed a wad of toilet paper in Lorraine's hand and then pushed the heavy door to exit the bathroom.

Lorraine was all by herself, everything blurring under the thickening tears. Then, suddenly, the silence was shattered again. "You better listen to that girl, Lorraine. God, you can be stupid!" The words rang out in an unmistakable tone like a smack in the face. No one else spoke so un-apologetically and with such force.

"Grandma?" Lorraine asked. But there was no reply. Was that all she got? When she thought about it, she realized it was all she deserved. Just look at her! Sitting on a toilet, blubbering making, a mockery of the strong women in her family. It had to end, right then and there.

Lorraine jumped off the toilet, rubbing at the spots on her jeans with her Princess Shout Outs! (which came in the evening out-kit along with a "morning after" Cosabella thong, a Durex for her pleasure condom, breath mints, a throw-away toothbrush, and a tiny Bond 09 New York perfume vial, $52.99 at www.princess.com). She dabbed at her eyes with some tissue, repowdered, glossed, and added a touch of blush.

"All right Grandma! I'm ready! Maybe I forgot who I was for about twenty years, but now I remember!"

Twenty-five minutes later the girls entered the Blue Zoo—four swirly skirts following a pair of slim white pants and a beautiful turquoise flapper blouse (and a nearly naked girl apparently wearing her mother's clothing). They were stunning, and the crowd was stunned.

Rich met them at the door. "Ah, the beautiful Princesses. A pleasure," he said, kissing Lorraine first on the cheek, and then each of the other girls on the hand, until he got to Tracey. He stepped in just the tiniest bit closer before pulling her hand, just a tiny bit slower than he had with the rest, up to his mouth, lingering long with his kiss, and then looking at her with an unmistakable stare. "Tracey." He said her name as if it were attached to a pile of jewels he were caressing in his palm. Ten minutes later they were making out, the same way he'd done with the high school girl the last time Lorraine had been there.

The crowd thickened into a mass of hair and arms and legs and a ca-cophony of voices. The music level rose several decibels as the band played Top 40 songs. Sitting chicly in back, the girls had nearly drained their dirty martinis. Rich already had his hand up Tracey's skirt, and her gaze trained expectantly in his direction in between kisses.

"I seriously can't drink these things!" Ashley the Invisible screamed to Lorraine, so that she had to hold her head back from the sheer volume.

"They are strong," Lorraine agreed, though she didn't feel drunk in the slightest.

What Lorraine *felt* was strong, but she wasn't sure just what to do with it. However, she didn't need to wonder long.

The sea of people parted, and there he was. Tommy was dressed sleeker, his shirt a little looser, his chest only hinted at rather than visible, his jeans a more time-intensive finish. But it was Tommy all the same. His scent—one thing he'd retained entirely—spilled inside her, filling her up until she thought she'd choke.

He looked her way first, and for a moment she thought she'd never be able to do this, never have the strength to fight him. She could see her life dropping away in shards, like a smashed piggy bank, the riches hidden inside her falling to the floor. That's what Tommy would do to her.

"Lorraine." She was paralyzed as his mouth drew nearer. But then something remarkable happened: When his lips touched her cheek, it didn't fit. They weren't right. In fact, they were all wrong! Sure, he was hot and sexy and magnetic, but those qualities couldn't overcome the growing feeling that it was just, well . . . over. She didn't want to hurt anymore. She wouldn't let him take her away. She would remember who she was.

"Tommy." The sound of his name coming from her mouth burned, like she was breathing fire.

"Miss me?" he asked in her ear, so that no one else could hear.

"No," she hissed.

Despite her response, he continued on. "See my new car outside, Lorraine? It's a Mercedes."

The bile rose in her throat. As she followed his gaze as it scanned the room, instinctively looking for other women, she could see, clear as day, how pathetic Tommy was. She held her grandmother's string of Chanel-like chain link pearls in her hand. They were a symbol of all her grandmother had wanted for herself, for her daughter, for Lorraine. Squeezing them tight, she said, "That's wonderful. I'm so happy for you." She'd been tested, and she'd passed.

"Wanna go out and see it?" Tommy was obviously the only one who couldn't see the change in Lorraine. Of course, she thought, he couldn't see it, because he'd never known her in the first place.

"No, I don't, actually." *Breathe, breathe,* she reminded herself.

"Ha ha." He grabbed for her hand.

"I'm serious, Tommy. I'm not going anywhere right now."

"Oh, I get it. You're waiting for that fucking loser with the pussy dog." His volume had risen and the band had stopped for a break, so a lot of heads turned their way. He was drunk; she could see that now.

"I'm not even going to grace you with an answer to that, Tommy."

He looked at her, anger tight at his jaw, red at his cheek.

As quickly as the look came her way, he turned from her, ignored the others, and went straight for Mallory, who'd been alternately ignoring them and piercing them with the evil eye. To Lorraine's shock, he grabbed Mallory and kissed her hard and long.

Mallory had really thrown herself into him. Her body was pressed against every square inch of him, her circle skirt encompassing his legs, swallowing him up, while his arms covered her entire upper half. They were stealing from each other. Only Lorraine could see it; only she could recognize the subtle differences between someone Tommy thought he loved and someone he wanted something from.

As she pulled her stare away from them, scanned the other girls, who looked sorry and ashamed, Lorraine said to Ashley the Invisible, "Well, Ashley, it has been a pleasure meeting you. Before you ask, Tommy was some stupid guy from around the way that I'd been obsessed with my whole life. But he wasn't going anywhere, never will. And I'm sure you understand, that's why it was just never going to work between us."

Stepping out from the cool air-conditioning, into the warm air outside, Lorraine should have felt uncomfortable. But quite the opposite! It was as if her chest, lungs, throat had opened up after being constricted the whole night long. The wide open space felt wonderful. She walked the familiar few blocks of Third Avenue, looking in at the dimly lit shop windows behind their protective chain gates. She always loved the big old fabric store with its bolsters of cotton, silk, and linen lining both side walls all the way to the ceiling. If she squinted, they looked like rainbows. It had been so long since she'd done this, since she was maybe ten years old. But the rainbows were still there, if only you knew how to find them. And as she squinted, Lorraine found a surprising smile creep to her lips.

Lorraine passed the bagel shop on the corner. It was still open. For the after-bar crowd around here, bagels were a popular snack; and despite diet trends, they were always piled three inches thick with cream cheese. Steven behind the counter gave her his giant grandfatherly wave as if it hadn't been nearly a year since she'd last walked by.

There were five guys sitting on the steps of a brownstone with paper bags, spilling that thrashing kind of heavy metal into the air from an open window on the first floor. "Wooh-hooh! Lookin' fine tonight!"

Lorraine smiled. She recognized one of the guys as Gino's friend. She continued walking.

After she closed the front door to her parents' home behind her, she heard a car. Looking out she saw Chrissy and Don, in a great big Lexus SUV. They were in love. Anyone could see that from the way they had to be connected to each other at all times. Chrissy looked tender, Lorraine thought, her hand snaking up and down Don's forearm, caressing it with intimate knowledge and care. And it was obvious she'd always been this way, and that she, too, had ignored who she really was to do what Big Bobby wanted. How had they both gotten that way? Where had they learned such submissive behavior?

The three of them sat on the hood of Don's SUV, the warmth from the drive seeping into their legs. Lorraine still felt that weightlessness she'd experienced outside the Blue Zoo. When you knew you couldn't go backward, at least your direction was clear. And that direction most certainly included Matt.

Don and Chrissy's presence gave her a hopefulness, if not a rosy outlook. She loved the look of them—unable to stop stealing glimpses at each other. Lorraine knew she had all that, too, but she wanted to be sure. She wanted to see Matt and comfort herself with the knowledge that she was in love with him.

And so the sight of him driving down her block was like a gift from heaven.

Even the way he addressed her friends, with respect and care and genuine happiness, reassured Lorraine. What she had with Matt was, if any-thing, amplified tenfold by what she had just experienced.

"Oh, I missed you baby. I couldn't wait until morning to see you." Matt kissed her and she knew he meant it. A rush of heat went through her.

Don, Chrissy, and Matt smiled conspiratorially before the couples parted.

"So what brought you here?" Lorraine asked teasingly, leaning into the leather seat of Matt's convertible.

He reached deeply into his pocket, pulling out a pair of delicately strung beaded chandelier earring. "You forgot these. And I couldn't have my baby go out naked . . . like that." He let the word *naked* linger between them until there was no mistaking his intentions. Finally he hooked the earrings gently through her pierced ears.

"Well, naked isn't always bad, is it?" She moved in close, softened the lines that had been etched into her face too long that night, and placed her lips softly over his until he took her in, his hands and body moving expertly.

At the sound of a car turning the corner, they parted slightly—noses just centimeters from touching.

"Lorraine! Quichy! Lorraine!" Her eyes bulged when she heard that name. It was Tommy coming for her.

The car came to a screeching halt alongside Matt's, so that no cars could pass by. Tommy tried the door a few times, pressing buttons with no luck, and then punching at them, before he gave up and just jumped out over the door of his own convertible. He was swaying. His hand found the passenger door next to Lorraine. "Lorr-*aine*, Lorr-aine," he sang the words to an indistinguishable tune. "I love you, Lorraine." He quickly quit that track, and blurted out, "Lorraine, I don't love Mallory. You know I don't. She paid me off, Lorraine-y. She made me part of that reality show, gave me a contract and everything. You know it's just for my career, Lorraine-y. It doesn't mean anything. I just had to stage hurting you really bad so we'd get the ratings. It's not that different from the reason you're on the show to begin with. We're the same, you and me—from the neigh-borhood! I told her that I love you."

Tommy didn't get to say anything more before Matt neatly knocked him out with a punch in the face, taking care to hold the back of his head so he wouldn't fall on the ground. Then he gently collected Tommy's limp body, deposited him inside his home, and draped an afghan over him, taking care to tuck in below his feet and at his chin. That's when Lorraine knew, for sure, that she was truly and deeply in love.

Hating only hurts the hater. If you can take that energy you have pent up inside of you and turn it into forgiveness, use it for good, then you will be better off. Ideas for using your energy for good:

1. Take up French cooking! It is a complex school of culinary arts and requires a familiarity with all sorts of new ingredients and lots of time-intensive bread baking.

2. Try weight-lifting! It requires so much energy, you will be too exhausted to hate anyone!

eBay auction block #20
Description: Excerpt from the book Lorraine used to get over the hatred she felt for Mallory and Tommy.

Opening bid: $22
Winning bid: $84 by Katharineprincess@princess.com

Comments: I really thought I was getting married! I hate everyone for setting me up like that. I hate Mallory! I hate NBC! I hate my ex-fiancé! I hate my parents. . . .

TWENTY

♥

PRINCESS OF PARK AVENUE SALON
BECOMES A GHOST TOWN

Lorraine was wearing a garden of a dress from the summer collection of Rebecca Taylor. She felt breezy, sexy. The collared, blousy top draped low, a wide macramé belt cinched her waist. Red always reminded Lorraine of glamour, and she'd always known that would be the color she'd wear to the opening. She was looking muscular from a regular two hours per day routine of weight lifting, which was good since she was eating a hell of a lot of heavy French cuisine.

Things hadn't worked out very nicely with the Princesses after Lorraine had found out all the dirty—and oh, boy, were they dirty—details about the NBC reality series, *The Royal Life*. Turns out the network wanted to add "colorful" Lorraine because the pilot hadn't tested so well with the bridge and tunnel crowd, or with lower-middle-class Midwesterners who couldn't relate to what they referred to as the "core" Princesses. When Mallory had spotted Lorraine, she thought she fit the bill exactly. But when the TV execs saw Tommy, they saw potential with a capital *P*. That was how they explained it to Lorraine in their great big boardroom hovering high above Rockefeller Center. The bachelorette night had been staged—as a matter of fact, Katharine wasn't even getting married! Lorraine had wondered at the other Princesses' lack of interest and even the fleeting nature of their jealousy. Now she understood.

What wasn't staged, what the man stroking his golf tee tie as if it were a kitten described as a pure stroke of *divine intervention*, was how Mallory actually fell for Tommy! Now, *that* was the magic of reality television. And then when he came crying back to Lorraine only to be too late, only to be socked in the face by Matt! *They'd all be billionaires!* was how he put it.

But that wasn't all. Guido was in on it. The show prompted his decision to offer Lorraine her own salon. It would have the kind of built-in publicity business owners only dreamed about. "Forget Paris Hilton. Forget Nicole Ritchie! Forget *Laguna Beach*. And who can stand another minute of the ditzy jokes on *The Newlyweds*, pu-lease," the executive said.

It didn't matter much what Lorraine thought of it all. Apparently, she'd unwittingly signed a waiver back when she was applying Mallory's Guido Nails for the first time. Oh, those cameras!

They screened a few clips of the show for Lorraine. "I'm just a hairstylist from the Bay!" It was mortifying to see herself edited into a caricature of herself, the very stereotype of Brooklynites that she tried to eliminate.

But there was no point in feeling stupid. There were always cameras following Mallory, so it would have been impossible to discriminate between the normal onlookers and those for the reality show. What was done, was done. *So you might as well enjoy it,* Golf Tie said, before standing and excusing himself from the boardroom.

As time marched on, Lorraine was able to get over her initial feelings of betrayal. After all, things had turned out so well. But sometimes, Lorraine felt sickened by the idea that she'd once again let life happen to her, just when she thought she'd finally been taking the bull by the horns. Behind it all, she couldn't let go of those words Mallory had threatened: *I made you, I can break you*. Could she really be nothing more than a pawn? The very question made her shiver.

Still, tonight was the opening of her very own salon, and no matter how she'd arrived, the moment was truly something to be proud of.

"You ready, gorgeous?" Matt asked, poking his head into her dressing room.

Lorraine turned to face the man she loved, the man she was finally ready to love, and watched as he pulled a long box from inside his tuxedo jacket.

"What is that?"

"There's only one way to find out, Lorraine." He watched her with obvious delight as she pulled the bow, loosened the ribbon, let it drop to the floor.

When she removed the golden box cover, Lorraine saw a beautiful charm necklace filled with antiqued-gold and brushed-silver charms. Upon a closer inspection, she could see each charm was designed especially for her. There was Pooh-Pooh, and Lena Horne, the tree they all sat under at the park, the Brooklyn Bridge, her father's cappuccino cup and saucer, and a calamari ring.

"Oh, Matt! It's absolutely the most wonderful gift! Please, put it on me." And as he fastened it, his hands brushing at the back of her neck, Lorraine felt like nothing—not the reality show, or even the salon— mattered as much as this. How happy she was, and knew she would always be.

Lorraine's cell phone rang. It was Mrs. Romanelli. It should have surprised her more than it did. "Well, finally! Good luck tonight and please, wear my long crocodile baguette!"

Matt grinned at her when she came back in the room.

"Let me guess, it was Romanelli?"

"Yeah, you know me and psychic Italian ladies!"

"The scary part is how I *do*."

They made quite an entrance, the two of them—dogs in hand, wearing high fashion and being snapped by photogs. They were a couple Lorraine might have looked at with suspicion and disdain not so many years ago. She knew they were just that to others now, and realized she had an opportunity to change what people thought.

The salon was beautiful, glamorous—rich with woods and brocades and antique mirrors. It was the perfect backdrop for the sea of glamorous, rich people who had come out to attend Lorraine's opening. There were gift bags filled to the brim with gift cards, jewelry, techno gadgets. Outside were two girls with clipboards and lines spreading out before them around either side of the block.

There were Guido, Tracey, Stacey, and Katharine. Mallory and Tommy canoodled in a corner, whether for attention or because they didn't really belong and had to cling to each other that way, Lorraine didn't know. Mallory's hair was up and hidden beneath a floral scarf that she had tied tight, with the long ends floating down her bare back. Lorraine thought she'd seen the look back in September at the spring fashion shows she'd worked, but couldn't remember who'd done it. Mallory really could make anything look good. But somehow, without the cameras for the reality show, Mallory seemed more naked, vulnerable, to Lorraine. How complicated it all was—the secrets and lies and false expressions of support and happiness. Where was the reality in *any* of it?

She surveyed the room as she answered a few questions from the press, and soon found the answer to her own question. Reality was sitting on a nook of seats in a corner, beyond the radar of the paparazzi and the Princesses and the free-service cards and the mindless chitchat. Her mother was wearing a fur stole around her neck, though it was high August. And Lorraine understood that this strange mink—still in its natural state, full face, moveable mouth with teeth, tail, and all—symbolized her mother's age-worn dream of glamour. Lorraine thought how beautiful her mother, whose face glowed with happiness and pride, was and how much she loved her. It was easy, somehow, in light of all she'd seen, to forgive her mother's relentless dreams of fortune.

Her father sat beside her mother, the strange mink staring him in the face, but he didn't seem to notice. Not with his wife and daughter so bright and lively before him, his son munching away at hors d'oeuvres as he attempted to pick up a girl at least five years his senior. "Did you know my sister owns this joint?" he asked, swaggering over to her.

Mr. Machuchi laughed at his son's antics. He was happy. He was always contented, always proud. But tonight he was radiant.

"Well, Mom, looks like I can send you over to Italy now! NBC says I'll be a billionaire."

"Ah!" She wiped the idea away with her hand. "Who wants to go to Italy when I've got everyone I love right here?" And then she patted Mr.

Machuchi's leg. "It was hard enough to get him to cross the bridge, much less the ocean!"

Lorraine's dad shrugged.

To Matt, Lorraine's mom said, "Never mind the money. I can tell the two of you are in love. And that's the most important thing."

Lorraine was thrilled at the change of heart her mother had obviously been experiencing. Still, she was not shocked to hear her mom whisper as they walked away, "He has a *Mercedes,* you know."

Old habits die hard. That was one thing Lorraine could understand.

And so, apparently, could Matt, who squeezed her hand at the sound of it. They both smiled. Some things would never change. And when so many things had in the past, that knowledge was a wonderful thing to ground you.

The questions and pictures and introductions flew by at record speed. Lorraine performed an impromptu color job on Ashley the Invisible, who turned up in another doosy—pants she'd obviously needed to hem but wasn't allowed to in case they'd be needed for a fashion shoot, worn with four-inch heels she could barely balance on to compensate. Needless to say, she was tripping and pulling up at her waist. It was uncomfortable even to look at her. So Lorraine thought she'd offer a pick-me-up— a complimentry hairstyling.

Mallory and Tommy looked so small and harmless in the corner, she thought maybe they were sorry. Perhaps they really felt bad about everything, and now just wanted to give Lorraine her space. She almost felt sorry for them herself, over in the corner, looking like misfits. Good or bad, they were intrinsically twisted into the events that had brought her to this moment, and she felt the pull of that connection—felt it slowly begin to soothe over the feelings of anger.

After the excitement of the party and the positive press that had surrounded it, the following day's opening was bound to be grand, Lorraine thought, as she pulled herself from Matt's Egyptian cotton sheets and forced herself to take Pooh-Pooh for a run.

So, Lorraine was completely dumbstruck when she arrived, ready to tackle the world—one strand at a time—to find there wasn't a single antique-finish oak chair occupied. What a difference from the evening before! She hadn't even been able to squeeze past Nicole Ritchie and her fiancé to grab a smoked salmon lollipop last night! But as she approached the desk now, she saw *nothing* but empty space.

Her receptionist, Chrissy's cousin Theresa, reached down to pet Pooh-Pooh, who threw himself on the wide wood plank floor belly up.

If only Lorraine could be as unaffected as Pooh-Pooh! She tried to remain cheerful. "I thought we were all booked up until 2010. Where *is* everyone?"

Theresa wasn't the kind of girl to beat around the bush. "It was that ho bag in the turban. The one kissing Tommy in the corner. Look." She pointed a Guido Nail down at an article in the paper laid out on the desk.

"COLORFUL" PRINCESS TURNS GREEN

Princess Lorraine, who celebrated the opening of her new salon, Princess of Park Avenue, A Guido Salon, just last evening, may be in for a rough start.

One of her most important clients, Princess Mallory Meen, claims Lorraine's famous "five-color highlights" have made her hair greener than Christmas. "I know that as a Princess I have a responsibility to let my public know when they may come into harm's way. I would never let any of my fans suffer the mortifying experience I am currently suffering."

Ms. Meen claims she will not be leaving her Park Avenue home until further notice, and plans to launch a lawsuit on Lorraine and the parent company, Guido Salons.

Lorraine couldn't read any more. As a matter of fact she couldn't even see. Spots of multicolored anger clouded her line of vision. *Green hair?* She'd never done that to anyone. People would surely know the claim was untrue, wouldn't they? It was such a messy lie, haphazardly thrown together, as if Mallory had wanted it to be so transparent, so easy, just to show Lorraine it would be that simple to toss her from the picture—as easy as it had been to paste her right in.

"Has anyone called about this?" Lorraine asked.

"Sure. They called to cancel."

Lorraine looked down to the red lines drawn over each and every name on the day's client roster, staring until they burned into her vision.

She just had to think logically. That was all she had to do. She had a fabulous salon here, in a prime Park Avenue location. She had great friends helping her out, a wonderful, very smart boyfriend. And a couple of enemies. Very powerful enemies. But she could outwit them, couldn't she?

The passion and anger she felt as she took an additional run with Pooh-Pooh to clear her head, figure out a plan of action, took her by surprise. Up until that point, she'd been coasting along. She'd been happy to have the salon, but she hadn't realized how much it meant to her. Now the salon seemed to symbolize everything she was fighting against in Mallory and Tommy. It seemed to encompass all the good in the world, everything that was pure and right in a society where people often got opportunity and luck when they deserved quite the opposite. It was the place that had put the smile on her mother's face, the first she'd seen in years, and the effect that had on her father, sitting so sweetly like the pointed teeth of a dead mink weren't two inches from his shoulder. It was her best friend Chrissy's, and her sweet friend Don's place of employment. And Guido—though he'd been difficult for a while there, and kept the reality show from her, deep down he was good people . . . just with some problems to work out. A lot of people cared about her salon. A lot of people had worked hard for it. And she was going to make it work. *But how?*

As she felt her muscles loosening into the pace of a quick jog, Lorraine breathed deeply, tried to take in what she could. Pooh-Pooh was always up for exercise, always up for anything she wanted to do with him, she thought. Maybe there was something in that—the idea was that he was a friend. She thought about her other friends, the friends she'd always had, and her family, too. Those were people you could count on—people who didn't change on you, who were always right there where you left them. She knew the answer to her problem somehow lay in that idea, but she didn't know exactly where. She needed an expert. Lorraine knew only a media coup could save her, but she realized she was way out of her league.

She could take it so far, but only the right person could take it all the way—really make things right.

She'd finished her run with one objective in mind, at least. She was going to phone the publicist Guido had assigned to the salon.

"I'm sorry, hon," Jane Jonstein said through the phone. "But I can't fight the Princesses. They're my main clients. And even if they weren't, that would just be career suicide. Slash them from your party attendee list, your product user list, and you might as well light fire to the whole office."

Lorraine was just walking back to the salon, freshly showered, and hoping by the grace of God that at least one client had shown. That conversation with Jane did nothing to lighten her mood. If no one was going to challenge Mallory, it seemed she would never be saved from this fate.

Pooh-Pooh started barking like mad toward the street, jumping so high she could barely keep hold of the leash. She tried the open palm move, the "Sit, Pooh-Pooh," command, but nothing worked. There was only one thing that got Pooh-Pooh this worked up: Her first name was Lena and her second name was Horne. Lorraine looked across the street to where Pooh-Pooh was pulling her, and nearly ran into a taxi. "Watch it!" the driver screamed and shook his fist.

It was just a blond girl and a guy sitting on a bench alongside the park. But wait, she recognized those fantastic highlights! They were hers. And that was no girl! That was Mallory! And next to her, with his head so close it was nearly touching hers, was Matt. Lena was dangling at the very end of her leash, barking back at Pooh-Pooh.

Lorraine was sure Matt would look up. He never ignored his dog. She waited, people shoving her and screaming profanities and asking "Why don't you watch your dog, huh?" and "Hello! What the hell? Did you forget how to walk or something?" Everything was loud—screaming loud—and yet way too quiet at the same time. If she could hear Lena's bark, then why wasn't Matt looking up? How could he be so distracted? There was one thing for certain: She was not going to take this. Lorraine was done stepping aside, letting things happen. From now on, she was taking the active role, not waiting for someone to stab her first.

The light turned red, and so she ran for it, in between cars and a couple of bicycles, Pooh-Pooh pulling her all the while.

She stood for a second directly in front of them, but with their heads down like that, they hadn't noticed. It still boggled her mind. How could anyone not notice Pooh-Pooh? Had she been such a fool to think she could find such a wonderful guy, that both of them would love each other and no one would get hurt? What in her life had ever prepared her to believe that?

"Having a good time?" she finally asked, hating the sound of her own voice, the jealousy and distrust in it. Apparently tuning in to her tone, Pooh-Pooh stopped licking Lena Horne, and drew back to Lorraine's side to show his solidarity. *At least that's someone!* Lena looked hurt, but Lorraine couldn't worry about that. She did feel bad, and wanted to tell her it wasn't her fault, but she forced herself to worry about more pressing things—like Matt and Mallory. "What? You've got nothing to say?" She was directing her anger at Matt. Lorraine hadn't yet looked Mallory in the face. She caught the glare from her oversize black sunglasses, was glad to know she wouldn't look her in the eye. Lorraine thought surely a demon was lurking inside of them.

"Lorraine, plea—" Matt was trying to say something, but he didn't get a chance.

Blind with rage having finally taken in the icy smirk on Mallory's too-perfect mouth, the mouth that could ruin you with a single syllable, Lorraine lost all control. "You know, your hair doesn't look all that green to me. Maybe you just confused your hair with the color your face was when you saw that I had all the things you wanted. You had money and power and every opportunity in the world. But you couldn't figure any of it out, could you? You couldn't figure out how to care about a person besides yourself! You didn't know the simplest things. You disgust me, Mallory Meen. I can't believe I ever wasted a second trying to find your good side, your emotions. You obviously haven't got any." Lorraine was shaking, and when she stopped speaking she could feel the blood pulsing up though her neck like a heartbeat.

Mallory licked her lips with a wide grin—a serpent's tongue lashing out.

And a long silence followed, during which Lorraine took in Mallory's skin, saw that it appeared scaly and greenish, it seemed like the evil she could conjure was taking over her entire being.

When Mallory did finally respond, it wasn't with a word or a laugh, but merely a sound—piercing and strange to Lorraine's ears, like the sound of evil itself. "Hissssssssssss," it sounded like.

Lorraine turned away.

Matt's plea was a spike in the tension: "Lorraine! Lorraine! It's not what you think! Come on, Lorraine! You know . . ."

She had no idea what Matt was saying. His voice sounded slow, like a spell; she could float along the sounds, but not make sense of them quite yet. She couldn't have understood what he was trying to say even if she wanted to. Lorraine was beyond that point. Could she ever go back? Ever find that happiness again? The Thanksgiving Day float had begun to rise—Up! Up! Up!—and take her with it, and she was just digging her feet into the earth, trying to stay grounded. Whatever she toppled over in the process, well, she couldn't worry about that just then.

Lemma lo, Lemma lood
Lorraine will eat spicy food.
She'll find the answer in a
glamorous girl
Who'll fix it all.
Mallory will fall.
True love will prevail.
And then our family will safely sail.
No more of this crap! Okay?

eBay auction block #21
Description: Spell reportedly written and left by Lorraine's grandma.

Opening bid: $100
Winning bid: $480 by grandmaghost@italianghosts.com

Comments: I could get in big trouble for leaving this kind of thing behind! We are supposed to be a secret society! Enough of your crap now, Lorraine! I have put in too much time on your case already, so please, in the name of all that is Italian, make sure you are totally over Tommy. And put a copy of *US Weekly* on your mother's kitchen table. We get so behind on all the gossip up here!

TWENTY-ONE

♥

GETTING OVER IT, PARK AVENUE STYLE

The telephone rang and rang, but Lorraine ignored it. She had to focus. She had to formulate a plan. Now that she was facing the possibility of losing everything, Lorraine thought, she could finally see how important it all was to her. There was no way in the world she was going to let it all go.

She took a seat at the window nook in her living room and dug into the takeout Chinese with a pair of chopsticks. The spicy Chinese chicken was just what she'd been craving—something different, something that could shock her system. She thought a shock might be just the thing to point her in a different direction—the direction that would save her.

After one particularly spicy bite, Lorraine screamed, "Whew!" She tossed her head back as she tried to wave some air onto her burning tongue. That's just when she caught sight of the billboard of her hands. She hadn't looked at it in quite some time. Now it seemed to tell her that the only way this problem would be solved was if *she* solved it. In fact, it just seemed to be egging her on to get started, reminding her that she held the power, had always held the power, to do anything she wanted.

The next morning was not the sunny start she had hoped to mark her fresh beginning. In fact, the Weather Channel forecasted the rainstorm would continue all through the day, possibly into the next. And it wasn't the sprinkly stuff, either. Nope—it was all extremes for Lorraine now, it seemed. The rain poured down so hard, she thought it might bust through her umbrella on the way to work. It did, in fact, blow the thing inside out—more than once.

Pooh-Pooh barked at the twisted mess of nylon and metal when Lorraine stuffed it down into the trash. After that, he decided to cut his run short, pulling them toward home way before normal. He was whining like the raindrops were daggers in his fur. She couldn't blame him—it was the kind of day you wanted to spend indoors.

But, apparently, she found upon entering her salon, not indoors at the Princess of Park Avenue salon.

"Good news. We had a blow-dry this morning." Theresa tried to sound cheery, but lost her energy halfway through punching the air, and dropped her hand to the desktop with a *smack*!

Well, that was *something*, wasn't it? Lorraine tried to convince herself one blow-dry might save her multimillion-dollar salon. "Who was it?"

"Oh, some Australian tourist. She'd read about the salon months ago in a travel magazine and wanted to check it out."

Lorraine didn't want to think about the fact that her salon wasn't even an idea months ago, that this client had obviously come in by mistake.

"Oh, and the accountant wants to talk to you."

"You mean Chrissy?"

"Well, I just wanted to sound a little more sophisticated. You know? This place is so classy, Lorraine. I just know it will all work out. It has to. It's so beautiful. And just look how beautiful you've made all of us."

The thing was, it had been so easy to make them look beautiful. The beauty was already there, inside them—all she'd done was bring it out. It was so obvious to her, so easy to see that in people. It pained her to think she might never have the chance to share that gift. If this all failed, there was no going back to Carlo. She knew she couldn't go back to exactly how things had been. When you'd changed, you'd changed. She shook the feelings from her head. She'd have plenty of time to feel like crap later—a long empty schedule of time.

As she walked the sweeping staircase up to the second floor, where Chrissy's office was located, Lorraine felt that her salon was a little piece of Brooklyn, right here in the middle of Manhattan. Everyone inside was like family to her. Everything was the way they liked it. They served her father's coffee. They offered pastries from the bakery on Seventy-sixth and Fifth Avenue, where she'd eaten her whole life. But here, now, there was something so regal and beautiful about the way it had all been revived and reinterpreted through her own eyes. They'd all said that to her, but now she really saw it, understood the truth of it.

"Knock, knock," she said as she rapped at the door.

"C'mon in!" Chrissy yelled back.

When Lorraine found her, she was sitting at the computer, the huge flat screen monitor reflecting light onto her face.

Boy, that must have cost a lot, Lorraine thought.

Chrissy's fingers were tapping away like mad at the keyboard. Then she stopped, swiveled the screen to face Lorraine. "Listen, Lorraine, I'm not going to sugarcoat this. Even with all the money that Guido put up to get this place going, you still used a great deal of your own savings—as you know."

This was not sounding good. Not good at all, Lorraine realized, feeling a heavy thump at the middle of her rib cage. She was staring so hard at the screen that the numbers displayed across it went out of focus becoming just a fuzzy series of harmless stripes. *How could those hurt me?* She sat up straight as she could, as if that might brace her for what was to come.

"The business model we created counted on a heavy stream of clients, paying an average of $400 per appointment. And without those—even these two days—we are already in the hole and digging ourselves deeper every second we sit here."

The words hung between them like a dead body they'd stumbled upon. Neither knew what to say. The music pumping through the salon was an old dance song—one of the girls' favorites. "Like the crack of the whip I snap attack, front to back in this thing called rap. . . ." Lorraine gave herself over to it. She started bobbing her head to the rhythm, singing.

Eventually Chrissy joined in. "Maniac brainiac winning the game, I'm the lyrical Jesse James, Oh-oh-oh-oh-oh-oh-oh-oh-oh yeah-eah-eah-eah-eah-eah, I've got the power."

Suddenly the Bobbsey Twins were smiling again. Here they were, still the best of friends, going through life together. Lorraine knew all this bad news would feel so much worse if it hadn't come from Chrissy, and she was grateful for that. Lorraine wasn't going to let her friend suffer without a paycheck, wasn't going to upset the security she'd always held dear at her old job. She would come through for her. And she promised Chrissy as much.

"I know you will Lorraine. Believe me, I do."

But it was going to be hard work. Mallory had obviously paid off others to say they'd been victim to Lorraine's awful coloring jobs. There were three more testimonies in that morning's paper. She could only imagine the back-room bargains Mallory proposed: "I'll get you into the premier of the new Ben Stiller movie." "Oh, you want that Louis V everyone's going to wait ten years for?" "How would you like to eat at that new Bouloud spot . . . now? For free?" Whatever she'd promised had worked. The results were staring right back at her in black ink: *The Green-Haired Monster Strikes Again.*

You had to work hard for what you wanted. She'd heard that so many times, but it had never really sunk in. Had she just thought it didn't pertain to her? She guessed you could call the effort she'd always put in with Tommy "work," but she'd never thought about it that way. The hard part had been when she had to give him up, force herself to see the badness in him.

Standing a few inches from Theresa behind the front reception desk, she tried to think of another publicist who might help her. Lorraine was no fool—she knew, just like no woman should attempt highlights herself, no woman should attempt to battle a publicity coup without the help of a publicist. And this retaliatory campaign had to be bigger than just protecting Lorraine's image. It had to be so big that nobody would even remember Mallory's lies. But who would help them if their very own publicist wouldn't?

Suddenly an idea popped into her head. "Theresa, I'll be in my office," she called over her shoulder as she jumped up the stairs. She was bubbling with the energy of promise. Yes . . . yes . . . it just might work. With every fiber of her being, she knew that all of her power, all of her strength, had come from her roots—generations of hard work, strong bonds, values. Just look at this place! It was breathtaking, and so . . . her! The oriental rug with the funky bamboo wall, the cool linen curtains mixed in with the antique treasure chest, and tons of great peonies! She'd made her own place in the city that the whole world was watching. Now she was going to make sure that serpent of a Princess didn't steal it away from her for kicks. Nobody was going to use her as a punch line anymore. There wasn't a person in the world Lorraine would lose herself for.

Lorraine waited for her computer to buzz and blink its way to life. Then she opened her Web browser and typed in the words *Publicist+Brooklyn.*

Power Publicist Carolyn Jennings wanted to meet Lorraine at Bemelmen's Bar at the Carlyle Hotel. As she sat and waited, a tiny cocktail glass—the kind you might have seen in the 1950s containing a murky sidecar—in her hand, she started to picture just what Carolyn Jennings might look like if she had a place like this on the tip of her tongue. There was a whole list of classic cocktails on the menu, and she'd chosen a sloe gin fizz. It sounded wonderfully.

Lorraine was spinning the base of the glass around and around, taking in the gold-leafed ceiling and the beautiful, enchanting mural lining the walls which featured dapper animal characters gathered around fluffy trees and park benches. The landscape had been imagined by the artist Ludwig Bemelmen, who, Lorraine had read online, called the Carlyle his home, as had Jackie Kennedy Onassis. The sips of the sloe gin fizz were warming Lorraine's body, slowing the pace of her heart. She was beginning to think that this place was magical. It sure felt that way in all its delicate detail. The leather under glass tables with golden rims; the dark, soft lights; the piano player tinkling songs that at the moment felt as if they were sending Lorraine into some easier time. She could see why someone would want to come here and never leave. It was that kind of place.

It reminded her—in spirit, you see—of another place she knew well—

her own home, the Bay. The warm, familiar side of Manhattan that Bemelmen's evoked was her favorite thing about her new home. She saw a
glimpse of the parallels between both of her names. She saw hope and
promise in the idea of having such distinct parts of her come together in
this magical way. It was truly that inspiring.

And that's when Lorraine saw Carolyn Jennings push through the
door, an Hermes scarf pinned perfectly at her shoulder, gold knots at her
ears. She was dressed in a slim black summer pantsuit that had an easy—
not constricted—look on her, and crocodile sandals. She looked right at
Lorraine, picked her out as if she were intimately acquainted with her already. Carolyn Jennings thrust her hand out, one chunky cocktail ring sitting next to one tasteful golden wedding band.

"Carolyn Jennings," she said, a dazzling smile forming at the corners
of her mouth. "Don't be surprised, I recognized you because that's my
job. I'm an expert, darling. I knew you'd come to me, too. I've been
waiting."

The waiter came by. "Ah, Mrs. Jennings," he said, smiling a knowing
smile, like maybe after hours they threw back kamikazes behind the bar.

Lorraine liked this woman. Right away she trusted her. After all, she
was from Brooklyn.

"I'll have a Chardonnay, Henry. This is Lorraine Machuchi, I'm sure
you know. She is going to be the most famous hair colorist in all the
world. Remember her." Carolyn waved her Fontainebleu pen around like
a magic wand as she spoke.

When Carolyn Jennings blinked, the heavy fringes of her lashes met
and parted in a graceful dance—just the way, Lorraine thought, you
would picture them doing on someone truly glamorous. Carolyn may
have just been the very first person to actually live up to those kinds of
expectations.

When Henry walked off to fetch the drink, a tray tucked weightlessly
underneath his arm, Carolyn pulled a thick folder from her lemon leather
tote. "First off, Lorraine, I want to tell you that I believe in you and everything you stand for. I've been watching you, I believe that you are the
poster child for a new revolution in this city. You are everything that Old

Brooklyn stands for, and you're just the girl to bring it back. Just look at you sitting in here! It's wild! Something, something big is about to happen. I can just feel it."

Lorraine wasn't sure what she meant just yet, but she was immediately drawn in. She wanted to hear everything. She wasn't sure if she felt that way just because she wanted to believe everything Carolyn was saying, or because she felt the same thing. Whatever the reason, she was hooked. Carolyn's teeth caught the light and glimmered; her skin seemed to glow. She was right . . . something was about to happen.

"Here's the thing. I invented Mallory and her little Princesses. I know it seems out of control right now, and believe me it is—a Frankenstein-ian sort of mess I've created. No one will launch a product without her approval. The other girls you could really just toss, but you'd still have yourself a Beyoncé, if you know what I mean. Mallory loves to boss them. She'd never give that up. In the meanwhile, you might as well forget about succeeding if you're not going to invite them. But the thing is, it's all gotten out of hand. And I know just why. Mallory watches all these little projects around her take off and become grand, and there she has all that power, but what has she done with it? Sell a couple million cocktail napkins? The girl is miserable. I know, it's ridiculous—everyone wants to be her, and the last thing she wants is to be herself. Seeing you rise up like such a star, claim something for yourself, carve out your own niche—even in the blinding light of her own star—that was too much for Miss Mallory Meen. And so, she set out to destroy you. The rest of the story, I'm sorry to say, you are already familiar with."

Carolyn's words shouldn't have gotten such a reaction from Lorraine. After all, she'd already known most of that. She'd guessed Mallory's feelings from the very beginning. But hearing it so cut and dried, was a lot to take. She'd never treated anyone with such a diminished attitude; Lorraine could never, would never think that someone just *didn't matter.* It was nearly unbelievable to her that someone could.

"It all sounds so awful. But it can't be as hopeless as my salon appears right now, Carolyn! It just can't! We have potential—I know we do. We just can't go the way of the Betamax. There is just too much—too many people—riding on this!"

"Lorraine, Lorraine! I swear on the Helmut Lang rack at the Bay Ridge Century 21 that we will fix your problem."

With a statement like that, Lorraine knew Carolyn was serious.

"Here's what we need to do. Let's call the first phase of this project 'discovery.' "

"Discovery?" Lorraine asked.

"Discovery," repeated Carolyn, uncapping her pen. "You see, often, the answer to your problem is right in your hands. You just have to take stock of all the resources you have. You know—Six Degrees of Separation."

Lorraine nodded. It was all so logical. Maybe Lorraine did have the means to fix this mess! At least having a plan made it seem like she was working toward something, moving in the right direction.

Carolyn wrote a list of the types of people Lorraine could consider. Each determined stroke of her pen was magical, and seemed to bring Lorraine closer to salvation. "These are your contacts," she said. The list read, *Family, Friends, Clients, Celebrities.*

"Start with that. I'll go through my contacts, too; let's meet up again when you've got it all filled out—with telephone numbers and e-mail addresses. It's a bit of legwork, but really, Lorraine, you'll see, once you organize it like this, there's always hope. Always hope. Relationships, people—how you treat them, the impression you make on them—that's always what matters in the end."

Lorraine could only hope that Carolyn was right as she watched her, with only the slightest raise of one eyebrow, summon Harold over with their check.

Lorraine reached into her purse, but Carolyn stopped her.

"Please, Lorraine. Allow me. You're going to be so big, you'll pay me a great monthly commission. A fabulous monthly commission. I'm not worried."

They both smiled. Carolyn was still a businesswoman in the cutthroat media industry. But she handled it well, Lorraine would give her that. She just prayed—again—that Carolyn was right.

★   ★   ★

She'd have to get to work on her Six Degrees of Separation . . . and quick. But first, there was the little matter of her green-eyed building-mate. The guy whose hair was getting longer and shaggier (and sexier) by the day since he'd started his furniture company full-time. There was something self-fulfillment could do to a look . . . and collagen's got nothing on it.

She wanted to be mad. She wanted never to forgive. But somewhere, in the back of her mind, she knew she wasn't being fair. After all, she hadn't even given him a chance to explain. She was mulling the idea of calling him over in her head as she returned from her meeting with Carolyn, when she saw that Matt was sitting outside her apartment door with Lena Horne—Pooh-Pooh barking from the other side. Each of them was wearing a sandwich board made from cardboard boxes and garbage ties (he was nothing if not inventive) printed with the words "I solemnly swear . . ."

"What? What do you solemnly swear to?" she asked. Lorraine stuck her hands at her hips, but she was softening already. She wasn't sure if it was a result of Lena Horne's whining or because things were looking a bit more promising thanks to Carolyn, but suddenly she realized she'd made a mistake in distrusting Matt. The guy was good people—even her father had said so.

"Turn the sign over. I couldn't fit it all on one side."

"Hmmph!" She tried to maintain her attitude, her edge, but her smile was giving her away. Lorraine bit her lip and crouched down in front of Matt. Lena Horne started licking her elbow like it was a lollipop. Lorraine reached for the cardboard sign and turned it over. "There's nothing there!" she said. Her nose was two centimeters from Matt's.

"Yeah, but I got you down here," he said. "Right?"

"Sure, yeah . . . you got me here. So what are you gonna do about—" She didn't get to finish. But that was okay, because Matt was kissing her. And she was enjoying it. Enjoying it so much she nearly forgot she was angry. Lip to lip, she remembered long enough to ask, "What were you doing with Mallory that day?"

"Lorraine, it kills me that you even thought for a second that I could be interested in her when I'm so in love with you . . . that I could ever hurt you. When you wouldn't answer my calls, when you acted like you weren't home—I could smell the Chinese food, by the way. You and me, we're not like that. Okay? I know you've been hurt. Bad. But I'll never do that to you. Never."

"You're right. You're right. It was just . . . I was just so angry and upset at that rumor Mallory spread about her green hair! I'm so dumb, I can't believe I didn't realize something was up when she was wearing that scarf on her head!"

Lorraine was curled up in Matt's lap, his hands stroking her bangs back from her forehead. She nearly forgot they were in the hallway until Pooh-Pooh took up the whining again, and she saw his tongue sweep out from under the door.

Before Matt let her go, he said, "What do you think I was talking to her about?!"

Lorraine felt like a moron. It was clear now that he'd been trying to help her, and she'd acted like a friggin' idiot! Trust was something she was going to have to work on. She didn't know quite how to apologize to him.

They both rose, and Lorraine fumbed, "I . . . well, you know . . ."

"Shhhh, Lorraine. You don't have to say anything. I know it will take you some time to trust again. And that's okay. I'm not going anywhere. In fact, that's what the other side of Lena's sign is about."

The couple were inside Lorraine's apartment now, and she thought it would be impossible to see the other side of Lena Horne's sign, what with Pooh-Pooh all over her like nobody's business (seriously, nobody wanted this business). However, in his excitement, Pooh-Pooh pulled the sign from its garbage ties and it flipped across the room. The cardboard smacked into the base of something that hadn't been in the room when she'd left it earlier. It was a beautiful coffee table, carved from mahogany, intricate rosettes at all the legs and across the surface. It was solid, stable—beautiful.

"That's a love table, Lorraine. And it's inspired by you."

She looked to Matt and smiled. As symbols go, the table was quite powerful. Staring into its delicate twists and turns, running her hand over the ins and outs of the carvings, Lorraine nearly forgot about the sign. "It's so beautiful."

"Are you gonna turn that sign over or what?" Matt nodded to it as he sat down on the couch right behind her. But when she bent down to flip it, he grabbed the board from her hand, jerked her up, and kissed her deeply. Matt tossed the sign way back into the kitchen.

"What the—?" Lorraine screwed her face up.

"Marry me, Lorraine, I love you and I want to have lots of babies with you. I want to finally take you on that Miami trip. And then I want us to live on the same block with Chrissy and Don . . . just like you always dreamed."

She looked at him, seeing all the parts of her life come together. "But that was a Brooklyn dream."

"And so is this," he said, "and so is this."

```
DOOR PERSON: "Sorry, you're not on the list."

TOMMY: "But we are the most famous couple in
  Manhattan!"

DOOR PERSON: "But this is Brooklyn."

MALLORY: "But I'm a Princess!"

DOOR PERSON: "There's only one princess who matters
  here."

TOMMY: "I know! And I love her, so PLEASE let me
  in!"

MALLORY: "What did you say?"

TOMMY: "You will never be anything compared to her!
  I already told you that!"

MALLORY: "But you didn't MEAN it!"

TOMMY: "I did!"

MALLORY: "You didn't!"

TOMMY: "I did!"

DOOR PERSON: "Step aside, please. Next!"

MALLORY: "But I didn't get my free B Girl shirt!"
```

eBay auction block #22
Description: Transcript of paparazzi audiotape recorded outside grand opening party of Princess of Park Avenue, A Guido Salon, Brooklyn location.

Opening bid: $550
Winning bid: $25,000 by malloryprincess@princess.com

Comments: This NEVER happened. And if it did, Tommy really DIDN'T mean it, and he DID love me. And he always will. Everybody loves me. And I still want my B Girl shirt because everyone knows Brooklyn is hot.

TWENTY-TWO

♥

"'CAUSE I'M REAL"
—JENNIFER LOPEZ

Lorraine handed out copies of the Six Degrees of Separation sheets to her mother, father, brother, Chrissy, Don, Matt, Carlo, Mrs. Stephano, and her awkward grandson Jimmy (whom, Lorraine could now see, definitely required the matchmaking effort of his grandmother), and Chrissy's grandmother—Mrs. Vioto.

Her dad was just finishing his last coffee order when the doorbell rang. "I'll get it!" Matt said and walked over to the door. "Romanelli!" He enveloped her in a hug.

Pooh-Pooh came barreling up to her. Lorraine felt like doing the same thing. It had been so long since she had seen her, and though she really hadn't spent much time with her, there was still an undeniable connection drawing them together that Lorraine couldn't explain.

Romanelli scratched Pooh-Pooh on the belly where he liked it and accepted his exuberant licking as gracefully as a queen before she embraced Lorraine in a great, strong hug. It was so like the hugs her grandmother used to give her. Lorraine found herself holding on tightly—probably too tightly. "Ah, dear," Romanelli said, her head shaking in approval. "You've been busy!"

She was so taken aback by seeing Romanelli here, now. The breezy summer dress she was wearing looked so chic and European—so striking amongst the rest of them. She hoped her mother wouldn't notice and become melancholy. "What are you doing home already? And how did you know to come here?"

"Silly girl, the year's up, and you're staying so much with Matt now anyhow! And why am I here? Well, darling, you need help . . . and honestly, your grandmother can be such a pain in the ass! Not one of you could remember to leave her that copy of *Us Weekly*, and so I had to bring it myself! She won't stop complaining about it already!" Mrs. Romanelli tossed the magazine onto the coffee table.

Nobody knew what to say to that. And so they all sat there in silence, until they started to laugh.

"Give me one of those Six Degrees of Separation sheets already. You don't have a lot of time, you know!" Romanelli took a seat next to Mrs. Machuchi. "Stella!" She handled Lorraine's mother's name like an opera note, lending to it the grace she gave to everything. "You must be so proud of your daughter."

Lorraine's mother had been growing, just like her daughter, and now her change of heart was obvious. "You know, Mrs. Romanelli," she said, holding her mother's friend's hand, and looking into the eyes of her daughter, "I always was."

She didn't need to say anything more—her loving look said it all. Of course, it didn't hurt that she was leaving for Italy in a week's time on an all-expenses-paid trip to the Richards familys Tuscan villa. But you got the sense that wasn't the only thing that had brought her to this point.

"All right, people!" Lorraine tried to rein them back in. "We got work to do here. No more chitchat."

Jimmy put his head down, as if absorbing the blame of the entire group. "Sorry," he mumbled.

They were all writing, every once and again someone calling out a name with enthusiasm, a name they hoped might save the day. "What about Jane Keller from the pork store? She once did a cabaret act in Atlantic City," Mrs. Vioto offered.

"Write it down." Lorraine tried to be encouraging, but things weren't going as smoothly as she'd hoped. Nonetheless, as she looked around she thought how lucky she was—all these people cared about her, wanted to help her. And when her eyes landed on Matt, he smiled at her and gave her hand a squeeze.

"Oh! I got it!" Jimmy shouted. Lorraine was shocked that Mrs. Stephanos sullen grandson could convey such energy. Maybe this would be good.

"Whatcha got, Jimmy?" Lorraine asked.

His mouth contorted into a lumpy grin, full of teeth. "The Beastie Boys." He sat back and crossed his arms, allowed his eyes to run over each and every person at the big table, as if he'd saved the day.

Lorraine grew excited. "You know them?"

"Well, no." Jimmy grew red. He'd gone from Donald Trump to a tiny radish in a few seconds. "But"—he swallowed the words—"they're from Brooklyn."

The group groaned. There had to be an answer, Lorraine reasoned in her head as she tapped her pen against her sheet of paper. Pooh-Pooh was moving around underneath the table, bumping her every so often. She took a look to see what exactly he was up to. Her mother would have a fit if he chewed any furnishings.

And there he was, chewing the *Us Weekly*, tearing it into bits with his teeth. "I thought we were past that, Pooh-Pooh," Lorraine said, wishing he hadn't done that in front of Romanelli. He'd been so good for so long, she hated to think this would be the impression he'd be giving. She pulled a page out of his mouth, and stole a glance at Mrs. Romanelli. But she should have known Mrs. Romanelli already knew the score. She was an old psychic Italian woman; apparently they had as much, if not more, weight than Princesses, if not within an entirely different medium.

"What have you got there, dear?" Romanelli asked sweetly.

"A page of *Us Weekly*."

"Oh," the group said, a collective sigh of defeat settling over them. What had they expected?

Lorraine put the magazine page down next to her sheet, and along with everyone else, bent back over it. There wasn't much writing, but there was plenty of foot tapping, chair shimmying, and shirt straightening. Though her "friends" portion was full (and she knew it would be worthwhile to call each and every one of the people on the list), it didn't seem promising that any of them would have any new ideas. Three-quarters of the people were sitting right there in the same room with her, and the rest already knew of her predicament. Jeez, who didn't? She was the talk of the town. *I'm the Green-Haired Monster*, Lorraine thought and rolled her eyes.

And that's when she saw it. Her eyes had landed right on the magazine page—right into the eyes of J. Lo. The page was called, of all things, Six Degrees of Separation. It was a little game the magazine played where they show how a celebrity is connected to the other celebrities. And although she'd been cut out of it, Lorraine recognized that hand next to J. Lo's. It was her own hand. The photo was from the APGBB ball! The idea clicked in like a Lego. Lorraine stood up with such force, her chair smacked into the wall behind. Her grandmother had done it again.

"Could it have taken you any longer?" Mrs. Romanelli asked with a laugh.

"There is one person more powerful than a Princess," Lorraine announced to the room at large.

"William Hung?" Jimmy asked.

All eyes turned his way.

"Who's that?" Lorraine's mom asked.

"The guy who sang 'La Vida Loca' on *American Idol*," Lorraine's dad answered—too quickly.

". . . or something." He cleared his throat and tried to return the attention to his daughter.

"*Not* William Hung," Lorraine said. What was wrong with these people?

"That big crazy blond woman on the MTV show?" Jimmy was nothing if not perseverant.

"Bridget Neilsen?" Mrs. Vioto asked.

Lorraine could only laugh at the people around her. And they called *her* colorful?

"You know it didn't work out with them," Mrs. Vioto said. "She went and got married to her fiancé after all. It's sad how things happen sometimes."

The knights of the square table all shook their heads in agreement about the sad state of unrequited love.

Lorraine gave them a moment of silence before bringing the attention back to the issue at hand. "Ahem," she cleared her throat. "As I was saying." She looked down to Matt, sitting next to her, amused at her frustration.

"Yes, what exactly was it you were trying to say, Lorraine?" He looked up to her with eyelashes batting.

"J. Lo!" As soon as she said it out loud, she could see it was definitely the answer. She looked to Mrs. Romanelli, stunned by the wonderful power of friendship, family, and love.

Jimmy raised his hand sheepishly. "Uhhhh, isn't she from the Bronx?"

Inside Carolyn's town car, everything was cool and soundless. There were telephones hooked up at three spots, their twirly cords dangling, and a prop-down desktop for Carolyn on one side. "I'm always so busy," she said, shrugging her shoulders.

They were taking Carolyn's car to the salon to meet J. Lo and the press. Carolyn wanted to control the way the entire coup was perceived from start to finish. The woman knew what she was doing.

When they pulled up to Lorraine's salon, it took her a minute to digest the scene in front of her. The crowd outside was so dense, the people were spilling a good two feet into the street. "How did you do it?" she asked Carolyn. "How did you get them all to come?"

Carolyn smiled that warm, dazzling smile.

The woman could have really been a movie star!

"Why, you did it yourself, Lorraine. J. Lo was thrilled to help you out. Said that where she came from, you don't believe a story about someone unless you see it for yourself. Said there was no way that could have happened, not with the way Sarah Jessica has been talking you up everywhere. If you ever wanna change careers, Lorraine, you'd be fabulous at public relations."

If Lorraine hadn't seen it with her own eyes, she'd never have believed it. As she pushed through the doors of her salon, sitting right there front and center, as gorgeous in person as on the cover of *People*, was none other than Jennifer Lopez. And right next to her, talking with her Guido Nails flopping here and there, was Sarah Jessica.

"Lorraine!" they said, simultaneously group-hugging as if they were old friends. Jennifer had her hair scraped back in the kind of high pony-tail Lorraine always admired her in.

"Oh my god! I can't tell you guys how thankful I am that you're helping me out like this!"

"Lorraine, you're helping *us*. You're the best hairstylist in town! And we're the first clients to have our hair highlighted in your new salon!"

It was a miracle. The most wonderful turn of events she could have imagined.

"You know," Lorraine said. "I didn't even know you guys were friends!"

"Well," Sarah Jessica said, "it's Six Degrees of Separation. I know William Hung. William Hung knows Jennifer . . ."

That Jimmy! Lorraine wasn't even going to try to figure it out. It was amazing how people pitched in and helped out when you were down. Just amazing.

As Lorraine performed the five-color technique, all cameras were on her, microphones in her face, flashes blinding, Matt watched with Chrissy and Theresa from the front desk. Lorraine thought she couldn't be happier.

"What's that shirt you're wearing, Lorraine?" It was Katie Couric, who'd been promised the very first question by Carolyn.

"Oh, this?" Lorraine asked, looking down at her shirt. It was phase two of Carolyn's plan, which she had promised Lorraine would be so powerful she'd have to pay her a "super-obnoxious retainer for it." "This is my B Girl shirt."

"Well, what's it about?" Katie wanted to know.

"Oh, it's a secret," Lorraine said with a smile. It would be a while until they unveiled the secret that would bridge both parts of her life—the New Old Brooklyn—with a second location for the Princess of Park Avenue salon. It would be a while until the morning when Lorraine woke up in her new Brooklyn address, letting Matt sleep in after so many years of waking with the international markets, clicked a leash on Pooh-Pooh, and walked out to glimpse the brand-new street sign that had been hung in her honor, up next to the 86th Street sign she'd seen every day of her life in the Bay. Park Ave, it would read.

A brand-new street sign always caught her eye. It was something simple, but still a surprise—especially if you knew all the details of the block with your eyes closed. The tiny surprises were what you treasured around there in the Bay, where things didn't change much. And that was no problem for Lorraine. Never had been . . . not for a round-the-way girl like herself.

And she thought, painting delicate lines of bleach onto J. Lo's crown, being a round-the-way girl didn't sound like such a bad thing. Not bad at all.